PENGUIN BOOKS

THE GRACE IN OLDER WOMEN

Jonathan Gash is the author of eighteen other Lovejoy mysteries including *The Possessions of a Lady* and *The Sin Within Her Smile*. He developed his love for antiques as a medical student when he earned extra money by working in a London street market. Gash's mysteries served as the inspiration for the Lovejoy series seen on the Arts & Entertainment Network. Mr. Gash lives in Colchester, England.

THE GRACE IN OLDER WOMEN

Jonathan Gash

PENGUIN BOOKS

PENGUIN BOOKS
Published by the Penguin Group
Penguin Books USA Inc., 375 Hudson Street, New York, New York 10014, U.S.A.
Penguin Books Ltd, 27 Wrights Lane, London W8 5TZ, England
Penguin Books Australia Ltd, Ringwood, Victoria, Australia
Penguin Books Canada Ltd, 10 Alcorn Avenue, Toronto, Ontario, Canada M4V 3B2
Penguin Books (N.Z.) Ltd, 182–190 Wairau Road, Auckland 10, New Zealand

Penguin Books Ltd, Registered Offices: Harmondsworth, Middlesex, England

First published in Great Britain by Century, Random House UK Limited 1995
First published in the United States of America by Viking Penguin,
a division of Penguin Books USA Inc. 1995
Published in Penguin Books 1996

1 3 5 7 9 10 8 6 4 2

PUBLISHER'S NOTE
This is a work of fiction. Names, characters, places, and incidents eitner are the product
of the author's imagination or are used fictitiously, and any resemblance to actual
persons, living or dead, events, or locales is entirely coincidental.

THE LIBRARY OF CONGRESS HAS CATALOGUED THE VIKING EDITION AS FOLLOWS:
Gash, Jonathan.
The grace in older women/Jonathan Gash.
p.   cm.
ISBN 0-670-86128-6 (hc.)
ISBN 0 14 02.4662 2 (pbk.)
I. Title.
PR6057.A728G65   1995
823'.914—dc20   95–2975

Printed in the United States of America
Set in Times Roman

The Grace in Older Women

1

'Will they see us?' she whispered.

My blood went cold in panic. 'Who? Who?'

'Anybody.'

Who else? She gripped my hand. The forest was silent. Not a bird cheeped, not a leaf crackled. 'We're alone, for God's sake!' I tried to make it sound romantic. 'Er, dwoorlink.' I'd nearly called her Mary. She was Beth.

We slithered down the slope, leaves skittering.

'I haven't got long,' she whispered.

Women always worry about what comes next. It would have narked me, but I was desperate for her. We sat, lay, then sprawled. Her husband was due back at twenty past.

Her breasts were cool. Odd, that. On the hottest days, women's breasts are cool. The sun just made it through the trees, dappling the undergrowth. The moans started so loud that I tried to cover her mouth with my hand, but she shook her face free and whispered that it was me, not her, making all the noise. It was beautiful as ever, the most wonderous ecstasy mankind can imagine. I loved her from the bottom of my heart, in the most perfect of all unions.

Afterwards we dozed in that post-lust slumber. I was awakened by her licking my mouth and eyes, asking if she'd been good. That's another puzzle. They always worry, as if there are grades of bliss. I told her she was superb. 'You were paradise.'

'Honestly, Lovejoy?' she said.

She was thrilled. I was thrilled she was thrilled, because it was touch and go whether she'd sell me her Bilston enamels that I craved. I know love, if nothing else.

'Darling,' she said mistily, then gathered her clothes to her exquisite breasts in alarm. 'Shhh! Lovejoy! What's that?'

'Squirrel?' Did squirrels make a noise, growl or something?

1

'It was a click.' She started flinging on her clothes.

Admiringly, I watched. Women's clothes are complicated, and they manage them with grace.

'A twig,' I explained. 'I'm good at nature. It's a beaver.'

She darted frantic looks for marauding husbands or, even worse, neighbours.

'Stupid!' she hissed. 'You don't get beavers here! Get dressed! Someone's coming!'

So? If people had any decency at all they'd politely ignore us. There wasn't anybody, of course. Women are scared witless of gossip. In three seconds flat I was my usual scruffy self: crumpled trousers, holed socks, shoes soled courtesy of Kellogg's cardboard, shirt with one perilous button, jacket frayed at cuff and hem.

'I mustn't be late, Lovejoy.'

'Right, right.' Women are always late, even if the clock says they're not. Dreading being late's their thing.

We tiptoed from the scene, gradually walking further and further apart as we approached the path from Fordingham. By the time we reached the old church we were clearly strangers, coincidentally strolling through the woods on a bright warm day. The only giveaway was Beth brushing imaginary leaves from her skirt every two yards. She reached the ancient churchyard where she'd parked her motor, drove off without a word. It's no good being indignant, but you can see what I mean. They always worry about what comes next, when the present moment is the danger. I should have remembered that.

At the old pond I paused. The path across Lofthouse's fields was clear of cattle. Nobody, except a girl coming from round the side of our disused church. Smart, colourful in a bright peach frock. I was tempted to try to walk with her, but she angled away towards the distant manor house. Oh, well. But the footpath wasn't littered with outraged bulls, and the chance was too good to miss.

In my ignorance I took it as a good omen, and plodded on towards the village at peace with the world, thinking of Bilston enamels. I'd only met Beth a week since, when she'd talked to the Village Society on 'Small Antiques for the Home'. I'd gone along for a laugh, and been stunned when she'd shown, voice wobbling nervously, a genuine Bilston. My chest had thrummed and gonged so hard I'd

2

almost collapsed in my chair. She'd left before I could shove through during the wine-and-wad session afterwards.

The day after, I'd caught her at the supermarket, having followed her. I made stilted conversation, I'd enjoyed her talk, antiques being me and all that.

'Oh, *you're* Lovejoy!' she'd said, colouring. 'I've heard about you from – ah. I didn't realize I was speaking to the learned.'

'Me?' I laughed a gay throwaway laugh. 'No, just interested.'

And went on from there: the glimpse of my deep inner yearning, honest admiration for her showing through, letting myself be drawn in despite my determined resistance to her allure. She'd invited me to her bungalow, shown me the Bilstons, fascinated when I all but keeled over at being so near genuine antiques. She'd got a mind-boggling eleven.

Don't laugh, because enamelling is one of the most difficult arts in history. Think a minute, and it's obvious why it must be so hard to do. Painting some metal with an opaque glass colour and heating it sounds easy, but you just try it. Never mind that the ancient Etruscans, the Chinese, even the early Britons all had a go. Alfred the Great's lovely Somersetshire jewel – he ordered it in AD 887 – looks a cinch, but the fake copy I once did drove me insane, took five months, and cost burnt fingers, eight metal splinters, and a fortune in materials. Adding insult, a charity woman talked me out of it for the Alder Hey Children's Hospital, which only goes to show how cruel they can be. And if you're going to try it, remember what the old enamellers used to preach before the spray method came in: you can't do it on big flat areas, only on curved – hence their liking for enamel miniatures – and the classic maxim that *every speck of dust leaves a hole in the colour.*

Bilston was the enamel Mecca. Once, collectors only thought Battersea. Now, the world is obsessed with Bilston and greedy for its enamelled plaques on silver and gold. If you too are crazy you should learn the Bilston colours, like they used a near peagreen from 1759 on. But the one colour that sends collectors demented is the famous 'English pink', as Continentals named the elusive, gentle, semi-rose hue that first saw light about 1785 and blows your mind.

Beth's small gold-mounted pendant of flowers and leaves had it, the chrome-tin complex, brilliant as the day it was made. Lovely,

lovely. It brought tears to my eyes, just thinking of how unfair life was, giving pristine jewels to an undeserving lass like Beth when they should have been mine.

Almost overcome, I reached my cottage in its overgrown garden. An envelope was on the bare flagstone in the porch. I brewed up, threw the letter aside. I recognized the handwriting. It would be the same old dear from Fenstone Old Rectory saying the same old thing:

Dear Sir,

Would you be able, for a small consideration, to speak with our parson concerning a fund-raising matter? I have been recommended to you by a person of your acquaintanceship, namely Mr Saughton Joyceson of Peckfold, Hertfordshire, who testifies to your honesty and integrity, and to your concern for worthwhile causes.

Thanking you in anticipation,

Yours faithfully,

Juliana Witherspoon (Miss)

It was the tenth begging letter I'd received from her in a fortnight. Church fund-raising, when I was broke? One odd thing, though. I retrieved the envelope. No postage stamp, no frank, so delivered in person. I'd have to watch out. If the geriatric herself had come to haunt the village's leafy lanes I'd better treat her as yet another predator, among bailiffs and servers of summonses.

Tea up. I took it out and sat on my low wall, which I'd finish one day, and swigged it with some jam and bread, but the robin and those little dipping brown birds came cadging so I only got half. I'd no more nuts for the bluetits. Let them go without for once, serve the thieving little swine right. They'd had my milk twice this week. They rip the foil cap so the bottles fill with rain. I get diluted rainwater while they get the cream. Life's just one damned thing after another.

2

Things are never what they seem. And I include every single thing. I could give you a million proofs, but Jox proves it best.

For a while I hung about the cottage. Its peace and tranquillity got me down so I hitch-hiked to town. There's a tradition in the village that anybody waiting by the chapel bus stop deserves a lift, but I don't trust to fortune. Women give me a lift if nobody's watching. Blokes only want to bully me into some parish council or club or sell me a secondhand motor as dud as my own. I always start walking.

Imagine my astonishment when a motor stopped. For a second I rejoiced, but it was only Jox. I got in with misgivings.

'It didn't come off, Lovejoy.' Not even a good day, hello.

'How do, Jox. It didn't, eh?'

He groaned, slipped his motor into first and pulled away. 'I had to hock my Jaguar.'

He pawns one of his three grand vehicles, so *I* must sympathize? 'Hard luck, Jox.' I'm pathetic.

'This is my brother's.' He nodded soberly. 'Charges me hiring fees. Tax, y'see.'

'Good heavens,' I said gravely, baffled.

There was more of this, all the way past St Peter's on North Hill. I won't go on, because Jox is the loser. Note that definite article: *the*, not just any old loser. Champion loser, is Jox. To realize the extent of his gift for catastrophe you have to know his background. It is formidable, for Jox was born rich, handsome, gifted, brilliant. He's only twenty-eight. He looks about ninety, on a good – meaning not specially disastrous – day.

Born into a titled family that owned (past tense, for Jox's calamitous skill is congenital) half of Lincolnshire, he went to famed schools, was tutored by geniuses, was an international athlete at swimming, hurdling and other sports of mind-bending dullness, gained a double first (whatever that is) at Cambridge University, married spectacularly some glamorous titled lass, got a spectacular divorce . . . Couldn't fail, right?

Wrong. Jox became an antique dealer.

With a residue of gelt, Jox got a small antique shop not far from Dragonsdale, between here and Fenstone. Rural to the point of somnolence. He could have done well – tourists on the way to John Constable's village, Gainsborough's house, pilgrims to Walsingham, all that. But Jox is jinxed. His fortunes plummeted, everything he touched turning to gunge. Like everybody who wants to 'settle down and run a small antique shop', he bought wrong, bid for fakes at every auction in the Eastern Hundreds, accumulated more dross than a town dump. And spent, and spent.

Until he was broke.

Then he borrowed, and spent. Finally getting the hint that the antiques trade was grimsville, Jox opened a small restaurant. It failed, gastroenteritis being what it is. His wildlife scheme ended when the local fox hunt found some ancient parchment that barred him. Those mediaeval monks had simply guessed Jox was on his way.

His real estate firm died when property developments crashed on account of a series of ancient footpaths somebody discovered. See what I mean? Folk who have everything just don't have it. The latest thing was this orchestra.

'Nobody wanted to play, eh, Jox?' I guessed shrewdly.

He almost wept, cursed at a little lad on a bicycle and honked his horn. Not a lot of patience, Jox.

'Play?' he cried, utter grief. 'It would have been superb! Like they did at Stoke-by-Nayland, that occasional choir and orchestra! Imagine playing in Fenstone's old St Edmund's Church. Like the Maltings at Snape – a musical Mecca!'

'Ta for the lift, Jox.' I tried to get out. We'd reached Benbow's auction room. I was fed up with Jox.

'That bastard of a parson scuppered me, Lovejoy.' I swear tears filled his eyes. Well, money does that.

'Wouldn't lend his church?'

'Fenstone parish council refused.'

'Tough, Jox.' I shook his hand off, made the pavement.

'It's that bloody village, Lovejoy. Ever since I set foot . . .' He shouted for me to hold on. 'Oh, Lovejoy. A ceremony tomorrow night, okay? Seven o'clock, the castle.'

'Can't, Jox.' I hate his catchpenny scams. Tourists and other maniacs adore them.

'Money, Lovejoy? And a meal?'

Grub? I'm pathetic, but hunger rules when your belly's empty. Mine gets emptier than anybody's. 'Castle, seven.'

He was still bleating as he pulled away. See what I mean, appearances? In Jox, you see a rich, educated, clever, sophisticated, talented geezer who couldn't help but succeed. The truth? Gloom and despond.

There was an element of truth in what he said, though. Before Fenstone, Jox was on top of the world. After, crump. It was decidedly odd. Maybe the place didn't suit him. I'm one of those who really does believe that some houses, streets, hamlets, countries even, are simply wrong for you. Like people, in a way. The place *knows* you're not right for it, and tries to tell you so. If you've any sense you listen, make a polite apology to the house or village concerned, and exit smiling. Otherwise . . . Well, I'm not one to get spooked by haunting thoughts. The least said the better. Moral: if a place doesn't like you, zoom.

Jox was daft to keep up appearances. A stiff upper lip is fine when you're building empires, but in personal life it only makes you look daft and talk funny.

Aye, Jox is definite proof that appearances lie. Things aren't ever what they seem.

Look at Queen Victoria. She was sober, frosty, sombre, right? Well, no. She was nothing of the kind. Victorian people *wanted* her to be like that, set her up in their minds just so. But it is on record that she shoved guards aside at a Mulready exhibition, the better to thrill over that artist's 'scandalously realistic' nudes, with their disproportionately tiny hands but luscious bodies. You don't hear much about William Mulready these days, but the Victorians knew lust better. Thackeray called him 'His Majesty KING MULREADY', above all the rest. And I know I keep on about the merriest grin ever photographed – on the lovely wrinkled face of the old Queen Empress rolling in the aisles at some drollery.

And look at Einstein. Everybody's perfect scientist, right? Not

7

really. The reappraisal joke is that MC squared means M for Misogynist and C for Cheat. Or some other things beginning with C. A swine to his family – including his shunned mentally sick youngest son, Eduard, and his illegitimate daughter Lieserl who the saintly Einstein pretended never even existed – he groped and ravished his way through fawning physics groupies all his life.

It isn't just people, meaning all of us, who prove my theory that everything's not what it seems. In the midsummer of 1993, the United Nations Human Rights Convention, presumably in the interests of human rights, barred . . . guess who? Only the most peaceable bloke on earth, the Dalai Lama. Wherever you look, preconceptions shatter. Stern old Isle of Man gave women the vote in 1881, long before even New Zealand got round to it. The Japanese Emperor Akihito, bastion of Japanese culture, prefers Chinese food. Constantine the Great, the first and holiest Christian emperor, wasn't. You wouldn't want to meet the likes of him in a dark alley, for the holy Constantine was lethal. He murdered Crispus, his own son, then his brother-in-law, little nephew, drowned his second wife in her bath . . . And the impression is that sharks in Australia's blue waters have killed millions. They haven't. Their total is 182, since records began when an Aborigine lady was eaten off New South Wales in 1791. And peaceful ancient East Anglia's villages aren't so peaceful or stable as they used to be. Why, look at that place Jox mentioned. Fenstone, hamlet of pestiferous Juliana Witherspoon (Miss), is in decline. Its population is dwindling fast, post office closed from atrophy, young people moving away, parishes merging, houses unbelievably standing empty. And Tinker, my oppo, whose antennae for antiques are worth any amount of electronics, and who does mundane (but not servile) jobs for me, passed through Fenstone itself last St Pumpkin's Day to pick up some antiques from a church robbery that I was brokering for some lass. He told me it was like a ghost village. No wonder the survivors were holding out their begging bowls.

Somebody was asking me something.

'Eh? Oh, wotch, Addie.'

She stood smiling, tried to take my arm and propel me somewhere. I shook her off gently, which takes some resolve, seeing I covet Adelaide Allardyce more than most. Her husband is a security man.

A born misanthropist, even now he was waiting in his car. As if people like me can't be trusted, the swine.

'Come and see this, Lovejoy. We're all agog about it.'

'It?'

'A colander. Two proddies came peering at it.'

A proddie is somebody who goes ahead of an antiques road show, which is a group of 'antiques experts' that travels from town to village, city to hamlet, offering to value (free of charge!) any antiques you might bring from your attic. They are loosely described as honest, and claim to act in your very best interests. Ahead of them barnstorm their proddies, putting up posters, bleating enthusiasm on local radio, flagging newspapers, stirring up eagerness. If you think of it, the proddies *have* to get us all searching our cellars for antiques, otherwise they'd get the sack. Their nickname is synonymous with unscrupulous.

'This way. Item 98, think it is.'

There's no point in hurrying through an auction viewing day. I take my time, drift, feeling the love that emanates from the few antiques hiding among the crud. There's always one beautiful antique, take my word for it. For always read every single time. Don't say I didn't warn you. If you go to a viewing day and see only an appalling mess of junk, and depart seething at time wasted cursing me for a fibber, then you've missed it. Serves you right for being unable to hear love shrieking in your earhole.

'Slow down.'

Addie tutted impatiently. 'You *amble*, Lovejoy.'

Women are great at impatience. It's not their fault. They're simply born with it. For me, hurrying is a terrible waste of all the seconds in between. Amble if you've a mind to. Don't gawp, ogle, rubberneck your way among the mangles, cupboards, flower stands, bureaux, old desks and boxes of decrepit toys. Looking never does much for me. It's feel that detects love. Simple as that. Eagle eyesight can't do it. Nor can those cunning electronic devices that folk carry about these days to peer microscopically at veneer or vaporize old paint.

Addie stamped her foot, pretty but pointless. I've been pushed by fearsome pushers and still stayed put.

Give you an instance: once, in Yorkshire, I saw a dealer inspecting a painting at a big auctioneer's. He had more gadgets than the parson preached about. Stereoscopic MacArthur microscope, water immersion and polarizing lenses, pigment anaylser, electronic impedance device to suss out precious stones – he was a walking laboratory, him and his briefcases. Even had a bonny secretary taking dictation as he probed and fussed. The reason I fell about laughing was that later I saw him bid, chucking away a fortune on a dud. The biggest joke was that next to the forgery was a genuine slip-inlaid celadon ewer. It had been made in Korea by firing the pottery piece on a ring of sand, producing the most gorgeous of colours, in the Koryo dynasty – which began over a century before our Battle of Hastings. It would have bought me a house, freehold, taxes paid. It went for a song, but not to me. Tragically, the four blokes I'd been trying to con – er, encourage – into buying it for me didn't turn up. The Japanese of the 1590s had sense: they invaded Korea and kidnapped the Korean potter families wholesale, kilns and all.

Drifting, I saw a few half-decent pieces that could be restored, mostly Victorian or Edwardian, but I'd not the money to bid. There was a lovely amber pendant, biggest I'd ever seen, carved in the form of a crucifixion scene, but it didn't feel right so I didn't stop to look because it would only have told me that Scandal was out of gaol and had resumed doing his stuff in Walberswick. He's our best amber carver, but can only afford amberoid – amber chips heatwelded together to simulate the real thing.

But this colander stopped me cold.

Some things don't need inspecting. They just glow like a star at dusk. I wobbled, crashed into a chair that almost gave. Adelaide caught me with a faint shriek.

'You all right, Lovejoy?'

A tweedy bystander, stiff country-gent collar, asked Addie what was going on. I heard her explaining, 'It's all right. He goes like this near a genuine antique . . .'

Feet thumped as people gathered, asking which was it, was it that painting over there that looked like Holman Hunt . . . I broke out in a sweat, same as malaria I'd had once when getting shot in indescribable foreign foliage.

'I'm all right,' I told Addie, and ta, mate, to Tweeds.

'Lovejoy's like this. Never forgeries. Only genuine – '

10

'Shut up, silly cow.' I would have clocked her one but I was still shivery from the colander.

'Can he really, well, *tell*?' a lady asked, fascinated. I could only see her shoes. They could have bought me, my immobile Ruby motor, and my prospects. Rare species had died to shoe her feet. She'd probably wear them twice.

'Every single time,' Addie announced proudly to the assembling multitude, her voice gaining decibels with every syllable. My secret gift was no secret any more. 'He's famous. We swear by him.' In auctions she bids like a rock'n'roll drummer. The essence of tact.

'Then why's he look destitute?' a manly voice intoned.

'Oh, well.' Addie was stuck, wanting to retreat. 'Lovejoy's, ah, affairs cost.'

To my relief a gravelly voice cut short Adelaide's broadcast.

'Lovejoy's shagnasty. Never the price of a pint.' Tinker, my barker, shuffled waveringly into view and hauled me upright. 'Come on, mate. Where is it?'

'There.' No point in trying to conceal the colander. Its price would now be astronomical, all the world and his wife poised to bid.

He all but dragged me to the table. I stared, for politeness. It didn't look much, but neither does the Mona Lisa.

Stoneware, a sandy brown, a simple pottery colander. That's all it was, the thing you strain vegetables with. Shaped, though, like a small basket, with plain holes all the way up its straight sides. The handle had two grooves. Nothing else to be said, except that it was the rarest piece of kitchenware. I'd seen one in my Grandma's when a little lad. Genuine, pure, lovely. I couldn't help smiling. Each little hole – all perfectly matched – had a small line grooved from it to the next horizontally, not vertically. The times I'd run a slate pencil along Gran's, hole to hole, making a grey-blue decoration.

Wasn't worth more than a week's wages, though, despite its rarity and pristine condition. Except to someone like me, who loved it.

'Genuine, Lovejoy?' from Addie, queen of the bloody obvious.

'Beautiful. Lancs., eighteenth century.' My voice wobbled.

'Imagine!' Addie shrieked, clapping, just in case somebody in the Midlands hadn't heard her first pronouncement.

'Price?' That man, peremptory.

'What it'll bring,' I said curtly and turned away.

'I asked you a civil question,' the man thundered.

Notice that people who aren't civil always say that, when they've been downright rude? I still hadn't seen his face. I felt for my hankie, decided not to bring it out because the women would holler it should have been washed last Easter, and instead blotted my dripping forehead with my frayed sleeve.

'*Isn't* it a *stupendous* gift?' Addie shrilled. 'Can you *imagine*? Coming over queer for a moment, then you simply *know* genuine? I've known Lovejoy for *ages*, ever since . . .' She coloured, ahemed.

'Lady, leave orff.' Tinker coughed, the burbling notes of his emerging phlegm magically clearing a space round us. His chest heaved, his old threadbare greatcoat swaying as his wheezes shook him into rigor. A fetor wafted away the delectable aroma of dust and must. Everybody wilted. 'Come on, mate.'

We got out, him marching me along the pavement like a squaddie to the guardroom. I shook my arm free.

'Where are we going, you stupid burke?'

'Forgotten, you pillock?'

'What? Forgotten what?' We'd reached Marks and Spencer's, stood there getting buffeted by prams and shoppers.

'The law, that's what. You're due in court.'

'Oh.' He was right. 'Have I got to?'

'Better had,' the scruffy old devil ground out. 'A bird's following you.' He jerked his chin stubble at the window. The girl in the bright peach frock was reflected at the bus stop, staring intently. Coincidence?

Anyhow, I'd no time. I had to get thinking about theatre glasses, as used by London's elegant ladies in 1750 to spy on other women making love.

'I say! You there! Lovejoy!'

The thunder man's voice, dopplering as he approached. I didn't even look. Tinker was right. The law wanted me.

3

Nothing gets very far from love. Antiques are already there, because they personify love like nothing else. Antiques *are* it. Look at 'opera' glasses, for instance.

As theatres and technology grew in the eighteenth century, so did innovations among theatre-goers. Gentry moved into boxes, snootily quaffed and noshed during the plays on balconies, far removed from the *hoi polloi* rioting with pies and beer in the stalls below. But grand ladies found it irksome to merely watch actors giving their all. They'd mostly gone for gossip, a chance to suss out the gorgeous apparel of rival beauties. Even with the aid of 'prospect glasses' – miniature telescopes – to observe the actors' dastardly deeds, shows could be pretty dull. These 'lorgnettes', as the French called them, could be put to more interesting use, especially if one's dear friend was in another box across the other side of the theatre. What could be more interesting than swivelling the prospect glass to watch her instead of Ben Jonson's play?

It could be more interesting still if one's best friend got up to no good in the gloaming of reflected limelight, just when she thought she was secure and incognito. And women crave to see other women at it – as long as they themselves go unnoticed.

But ladies who planned assignations in theatres learnt cunning. They came with fans, wore masks, adopted fanciful garb, used screens, employed disguise. And gentlemen took umbrage at being overtly observed while in some deep sexual intrigue. It became especially troubling when the lady concerned turned out to be no lady at all, but some tart picked up in Covent Garden. Duelling was in the air. Reputation was everything. Scandal was a fitting reason to go about killing people who spread it.

Enter the inventiveness of Georgian London. Lorgnettes were hidden in the handles of the gentleman's walking canes, in ladies' fans. Prospect glasses were sold that folded, or shrank to minuscule proportions. All clever stuff. But the worrisome fact remained, that if you wanted to spy on a friend making love in the theatre's cosy dark, you still had to dangle out at an ungainly angle and ogle with your mini-telescope in an unseemly way. You simply could not pretend, when pretending is the woman's love game, always has been. Another urgent call on Georgian instrument makers.

They solved it brilliantly, with a thing called the polemoscope. The French, always in the running when improving wickedness, called the polemoscope a *lorgnette de jalousie*, the 'jealousy glass' of London.

Basically simple, you can make one yourself. Take a tube (cardboard if you like) and make a small telescope out of it same as usual. You cut a long oval in the tube's side, and glue a mirror inside at an angle. Then to the theatre and, affecting great interest in Mr Shakespeare's tragedy, you raise your jealousy glass. And you see, not the stage play, but the goings-on in the box immediately to your right or left. *And nobody knows*. Folk can glance slyly at you all they like, but all they see is you staring with wrapt fascination towards the stage. Actually, you have a bird's-eye view of your friend's passionate scene in the adjacent box and can focus on every ravishing grab and grope. Polemoscopes sold well.

The ones that collectors favour most nowadays are the jewelled ones, plus the rarities. The great Wedgwood did some All things being equal, the smaller the better. Go for the ones concealed in toothpick quivers, pendants or hidden in watches – this last the rarest.

'In, Lovejoy,' Tinker was saying, pushing me.

'I'm going, I'm going.'

Across the street the girl in the peach dress was walking purposefully along the pavement. So what?

'I'll be in the Drum and Dog, Lovejoy,' Tinker said, pity in his voice. For himself, note, not for me.

'Put your beer on the slate. I'll pay at weekend.'

'We broke again?'

Not even worth answering. I went in for my big scene.

Most things actually aren't. Antiques taught me that. It's a sort of law with me. It's simple, but complex inside, if you follow. Most things aren't.

Start with antiques. Antiques aren't, because mostly they're fake, dud, Sexton Blakes, simulants, repros. Estimates vary, but the lowest is ten per cent at any famed auction. Choose any great art gallery in the world, forgeries are a tenth. And the highest proportion? The sky, the sky. Old Master drawings are all fakes until proved genuine. And I do mean *proved* squared, cubed, finger prints of Michelangelo attested by Scotland Yard, and the certificate of authenticity treble checked. And then don't bother, for an Old Master drawing is sham. Only a true divvy knows.

It goes for other things too. Marriage, cynics could say, is a partnership of deceivers based on convenience. Government isn't. Policing isn't. Truth usually certainly isn't. Holiness positively certainly isn't its beautiful self. But the real front runner for being definitely not what it's cracked up to be is Law. Lawyers, laws, legalities, The Law in all its grandeur, is one enormous fraud. We don't have Law, we have lawyers. Sadly, lawyers've won the game. One or two judges, maybe a politician here and there, is aware of this terrible criminal conspiracy, but they're as helpless as the rest of us. I entered the law courts without misgiving. I've misgiven so often there was no point.

'Lovejoy,' I reported.

The goon looked up. 'Hello, Lovejoy. Thought you was still with that rich bird in Wales.'

Some memories make you wince. I winced stealthily, not to give him satisfaction. Den Heanley's a stout uniformed bloke with a walrus moustache, fancies himself at nine-pin bowls of a Saturday night at the Welcome Sailor, sails off Southwold. He has a cousin in Zurich's police, so he knows I killed my missus once, he says. He has a wayward daughter, sixteen, who manages illicit chemicals and university students. He's worried sick, his wife suicidal over the girl. Outwardly, he's the avuncular custodian of our legal portals, ticks names off a tally list.

'I've no money for bribes, Den.'

'*Fees*, Lovejoy. The law's against bribes.'

'Ha, ha, Den.' I looked about. 'Where do I go?'

'Through there, and – '

'And wait,' I finished. 'Chance of a cupper?'

Taking his pen, I signed *Winston Churchill, 1, Hyde Park Gate* and walked through. Nobody else waiting. Distant voices pontificated, echoed. A door slammed. Footfalls thumped. Silence. More fairy voices, a stern bass intoning somebody's name.

Quarter of an hour. Another. Half an hour.

Rising, I returned to Den. 'How much longer?' A posh suited bloke advanced.

'Lovejoy? I called out, and you ignored me! That's the action of a bounder!'

'Sod off,' I said. It was the thunder man from the auction. Medium height, furled brolly, waistcoated double-breasted suit worn with such assurance you could almost believe they were still in fashion. Moustache like that old comedian. He'd have his bowlers privately made (sorry, built; you *build* bowler hats), Bates's of Jermyn Street, London.

'Guard! Make this hoodlum speak in a civil manner!'

'Yes, sir.' Den's eyes gave me an imploring look. 'Lovejoy. This is the chief magistrate, Mr Ashley Battishall.'

'Sod off.'

'Heanley,' the thunder man thundered. 'Bring him to me the instant he's given his evidence!'

He strode off. Unfortunately, you need really long legs for a good stridey exit. He tried, didn't make it. And I think bowlers are only for squat navvies or tall effete gentlemen who are deadly shots and can ride dromedaries.

'He ever ridden a dromedary, Den?'

Den sighed. 'Don't start, Lovejoy.' He perked up with a smile at a distant echo. 'They're calling you.' He pointed with a pencil. I hate that. 'If you get done, Lovejoy, it's Bill Tyrone on the cells.'

Bill, custodian of us honest people penned in our town dungeons, gets me fish and chips from Sadie's.

If it's all right with you, I won't go into detail about the court. The ritual's repellent, their tricks hideous, the whole charade disgusting. Lawyers can't see it, of course, because it's their livelihood. Makers of poison gas must have their own rationalizations. Juries listen, or don't. Judges listen, or don't. The mouthies talk, trying to seem lifelike. My bit concerned a polemoscope.

'Would I be right to say you gave the defendant one of these instruments?' the barrister asked when he could be bothered.

'Aye.'

'An antique?'

'No.'

That made his team shuffle papers and glare.

He cleared his throat, to put the knife in. He flapped a paper at me, an irritating fly.

'To the police, you stated it was marked London made, 1878. Do you deny this?'

'No.'

'Yet now you say it isn't an antique?'

'Yes.'

The magistrate cut in. 'Could you explain, Lovejoy?'

Him I knew from last year. I'd sold him a mahogany smallboy without veneer. Lovely. Because he was a magistrate I'd told him it was a reproduction I'd made, but he hadn't minded.

'Antiques begin in 1837, m'lord. Things made later aren't.'

'Aren't?'

'The Customs and Excise lot started to con the public into believing antiques were defined as a century old, so they could charge money on more things. Then people started claiming anything older than seventy-five years, then fifty.' I paused, but nobody spoke. I added helpfully, 'I don't trust moving goalposts, Your Honour.'

'The, ah, device was marked as London, 1878?'

'Yes.'

'Very well!' The barrister flung his paper down to put the fear of God in me. It didn't work, because the fear's already there. This wart was a pillock. 'Why did you give it to the defendant, Packo Orange, a rival antique dealer?'

'So he would keep quiet.'

'Quiet about what?' He looked blank.

'About a sympathy.'

'Explain!' He stood akimbo, jowls dangling.

'I already have.'

'Lovejoy.' The magistrate was getting tired. An old bloke, he's our town's contract bridge champion, hangs anybody who uses the Culberston system. 'What is a sympathy?'

Packo wasn't in court, which was a pity. He'd like this. No greater raconteur than Packo Orange. He was probably pulling his usual trick of dying in the cells. He's an elderly mate of mine, paintings faker in Dedham. Looks exactly like a garden gnome, beard and all, yet cohabits with a succession of young blondes. His worn joke is that he changes them when the ashtrays are full. You are expected to laugh.

'A sympathy's a painting, m'lord, done using sympathetic inks.'

'Lovejoy,' he admonished wearily, as if I'd gone two no trumps without a knave for entry and only one point.

'I'm telling you!' I said indignantly. 'The auction had a blank painting, a sympathy, on sale. I wanted it badly. The dealers laughed, thinking it stupid, but they're thick as a well wall. Packo knew it for a sympathy. So I bribed him to keep out of the bidding.'

'That is illegal!' somebody interposed.

My turn to be weary now. We have this hopeless law about the conduct of bidders in auctions. It stands virtually unused.

'What did you bribe him with, Lovejoy?' the old beak asked.

'The polemoscope, and the Coke recipe.'

'The what?' Everybody woke up at that.

'The recipe for Coca-Cola, sir. Packo was thinking of marketing some, though it seems a waste of time to me.' The news seemed to have thrown them. Consternation was about. I helped it along, seeing they were interested. 'I told him to convert it all back to imperial measures, because the Coke company do it in metric nowadays. But that's not my fault, is it?'

Nobody answered. Two lawyers were whispering. Then, 'Recipe? Is it not secret, Lovejoy?'

'Oh, aye. Packo thought 19.94 grammes of alcohol was too much – you end up with a hundred litres.' I paused, adding helpfully, 'That's knocking on twenty-seven gallons, Your Honour.'

They held the wary silence, a Byzantine court wondering who had the sword.

'And 4.48 grammes of coca leaf, same as they used to. I showed Packo how to do it. Have you ever tried measuring out 77.4 grammes of glycerine? Phew! I can't see why 44.8 grammes of phosphoric acid doesn't rot your guts.'

'Isn't this unknown?' the old man squeaked.

'Yes, Your Honour. But everybody knows it. Like the pope's

secret telephone beside the high altar, St Peter's in Rome.' The old bloke shook his head. 'It's Vatican extension 3712.'

'Mr Moore? Relevance?'

'It's just me, m'lord,' I said kindly. 'My mind's a ragbag. Things stick. Like, Italians are supposed to rank the world's most scoundrelly blokes. And, a male contestant was barred from the Miss Australia Quest contest, even though he'd won a local pageant hands down.' No response. I went on, 'The US shows eight times more violent acts per hour on children's TV programmes than in prime time . . .' I petered out.

'Return to the sympathy,' the barrister bawled.

'Look.' I was narked. He was making a mint, standing there showing off. It was me sinking into destitution. 'Any nerk knows that some chemicals change colour when heated. They knew it back in 1829, when that sympathy was first painted.'

'Lovejoy,' the magistrate queried. 'A *blank* painting?'

'Yes, guv'nor.' I didn't mind him. I was getting fond of the silly old sod. 'Dissolve zaffer ore in aqua regia acid. Dilute it four times, and paint on a blank surface. You see nothing, right? But heat it, and you see a luscious sea-green colour. Let the paper cool down, it vanishes again.' One of the lawyers was scribbling, taking it all down. I smiled, knowing an embryonic crook when I see one. 'Warm it again, the green painting reappears. Use zaffer in spirits of nitre, though, it'll do the same in red. Combine the two, you get other colours.'

'A sympathy is a painting that emerges only when heated?' he summarized. 'Thank you, Lovejoy.'

'Not at all. The ones ladies of olden times loved were landscapes, bare of trees or flowers. A lady feeling particularly low would bring out her plain landscape painting, place it by the fire, and watch the spring grass and trees cover the scene in foliage and flowers. Her own springtime!'

'So you persuaded my client to a criminal act,' the barrister denounced in phoney rage, 'to acquire this sympathy!'

'Yes.'

That stopped him. 'You admit it?'

'Yes. I wanted to make several forgeries of it.'

'*Forgeries?*' three of them said together.

Courts make me fed up. 'I did eleven.' I shrugged. 'Make one sympathy, you might as well do several. The price of frames is frigging criminal, though. You lawyers should check the framers on East Hill.'

They shut me up, dunno why, demanded times, dates, where I'd seen Packo Orange selling his own forgeries – he did a nice one of a John Constable, *Landscape Noon*, but from the opposite view. I waxed eloquent, telling them Packo was straight as a die, but the Law had it in for him whatever anybody said.

Out, after four wasted hours. I left the back way, so avoiding Den and so, I believed, keeping out of the way of that magistrate, him and his frigging furled brolly. I'd had enough law to last me for one day, if not two.

Addie caught me up as I reached the Arcade, and told me in breathless excitement that she'd almost practically virtually nearly managed to buy the colander but been outbid by some idiot in a bowler hat.

'Did you get the name, Addie?' I knew she took everything down at auctions, who bid for what, prices.

'Yes.' She eyed me with smiling calculation. 'Lovejoy! You want something I have!'

'I can always ask one of the whifflers,' I told her airily.

'What will you do for me, darling?' she said, coming all little-girl winsome.

'Forget it,' I said, narked. Then realized my voice hadn't managed to say anything at all. 'Forget it.'

She ran the tips of her fingers along my shredding lapel, looking up. 'You don't really mean that, do you, darling?'

A motor horn sounded three peremptory blasts. Hubby, revving angrily across by the other kerb. God, he'd a glare that would melt glaciers.

'Give it me, Addie.' Any woman can pull any bloke, whatever they pretend. And a woman with valuable information about antiques could pull me any time she wanted.

'The priory, Lovejoy. Eight, tomorrow,' she said softly, then sprang back. Wearily I waited while she did the purity scenario. 'Certainly not, Lovejoy!' she cried, stamping for her hubby's benefit. 'A partnership? Out of the question, and that is final!'

She marched to the car and embarked. It pulled away, him smirking as they glided past the war memorial.

Eight, the priory. I joined Tinker at the tavern ten minutes later. He handed me a letter. Familiar handwriting, Juliana Witherspoon (Miss) had struck again. I was about to chuck it away when Tinker restrained me.

'Best look, son,' he croaked. 'It's threats.'

He'd read it without opening the envelope. I wish I knew how he does it.

Dear Lovejoy,

Kindly respond, or I shall take grievous action. Your assignations with a lady are known to me. I shall expose your perfidious nature to her relatives. Six o'clock, please, at the town library, tomorrow.

I remain,
Yours faithfully,
Juliana Witherspoon (Miss)

Threats *and* please? So courtesy was hanging on by a thread even yet. Well, Beth's Bilston enamels still beckoned, and she'd kill me if I let J. W. (Miss) run amok with her glad tidings.

4

Tonietta, when I finally found her, was pushing her cart through the shopping precinct and ready for a fight. Mind you, I've never seen Tonietta tranquil. She's always girding for Armageddon. This time she was readying to scream the town down over somebody pinching her pitch.

'You fucking frigging shitting bastards I'll marmalize the lot of you. . . !' et Tonietta cetera. From there, her invective goes downhill. Take it on trust: Tonietta is dynamite, abusive, and usually wrong about everything except tortoise-shell. She hates her two sisters, both carnivores, and I have teethmarks to prove it. She doesn't speak to her mother. On rare occasions, she'll communicate with the world through her dad, a pleasant patient man who tries to cobble his family together using birthdays as excuses, but failing often. He's a museum archivist.

Patiently I waited her rage out. Long wait. Nobody had pinched her pitch, of course; there were only three other barrows in the square. One I knew vaguely, Connor, a seller of hot potatoes with cheese fillings. Another was Lucille, the fish lass from Lowestoft, looking the part under red-and-white striped awnings and straw boater, neat pinny. And Gravity Woodward, a morose globe-hater who takes racing bets on commission while disguised as a tree that speaks morose hatred in a little square of greenery encouraging you to throw coppers in the charity fountain. The flyers – sudden sellers who whirlwind through markets offering discount fruit on its last legs and who hadn't a legit hawker's licence between them – weren't in today.

Tonietta fired off one last salvo at Lucille and set up her cart by simply halting and opening the top. It lets down into a small counter. She smiled beatifically.

'Hello, Lovejoy. You know Jox is looking for you?'

'Aye.' I eyed her wares. Trinkets, some tortoise-shell.

You go a long way to get more lovely material to work with than tortoise-shell. Some major antiques were made of it. Like, Henry IV of France was nursed in a cradle made of a tortoise's inverted shell, one complete thing. Some writers claim that the ancient Greeks and Romans manufactured musical instruments from sea turtle carapaces. I've even done a fake one myself, a lyre from dried cracked old shell, copying the musical shape from a vase in the British Museum and selling the final instrument for Jellbone's missus after he got done for robbing two Bavarian antique dealers of a valuable Cozens watercolour in Coggeshall.

'I've some pale shell, Lovejoy.'

Dealers call pale tortoise-shell antiques 'blondies'. It is highly prized. The shell itself is sold by the pound, best from the Caribbean but sometimes the Far East. White shell – I think it a sort of dusky amber colour – costs ten times as much as the so-called 'black', which is grubby brown to near black. The horrible thing is the way it's collected. The islanders catch a turtle while it's laying its eggs, turn it on its back, then do one of two ghastly things. They light a fire on its living belly, or they lever it into a cauldron of boiling water so it can thrash and bleat and flail . . .

'Sit down for fuck's sake, Lovejoy.' Tonietta abused me roundly, giving me her folded stool. She rammed my head between my knees so I could recover. 'You're always like this dying on me you squeamish bastard I'm sick of the frigging sight of you you pillock that's three pounds twelve shillings and elevenpence,' she continued brightly to a lady with a little girl. Tonietta talks in old coinage, before the Great Decimal Deception conned us and made the Treasury rich. She meant three sixty-five, give or take. 'Original genuine tortoise-shell pendant, in silver plate. I've some beautiful combs . . .'

The poor turtles are sometimes dissected free of their shell while still alive, then, bleeding and naked, are chucked back into the shark-infested waters where, in time, they grow another shell but of poor quality. It's an industry. On the lovely wave-washed moonlight shores of the tropical islands, you get served turtle steaks cooked in the poor thing's carapace. A turtle dies slow. It dies slowest, they say, in Madagascar, where they can keep a sea turtle alive during the very act of dissection so it can actually scent its own turtle soup cooking . . .

'What's the matter with Lovejoy?' the little girl asked.

'Drunk, love,' Tonietta said smoothly, crouching to be friendly while the tot's mother paid for the pendant.

'Lovejoy? She's telling porkies, isn't she?'

'He'll be better when he's sober.' Tonietta straightened, less friendly.

'Lovejoy drinks when one of his aunties tells him off,' the mite foghorned. 'Your aunties don't stay long, do they, Lovejoy?'

'Not usually, Brenda.' I babysit for Brenda and her cousin Henry. They're from the village.

'I liked your last auntie. She has a dog,' Brenda said, loudly confiding to the world. 'She's married to the vicar but bounces in bed – '

'Thank you!' Brenda's scarlet-faced mother shrilled quickly, grabbing her change and dragging away Brenda Blabbermouth, who complained she wanted to stay and see me be sick.

'You better?' Tonietta can be kind when things were going her way. 'I'll get you a coffee.'

'No, ta. I'm okay.'

For a while I pulled myself together, watching the passers-by shop. The precinct forms the centre of our town square. For a kingdom's most ancient recorded town, the square is brand new. Paved, a few covered ways, two arcades, a fountain, shops abutting, stalls and itinerant barrows, buskers here and there, it's pleasant. There's even a caff, trying to look continental with white plastic tables and chairs in clusters. Pigeons, of course, lending droppings, ectoparasites, and authenticity to the scene. A girl from the music school was playing a violin with intense preoccupation, some Purcell air I think, a cap on the flagging by her feet.

'What pale shell, Tonietta?'

'This.'

And she pulled out a small fan, a tiny thing. It beat a chime in my middle that practically put me on my feet again better than any pick-me-up. It folded, had fewer than a dozen sticks to it, and was mounted with traces of gold. Definitely the real thing, but sadly broken, five of the blades badly fractured, almost as if somebody had trod on the lovely creation. Late seventeenth century, rare. No carefully sculpted holes in it that would have been the giveaway sign

24

of the 'quizzer', the quizzing fan that allowed a lady to conceal her face with gracious modesty but peep at everybody. Of course, a turtle carapace has thirteen great scales, with littler scales towards the edge, so you are limited by size. This was genuine, not merely workbench sweepings held together by melted gelatine.

'Who's the duckegg that danced on it?' I hadn't touched it.

'I have this new feller, Lovejoy.' Unabashed, she did a brisk sale, a plastic comb. 'He's a driver, Hook of Holland ferries. He stood up, sudden.'

'This is English.' I held my hand like a child does playing cowboys with imaginary pistols. Four inches, tip of the middle finger to where your thumb forms the pistol hammer at your index finger's palmar crease. 'The blades were only four inches long. Then they lengthened to nine, end of the first George's reign. They went giant in the 1740s, up to two feet, but then folk saw sense. Nine to eleven inches became a sort of norm.'

'Real shell, then?'

She was thrilled, but kept on serving. Connor brought her over a huge steaming spud. My belly rumbled a begging plaint but he shuffled away without offering me a mouthful.

'Aye.' I touched it then, at least as thrilled as her. 'Sorry, pal,' I told it in sincere apology, and looked at its venation against the daylight. You could hardly see the pallor of veins in it. 'You're beautiful, a darling. You deserve the very best.' A tortoise-shell fan this old was beyond belief.

'Will you mend it, Lovejoy?'

'Aye. It'll take a while.'

'I'll bring it. Got to have it photographed first.'

She didn't trust me, after all I'd been to and done for her. Well, nearly been, and nearly done. (Tip: when entrusting some antique to an 'expert', do two things. First, *weigh* it. Second, *photograph* it. Then when it's returned, so-say cleaned or whatever, you have a couple of measurements to check that it hasn't been swapped for a fake.)

'I'm at the library meeting some old crone. Then the priory ruins. Six o'clock and eightish.'

'Don't tell me, Lovejoy,' she said, sure of herself now I was hooked on her priceless fan. 'The geriatric at six, the married bitch in the dusk at nightfall. Have I got it right?'

25

'If it's Lovejoy, dear,' a voice tweeted, 'it's *never* what *I'd* call the right way round!'

Cyril stood there, a riot of coloured sequins. He and Keyveen had lately become our town's most flamboyant flamers. God knows where they get their money – and their household furniture, paintings, jewellery.

'How do, Cyril,' I said miserably. I never know what to say to this pair. They spend their time scrapping about intangibles. Keyveen is always bitter about something. Cyril is, according to him, the showpiece. Today's garb was a drum majorette's tall military hat, glittering cloak, and a Hussar's fitted riding trousers with a magenta stripe into circus boots. He looked a prat.

'Three hundred,' Cyril cooed.

Scanning the pedestrians, I saw Keyveen glowering and my heart sank. They'd have heard every word of my chat with Tonietta, seen my response to the antique fan. They already knew what to offer. Keyveen's Irish, sullen and always working something on a calculator.

'Ignore Keyveen, Lovejoy,' Cyril said. 'He's in a most terrible *sulk* because I stopped him dancing during breakfast. Can you imagine, the Moonlight Saunter with your crispies?'

'Oh, good,' I said lamely, going red because everybody was looking and grinning, but everybody knows Cyril and his mate.

'Wrong, Lovejoy. Indescribably *bad*.'

'That what you're offering?' Tonietta asked.

'Six, then, you slush-mouthed cow.' The cloying sweetness of Cyril's voice is often at odds with his words. 'And I mean that description most sincerely.'

'What d'you think, Lovejoy?' she asked me.

'Double.' The price was an insult to the lovely masterpiece. Think what had died, and how. Cyril and Tonietta were bargaining over the last mortal remains of a beautiful sea creature, one of the oldest species on Planet Earth.

'Twelve hundred,' Tonietta said, breathless. 'And you pay Lovejoy's repairs.'

People gathered. Keyveen was pacing, guessing things weren't going Cyril's way. I wondered if they had some sort of concealed mike.

'All right, you thieving rotting corrupt evil bitch.' Cyril maintained his cherubic smile. He turned to me. 'Lovejoy? Remember this moment. I still haven't forgiven you for saying my last hairdo looked barmy. Now, it's war. Do you hear?'

He saw me try to duck beneath the stall, looked round, glimpsed the besuited magisterial figure stalking through the square, and smiled beatifically.

'Yoo-hoo!' He waved, pointing at me, shooing people aside so I could be seen. 'Lovejoy's here, sailor!'

My heart walloped as far as it could go. Cyril screamed with laughter as the gent marched towards us. Bowler on, moustache abristle, brolly stabbing the flagstones.

'Cyril,' I said, but I don't know how to threaten like him. 'Tonietta,' I said, but I don't know how to beg like her.

Both were smiling, counting gelt. I felt sold. Across the square I glimpsed Beth, gliding towards the car park. My hopes lifted. I stood up, smiled, got in a quick wave, but she instantly turned away. Ta, Beth, sweetheart who had begged me to use foul language while we shagged among the daisies, how long ago? Keyveen intercepted my desperate gesture and beamed.

Time to grasp the nettle. I set my shoulders, smiling my best ingratiating smile.

'Mr Battishall!' I exclaimed. 'I tried to find you, but that Heanley's never there, is he? How can I help you?'

'Job,' he barked. 'Car. Two minutes. Post office.'

Not all bad news, then. I cheered up a bit. 'I wonder if it can wait, sir? It's getting on for four now and I have my sick uncle to see to in the village. Needs his tea about now.'

'Nobody indispensible! Get organized! Two minutes!'

Well, I'd tried. I'd made enemies, some old, some new, made not a penny, and failed to endear myself to practically everybody. Uselessly, I'd wriggled as best I could and still lost out to fate. I finished up getting driven out past the decaying village of Fenstone and to Dragonsdale by Mr Ashley Battishall to his mansion house for tea and crumpets.

5

Except it wasn't a mansion house. Once, it had been grand, lovely, old, a place that might welcome you, say everything's all right now you're home. Queen Anne if it was a day, the great place was imposing, chimneys elegant, red brickwork warm, windows stylish without those windows phoney walled-in to avoid the iniquitous window tax of bygone times.

It looked glorious, felt cold as charity.

Mr Battishall skidded to a halt, showering gravel. A wrinkled bloke, small and dapper, came forward smiling.

'Bags, sir?' he asked, chirpy, then his smile faded.

That look I'd seen a million times. It announced: I recognize you. Without a groat, no tips, no luggage – get lost, mate.

'Lovejoy will not be staying, Nick,' Mr Battishall said, striding to the grand balustrade, leaving the motor running.

'I'll not be staying, Nick,' I said, following at an unmilitary step.

We entered what could have been a beautiful home. A discreet notice said it was the Dragonsdale Guest and Residential Hotel. I apologized to the old place. It felt ashamed. It was cardboarded off into flatlets, a sort of pigeon coop for, well, those who want to be pigeons cooped.

The carpet was a modern Chinese mass product, not bad but still only that. The woodwork – panels, skirting boards, pelmets even, staircase, bannisters – was replaced by imported softwood and chipboard. It felt an utter disgrace.

'Hard luck, love,' I said, then realized I'd spoken aloud.

'What?' Battishall rounded, bristling.

'Your house. Poor thing's been ruined. Gutted,' I explained, 'and falsified.' I swear the old manor straightened up. I felt it go: *Tell 'em, friend*.

'This mansion is restructured on the best architectural precepts, designwise, from reconstructional necessity.'

'So's the bloody council's car park.' They'd recently demolished a wondrous ancient building – this place's contemporary – on Balkerne Hill, to make a flat spread of concrete for council workers to park their limos. 'You desecrated her. She was exquisite, once, I'll bet. I'd give almost anything to've known her then.'

'You are stupid, Lovejoy,' he said. A maid came forward to take his bowler, brolly, leather gloves. 'Is Mrs Battishall in, Lily?'

'Yes, sir.' She avoided my smile. Like Nick. 'In the guest drawing room, sir.'

He strode across the imitation parquet flooring and knocked on an imported kiln-dried pine double door. God, I was already sick of the place. He listened. After five minutes, a faint voice said, 'Enter.'

A lady reclined on a phoney (meaning made yesterday) chaise longue. She was straight out of a domestic Ealing comedy of years ago, desperately trying to be young with wispy attire and makeup that had probably taken hours. Dyed blonde hair. Enough jewellery to float a Zurich loan – were it genuine. I wish I'd had some quality sunglasses, to check the polarization of her false diamonds. She didn't wear a tiara, but it had been a close call. Oddly, a curtained painting – I could just see the frame – hung above a cornish. A votive candle burned there, quite like an altar.

'This is the person, Roberta. Lovejoy.'

She extended a languid hand. I didn't know what to do. Genuflect? Stoop to kiss her digits, or just say wotcher? Clearly she expected some sort of grovel.

'Er, how do, missus.' I wished I'd had a hat. I could have rotated it in my hands, peasant before gentry.

'Put him where I can see him, Ashley.'

He almost tiptoed, beckoned me to cross a synthetic rug and sit opposite the lady. I couldn't help gaping. Battishall's manner was transformed. From barking military country gentleman, to an instant serf. She lay back exhausted on the cushions he leapt to arrange, and indicated a glass of milky fluid. He sprang to lift it to her lips so she could drink without expending too many ergs.

Was she dying, then? Or simply crashed out from night-long wassailing in this genteel guesthouse? These things worry me because I never know where I am with women at the best of times. Now here was Madam Frailty making her servile hubby bring me here, when I

29

could be elsewhere being ravished by Adelaide or protecting my assignations with Beth by chatting up old Juliana Witherspoon. Both would have been useful pursuits. And I had fake mediaeval pieces of jewellery to make by noon tomorrow, for Slicer. He's called that because he likes to cut people – cut as in slice, not as in ignore.

The firedogs were fake, epoxy resin monstrosities done down Aldgate. God, but the manor had been diced up. I wonder they hadn't taken the brickwork. Then I noticed the faint indentations by the window, a giveaway, and knew they *had* taken the frigging brickwork. There's a terrific market for it. You can always tell, however good the plasterers are. Something to do with oblique light.

'How?' the lady managed to whisper.

'?' I went, not even knowing what I was here for.

'How do you do it?' La Battishall was prompting an awestruck courtier before her august majesty.

'Divvying?' I might have known. Everybody wants me to do it, scenting money. 'Near an antique, I feel queasy, malaise, like flu's on its way. Duds don't do it, unless they're particularly repellent like your house.'

'*What* did he say, Ashley?' She moved an inch.

Ashley hurtled to hold her. Even the bloody cushions were replicas, supposedly Victorian but unhumanly machined.

'He said our lovely mansion was . . . not nice, dearest.'

Tears filled her eyes, pools of reproach. She wept at the horrors out there and the pain within.

'Lovejoy!' Still quiet, trying for sibilance, he glared, at attention but quivering. A horse whipping was the way for daring the truth here. 'You will speak with greatest possible respect to Mrs Battishall at all times. Am I understood?'

'Aye. But look at it, for Christ's sake.' I rose and crossed to the window. 'Can you imagine what this building was like? Lovely proportions, gables, brickwork perfect, everything in delicate balance. Instead, you've raped the poor thing, reamed it out like a petrol motor's cylinder, and sold its very arteries, veins, lifeblood.' I drifted back, feeling really down. 'You've not even done a post mortem. You've vivisected, and left a bonny husk, you rotten sods.'

For a second the image of a sea turtle rose but I wiped it out. I'd had enough giddy spells for one day, and I still hadn't recovered from

Beth in the woods yet. I was hungry as hell. Battishall talked of manners, but he hadn't even offered me a cup of char.

'Is he being horrid to me, Ashley?' she whimpered.

'For the last time, I assure you.'

His glares were getting me narked.

'Look. Your husband's a legal eagle, so can put the screws on me. That doesn't mean I have to admire the crime you've committed gutting this lovely old house. Because, in fact, it makes me puke.'

'Ashley!' she screamed faintly, swooning.

'Is that it?' I didn't sit down, moved towards the door.

'Stay!' Battishall thundered, repeated it in a whisper.

'What for?' I watched them both. It was an act, her snowflake fragility, and him the great panjandrum becoming the bootboy in her parlour. Pathetic. Like me, I suppose.

Her tears flowed. She held out a hand. He sprang, gave her a lace wisp – manmade fibre, meaning of course anything but manmade in today's sham world. 'Tell him, Ashley.'

'Very well.' He rose, jerked his head at the armchair I'd vacated. I stayed still, noticing now that he wasn't immense as he'd seemed before. In fact, he'd definitely shrunk.

'Do listen, Lovejoy.' Her lips fluttered. 'It is vital. The hope for the world.'

My mind went, *Eh?*, but my heart had done its plunge. Antiques is a loony game, with blood in it. I've had anything and everything brought to me. Everything from the Holy Grail to the Crown Jewels, every barmy scheme you could imagine. Some scoops aren't quite so daft – I mean, Roosevelt and Churchill both wrote scripts for the movies, Hitler painted (if that's the word for those things a mighty London auction house auctioned off lately). Celebrity sells. They'd sold everything they could remove, cut, tease, yank out, of this mansion house, replacing it with modern gunge. And even the space too, if they had paying guests lodging among the rafters. I didn't mind them claiming that civilization hung in the balance if they'd got some precious antique. I've seen blokes weep at missing a cigarette card or a Huguenot twine button for a set. I've done it myself, twice hourly if it gets results. I remember making love to this woman who had a Regency commode, with only an hour to go before a buyer came from Sotheby's. You should have heard the promises I made to her. I moved me to tears. I wish I'd been on tape, maybe learn a few things. You forget what you say in the heat of the moment . . . Where was I? Fate of the world, these loony Battishalls.

'We have a responsibility, Lovejoy,' Battishall began, glancing at his recumbent lady. 'We have invested heavily, in . . .'

'Preservation,' she sighed.

'Preservation!' he agreed with pride. 'We have run short of capital, Lovejoy,' he went on portentously. 'This is the most significant project on earth. Once known, the world will be agog!'

Oh, aye, I thought. The lady drifted out of her decline to join the general hilarity, exclaiming feebly, 'The world will be a place of peace and love. True civilization restored, the glory of yesteryear!'

Straight out of Mrs Gaskell, whose writing I like, but you can't really say her stuff aloud and expect to be taken seriously. Except Roberta Battishall was gorgeous. If she had access to some antique valuable enough to gut her home and hearth for, then I could at least listen.

'And now we need funds to continue our onward march!' Good old Ashley, recovering rank. 'Our righteous duty, Lovejoy!'

Righteous duty snuffs out more lives than somewhat, so I'm not strong on those. But an antique is an antique is an antique – sometimes.

'Funds from where?' As if I didn't know.

'From a particular antique, Lovejoy. Our last one, which we need to sell for the highest possible sum.'

'You have it?' I stooped to grovel, eager as a hound. Yet I hadn't felt a single chime since entering the place, so there wasn't one within a crook's reach. 'Here?'

'Not yet, Lovejoy. But we shall. It's a horse, Whistlejack.'

Who now cared? Not me. His horse could have sired a million Derby winners and I still wouldn't give it time of day. Horse racing's the dullest sport known to man. I once was invited to Epsom for the Derby, when involved for a short time with a wealthy lady who had a string of thoroughbreds. It was yawnsome. I'd sooner watch a hen sit . . . Hang on, Whistlejack?

'Stubbs painted a lifesizer called *Whistlejack*.'

'Correct. It will be ours. You will sell it.'

'How do you want it sold?' As if I didn't know.

'With your help, Lovejoy.'

'What sort of help?' A.I.I.D.K.

'Well, ah . . .' For the first time a little uncertainty crept in. 'Not what you might call *direct* help, Lovejoy. Kind of . . .'

'Bent help?' I said kindly. Criminals hate words like crime, fraud, deception. They prefer slang, especially upright bastions of the law like Ashley Battishall and their lovely if ageing ladies that are keen to restore civilization to its former grandeur.

He brightened. 'Exactly, Lovejoy! Capital description! But stay mum. Right, dearest?'

'Yes, Ashley.' She was almost inaudible.

'Can't you give me a clue, just so's I could get things, er, bending?'

'Afraid not, old chap.' Old chap now I was on his side. 'You'll be informed the instant it arrives.'

Arrives? On its way, then? He wrung my hand to seal the bargain.

'One thing. What precisely do I get out of this?'

Roberta hid her face in her frail hands, sobbed at the outrageous mention of such base stuff as monetary profit.

'You, Lovejoy, stay out of gaol.' He stooped to apologize to Roberta, the sordid world entering her drawing room.

'Gaol? What have I done?'

'Your central magistry file is a foot thick, Lovejoy.' He didn't need to bawl this bit. 'I have compiled a summary on your criminal past. You will not survive a week if I choose to act. One word, and the police will be investigating you for the next seventy years.'

Roberta was peeping from her phoney lace handkerchief. I swear she was gloating, thrilled at threats, at her Ashley crushing my opposition.

I nodded, know defeat.

'That's my man!'

Was it? Was I? I looked at them both. Triumphant, sure, but a serf is a serf. Only very rarely does servitude become loyalty. They'd made a mistake, and mistakes have to be paid for sooner or later. You'd think people in their position would know that. People in my position do.

'We welcome you to our cause, Lovejoy,' Roberta said. She extended her hand. This time I went to take it, for the sake of appearances. I felt a distinct pressure of her fingers on mine. In fact, if she hadn't looked so delicate I'd have said it was just this side of a clutch. 'You will move in, two days from now,' she added.

'Move in where?'

'Here. On my husband's orders.'

He managed to look unsurprised, but it was close. First he'd heard of it.

'Sorry, love,' I said quickly. 'I've antiques to suss – '

'Mrs Beth Pardoe can wait, Lovejoy,' Battishall said.

Which made me gulp. 'Right. Two days, then.'

They let me go. I was told to wait at the servants' entrance, for a radio taxi to come and take me to Sudbury railway station. As I left the room, a maid arrived pushing a tea trolley. It was laden with enough grub to feed a regiment. Sandwiches, a huge trifle, cakes, tarts. I drew breath to beg, but the maid frowned me on my way. However close to death's dark door, the lovely Roberta was quelling any lingering anorexia. I went to stand outside and wait, thinking about Whistlejack.

Now, the horse called Whistlejack trod the springy turf about 1762, and pegged out soon after. Two legit honest genuine canvases of this nag exist by the great Stubbs, one a lifesize painting of epic proportions, the other a small rather mundane thing showing a groom with Whistlejack and two stallions. Neither oil belonged to Battishall. Or was somebody stealing the lifesizer for him this very minute? He'd said its arrival was imminent. But it *couldn't* be thieved, not the huge portrait. So somebody was going to work the shuff, were they? (Tell you about this marvellous trick when I get a minute.) Which raised the question of who was a faker good enough to duplicate Whistlejack's loving portrait. Two, in these parts, Packo Orange, in gaol. The other was me.

The taxi took its time. I was late for Addie, and the determined Juliana Witherspoon. I wish now I had been too late.

6

There's a thing called morale. Elusive, but there when it is, if you follow. It's the stuff that makes banks obey you, and women place their implicit trust in your every word.

But:

Its absence is misery plus everything worse. Without morale, you might as well stay at home. My own tactic, seeing I lack morale most of the time, is to give in. If my opponent's a man, I might brave it out. If it's a woman, I chuck the towel in straight off. Instant surrender. The reason? It's a woman's world. They say it's not, just so they can get the upper hand quicker, but they know and we know. Life is their game. Women have the referee's whistle. You might say I'd given Juliana W. the sailor's elbow, but that wasn't true. I'd only rejected her scheme of funds for her parish church's wonky spire. I'd not really spurned her *qua* her. And believe me, a crone is never a crone. There's a grace in older women that is missing from younger ones. I'd even go so far as to say that older women are preferable. Comedians joke that they're more grateful, but it isn't that. It's the older woman's sense of looking, saying something worth listening to, their friendliness even. And their understanding, which goes a long way with rubbish blokes like me because it can lead to something so precious that it cools your soul like sweet rain. That something is called mercy. Show me a dolly bird who has any. But an older woman, just occasionally, has a depth of mercy to sanctify a saint . . .

'Piss off aht of it, Lovejoy,' the girl said. 'You make me frigging sick, you gormless festering pillock.'

It had come on to drizzle, the railway lights reflecting in the platform. I sighed. Back in the real world.

'Well, I'm broke.' I tried cadging off her, but nobody cadged off Inge and lived unscathed. She's a real Valkyrie, Brunhilde, whatever the term is for a five-ten blonde that could make three of me

35

sideways. 'I've got to get to the library for six.' Or was it the priory at seven? Or the castle?

'Tough tit, prat.' She's from one of those ladies' colleges in Cambridge University, has to keep down with the Joneses. She spits, belches, drinks pints. Can't see the point of her behaviour myself. Going for the vulgarity stakes might be tolerable when you're gorgeous, but she has weirdness as Tinker has wrinkles.

The train came in. I had a quick think. 'If you see Jox, tell him sorry but I tried.' And trudged off, or started to.

Her telescopic arm yanked me into the compartment. 'Jox? The way you spoke I thought some whore – '

'Elegantly guessed, Ing.'

'Ing-*errr*, you poxy frigging moron. I'll pay your fare.'

We conversed, each in our own way, all the way home. The point being that she's demented over Jox. He can't stand the sight of her. It's a shame. They'd make a smashing pair.

'Look, Lovejoy,' she said, worried she'd only reached third gear in her invective and we were already pulling in. 'Can I come with you? Meet Jox?'

'Look, Ing.' Women always worry you. Lovelorn women are the pits, worse even than weepers. 'It's only another of Jox's penny scams. You know what he's like.'

'Please, Lovejoy.' Tears started her sniffing. 'If you'd only put a word in for me, I'm sure he'd see me as I am.'

'Bus fare?' I bargained. I was already late for whoever it was.

'Yes!' She rummaged eagerly in her shoulder bag, and we made the ten furlongs to the castle as the town lights came on.

Jox was holding his awards ceremony on the ramparts. A small gathering of tourists stood observing Jox's lunatic goings-on, taking photographs. I was clemmed, so had to go through with Jox's craziness for grub money.

'Lovejoy! Nick of time!' Jox advanced, grinning. He wore a velvet jerkin and leggings, tall thigh boots and a cavalier hat with plumes. Inge groaned with lust. He shoved her aside. She looked thrilled.

'What're you doing tonight, Jox?' Me, asking for orders.

'Knighthood, Lovejoy. Plus a deputy lordship. Garb up, over there.'

Under the wooden drawbridge before the castle doorway lay a

heap of mediaeval serf's clothing. Glumly I donned it, piled my own damp clothes, and stepped into the drizzle.

The castle is down to its keep nowadays, but was once a major structure. Spotlit at nightfall by our stingy town council – two glims of faltering candlepower – the castle would look splendid except for its grim disrepair. It stands in our town park by the war memorial. Here, two knights withstood seige for King Charles I during the Great Civil War, and when Cromwell's lads took the town stood to be shot to death on the greensward. Lovers use the place for snogging, and bands for parping their Sunday umpahs. There are pretty flower gardens, but that's it. Except for Jox's schemes.

By the time I joined him he was already reading out some citation from a parchment from a heap of old stones. He had a phoney sword. A stout Scandinavian stood humbly before him, head bowed. I wore a cloak that stank of mothballs, leggings, black slippers and a beret, and stumbled across to join them feeling a right prat. A lass weaved adoringly with a video camera.

'. . . be it known for ever and appurtenances hitherto,' Jox was intoning, 'that Sven Stromberg Hassellblad be henceforward and hitherto aforementioned as Sir Gallant Kingscouncil of Coggeshall in this noble and loyal county by authority and investiture pursuivant . . .' et fakedom cetera.

On his signal I stepped forward with the cushion, part of my set. On it was a mock-up Order of the Garter, done by Slicer's cousin in Norfolk. They're only resin-cast bronze, from the modellers in Charlotte Street.

He knighted Mr Hassellblad with a flourish that almost took the bloke's ear off. A sash, the dud insignia of the Garter, and it was 'Arise, Sir Sven!' to a scatter of applause. Inge watched the phoney ceremony in tears of admiration, loving every minute. She'd have given Jox an Oscar for his performance, if not more.

After that we hurriedly changed back, thank God. And I became the Superintendent of the Olympic Games. We walked briskly to the rear of the castle, where the spotlights barely reached. Two lamps trailed wires from a generator that coughed and wheezed nearby. The camera girl followed us. Jox was now in a smart suit, tall and imposing. A midget flagpole stood by. Jox whispered me instructions about the ceremony. Luckily it was one we'd done before.

Slicer, mournful as an undertaker in bowler hat and winged collar, was on hand with the Stars and Stripes. He had a battery-operated ghetto blaster. Jox ascended the old mounting stone. I had the medal. An elderly lady, dumpy, singularly old-fashioned and with puffy ankles, stood proudly before the flagpole.

Jox nodded. Loud music made me leap a mile, Aaron Copland's *Common Man* blaring. I swear the gardens wilted. Jox wafted it to silence. Another parchment.

'Be it known that Hilda Fratrina Benshawk of North Carolina today won the Olympic freestyle fifteen hundred metres and is champion of the world from heretofore. The United States of America!'

Hilda came forward. She could hardly hobble, but gamely made the mounting stone. Jox vacated it, helped her up. I stepped forward with the medal – Slicer's manufactory, Olympic circles, gold glistening, silk ribbon – and placed it on the lady's neck. I stepped aside to avoid her drenching tears and stood at attention for the US national anthem. The watchers stood in silence, hats doffed. Applause. We helped the lady down.

'Thank you,' she said over and over. 'I'm so proud.'

It was handshakes all round, with her husband advancing along camera angles and blinding us all with flashes. Then came the fee, which Jox snaffled, promising me with nods and winks. I edged him aside to get my food money, but he edged away faster. Inge went after him like a sprinting hippo. Slicer collected the gear in a handcart, ominously reminding me I owed him a mediaeval fake by tomorrow dinner time.

'I'd like to invite you and your officials to dinner, sir.' Hilda caught me.

'Thank you, Hilda,' I said, dazzled. 'I am honoured. The officials are due elsewhere. If you're sure?'

'Vernon here insists, don't you, Vern?'

'Sure do.' We all wrung hands once more for the road, and were joined by several others.

Everybody was talking. Working out what Americans say is hard work, but luckily they shun nuance so a streamlined syntax shows above their accents. They belonged to a touring charabanc.

'This was my dream,' Hilda said, proudly wearing her medal. 'I missed the Pensacola final when I was eighteen, didn't make the cut. Never got to the O-lympics.'

'Yes, you did, Hilda,' I put in. 'You just got the gold.'

We went towards the George carvery, joyance unbounded. I barely made it from hunger. The carvery lets you fill your plate as many times as you want. I did six trips, and for the first time I could remember was replete.

'You must have been a war baby, Lovejoy!' Hilda said in admiration as I scoffed the last load.

That set me roaring with laughter too. Dangerous, because I almost started reminiscing on Jox's many titles and awards. He'd lately dished out three Congressional Medals of Honour, a barrow-load of Victoria Crosses, and, during the recent European Games, made two people Count of Monte Cristo and no fewer than six ladies Countess Pompadour. There's an old geezer called Doothie, lives in a caravan on the estuary, who copperplates his manuscripts, the only calligrapher with a watercooled overheated quill. I didn't say this. I spoke a little heartfelt prattle when Hilda smiled rather sadly – by then Aldo the carvery boss was plying us with limitless wine – and said groggily,

'Lovejoy, I expect you think this is all kinda silly.'

'Silly? Why should I?'

'Us, the whole holiday thing. These parchments that are pretty but kind of well, made up. Play, y'know?'

'No.' I took her hand gently. It held her wholemeal roll. I removed it, pinched her butter and wolfed it. Never look a gift horse and all that. The rest were all yakking, laughing, joking. I helped her to finish her plate in case she ran out of appetite. 'I'm an antique dealer. I find dreams.'

'Dreams? You *find* dreams?'

'In the strangest places, love. Once I found a genuine ancient Etruscan bronze statuette for a politician in Newark.' I grinned, enjoying myself now. 'He wanted to present one to some visiting Italian mayor. I searched for three months, the clock against me. With two days to go I finally found one hanging under a wheelbarrow in a garden centre.'

'How did you know to look there?'

'Felt it, Hilda.' The wine and food made me indiscreet.

'Feel?' She had great spectacles. I gazed into them, laughing, gazed at everyone. We were all on one long grazing table.

'Aye, love. Your pendant's older than you by a hundred years, love. Did you know?' Glancing down the table, I picked on Vernon. 'Your husband's got something in his pocket worth maybe more than this carvery. And that lady with the brooch . . .'

A silence had started up. They were staring, no longer grazing and gazing. I wondered if I was sloshed. Vernon cleared his throat. The rest of the carvery was still noshing, bustling with a genial clatter. It was only us.

'What?' My stupid grin froze.

'You see, Vern?' Hilda breathed in something like triumph. 'I *said*, didn't I?'

'You did right, hon.'

Then they all started talking at once, and I got woozy. I think they took me home. I remember promising to come for breakfast, meet them at the Welcome Sailor, talk over the Survey, give them a fortnight, show them round . . .

Vaguely I remember them stumbling about my dark cottage, Vernon cursing, somebody saying, 'Hey. These goddam Limeys never heard of electricity?' and the woman with the brooch saying, 'Hush up, Elroy. *We* had it hard in Des Moines . . .' And a flashlight blinding as I fell on my unmade divan.

Then I was alone, peaceful, in the arms of Morpheus. For how long, I don't know. A vague internal signal that it was midnight, and suddenly a slab torch clicked whiteness on bright as day.

The peach dress girl was in my doorway. A draught blew in. She now wore a smart suit, ready to take over ICI, held the lamp out like an infected handbag. I gaped, bleary.

'If it's a valuation, love, tomorrow, eh?'

'Good morning, Lovejoy. May I trouble you?'

Morning, when I'd just got to bed? Why do they say May I Trouble You, when they already have? It's like the Inland Revenue asking, May I? I whimpered. 'Not now, love.'

'I apologize. But it is a matter of life or death.'

This intrigued me so much I dozed off, but she spoke the magic word.

'I am Miss Juliana Witherspoon, Lovejoy. Antiques.'

'Eh?' Suddenly I was sitting up. 'Where? Whose?'

'A . . . a friend's.' She bit her lip. Really did gnaw her lower lip. I watched, fascinated. You don't often see people do it. And thought, oho. Her lover in trouble? 'Time is of the essence, Lovejoy. It's his last one, you see. I think it may get stolen. I wish you to prevent the crime.'

Prevent crime? Novelty upon novelty. I gauged her. She looked in deadly earnest. And beautiful. This bird would not give up lightly. True to form, I surrendered.

'Got a match, love? I'll brew up.'

7

Portents really exist. Sometimes, you just know an offer spells doom, this woman is born trouble, that date will prove your downfall. Me, I go anyway, drawn by hope which, combined with a perennial lack of willpower, leads to disaster.

There was once a Vandal King who ruled North Africa – we're talking *Anno Domini* 410. However you define that ghastly word power, King Genseric wielded it with horrendous effect. History books call him 'the most terrible'. No wayside pansy he. He ravished Hippo, stormed Carthage, invaded Italy, engulfed Rome itself. But deep down he was a troubled man, for Genseric the Vandal had a recurrent nightmare. Served him right, because he invented a fashionable kind of genocide that persists to this very day: the social policy of Christians massacring Christians. An Arian Christian, he decided to massacre Christians of orthodox Roman inclinations, just like on tonight's – or any other night's – six o'clock news. So King Genseric surged through the Roman Empire, terrorizing all but whimpering in his sleep.

He knew no physical fear. Why should he? But night after shivering night, this monster drifted into sleep . . . to find himself, in his dream, suddenly gliding through a serene palace. Forward he glides, thinking this is nice, all peace and quiet, towards a tranquil old gent. (Phew! Okay so far! King Genseric always started a sweat of relief about here, because it hadn't happened yet. Maybe tonight he'd make it unscathed . . . You know the feeling.)

He glides. The old man smiles kindly. He is bearded, benign. No worries! The trembling but mighty Genseric is reassured. Will it be okay this time? The white-haired old figure, benevolence itself, stoops to offer some fruit. Hey, we're all pals here. King Genseric thinks, made it! He leans forward – *and looks into the old man's eyes.*

42

Horror! He sees a pit of stark terror, feels himself falling in, oh Jesus, no not again, falling, falling . . . He shrieks awake, gibbering and screaming, et ghoulish cetera. Night after horrible scarey night, he never escapes that ghastly pit. That's all it was, the whole scene: mighty Genseric, sweet old gent, the frighteners.

Which is where it should have ended, a mere footnote. Everybody has a nightmare, so what? Except out in the world there was pillaging to be done, and hollow-eyed King Genseric knew his duty.

Cut to Nola, in Europe, to the shrine of St Felix, where one Paulinus humbly tended the flower garden.

Now, Paulinus was interesting. Snowy-haired, gentle, this creaking geriatric was kindness itself. Once, he had been governor of a Roman province, no less, a consul of Rome before his thirtieth birthday. So no slouch, our Paulinus. But he was deep. One day, he chucked it all up – the power, the riches – and became the priest at the shrine of St Felix. Life was serene. Until rumours came of the whole Roman Empire being stormed by the Vandal hordes of sleepless You-Know-Who.

Refugees poured past, fleeing their wrath. Vandal looters swaggered about, dragging coffles of slaves. Turmoil, death, trouble reigned. In this mayhem, old Paulinus sold all his wealth to ransom back the slaves, incidentally including St Felix's sons. Finally he'd spent up. He'd stripped the shrine bare, given everything.

On that last penniless day a weeping widow came.

'Please, Paulinus. Ransom my son! He's taken in slavery!'

'Sorry, love,' says Paulinus, sad. 'I'm skint.'

She begs on her knees. 'Have you nothing left?'

'Goodness!' says Paulinus. 'I've just remembered! I *have*!'

He plods off to the Vandal captain, *and sells himself*. He makes a good case. Getting on in years, but he's an excellent gardener, skilled grafter of trees, grows superb vegetables, can write, you ask anyone. The Vandal captain says it's a deal. Paulinus ransoms the lad. And is chained into the Vandal galleys. The fleet rows away from smouldering Europe, docks in North Africa. Paulinus is sent to slog in the gardens of a Vandal prince. (I'll bet you guess the ending.) For completeness: Eventually, King Genseric comes to dine, chats with his daughter, his son-in-law the Vandal prince. Ho, King and Dad, says the princess, why not try some lovely salads and things, because I've this gardener, a slave from some dump in Europe, a dab hand with greens, never seen fruit like what he grows. Great, ho daughter, says Genseric. Slaves, cries the princess, tell the old sod Paulinus to get a move on, bring the very best produce. This isn't some casual caller, this is the mighty Genseric before whom empires tremble, so quick about it. Frightened slaves scatter and sprint.

Enter Paulinus with a basket of fruit, stoops down, offering it. King Genseric says hey, this looks the best. Says ta. He leans down – looks into the old man's eyes . . .

Shriek! Horror! *The nightmare's gone real!* Mighty tyrant Genseric is a blubbering wreck. Well, you can imagine. Consternation, guards pouring in, the princess hysterical, the Vandal prince thundering out Who's done what to Dad? while soldiers and slaves mill about, during which saintly old Paulinus, kneeling with his trug, wonders, what the hell happened, I miss something here? Then the princess howls, 'What's in that frigging basket? That old slave sent Daddy demented! Execute him!'

Happy ending for once. Paulinus is leapt on and, knee-deep in shackles and assorted ironmongery, admits all: ex-governor, Roman consul, etc, etc. King Genseric, badly shaken, goes phew with relief, recovers his cool, orders Paulinus freed, and sent home with a galley-load of freed slaves. It's back to St Felix's shrine. When kindly old Paulinus eventually passed on, people of every stripe followed his coffin weeping, 'even Jews and Infidels' adds Gregory the Great – among, presumably, the few surviving Christians.

See what I mean? Portents. If you're a king of mighty armies like Genseric the Vandal, I suppose you can escape blame by munificent gestures. But somebody like me's for it. Maybe subconsciously I was trying to shun this portent, knowing it would be fatal, but I still didn't have the sense to tell Juliana Witherspoon a deafening no.

'Look, miss,' I said to her blinding torch. 'I kip naked, so wait outside, please.'

'No, thank you.' She stood like a sentry, feet together. 'I fear you may evade your duty, Lovejoy. I shall wait.'

Narked, I struggled to sit up. You can't be angry at a woman when lying down. I've often tried. 'I didn't invite you – '

'Your reprehensible behaviour in avoiding my requests have eradicated your rights, Lovejoy,' she had the gall to say.

44

'That's bloody convenient,' I shot back. I'd never get to sleep now. 'What time is it?'

'Ten to six. We have a journey ahead.'

Six o'clock on a cold rainy morning, and her bloke's antique due to be stolen. Why the hurry, unless he lived on the Isle of Mull? Another lip chew. It was worth a gnaw. I could see that.

She stepped to the door, raised her lamp, saw the shambles of decrepit furniture and old clothes between the divan and the door, and nodded. Her conclusion: nobody could reach the back door without a hang-glider.

'I shall switch off the light,' she pronounced firmly. 'You will please dress. My car is in the lane.'

'That'll ruin my reputation.' My drollery fell flat. The place went dark. I groped for my things. It's as if my mind gets mad about things but the person I am simply does as it's told. It narks me. I wish one or other of me would make things easier, because one day both of me's going to come a cropper. I dressed quickly, because a naked man looks stupid; it's naked women look brilliant.

'I'm death until I've swigged my morning tea.'

The torch lit the cottage. She tried to smooth her face, but the light caught her in mid-hate.

'Why so . . .' She coloured, tried to end in a way that wouldn't offend her mam. 'So *unkempt*, Lovejoy?'

'I haven't time for housework.' I was double nasty. 'Birds keep barging in and molesting me in bed so I'm worn out.'

'That will do,' she said sternly, and watched as I got some crumbs, a morsel of cheese and laid it by the porch.

'Bluetits and my robin,' I explained.

'Lock the door, Lovejoy.' I'd never met a lass like her for giving orders – well, actually I have, but I meant today.

'No locks. Women keep battering in and molesting me –'

'Stop it, Lovejoy!' She went nuclear. I blundered into her on the path. 'Your duty is to protect Father Jay!'

Who? Miserably I followed her out to her motor while she ballocked me for not having a gate. I explained that these women kept battering in, et cetera. It made her hiss in fury like a snake. That's woman's logic – turf you out of bed, deny you breakfast, haul

45

you out before cockshout, then blame you for having a non-gate gate and not doing your cleaning.

Spirits low, they went lower. A priest, at this ungodly hour? And in trouble? They're supposed to help us, for Christ's sake, not the other way round. And why was she so desperate to help the bloke? Only a lover, actual or potential, can drive a woman so, and a priest was way out of reach, right? Unless . . . well, things change.

'Can we call in Fenstone?' I asked, clambering into the scented interior. 'Only there's a bloke called Jox owes me – '

'That gentleman brings the village unwelcome attention,' she said. 'Do not associate with him while you are engaged upon this undertaking.'

'I'm not engaged upon any undertaking, Miss Witherspoon.'

Women have a distant smile that isn't a smile, but shows secret scorn at your pathetic resistance. She did it. I watched, gloomier than ever. It always implies threat. I wish I could do it. I've tried in the mirror, failed. If ever I learn how, I'll do it to everybody, then let them watch out. She fired the engine, and we hurtled – and I do mean streaked like an arrow – north through Suffolk's dark leafy lanes. My cheeks dragged at my skull from the G force. Only the seat belt kept me in the damned vehicle. She drove with a cool disregard for limits, scared me to death. Her one comment was 'Tut tut' when a herd of Jersey cows lumbered across our path. I thought we were going to smear them and us, but with a horn blast she set them scampering clumsily any old where, their demented collie scurrying after to round them up.

Not that I wanted to linger. Countryside's grim and horrible. It lies there with nobody much in it, waiting, ticking off the days like one massive timepiece. I'm convinced it only looks pretty the way demons and sirens are said to take on a winsome guise, to lure honest people away from reality. How ruralists have the nerve to stock up with jam butties and tea flasks, then march along lonely riverbanks and ancient trackways enjoying woods and fields, God alone knows. I can't understand. If ever I get the money I'll be out of our remote rusticity and never ever leave the comfort of dense town houses, crammed humanity and shops. Where nature lovers see 'scenery' and conservationists see 'survival', I see only things sinister.

'I beg your pardon, Lovejoy?' she asked, as we slithered to a stop. 'You said "eating everything".'

'Ah. Countryside. Everything hunts everything.'

She opened the car door. 'That's simply Nature, Lovejoy.'

Oh, aye, I thought. Putting a nice word to anything makes it okay then, does it? Assassination, murder, carnage, they all sound respectable. It's only their import chills your spine. I disembarked in the cold wind. She dowsed the motor's glims.

We were in a narrow lane near a lych gate – modern. The original old gate had gone. There was just enough coming light to see by, the eastern skies shredding black clouds but leaving the pieces there as a warning. More rain due soon. Vaguely I could see the sombre mass of a church thickening the shades beyond the trees. Down the lane, I guessed hopefully, a huddle of houses, cottages, maybe a farm or two. . . ? Until I realized this must be Fenstone, that huddle of vacancies, one of East Anglia's dying villages. In Juliana's careering arrival I'd noticed one or two wattle-and-daub cotts, one shop front, a walled garden, in a blur.

'This way, please.' Her torch went ahead up the path.

Incredibly, a vestry light was on. She knocked, and we entered light and dryness. I shut out that widespread malevolence of field and flower.

'Good morning,' he said.

'Father Jay Smith, may I introduce Lovejoy,' Juliana simpered. She didn't blush, but it was a near thing. 'Lovejoy, Father Jay.'

'How do, er, Father Jay.'

'How do you do, Lovejoy.'

He was of average height, thirtyish, with springy hair and a pleasant open face, though I never know why we say things like that because all faces are open, aren't they? He wore a cassock, and had been reading his breviary. Juliana went instantly into apology.

'Oh, I'm so sorry! Were you. . . ?' She writhed in abasement

The priest smiled. 'Just finished my office, Miss Witherspoon. Vest for mass in a few minutes.'

'If there is anything I can ever . . .' She halted in near-blunder. I looked away. Another's pain spreads like ripples on a pond, goes on and on affecting every molecule in the water. I couldn't see the problem. Celibacy's all very well, but it's not gospel, is it? She was gorgeous, he looked hale, so why not get on with it? There's enough problems in the world without inventing more. I joked to staunch the wound.

'Miss Witherspoon overtook Fangio at Bures.'

'Miss Witherspoon is kind to trouble.'

He smiled his appreciation, gestured us to seats. The vestry was spacious, but the furniture was reproduction. Old pock-marked linoleum covered the floor, the flagstone edges making indentations. Cruets of wine and water stood on a small chipboard stand, Woolworth's best glass. This place also felt gutted, breathing as if comatose and with a terrible emptiness. An ancient church all right, but I'll bet even the pews were sold. It was walls and a roof, and nothing.

'Where is it?' I asked. If the priest was bound heavenward, I'd have starved to death by the time I reached any grub.

He went blank. 'It?'

'The antique.' I glanced from her to him. Some mistake?

'Oh.' Eyebrow play, looks darting. 'The antique?'

A door in the main church boomed. A shuffle began, some ancient dragging to morning mass. You don't get many papists in East Anglia, so I expect he wouldn't have to struggle to find a pew. In fact, I was rather surprised to find a church of that persuasion still at it. We've hundreds of churches dwindling year by year as congregations empty into modern life. His quizzical smile showed he'd sussed my thoughts.

'Not being critical,' I said hastily. 'Times are changing.'

'I know, Lovejoy. This church was of a, ah, former denomination. I came three years ago. I think I have found paradise early, so fond I am of this village.'

'Hard up, eh?'

'Lovejoy!' Miss Witherspoon in outrage.

'I'm sympathizing!' I shot back indignantly. 'For Chri . . . Goodness!' I completed piously with a feeble grin. I'd have to watch my language, but you've got to talk, for Christ's sake, or nobody would say anything to anybody. Then where would we be?

'It is true, Miss Witherspoon,' he reproved her sadly.

She subsided instantly, bowed her head. See? Subservience for him, vituperation for me? I began to regret having come. Not a single antique in the place, from its feel. Sorry, old church, I mentally apologized. But if all your church silver, your ancient pews, fonts, lecterns, misericords, have been ripped out, what did the exquisite Juliana fetch me for?

48

She glared hatred, but only because the priest's sad gaze was fixed on some distant sorrow. Miss Witherspoon was truly smitten. She would kill to avoid seeming unpleasant in his eyes.

He sighed. 'The world has shrunk, Lovejoy. Less than a dozen parishioners. If it wasn't for Miss Witherspoon, and Mr Geake, my other churchwarden, I'd not survive. This week three more families leave. Fenstone is dying.'

'It will grow again, Father Jay!' Juliana cried fiercely.

'We can hope, Miss Witherspoon.' He was suddenly tired. I felt a bit sorry, but not all that much. I mean, I'm always on my uppers. He at least had a roof over his head. He spoke directly to me. 'I've no illusions. Folk see a priest nowadays, and ask why he enjoys such privilege – his keep, rent-free position, security – when they are out there earning their beans, children to clothe, battling for jobs.'

'Well, that's people.' I smiled to show I didn't think that, I was on his side. Well, he had an antique.

'This great old church is crumbling. We've tried various schemes but been unfortunate – '

'It's more than misfortune!' La Witherspoon interjected. 'It's a plot!'

'Look, padre.' Talking with priests makes me uncomfortable, but I had to say it. 'East Anglia's famous for dying hamlets. Young folk want out. They don't want to slog in the fields twelve hours a day. They want town life. In Lincolnshire – '

'I do not claim we are unique, Lovejoy. Only that it's happening to *us*.' Juliana nodded with vigour even before she'd heard him out. 'Our church appurtenances have been sold. I auctioned our last treasure in Norwich last Michaelmas – an Elizabethan vestry chest. It was stolen on the way. Are you all right?'

'Fine!' I must have groaned aloud with baulked lust.

'It was photographed for a book on antiques,' Juliana complained. 'A very unusual design.'

'Then there was the fire. We couldn't afford the rewiring, so I did it myself. It caused a fire in the presbytery.'

'The antique you want me to guard?' Why I'd come.

'I will have it collected tomorrow by the auctioneers.'

'Why not have them collect it today?' I asked. 'You're daft to leave an antique lying around.'

'Because today's Sunday.'

'Ah, yes.' I cleared my throat. 'I forgot. I was just on my way to morning service when Miss Witherspoon called.' I stared defiantly at her. I was bloody sick of piety. Because she wanted to ravish this defenceless priest I was out in these wilds starving to death. She could get on with it. 'Where?'

He raised his eyebrows. 'The painting behind you.'

'No, it isn't,' I said, fed up. 'If there's a painting behind me, it's a fake.' I rose. 'I'll be going. Thanks for . . .' He hadn't done anything except ruin my dawn.

'You haven't even looked, Lovejoy!' They said it together.

'Chance of a lift?'

'Of all the. . . !' the bird started up, but the priest must have shushed her. She fell apoplectically mute.

The painting caught my eye, as paintings will. Even daubs halt you in mid-stride. It was a good forgery. The colours were right, including the woad blue. A woman seated at a window, a little girl in pre-Carolean dress at her knee. They were staring out in sorrow shared. I thought of Frank Bramley's *A Hopeless Dawn* painting, Tate Gallery, but this was a faker's attempt to do Elizabethan. Little knowledge and mediocre talent. One thing he'd done right, though, was get the pigments correct, which for a forger wasn't at all bad. Most make tragic mistakes with wrong colours. I've even seen Turner lookalikes done in acrylics – *and sold*! Unbelievable. Except not quite as unbelievable as all that, in an age when forgers openly boast that every thing can be made from any thing (and note those word spaces).

Woad's funny stuff. It grows frankly as a weed. Rum-looking, even for a plant. When you first see it you're downright disappointed. Especially thinking of those Ancient Brits with painted blue faces attacking Roman legions, that embarrass schoolchildren by reminding them that we were once almost as barbaric as we are now. For a start woad's not blue. And you never see as many branches on a plant. And it's *yellow* flowering, with green leaves. Only two feet tall. I like to sit on a summer's evening watching insects. They fly at the yellow blossom and pop each flower. Sometimes on a quiet evening you can actually hear the petals pop apart, like whinnymoor broom flowers do. Our old villagers use the seeds for roasting into coffee. (Don't try it. It tastes horrible, and it makes you nod off all the time.)

The Romans and Greeks, of course, used it. Its flowers dye yellow, but its leaves when festered in water for fifteen days dye the loveliest blue you'll ever see in your life. Not as stark as ultramarine or lapis lazuli, but a gentle mild blueness you can't help but love. Add the two, and your wool dyes green.

Anciently, whole countries flourished on woad. Like in France, where Toulouse's rich architecture came directly from exporting the stuff in little rondels a bit bigger than a golf ball. Until about 1562, when holiness raised its ugly head and religious wars sent the Protestant woad merchants diving for cover and the industry vanished. Oops. I remembered where I was.

'Who did it?' I asked. A forger nearly as good as Packo?

'Some ancient artist long dead, Lovejoy. Anonymous. What's the matter?'

The pong of linseed oil was the matter. Frankly, the daftness of forgers takes your breath away. Little girls have the best noses. Ask one if a painting smells. She'll wrinkle her little two-year-old conk and go, 'Poooh!' She'll even tell you if it's the same aroma as your linseed stand oil. It takes, I assure you, nigh two years for linseed scent to vanish, so it's a good test. We've all got noses. There's no excuse for getting ripped off.

'Doesn't feel right. It stinks oil. You've been done.'

'But . . .' He turned to Miss Witherspoon in perplexity. 'Wasn't it walled up two hundred years?'

'It certainly was, Father Jay!' she pronounced sternly. 'I had heard this man was honest. Now I can see he's a conniving dealer who wants this painting himself for a song!'

Patience evaporated. 'I've told you the truth. I've got some rich Americans to see.'

'Americans?' I swear Father Jay went pale.

'They want me. For breakfast,' I added pointedly.

'Oh. Not here, then?'

'Why would. . . ?' I caught myself. I'd almost asked why anyone in his right mind would want to come to Fenstone. 'Er, in town.'

'Please don't have any truck with Lovejoy. He's a crook.'

That was when I left them to it. I'd had enough. It was barely dawn. I was stuck in the wilderness, hungry as a hunter, no nosh bars anywhere, and a million miles from civilization where Addie, the

51

Yanks, waited – I hoped. In an earlier, more condign, age I would have gone to the nearest church door and knocked, asking for food to stave off my gnawing hunger pains. Not now, not now.

Naturally, I couldn't resist peering into the church. A stout balding gentleman with a pronounced shuffle – stroke? – was lighting altar candles. He looked vaguely familiar, but it was hard in the gloaming. Then I thought, tweeds, country gent, the auction, Addie Bigmouth explaining why. Otherwise, empty. The poor box beckoned, but with true nobility I walked away, hoping never to see Juliana Witherspoon and her priest ever again.

8

There was enough light to see the mighty metropolis of Fenstone was rousing, when I found a bus stop. No bus. Maybe eighteen cottages, once-splendid houses abutting the road, no pavements in rural fashion. The bus shelter was falling. I mean literally, its glass shattered, roof holed. No timetable to show when, if ever, the last train to Marienbad was due. I walked about. The pub was forlorn, announcing a 'good pull-in for travellers' in a flaking, frankly disbelievable, notice. One in three of the cottages was vacant. Faded FOR SALE signs bleached. Fenstone hadn't grown astride a trunk road, so no traffic was through. A man leading a massive shire horse came by.

We exchanged greetings. 'No caff hereabouts, is there?'

'Na, son. Ta'll get nothing at the Bull. Closed for good.'

'Shop, then?' Some sell milk, boxes of orange juice with a straw.

'Got none now.' He stopped the great beast by leaning back on its chest and slithering his boots until it understood.

'Bus?'

'Noon, to Dragonsdale, Tuesdays and Thursdays.'

He was wondering what I was doing there. I explained, 'Been to your church, and I want to get home.'

'Left before prayers, then.' He grinned. 'Services to nobody. Empty since Reverend Fairhurst died of his accident. This stranger's not filled it, with his rituals, all smells and bells.'

I found myself grinning. East Anglia's religious issues were decided by the Civil War, for good. 'Nice bloke, though.'

'Foreign, they do say.'

Odd, I've a cracking ear for accents. I'd bet my next meal Father Jay was as indigenous as us. 'He's had troubles.'

Never question country folk, you'll get nowhere. Leave a space, and answers come a-flowing. Upset over Juliana's crummy forgery, I'd flitted without hearing of their impending robber.

53

'Ar, has that! Church's things lost. Him and his wrong services.'

'Well, churches nowadays . . .' Me, leaving a casual space.

'He'm Fenstone's bad luck, son.' He spat a parabola, the grot splattering on a fragment of pane. Tinker had a rival, the Fenstone champ.

'Bad luck! A holy man?'

'Aaah.' A local yes, with mistrust. 'With him, Middle Snoring's come nigh to vanishing.' Middle Snoring was Fenstone's old name. 'Post office, gone! Go to Dragonsdale for a stamp. Our lady's farm had a fail lately, all bad luck.'

'Your farm! Failing!' I tutted.

'Her got new animals, goo-an-acko. Wool fit for a king, nigh's good as East Anglian sheep. All to nought, that.'

'Hard luck.'

'Luck?' He nodded the way Suffolk shows apoplectic rage. 'Took sickness, they. The Ministry come in from Lunnon, closed the herd.'

'Still, you've got your church.' I was starting to wonder now. It didn't only seem to be Jox that suffered in Fenstone.

'St Edmund's? How she lasts I dunno. If it weren't for Miss Witherspoon there wouldn't be no church at all. What she makes from visitors wouldn't keep a gnat in beer.'

'Oh, I dunno.' I was only talking, not really hoping. 'Some villages attract tourists in summer.'

'Aaah. But who wants their likeness these days? Fenstone's not had a Ringing Day these three years. That Jox tried, but folk're saying it's cursed.'

A mist was slowly spreading from the fields opposite. A river vale lay there, where the track fell away. The gleam of daylight by the lych gate had gone. The faint gold light in the church windows lessened as the mist climbed the buttresses. I tried to ignore it.

Ringing Day is November Fifth, that folk mostly call Bonfire Plot. A relieved parliament ordered bells rung to celebrate Guy Fawkes getting caught before he could blow everybody to blazes. It's a time of bonfires, fireworks, parkin cake and general wassailing. No more in Fenstone.

'Can't your policeman help?'

He snorted derision. The shire was restless, snorting, not liking the mist. 'Police? We'n't no bobby these nine year.' He looked round. 'Best be off before I'm blinded.'

54

'Mist comes every morning, does it?' This sort of thing happens. East Anglia in some areas is flat as a pancake. Village lads wear joke T-shirts, EAST ANGLIA MOUNTAIN RESCUE.

'And evening, this time of year. Cheers, son.'

'Morning.'

Now, 'likeness' means a painting in old speech. I looked hard at St Edmund's. Its old name, Parish Church of Middle Snoring, had been painted over. Who'd change an interesting old name to a boring new one?

Which made me start listing failures in Fenstone, apart from Fenstone. Jox's orchestra, antique shop, restaurant, wildlife scheme, estate agency, others I didn't know about. And now some lady's farm of, what creatures, goo-an-acko? What the hell was a goo-an-acko, with its wool fit for a king?

No cars coming. I started a long lonesome plod, away from Fenstone and its eerie creeping mist, thinking as I went.

Names are odd things, when you think of it. Women usually hate their forenames, though they tolerate their surnames well enough. Villagers are almost as bad, especially when their village name's a national joke. But when you've grown up in this creaking old kingdom of ours, the laughter of tourists is simply a surprise. I mean, a Canadian lass laughed on hearing of Middlesex. You've got to make allowances. But do Canadians roll in the aisles at Newfoundland's Blow Me Down? Or Americans fall about at Intercourse, Pennsylvania?

There is a Little Snoring in Norfolk, and a Great Snoring. Cornwall has Goongumpus. There's North Piddle, for grinning motorists to photograph each other peeing nonchalantly by the name sign. Essex has a village called Ugley. It's a pretty postcardy place, but I'll bet they wish they had a quid for every time a visitor's asked their bar ladies, 'Are you an Ugley woman ha-ha-ha?' There's our mega-famous original Gotham. Notthinghamshire. The village of Lover is popular every St Valentine's Day.

With a name like mine, I'm only thankful I don't come from Wormelow Tump, Cold Christmas, Swine Sty, or Maggot's End. Names make you careful. I almost got in a scrap about the name Pratts Bottom, south of London. There's a serious market in signs stolen from villages with names like Shellow Bowells. I'd hate to be their parish clerk – you'd need a standing order with sign makers for replacements every fortnight. The undisputed leader is Anglesey's little Llanfairpwllgwyngyllgogerychwyrndrobwllllantysiliogogogoch. Its railway platform sign is the one most at risk – if you could find enough stalwarts strong enough to carry the frigging thing. Muck, I'm told, runs it close. The point I was making, as I trudged finally out onto a road with actual real motors running between civilizations along it, is that to us they seem pretty dull. To people who've never heard of them, they're worth a detour, cameras at the ready. Tourists flock, camcorders whirring, to buy T-shirts and porcelain mugs, ice creams, patronize the local taverns and maybe send franked postcards to give the lads a smile back home.

Middle Snoring had chucked away its birthright, and money, by changing its name. I could have got a lift from the tourist charabancs that would have been thronging the place. But, 'Fenstone'? Who'd go out of his way to be photographed there? The village of Crackpot, the equally famous Fattahead, though, you're talking visitors by the score. For ever, wallets at the ready.

Mind you Whistlejack's an odd name, too, even for a horse.

By the time I'd got a lift – a couple wanting to buy a boat at East Mersea (which incidentally lies south of the northerly West Mersea, so not even humdrum names are safe) – I was sure of one thing: Fenstone, lately the village of Middle Snoring, was not simply atrophying. It was being strangled.

The village's killer was not Juliana Witherspoon, for she seemed to be fighting might and main to keep the church going. And she was doing her bit for the lone stray tourist with her proffered 'likenesses'. Jox, fabled doomer, was also trying, in his stalling way. And some lady with her strange animal farm.

Not only that, but that painting had been quite a good tilt at forgery. Should I visit Packo Orange in gaol, ask him a thing or two? I'd definitely suss out Juliana. And see Jox. And excavate Fenstone, and its lonesome parish priest. And get something to eat, to survive long enough to do all these. Still, I wouldn't suffer the ultimate hunger, for Sundays spelled Sabrina, thank God. At two o'clock we'd make smiles. Before that, there was the tomorrow auction.

Due about elevenish, today. (Tell you more in a sec.)

The couple dropped me off at the bowling place in Leisure Planet, where they intended to nosh. They didn't invite me to a burger, I noticed, thanking them and piking away. That's what you get for being nice to people for umpteen miles. Sometimes I wonder where gratitude's gone. Ten past ten by the town hall clock. Still in time. Then I saw a long mobile home pull in, engine coughing over the greensward. The legend SEX MUSEUM was emblazoned on it. I felt a wash of relief. Food, in the nick of time! Thank God for nutters like Tryer.

9

The engine wheezed, choked explosively, gave a final gasp. Tryer slammed from the door, smiling when he saw me waiting.

'Just a minute, sir!' he croaked – he has this gravel voice from years of fairgrounds. 'We'll be open in . . . Oh. Lovejoy.'

He's as blind as a bat without his bottle specs. Tryer rhymes with sigh-er, meaning one who tries (and, by implication, never succeeds, or his nickname would be something like Champ or Hero). I've known him since gaol.

'Disappointed, Try?' I cracked cheerfully. Never look desperate or hungry, or you get scorned. It applies most when meeting women. He has Chemise, *Deo gratias*.

'Thought you was a customer, Lovejoy.'

'Chemise in?'

'Aye. Just brewing up.'

'Chance of a cuppa with the belle of East Anglia?'

He grinned, sheepish. Chemise is really ugly, but if you've tact you don't remark on this. I like her. Tryer's besotted since they met last year and invented the Sex Museum. Local peelers move it from town to town, not wanting sordid exhibits in their little patch, thank you. Makes me wonder how some people manage to breed.

'I'll put the music on. Go in, Lovejoy.'

Tryer has this wailing music, his idea of enticement to the multitudes. It comes from a faulty compact disc player that blares out over a Tannoy thing, loudspeakers and dangling wires. He started unrolling a dirty banner. He always has a fag between his lips, goes unshaven. But, I thought enviously, he has Chemise, regular grub, and a career crusading against the ungodly. Can you ask for more?

'Take that end, Lovejoy.'

It read ADMISSION FREE EVERY SECOND PATRON. Quite clever, because couples will go in for a giggle, and loners wait then slope in silently. Hence, it's only rarely a customer gets in for nowt.

Chemise put her head from the side door as we got the banner tied along the vehicle.

'Wotch, Chemise.'

'Lovejoy! I thought it was your voice!' She was delighted to see me, and embraced me with a savagery you don't often get outside of total war. I almost vanished into her cleavage, struggled up after a prolonged asphyxiation.

'Hello, love.' I sucked fresh air in, reeled about a bit. 'Business good?'

Tryer watched, smiling foolishly at his loved one as he hung out shingles of admission prices. It was a daft question, really. More rust than last month, I noticed. The tyres were bald as a bladder. The engine was already pooling oil on the macadam. Times were hard.

She grimaced. A pretty woman can get away with doing that. Chemise's grimaces are a tribulation because she starts with a handicap. Yet I really do mean I like Chemise, in the sense am fond of. The Sex Museum is her idea. It's kept them in bread since they paired off, which is a novelty for Tryer. He's like Jox but without the money, if you follow. She's average height, has uncontrollable brown hair, a figure that's oddly lopsided as though she's had some auto accident, with legs of skeletal thinness and large feet. Her cleavage is something else, but her shoulders are also kiltered. Buck teeth, a forehead with permanent wrinkles. But I like her, so that's that. I don't honestly understand why women score off each other about appearances, because every woman has her own beauty, Chemise included. It isn't necessarily what you see, what's to grab in the throes of orgasm, a snooty comparison of shapes. It's not even the business of smart fashion – her dress costs thousands, little Cinderella's only discount sale garb – that competition thing women do. It's the woman's gracious merciful *self* that counts. And the one with grace wins hands down. Women don't know this. They think everything is youth, shape, and marvellous clothes. Try telling them, they think you're having them on.

'Business? Awful, Lovejoy.'

'I'm hungry, love. Any use asking?'

'Don't be silly. I'm just getting rid of some extras. Help us finish them off. Come in.'

See what I mean? A gorgeous woman could become Lady Bountiful, dishing out grub to ruffians like you. With Chemise, it's come and help her get rid of excess grub. Grace and mercy go together, so I went in.

The trailer's in two sections, one for living in, one the Sex Museum. Her microwave's often on the blink but this time was going okay. Those gas cylinders always worry me in case they go off with a bang. And a loo, a shower behind a plastic curtain, two bunk beds that fold into bench seats.

'Everything but hope!' She did another grimace. I think.

'More than me, love.' I sat down while she brewed up. She had breakfast ready, beans, eggs, potato cakes reheating, cereals, bread, and a toaster. My mouth watered while she cooked and Tryer clumped about on the roof. 'Got anything new?'

'You mean *old*, Lovejoy.' She smiled, exquisitely beautiful. Her eyes became brilliant with humour. 'I know you.'

'Well, I can ask.'

'Some odd old items, Lovejoy. Job lot, an auction. He only bought them because they were at the end of the sale.'

'I look?'

'Have your breakfast first, Lovejoy.'

She called Tryer. It was agony, waiting with a steaming hot plate of grub in front of me dragging my mouth down and my hands twitching. As soon as Tryer sat at the let-down table I was off, whaling in like a stoker shovelling coal. I ate everything within reach. She started buttering another load before we'd finished the first, talking all the while of the places they'd been, how poorly they'd done through the Midlands, police.

'It's the bloody watch committees, Lovejoy,' Tryer said. 'They had us out of three towns on the trot before I'd got the handbrake on. Right, darling?' He calls her darling without embarrassment, a rare thing for our level of society.

'They know us, Lovejoy.' Chemise was really downcast. 'It's this new morality.'

'No, love. It's your name.' My mouth was crammed. Speaking, I lost vital crumbs, which narked me. Starved of calories, here I was spraying the damned things into mid-air, but I had to sing for my supper. 'Worst name you could choose.'

'Sex Museum?' Chemise and Tryer looked mystified. 'But it *is*.'

'And how often do the peelers move you on?'

'Two out of three,' from Tryer. 'Bad spell, four in five.'

A thunderous knock deafened me on the panels. A voice boomed, 'In there! Watch committee! Open up!'

'See?' Chemise wailed. 'Now look! They're here.'

'Hold on, love.' I got up, swallowing fast. 'Stop there, Tryer.' I didn't want him interfering. Lies were called for. My game.

The bloke standing there was typical. Clipboard, waistcoat, a clerk's view of the universe. Pinstriped suit, for God's sake. I thanked heaven. The watch committee had played into my hands. They'd sent me a duckegg.

'Yes?' I wished I had a napkin to dab genteelly at my mouth, but Chemise doesn't run to such. I'd have to tell her when I'd got rid of this nerk.

'Get this off this car park!' Like all his kind, he bawled the command, though I was well within earshot.

'Why?' A gentle puzzlement lighting my countenance.

He was narked, having to look up at me. He tried to thunder. 'Your Sex Museum is a disgrace! As the authorized watch committee officer, I order you off! This town is respectable!'

'Sex Museum?' Now I was baffled, frowning. 'This isn't a Sex Museum. Whatever gave you that idea?'

'Your banner!' He mocked me, beads of sweat on his forehead, almost dancing with rage.

Stepping down, I looked. My brow cleared. I could have filled the Shakespeare Memorial Theatre, my acting felt that good.

'Tryer?' I called, truly sincere sadness slumping my shoulders. 'Those kids again. Come and see.'

He emerged, mystified. 'What?'

'Them desecrators've draped the exhibition.' I pointed. 'It's a damned shame. Every time our Humanistic Encounter Exhibition reaches town.'

'What exactly are you implying?' the committee man bawled.

'It's no good, Lovejoy,' Tryer said dispiritedly.

But I was halfway through a meal. God only knows where I'd get the next. I halted, determined, St Alban facing doom.

'No, Tryer,' I said firmly, trying to signal him to shut up for Christ's sake. 'No. We must stand firm.' I turned, tearful, to the goon. 'Sir, I wish to protest about your town schoolchildren and your security services. No sooner does our travelling exhibition reach your town than we endure insult. It was the same at Ipswich.'

'Ipswich?' He glared at the banner, back at me.

'Insult after insult. The Arts Council predicted this!'

'Arts Council?' he said, eyes darting uneasily.

'Of course. We are supported by the Arts Council,' I said gravely. 'This exhibition is aimed at disadvantaged minorities who, poor things, can't encounter others similarly oppressed by humanistic relationships.'

'Lovejoy,' Tryer was saying. 'Give up. I'll move on.'

Nobly I faced the ungodly, smiling with proud heroism. God, but I was good. I felt myself welling up. 'No, Tryer. How could we face the Minister for the Arts? Didn't he promise parliament to speak out *for* travelling exhibitions that help the suffering?' I gazed at the official, brimming pure soul, and spoke with quiet martyrdrom. 'Sir. Your vile and unlearned youth with fascist malevolence defiled and desecrated our attempts to help those in need. But even with such horrid opposition, we will open our doors. *In one hour!* Even if you bann us!' I finished in ringing tones.

A crowd assembled at such goings-on in the Leisure Planet car park. Some carried skateboards, sports bags. I appealed.

'See what the town's yobbos have done! Defaced our exhibition! Just because it is concerned with living life!'

'Shame, that,' a bloke muttered.

A lady piped up. 'There's too much interference from the town hall.' Women get more bitterness in their voices. I could have kissed her. Agreement rose. More people paused to listen.

'Thank you,' I said fervently. 'You see, sir? These good family folk can see it instantly. You let your vandals replace our banner by this monstrosity! And blame us!'

'He's right!' another lady chipped in. 'They sprayed the public lavatories last week. It shouldn't be allowed!'

'I know the town hall is overworked . . .' I knew I needn't complete the sentence. A roar rose from the onlookers.

'Over bloody worked?' a man exclaimed. I'd touched a nerve. 'The town *hall*? A load of parasites, I'll tell you.'

'What about the trees on the bypass?' the first lady demanded, angrily prodding the council man. 'Tell me that!'

'Landscapes and gardens is a different section – '

'Too many bloody sections at that bloody town hall, if you ask me!' from a beer-face.

'Ladies and gentlemen,' the clerk tried, desperate. 'I do assure you that – '

A crone said grimly, 'He's trying to get out of it!'

'Please.' I appealed to everybody. 'If our original notice could be . . . We don't want to cause bother.'

'Right!' The clipboarder grasped at a straw. I thanked people, smiling sadly as they started to disperse. He took out a pen. 'What was on your notice? The wording? I'll replace it.'

Hell fire, I thought in despair. What had I called us? 'Er, Encounter Exhibition.'

His eyes narrowed. 'That wasn't what you said.'

I said, quiet but resigned, 'If it's too much trouble – '

'No, no! It will be ready in half an hour.'

He wrote and vanished, like the poem's angel. We went back in. I attacked my congealing fry-up.

'Here, Chemise. Where's the toast?'

'Coming!' She hurtled about the confined space. 'That was marvellous, Lovejoy! He's right, Tryer. Our name's wrong!'

We dined with more speed than elegance, then went through to the Sex Museum in the trailer to see Tryer's mysterious job lot.

It's not bad, as displays go. It consists of bays just wide enough to stand in, the partitions crudely tacked to a frame. Chemise put the light on. No windows, just overhead glass for enough basic glim.

'It's been rearranged since last time, Lovejoy,' she pointed out. 'See the dildoes? First two alcoves.'

' "Dildo Through The Ages".' I read the card. 'Er, good.'

The implements were all newish. Wooden, with belts and without, leather, plastic composition, bakelite, even beeswax phalluses, small to gigantic, anatomically precise to bizarre.

'Automated sex dildoes are separate from the manual.' Chemise led me. 'Tryer doesn't agree. But the electronic and battery *must* be separate. Different concept, right?'

'Right, right.' I had to agree, being unable to see the point of the entire thing, but Chemise thinks it's the only career. For all I know it might do a deal of good.

I felt off colour. Maybe I'd eaten the meal too fast, or maybe I wasn't getting fed often enough. But I started sweating.

'Are you all right, Lovejoy?'

'Aye, fine.' I wasn't. I laughed to stay her worry. 'Just all this passionate sex with none coming my way!'

Then I was down with a bump, clammy and woozy. She called for Tryer, dashed for a flannel. By the time she started laundering my face I'd sussed the problem.

Near where I was slumped on the trailer floor stood some small boxes. Nothing special, just various shapes dusty and worn. They were on a shelf Tryer reserves for erotic postcards. This was the cheapest section. You can still buy these postcards for a postage stamp. This won't be the case for long, because they're getting rarer with every tick of the clock. Tryer has all the common ones: 'Hold to Light' cards – you peer through a pinhole and see a lovely girl bathing or being passionate. Each card seems innocent, with maybe a sailor holding up a lifebelt at a porthole, as in W. H. Elliam's famous example – still priced at three pints of beer, no more. Go for them today while they're dirt cheap. Tomorrow's too late.

The next alcove held a display of nipple jewels and penis rings, rather clumsily pinned on a cork board, with descriptions written in a painstaking scrawl. I'd told Tryer the details of them some time back. Most were cheap, though one was 14-carat gold. Penis rings come in two sizes. One is small, the size of a sleeper earring, for putting through the foreskin or under the glans penis, very like a nipple or an ear is pierced. Usually engraved with a sentimental inscription, though why anybody'd want it decorated beats me. The other sort's larger, to go round the penis. This embellishment is coming back into fashion, would you believe, and women – especially wives, odd to relate – are the instigators, who want to doll up their blokes. Ask any specialist jeweller. It beats me. I always want to know if it's painful. Shops in exotic cities sell them to males of a certain proclivity who intend to declare mutual betrothal in unusual ceremonies. The real oddity is that women mostly buy them for an illicit 'marriage' ceremony, in which the ring is slipped over their secret bloke's organ, to the accompaniment of prayers, chants, incense from a thurible, and blessings. I went to one where a respectable married woman wed a boatman down the estuary; they were lovers and wished to plight their troth unknown to the outside world. There was quite a party afterwards, consummation on the floor right there and then, ring in place. I wanted to ask the bloke if it hurt, but the girl I was with whispered I wasn't to and how dare I ask. Propriety gets everywhere these days, so I'll never know. You can tell these 'shafter' rings from their relatively larger size; they're usually jadeite or nephrite jade, with bright green preferred. I've seen them in onyx, cheap old serpentine, and genuine gold. Silver's in vogue for dark skins, they say, with alabaster long in fashion among Earth groupies, for occult reasons.

The other bays were more mundane: iron chastity belts (two hundred quid, as this goes to press), whips, bondage instruments, cuckold's horns, the inevitable faked Japanese woodblock prints, and posters from exotic films. Tryer had introduced a small video stall, where folk could buy movies. This alcove was marked 'For Educational Instruction Only'. A section on love chairs, conversation chairs, and love positions was badly illustrated by modern pictures torn from magazines. On the whole it was pretty poor, and badly displayed. A kid could have done better.

'Why not have some rope, an obsidian blade and a twist of bark, for a Maya ritual? Nick the pictures from books.'

'Of what, Lovejoy?' Chemise asked.

'The Mayas. Central America, AD 250 to 900. Bloodthirsty lot who beheaded their losers at football. The King slit his, er, thing, passed a rope through, caught his blood on some bark that he burnt. His missus did the same rope trick through her tongue's frenulum. The smoke gave them visions – with a little help from hallucinogens.'

'That's simply beautiful,' Lovejoy!' Her eyes shone.

But those boxes. Chemise was still dabbing me. I shoved her away, managed to stand.

'Get off me, silly cow.'

'Lovejoy! You just take your time! Do – you – hear?' Chemise gets self-righteous when a bloke's off colour.

'Can I look? I think you've got something, love.'

'What's up?' Tryer entered, the trailer tilting to a cant.

One box was large; held a few old cards, nothing else except a small bronze. It was nineteenth century, French, showing Diana. Somewhat corroded, but nothing to worry about. She was seated, arms raised almost as if sleeping, yet with her knees flexed and her naked form all curves. Lovelier still, the name Denecheau was underneath. It was worth the Sex Museum and the trailer. She was good enough to eat.

Another box held two corkscrews, both German about 1899, give or take. Don't laugh. One was the famous Folding Lady corkscrew – the torso was one 'arm', raised legs the other, and the business bit standing erect between. The second, its fulcrum rusted, was the well-known Amor, one 'arm' being a soldier, the other a lass. Open them, they assume one position; close them with the screw between, they get up to no good. Collectors give about a fortnight's wage. Nothing in a couple of the other boxes except yellowed cuttings from newspapers needing sorting out.

Then a Japanese print, folded (pity; reduces the value by half). Modern posters or comic-book glossies of starlets had these olden-day Japanese equivalent. Only, they made them by woodblock prints of Kabuki actors. This was on lovely fine paper; a rare *surimono*, one done especially for an admiring patron. I think they're gruesome, those faces, but I was looking at a new trailer. It showed an actor depicting a made-up woman character. Another superb find. Tryer had made it, all in one go. But it was the last that was the true winner for Tryer's flying-tackle guess.

It was jade. And I do mean real, honest and true jade. Everybody knows jade, but forgets there are two sorts. One is jadeite jade – comes in any colour you like, but only became the expensive front runner in the eighteenth century. The most valuable isn't the orange, white, bluish, red jades, but the 'imperial' emerald-green jade. It's still carved, of course. But there's a trick for jadeite jade. I took out the loupe I'm never without. And looked close at the little bell shape, moving to the light.

Modern jadeite carvings tend to be polished with diamond powders, otherwise you can't get that lovely iridescent sheen jadeite gives. This looked matt, which I actually prefer because it's older, and felt almost greasy to the thumb. I had to keep my breathing going so I didn't keel over, for just visible were minute discontinuities, quite like crazy paving cracks. That's what stops it from taking a perfect polished gleam. It was ancient jade, predating the modern period where everybody wants 'perfection'. It was a bell, imperial emerald jadeite jade. Nephrite jade, however, is usually green or brownish-pale, less favoured, and only moderate value, even though it's often brilliantly carved.

'Jadeite.' I was overcome from delight. I felt floating. 'This was carved by a bobby-dazzler so long ago it doesn't matter. Look!'

I inverted the bell to show the carved interior. Two concubines, partly clothed, were depicted on the inside of the bell's lumen, arms spread, limbs amorously disposed. The clapper was free-swinging, carved in the form of a bifid male organ. Each swing gave a musical tinging sound, the shafts piercing each of the concubines in turn, once each oscillation. A fortune, from any collector of erotica.

'What's it for?' Tryer, ever the tactless genius.

'It's for hanging on oneself or the lady, in certain . . .' I cleared my throat. 'Actually had a variety of uses.'

Chemise smiled her beatific smile. 'What exquisiteness! Musical love! What elegance!'

'What d'you mean?' Tryer asked, looking.

'It means you can buy the frigging town, Tryer,' I said, but wry because this miracle never happens to me. I only make discoveries for somebody else.

'Lovejoy,' Chemise said, moved. 'Thank you, darling. Is there anything I can do for you?'

Right offer, wrong moment. 'Any chance of a coffee?'

'Ten gallons, for you,' she said.

During nosh, I told them about the corkscrew, and the little bronze, but kept coming back to the jade piece.

'Where'd you find it?' I asked. You never ask this of another dealer. It always leads to trouble.

'Suffolk,' Tryer said. 'Fenstone. I was clearing a neighbour's tied cottage. A lady's farm's in Queer Street.'

Fenstone was popular lately, for a village sinking slowly in the west. 'You lived at Fenstone?'

'Used to. That was where I met Chemise.'

'Yes!' She was glowing, as only women suddenly rich can. 'Tryer's holy well. Didn't you hear about it?'

'Nobody heard about it,' Tryer said bitterly. 'That bloody parson cocked the whole scam up.'

'Parson? You mean that Smith?'

'Him.' Tryer looked venomous. 'I invented this holy well. Built a grotto, me and my sister's lad from Breakstone. Lovely. I put it about that the Virgin Mary appeared there. Wishing Well stuff, printed histories. I had touring agencies interested. They'd have flocked in.'

'It got scuppered, eh?'

'He got my lease cancelled. Said it was blasphemous.'

'Oh, Tryer, don't keep on.' Chemise was exasperated. This was obviously old ground. 'Lovejoy's divvied the job lot. We've made it! Let's be thankful. Anyway, how d'you know it was Father Jay?'

'Because his parish council had us evicted, that's how!'

No good. I said I'd best get off because I had to go to an auction. Chemise rushed after me. She'd wrapped some slices of toast in kitchen foil, and gave me a kiss and three apples. I said so long. I couldn't help thinking what a lot of useful con tricks had died the death near tranquil little Fenstone. So tranquil, in fact, that it was being *made* comatose. Where had I seen that stout, limping, balding bloke before, the one lighting the candles? And who was the lady with the farm in decline?

10

Hoping I'd got the day right, I went along the Roman wall as far as the Balkerne gateway. Now fashioned into a tavern, it overlooks the river slope, where schools abound and cattle graze. I like it because you can see countryside without having to suffer its terrible terrain. It makes me smile with wicked glee, very like a kid looks at a tiger, secure enough to taunt the caged menace.

The pub's called the Railway Vista now – you can see the station a mile off – and has a cellar that was part of the Roman wall. Cool, door a mile thick, safe from prying eyes. It's there that the tomorrow auction would be held, eleven o'clock. I hung about outside, judging the town hall clock. I saw Litterbin Bell go in, leaving his blonde dolly bird in his huge Lagonda. She sat there la-lalling to the radio, gorgeous and vacant as a balloon. Litterbin's made a fortune out of rubbish, having started rooting in dustbins. He wears capes now over hand-tailored suits, spats even, hand-lasted shoes, smokes cheroots, fawn kid gloves in his shoulder bar, movie-spiv tash.

There are usually only six in a tomorrow auction – you'll see why when I can get round to explaining. This is Big John Sheehan's decree. He's a quiet Ulsterman with power, has a Praetorian Guard, and rules the roost hereabouts in bent activities. Only occasionally does he launch into antiques, but when he does it's essential to know his wishes. In fact, it's vital to guess what his orders might become in the near future because if he gives a naff order he's likely to look for blame among those around him. He trusts me, knowing I'm too scared of him to do anything but obey to the letter. Usually, I mean.

Corinth arrived next, attractive, early forties, in a pastel green suit, matching everythings, expensive hairdo, amber bracelets. I love Corinth. Well, I would if. She took her name from some film years ago. She talked earnestly with a neatly dressed man her age. He's her secretary, Montgomery Mainwaring, who cohabits with Corinth in a splendid house at Aldeburgh beach. She deals in Regency furniture, paintings, English porcelain. I've never quite worked out their relationship. Speculation is rife. I saw her tick off her instructions, Montgomery nodding. Then she snapped a goodbye, and walked off towards Luciano's coffee bar on the theatre corner. Big John doesn't allow women in auctions, deals, murders. I was there when somebody once asked him why. Big John was astonished, said, 'What *for*?' Couldn't understand why anybody'd let a female decide the next crime. It's his upbringing, gentleman of the old school.

Montgomery, Litterbin, me, Sheehan himself, making four. A Rolls was illegally parked asplay the cul-de-sac, so a fifth was already in. I stood among the trees by the theatre – on show nights patrons emerge with interval drinks, a pretty sight. It gave me protective colouring. I wanted to know who, because I'd a vital question about funny names. I saw Bog alight from a taxi, smiling as if at admiring crowds. Bog Frew's an ageing thespian given to declaiming Shakespeare speeches. He never was any good, but his dreams flirt with reality and they tend to merge. He has a terraced house near the bypass, one room crammed with stage memorabilia. He'll tell you barefaced falsehoods like, 'Oh, that poster? Me and Larry – I was very young, o' course – went a bomb at Strateford-on-Avon. We did the Bard's Scottish play, y'know. Macduff, me. The critics *raved . . .*' Not true, none of it, but where's the harm?

Six, was that enough today? I went in at one minute to eleven, through the taproom bar, made it downstairs just as Tomtom, one of Big John's goons, was closing the door. He hesitated, let me through, and there was the tomorrow auction, ready for off.

They stood around in an awkward circle, like the Privy Council. Big John was talking with a thin small coloured bloke wearing, would you believe, sunglasses, in a cellar? Sheehan has an Ulsterman's typically mobile alert face, with steady eyes for worrying you if you dare look in. I leant against the old Roman mortared walling. It warmed me like a cherub's smile.

'Who asked Lovejoy?' Big John asked the air.

Silence, so we could all freeze in terror in comfort.

'Er, I came to, er, ask, John, please. . . ?' My voice broke like when I was a lad, yodelling in spite of trying to keep it steady. 'Er, if that's all right, er . . .'

My speech was as grovelly as I could make it without actually kneeling to supplicate. Was it too late to fling myself down?

'How did Lovejoy know it was now?' Sheehan's quiet words fell like a pall made visible. I saw even the stranger blanch. John's voice goes softer the more menace it contains.

'Er . . .' I heard my frantic yodel, cleared my throat, shoved it to a bass, started anew. 'I overheard somebody, dunno who, in the Drum and Dog, say about Sunday, eleven o'clock. I waited outside . . . Well, see, they're usually here, John.'

Best I could do, and with enough truth to make it stand a rough test. A lie has to be either so far beyond credulity that its bizarre lunacy might just carry the day, or so close to truth that it seems probable right off. I'm good at lies, except when I'm scared, which is usually.

'Shut it,' Big John told nobody. 'Fine the beater, both seven days.'

'Right, John.' Tomtom, pale with relief, sloped out.

We all relaxed, me almost screaming that I'd got away with it. Actually, Tinker had told me about this gathering. But I'd saved his hide, even though the poor old Drum and Dog would have to bolt its doors and lose a week's trade. The beater – the looker-out outside, who should have detected me lurking away by the old wall – would be one of Big John's own. He'd lose a week's everything – money, status, car, home, credit. A terrible punishment. But I was in the clear.

'C-c-c-can I stay, John, please?' I almost said sir.

'Got a question?'

'Yes, please.' I was sweating buckets from deliverance.

'First is,' I heard Sheehan start up, 'stained-glass windows from the Black Moat House. Montgomery's bid.'

'Thank you, Mr Sheehan,' Corinth's assistant stepped forward, wisely addressing his remarks to Big John. 'The robbery I propose concerns moderate cost and minimal risk. The Black Moat House is an ancient pile in coastal Suffolk due west from Thorpeness. It has earned historians' attention these many years. Visitors are attracted by its windows' quality.'

He patted his pockets, quite the forgetful major wanting map references. Military bearing, with a smart tash and a brisk manner, he'd been used to authority, which raised interesting thoughts about why he was subservient to the beautiful Corinth.

'The windows were designed by Lalique's assistants. French design, glamorous rather than overtly exotic – '

'Hush now,' Big John said as if calming a babe. Montgomery clammed as if gagged. 'There any doubt they're French?'

'No, Mr Sheehan. I can bring evidence, if you wish.' Montgomery Mainwaring was desperate to expound, but Big John knows only money. His convictions are absolute, though. Montgomery had better be right.

'Right. How much?'

'I am authorized to bid nine,' Montgomery said, looking round. 'That is for a clean removal, all windows intact.'

'How many windows are there?' Bog Frew asked, trying to sound bored, but excited at the value of leaded windows.

'Four large, three small.'

Bog winced. The price was steep. Litterbin chipped in. He could never resist scraps, however the word's defined.

'They worth it, though, eh?' he said. 'Continental stuff's going a bomb down the chute.' The chute is the Channel Tunnel. 'Go on, then. I'll bid ten. I'll suffer, you dance.' He said it as if we'd forced him to make the offer.

'Any advance on ten?' from Big John.

'Eleven,' Montgomery said. He was calm, give him that.

It was me invented the system of numbers. Some years back, money got ridiculous from politicians doing secret things that eroded the world's money. Revaluation, inflation, devaluations, worrying the life out of everybody. It got stupid. So I started quoting everything in the average wage. Government statistics include the average annual wage, meaning enough for a family to live on for a year. Money has to be translated into time, or it means nowt. Within a twelvemonth antique dealers everywhere were quoting in multiples of the average annual wage. It's the only sensible means of measuring the importance of the paper stuff we distinguish by the name of gelt.

'All done?'

Litterbin looked restless, but conceded. Big John knocked down the seven stained-glass windows of the Black Moat House to Montgomery. Now, this was a tomorrow auction, note. The windows were still in place. And the House's owner had no part in these proceedings except to wake up one morning to find their beautiful windows stolen, evaporated with the foggy foggy dew. The money Montgomery'd bid would be paid up front, the day *before* the theft was due – hence the term 'tomorrow' for this arrangement. The money is always cash, paid on demand to Sheehan's goons, whereupon the next day the lovely windows would magically appear in Corinth's 'cran' – the place where she usually stored illicit antiques.

That's the tomorrow auction: thieves (I exclude honest blokes like me) bid for a theft of certain objects. Always antiques these days, because of their unlimited – meaning unchangeable – value to one and all. Now it was up to the successful bidder to hire crooks good enough to nick the windows, after which BJS would refund Montgomery's cash deposit less a tenth. There are scores of variations, but you get the idea.

'Next is a dressing table, made in Copenhagen. F'rook?'

'Thank you, Mr Sheehan,' the little sunglasses chap said. 'How do you do, those I have not met hitherto. This table is dear to me. It stands in the abode of one Dame Millicent Hallsworthy. It has palisander veneer, most unusual, dated approximately 1790. By J. Pengel, Danish. One might almost believe it to be English manufacture, but its superior Greek fret and its brass swag over the front of the lower drawer . . .'

He faltered. Big John was glowering. I cringed.

'Superior what?' Quiet voice, far too quiet.

Farouk looked bewildered, scared out of his wits. 'Superior Greek style fret . . .'

'Superior. *To what?*'

'Er, please, John,' I put in, timid, but not wanting blood on the carpet before I'd said my piece. 'I think Mr, er, Farouk means the fret is *placed* superiorly, meaning on top of, not meaning of quality superior to the old London makers.'

'Superior?' The word gnawed.

'Yes, John. It's in the Oxford English Dictionary. Honest.'

'Oh, right.' He glowered round to make sure of whatever he wanted. The shaken visitor continued at his nod.

'Ah, Dame Millicent is a daughter of a Polish refugee, self-titled. She turned to an agricultural life. She purchased the Cockcroft lands outright when that family . . .' He ahemed in gentlemanly fashion so we all knew he was being nice about a clone of sinners '. . . relin-

73

quished their property. I saw this piece of furniture on a visit. Cockcroft Manor's security is moderate.'

'Cavern?' asked Big John.

'Easy, John,' said Cavern. He's a prematurely wrinkled Morne bloke. You don't mangle with Cavern. Big John once sent him into a gaol to punish some inmates that Big John wanted corrected. Cavern slipped in, inflicted the necessary, and was home the following day without a scratch. I like the sense of security that comes from agreeing with Cavern *et al*.

'I bid one,' Farouk said.

'Two.' Habit said the bid for Litterbin.

'Three.' Bog Frew did his I-don't-care pose, fooling nobody but himself, as Farouk capped Litterbin.

Silence. Sheehan gave it the nod. Farouk looked dismayed, but I wondered. His sort of quiet reflective type never looks dismayed, however downcast he might be. So he wanted us to believe he was dejected when he really wasn't. Now why would an antique dealer propose the theft of an antique from a country house, pay local thieves to steal it, yet not really want it?

We pressed on, me shelving the little problem. Antiquery's full of these twists. You can never remember half of them. I'd have to ask Tinker what Farouk was up to.

Sheehan next allowed some Louis Comfort Tiffany glass to be stolen from an East London museum, but said Bog Frew would have to make his own arrangements because this wasn't his area. Tomtom would give Bog a couple of names, contacts. Besides, Big John couldn't care less about foreign stuff. It broke my heart to hear of pieces so lovely as Tiffany Glass Company of New York – leaders in the Art-Nouveau style, late nineteenth century. Oddly, these glorious American antiques are far more admired by non-Americans than by the Yanks themselves. The Tiffany firm had a workman called Arthur Nash, whose colours and designs are brilliant. I'd seen the collection – only eight pieces, only one night guard. I'd wondered whether to try the place myself, just for one of Nash's Tiffany 'favrile' pieces, which are simply glass shapes like balls, vases, fruits, decorated by flowers or vines. Louis Tiffany coined the name himself, bright lad, and did the same shapes on metalwork and even pottery. I wondered whether to try to 'chop' (meaning to share) the scam with Bog Frew. I'd heard lately he had lost heavily on horses. Again.

Big John denied Montgomery permission to do our town's museum for Roman coins, on the grounds that it was done far too often. But he allowed him a theft of a vintage motor from a Berkshire museum. There was enthusiastic bidding for this, the maniacs. Car addicts are really odd. Bog Frew wanted a lovely flintlock fowling piece by Manton stolen from the Rotunda Museum in Woolwich, and sulked when Big John said a flat no because it belonged to the Royal Artillery, the 'Gunners'.

'Any separates?' Big John asked.

'Er, John. Sorry and all that . . .'

His gaze interrogated Cavern, who shook his head to tell his gaffer this was the first he'd heard of an extra proposal.

'Yes, Lovejoy?'

'Er, John. There's a big painting, Stubbs, a horse. Down the estuary. I've been wondering if . . . Nothing definite, you understand, and I'd have to get the gelt together, maybe syndicate it, like, and I know it's early days . . .'

'Picture?' He wouldn't know a masterpiece if he fell over it, but his shrewdness can't be bested. 'What's he saying, Cavern?'

'Propose it, Lovejoy. Then bid. With,' Cavern added, secretly rioting in mirth-filled glee, 'money on the nail.'

'I know, John,' I said, desperate. 'But can I give notice that I want to propose it next time? If that's all right?'

Sheehan thought a second. 'Put it on hold? Right, Lovejoy. But you'll pay a half extra when you bid.'

I dabbed my sweaty brow. 'Thanks. Really good of you, John.'

'Called?' he asked.

'*Whistlejack*,' I said, looking to see if anybody present jumped in surprise.

Montgomery did. Bog Frew turned slowly to look at me in utter astonishment, but he was an actor, right? Farouk didn't, possibly being the dog that did not bark, as Sherlock Holmes remarked. Only Litterbin's response seemed normal. He guffawed.

'What a frigging name!'

Practically grovelling in gratitude, I fawned my way out into the cool daylight, every muscle trembling. I was standing by the Roman wall recovering when Montgomery came by. I could see Corinth at a café table, smoking her head off.

'Lovejoy!' False heartiness. 'Chance of a word?'

'Sorry, Monty. I'm due at a meeting. Clients waiting.'

He smiled in polite disbelief. 'Ring me. Pretty urgent, what?'

'Ta. What about?'

'Good idea that, about *Whistlejack*. I'll tell Miss Corinth.'

So we went our separate ways. I felt I'd done superbly, for now *Whistlejack*, the famous Stubbs painting, could not be stolen, for Big John Sheehan's writ ran throughout the whole Eastern Hundreds. I hadn't lost my touch for disaster.

Hurry now, to fit in everything before twilight, when I'd have to do the burglary. Sabrina time.

11

One thing you can be sure of: antiques and sex are scarey. Which one's more frightening than the other, I don't really know, but they run it close. Which is why I walked past Sabrina's house without looking, then stro-o-o-olled slowly past the remnants of the Roman wall that borders Castle Field, carefully not looking across the road to where the luscious Sabrina palpitated behind her window. Two o'clock, on the dot, and Sunday, as she'd ordered.

The curtains were drawn upstairs, signal for go. Her Jaguar, size of the Norwich express, was backed into the driveway, not bum outwards. Signal two. And the flowers in the windows downstairs, blue: signal three. I went towards the house only when nobody happened by walking their dog, across the small lawn and darted inside, the door opening the instant I made it.

'You're only just on time, Lovejoy.'

What's the answer when a woman says that? Early, I'd be risking her reputation. Late, disaster.

She enveloped me, mouth seeming rimmed by lips a foot thick, breasts slamming me against the wall. She clicked the door lock as we groped and clutched. It was two o'clock Sunday all right. From the corner of my eye, as passion took over, I caught sight of the printer's proofs of the next Aldeburgh auction lying tantalizingly on the couch, but I was already too far gone and my vision blurred. We made the safety of her outhouse before paradise obliterated my remaining senses.

We'd met in odd circumstances. The trip to the Cornish holiday resort was by reason of some antiques catastrophe. I'd tried to organize a syndicate to buy an Adam Revival cabinet known to have been exhibited at the 1867 Paris Exhibition. Cruelly, some New Yorker bought it for quarter of a million slotniks, leaving me owing frightening interest on a loan I'd thought cast-iron. This Leslie Mulrose bloke I'd come to Cornwall to meet was a heavy roller, gave loans on antiques. I'd arranged to meet him at his hotel. I had three forged sale notes on me, all relating to imaginary furniture in the Midlands, as convincers.

I'd been nearly basking on the bobbing briny – meaning I was staring out to sea from the sand – when Sabrina happened by. She was carrying her succulent self and a catalogue from Greenhalgh's Original Antiques Auction (every word of that title's a laugh) in Aldeburgh. For a moment I was startled, thinking she'd come after me about an overdue account and a dropsy I'd done – that's moving a good antique from a mixed job into some dross, so you get it – and the good little one – cheap. It takes sleight of hand.

We got chatting. I made sure of that.

'Go ahead,' I grumbled as she borrowed my beach parasol. 'Let me sizzle.'

She laughed pneumatically like they do. 'This sunshade is mine.'

I'd nicked it by pretending I was Number Forty-two. 'Okay. But don't start complaining I should pay. You're the rich auctioneer.'

'How – ?' She remembered her catalogue. 'Quick eyes.'

'Here on your tod?'

'No. My husband.' She indicated a figure zipping along the ocean, skis behind a speedboat. 'He does hang-gliding, scuba diving, that.' She gave me a wry look that spoke volumes. 'Burns off his excess energy.'

She spoke dismissively. It made me swallow. 'Heavy duty in the City?' Sympathy wins women.

'Leslie's in banking regulations, investors amok at the drop of a decimated cent.' She smiled. 'I exercise differently.'

More swallowing. She looked, sounded, was massively voluptuous. More than ample, and that hidden languuor women promise with.

'Lifting antiques about all the time, eh, Mrs Mulrose?' Her catalogue wore a 'For The Personal Attn Of' sticker.

She looked startled, cottoned on and smiled, perfect teeth. Then she started, telling me tales of minor antiques scams, to impress me. But she laboured under a handicap: I knew who she was, while she'd not a clue about me. I'd heard the lads talking of this superb blonde auctioneer with an accurate memory for faces, names, bids, names of substitutes. This was the famous Sabrina Mulrose. The lads all over East Anglia lusted after this delectable lass. They'd give anything, antiques excepted, of course. I was here to meet Leslie Mulrose. I hadn't connected the surname.

Within minutes she had me smiling then laughing. By the second drink – she quaffed it faster than I ever could – I was learning of the auctioneer's viewpoint. To this day I don't know what prompted me to ask my question outright. Was it delight at being one up on an auctioneer? A chance to show off, laugh at her expense?

'I read once you lot have trouble with antiques scruffs. They can, what's the word, divine whether something is a fake. Is it right?'

'Divvies, you mean.' She tossed her hair from her nape with a hand. I watched, mesmerized. I believed the lads now. Before, I'd taken it with a pinch of salt because they're a randy lot. 'We've one in our region. He's a swine, always broke. Cadges off women, a born thief. He's been too scared to come to our auction since I came.'

'He has?' I was double narked. She could only be talking about me. Scared? Of *her*?

'I've a degree in fine art, an MA art history. I've written two books on antiques. I contribute to *Antique and New Art*, specialist auction articles.'

Gradual graduates. Who profit by degrees, as it were.

It was then that her husband Leslie skimmed in to the beach and waved. She waved prettily back, extended herself elegantly sky-wards, brushed sand off. I couldn't take my eyes from her.

'See you, Mrs Mulrose,' I said, working out how to come on them accidentally in the bar, pretend surprise.

'See you, Lovejoy,' she said.

My face burning, I sat watching her retreating figure. I hadn't told her my name, clever cow. She fell in with her hubby, him explaining with swooping arms how he'd hung on to that rope and flown like an albatross.

That was the start of it. Needless to say, good old Leslie hadn't lent me the money, but me and Sabrina went on from there. While her husband went out flippered and sealskinned to inspect the seabed's detritus, she'd had the gall to ravish me on her hotel balcony within clear view of the ocean. 'It adds spice, Lovejoy,' was all she would say when I remonstrated. She meant risk. God knows how many I was, in her ordinal list of lovers. She was scarily frank about her previous blokes. And the reason I had to come when summoned, so to speak? Two reasons. She dissuaded Leslie from lending me the gelt, then offered me a lump sum, which saved my skin. Second, she was eager to run a scam in the Aldeburgh auction, and had been waiting for some gormless dupe like me.

The means? She was the one who checked the secret proofs from Greenhalgh's printer, before the auction viewing day. Which gave her a head start on any legal honest bidder like you and me, because a cataloguer can change descriptions enough to deceive. Tell you about it if I get a minute. Since then, me and Sabrina had been active in, er, making such adjustments after clandestine encounters. She was thorough, precise, demanding.

'The last thing I want, Lovejoy,' she'd told me when first we made smiles, 'is for Leslie to find out that you do this to me. Understand?'

'Yes, Sabrina.' *Me* doing. . . ? Who was doing what to whom?

'He wouldn't tolerate you messing about with me like this.'

'No, Sabrina.'

'He can be vicious, Lovejoy. So obey my signals to the letter when you start seeing me regularly at home. Understand?'

That was the first I'd heard of her permanent interdict, to coin a phrase. It had been over six months ago, and I'd come once a week, Sabrina's Sunday seduction. Only twice had Leslie failed to sail, fly like a bird or dive like a duck. Then, we'd met the following day when Leslie was beavering for dinars on some London heat seat. Sabrina hadn't paid me a groat yet. 'It's in a numbered account, Lovejoy,' she told me huskily whenever I asked for my cut. 'I'll pay it eventually. Now, where were we. . . ?'

Answer: where me and Sabrina always were, in her spare room, outhouse, on her stairs even. She never took me into her own bedroom. Some fine sensitivity, perhaps.

'The catalogue, darling,' she said. Her voice always goes kind of sleepy afterwards, though she's wide awake. It's the same with a lot of women. Even Liz Sandwell and Margaret and Josie and Cerise, and the wood nymph Beth, even when she was worried sick we'd be startled by forest ramblers.

'I'll get it.'

'No. Let me.'

Which meant a wait, while she padded about, returned with the proofs. She kept hold of it, as always.

'This stool, Lovejoy. The lady wants a massive reserve price.'

'Oh, aye.' Casual, but that knowing heart of mine pounded.

'Funny thing. Looks old, walnut, round top covered in thick faded embroidered fabric, might have had a coat of arms.'

Now, don't mock stools just because they're not chairs. Truly old ones are rarer than chairs, believe it or not. The great find is always the tabouret, a round-topped stool like this might be. Sinful old James I brought with him the continental politeness of letting the wives of important lords actually sit down in his presence, the famous 'tabouret etiquette' of that age. Quite a concession. Charles II favoured it, too, but the courtesy died out with the Georges, whereon round stools petered out mostly until Victoria. I'd go so far as to say that the stool is more of an historical indicator than almost anything else, from monarchs down to the level of my labouring ancestors. Mind you, if you happen to snap up one of Queen Mary II's own set of eighteen from Windsor Castle, complete with its original green damask covering, you can start your own antiques firm straight off. The familiar music stool that can be adjusted on a central pillar screw is one of my real favourites. (Tip: seek out the ones that the Victorians, after about 1847, cased in with a wooden sleeve. They did this because that screw, sliding erotically into that plush circular top, clearly suggested something unthinkable in the Victorian with-drawing room. The wooden-sleevers are a lovely unusual craftsman-ship.) Hepplewhite in 1778 wanted stools taken back to stark simplicity, delectable mahogany, or japanned 'to match the suit of chairs', he said. My mouth watered. A dressing stool matching a set of chairs –

'Eh?' Sabrina'd mentioned her this-week scam.

'. . . send somebody to bid, make the bid come from you.'

A think. This was the wrong way round. 'No, love,' I said patiently. 'We pick out the good items, get them for a song by distorting the catalogue description, see? As we always do it.'

'Not this time, lover.' She leant over me, talking, me recumbent. Her breast curved eloquently near my eye. 'We give it a poor description, true. But this time you send your terrible old tramp to bid a fortune.'

Her breast made me inclined to agree. 'Why?'

'Because of what you just said, Lovejoy. Hepplewhite, the matching chairs. It occurred to me as you spoke.' *Spoke*? I hadn't realized I'd been talking out loud. 'We con folk into thinking there's a matching suit of chairs somewhere!'

'And lose the tabouret?' Reason's a mistake with women.

'And gain. . . ?' she prompted, going on when I said nothing. 'We learn who the rich cow is, see?'

'The vendor is anonymous? You said a lady.'

'Yes, but through that mare Corinth's pimp.'

You have to sigh. I don't understand why women hate each other. I mean, she hardly knows Corinth, and here she was slagging off . . . Hang on. 'How d'you know the vendor's a bird?'

'Montgomery let it slip when he brought the stool in. Reverence,' she sneered, 'for titles is the bane of antiques. Mind you, he's only doing what the rest of the trade's been up to these past weeks, clearing out a decaying village.'

'Any idea which one?' I asked, dreading the answer.

'The one that changed its name,' she said. 'Fenstone.'

'That old dump,' I dismissed the whole thing. 'Any more?'

'A coffee biggins is in, genuine silver they're saying.' Her gaze slipped gently down her breast and met mine, a feat. 'Here it is, One-one-nought. How much d'you think?'

'A fortune.' Silver is slowly recovering. A biggins would temp Big Frank from Suffolk, silver maniac and bigamist.

'I want it, Lovejoy. Myself. Can we blam the bid price?'

'You'll bid through a nominee?'

'Of course.'

This really hurt. I could do that brilliantly, yet here she was, naked as Eve when God got narked, getting somebody else to do her clandestine illicit bidding. 'No trust?'

She smiled. My vision couldn't get past her nipple. 'Lovejoy. You serve one purpose. My employees serve another.'

Only one purpose? It was a crude admission, that I was utterly superfluous to tender-hearted Sabrina, except for my antiquery talent. Love was out, even carnal lust was incidental. I was a pawn. But what bloke isn't?

George Biggins was one of those dazzling intellects who suddenly explodes into history. Tragically only remembered for his coffee percolator nowadays, back in the 1790s George shone. He was a musician, inventor, a clever mechanic – this at a time when Great Britain was knee-deep in genius mechanics – and a clever chemist. Equating this outstanding polymath with a coffee pot's like honouring Shakespeare for walk-ons. George's name was synonymous with the coffee percolator soon after he made the first one in the mid-1790s. It's a simple cylinder with a snouty pouring lip, a three-legged lampstead beneath. With decoration of the time, nothing unusual.

'Has it a strainer?'

'No. Should there be one?'

'Not if it's a true biggins. He pegged out in the early 1800s. Henry Ogle patented a modified biggins with a strainer in 1817, fifteen years after George died. You see the hallmark?'

Her breast was blinding. I could hardly speak, swallow, think. A breast, sloping like that when a woman leans over, has cruel effects that damage rational thoughts. My mouth was watering. It's not fair.

'Yes. I think it's 1798.'

'Oh, is it really?' I said, voice quaking.

Sabrina was casually paying no attention but probably rolling in the aisles inside.

'Give it to me, I'll ditch the hallmark.'

To 'ditch' a hallmark is not to get rid of it. It's to add metal round a genuine hallmark so that people will assume the hallmark has been added later. Many silver items – coffee pots, tea urns – were imported from the Low Countries, and escaped being hallmarked. They're around still, common even in fly-by-night roaming antique fairs. It's become quite the thing for an unscrupulous dealer to simply impose some famous London silversmith's hallmark, complete with the period assay mark. Duty payable from 1797 was a shilling – twelve whole pence! – per ounce of silver, so it was worth evading. Needless to say, an *un*hallmarked piece of silverware costs peanuts compared to a genuine item with a London master's mark.

'Will you, darling?'

Now, our law says you can't buy a Regency silversmith's die, even if genuine, and use it on silver, even if that's genuine too. But villains do this. Big Frank does, on the rare occasions he's not getting married again. The alternative is to 'float', as we call it, a hallmark from some relatively unimportant, cheaper, silver piece – like a church communion patten – and stick it on the desirable costlier piece. It becomes a small recessed hallmark set in a circular 'ditch' with raised shoulders. Once a dealer glimpses that, he walks off, because it means the silverware's a boring old piece with a fraudulent hallmark.

To make dealers ignore a genuine Biggins biggins, I'd need to add silver round the hallmark skilfully enough to make it look as if the genuine hallmark was floated on. Then, when the auction was over, I could simply remove the silver shoulders and sell the silverware at a price justifying its pristine original glory.

'Will you do it for little me?' Her breast stroked my face.

For a second I felt narked at being forced into doing something I didn't really want to. I drew breath to tell her to go to hell and leave me out of it.

'Course, love.'

She laughed a throaty laugh. My speech was silenced by her lovely shape. She tapped my face in mock rebuke, and dropped the proofs on the carpet. I heard them go, then she was superb, honest, truthful, and goddess of everything.

Which encouraged me to risk burglary on Sunday night, something no self-respecting footpad ever does, in his right mind.

12

Once, my motor was active, meaning it went. Now, it rusts in the garden undergrowth, lamps unlit, its corrosion crackling in the evening mist, bits crumping to the grass. I've given up hope of ever getting it going. Its main value is a possible sale, until the sums Sabrina's accumulating for me arrive. I asked her for a sub. She said it was out of the question.

'We can't forever disinvest for no reason, Lovejoy.'

'I have a reason.' Namely, me, hunger.

'An inadequate reason is no reason, Lovejoy.'

Which is where I'd been earlier, except now I was walking away tired and despondent with three new problems. First, who was the lady from Fenstone? Second, how to find time to do the biggins ditcher. Third, how to burgle the Dragonsdale Guest and Resident Hotel. I'm not too bad at burglary, but haven't the panache of the seasoned eaves walker. Some lads I know could do the place over without breaking step, but for me it loomed like the Tower of London.

With my last coins I phoned Margaret Dainty. She was out, her machine politely saying to leave a message. I would have called Dolly, but she was on holiday with her husband, the selfish swine. Janie was in the Orkneys looking at some of the more important grass on one of her estates, thoughtless cow. Beth was being apprehensive somewhere, and so would remain, until she felt lust stir and would then breathlessly demand panicky ravishment out in the untrodden wilds. Helena, my assistant, was due back soon from Brasenose College, Oxford. She undid the erudition with me in vacations and learnt life, subsidizing me in the process. I was without visible means.

By the time I reached town and the Misses Dewhurst's Lorelei Sweetmeat Delicatessen and Tearooms I was dispirited. The bell clonked over the door, going on for five o'clock. They'd soon be closing for evensong at St James's on East Hill.

'Afternoon, Priscilla.'

'Lovejoy! You dear!' Priscilla Dewhurst clapped her hands with real pleasure. She was behind the counter busying herself with clotted cream for two lady customers to gossip over. 'Philadora! See who's visiting!'

They are quite like twittering birds, who could be bookends in another life. They had arrived last summer from the northern cotton mills, where they had worked through a million incarnations, not far from where I was born, actually. As the mill towns collapsed, they'd joined the diaspora and come to breathe moderately clean air here. I'd sold a collection of miniature industrial engines for them. It had given them life security. They have an unbelievable brother who's a town crier somewhere in Lancashire. At first I was the only one who could tell what they were saying. Now, they tailor their dialect and haul out their aitches.

'Lovejoy!' Philadora also came to peck my cheek. 'You're just in time!' She lowered her voice conspiratorially. 'Reverend hates late-comers! Why, Mrs Whitehorn – '

'Philadora!' Priscilla's reprimand shut her sister up. 'Lovejoy wants his tea, not gossip!'

'Actually, Priscilla, I can't stop – '

'Nonsense! What have we done, for heaven's sake?'

They made me sit and served me a nosh, which more than saved my life. It brought me a tranquillity I don't often feel. Just listening to the two dears battling and laughing gave me rest. They occasionally threw a question, what about this weather, how was my cottage and weren't the nights chilly. It was so genteel, this the one place where I'd not get caught by Tinker. Sabrina owed me a fortune; I'd done maybe a hundred auction lots for her. She must have culled a mint. But debts were my trademark. I didn't want to get caught. By now I probably owed every pub in the parish. Tinker lives on ale and the occasional meal. He can chalk up a slate faster than a football team.

The Misses Dewhurst were my one last chance of reaching Dragonsdale and Fenstone. They were also my first chance, truth to tell, because they would fund me any time, but you can't go cadging off the undeceitful, can you? Different if they'd been crooks.

When the customers had left, they came to sit with me, giggling at such boldness.

'This isn't proper, Philadora!' Priscilla said, hiding her face. 'Entertaining a visiting gentleman to tea!'

'What would . . .' Philadora had the grace to colour, but managed to get the unthinkable out '. . Mrs *Heywood* have said?'

'Oh my *goodness*, Priscilla!'

They squeak when they titter, rocking on the chairs, as if they – them, not the chairs – have wooden joins.

'I'm grateful,' I said. 'But look. I haven't any money for this.' They'd given me a bowl of clotted cream, a plate of scones, jam, butter, tea strong enough to plough.

'How dare he, Philadora!' Priscilla flung her head back. She had to clutch her mob cap to keep it on. 'How *dare* he!'

'Yes. How dare you, Lovejoy?' the other said soulfully. 'You practically *gave* us this entire business!'

'Thank you,' I said awkwardly. They like to watch me eat, God knows why. They never have any themselves. I'd come on their opening day, and tried to pay, start them off on the right foot, but they'd threatened me with fire and brimstone. Having to cadge off them now was making me disconsolate.

'Lovejoy, dear. Please don't mind. When is your birthday?'

Philadora inhaled at such temerity. 'Priscilla! *Should* you?'

'Thirtieth of September, last I heard.' I was fast running out of scones. They had parkin in the counter case, but I didn't look. 'Gemini?' I knew they were into the zodiac. They even had a window notice each dawn, TODAY'S STAR SIGN.

'There!' Philadora was triumphant. 'Libra! I knew it! Haven't I always said Lovejoy's a typical Libra, Priscilla?'

'You were a *little* unsure, Philadora,' her sister observed sweetly. 'You always inclined to the view that Lovejoy was Aries.'

They set to bickering in the politest manner. I noshed and slurped, until Priscilla saw I was down to crumbs and rushed for the parkin. They cook it right, the oatmeal crumbly, the treacle not too sticky. Supermarkets in the south sell it nowadays, but it's horrible. You'd think they'd get their act together, use the right recipe or whatever.

'Lovejoy, dear. What *time* were you born?'

A think. I remembered my Gran saying. 'Ten to midnight.'

'There!' All excited. 'Aquarius or Gemini, Lovejoy!'

'A choice?' Nothing fills you like parkin. Its oatmeal settled in my belly with an audible thump. I grunted with pleasure. Had they found a way to put the clock back?

'It's our scheme, Lovejoy! From studying ancient Persia's astrologial diviners.'

'Oh, aye.' I eyed them warily, wondering if they'd gone doolally with the strain of this teashop. 'Er, look, loves. Me and astrology aren't – '

'Oh, shush, Lovejoy!' They were really motoring. 'We will launch our New Astrology! Though,' Priscilla continued, abashed, 'it is really the *oldest* astrology, you see?'

'No,' I told Philadora. 'Sorry, I don't.'

'We've discovered people have two zodiacal signs!' Their heads were shaking in firm negation. 'Not merely one. A main one, of course. Plus an obverse. You have a choice of obverse.'

'Determined,' Priscilla added, 'by your Libra primary. Aquarius or Gemini, Lovejoy.'

'Don't you know which?' And who cared? I didn't believe in the Libra I'd already got. Why add to it?

'You *are* a problem. Fourth sign from Libra, earlier or later. Balance, you see?'

Well, no, but what can you say when you want to borrow their motor for a burglary? 'Er, yes!'

'You're nearer the start of the Libra zodiacal span. More Gemini than Aquarius.'

'Great! Well, ta for the grub, loves. Incidentally, can I borrow your car, please? I won't be long, honest. I have to deliver a rare antique to Harwich . . .'

They both smiled in definite refusal. Groan.

'No, Lovejoy. You can't *borrow* anything at all.'

There's always a first time. I sighed, said my thanks and started to leave. They said wait a minute. Priscilla fetched the car keys and gave them to me. I looked. What was going on? They'd just said no. Had I missed something zodiacal?

'Dear man doesn't understand, Priscilla. Explain.'

Priscilla's eyes were bright. 'Lovejoy, we need a partner. A gentleman, wise in the world's ways. We have no pretensions.'

'Oh dear, no!' from Philadora. 'None!'

'We manage well, drive hard bargains with the suppliers. And,' with lips thinned in resolve, 'we *savage* accounts!'

'Excellent, Priscilla. Well done . . .'

No good. I had to listen or I'd never get away.

'Needing a partner, we turned to our first love.' She misinterpreted my astonished look and said quickly, blushing, 'No, no! To our astrology, Lovejoy! It proved we needed . . . you.'

'Me?' I looked about the Lorelei Sweetmeat Delicatessen and Tearooms. 'Look, loves. Me and chintz – '

'Oh, Lovejoy!' Philadora scolded. 'Not to work here. Partnership by merger! You do your . . . *things*, we do ours. Sharing resources! We contribute to your wellbeing – food, use of car. You contribute to us!'

'What?' I asked, guarded. 'Contribute what?'

'Your expertise! We could have been destitute!'

'Forget it.'

'No. The Obverse Zodiac has spoken. We require a Libra gentleman with Gemini obverse, balanced by Aquarius.'

Lost, I said, 'My, er, obverse says I'm your partner?'

'No other, Lovejoy!' They beamed. 'Take the car, partner!'

They saw me to the door and waved after me fondly. They stable their tiny Morris Minor, an extinct coughing species on four bald tyres, across the road in a lock-up garage. I found it, got it enthusiastic after cranking for ten minutes, and drove off to do over the Dragonsdale Guest and Residential Hotel.

Sometimes when you expect the worst, it turns out to be acceptable. A party you're dreading – horrible folk, feared talkers – proves interesting, the people tolerable. The auction you're scared of proves a doddle. The woman who finally corners you is the most exciting you've ever met, and so on.

This isn't to say I recommend burglary instead of a pleasant riverside walk. I don't. It scares the hell out of me. But for once I'd worried unnecessarily. Come dusk, I drove into the village and parked the Morris Minor in a tavern yard, and walked to the hotel. I fell in with one of the residents returning from the pub. He was a smart, elderly bloke in a worn cardigan, corduroys and boots, who told me interminable tales about heavy calibre handguns and 'small modern things'.

'No bloody good winging the blighter, is it?' he kept asking fiercely. 'Sod just keeps on coming. The old wide calibre actually stops the bugger, see? Learnt that in the Western Desert!'

'Mmmh,' I kept saying. 'I see.'

'I'm Jim Andrews,' he said. 'Displaced person, refugee from family. Live at the Battishalls' dump now. Going to see Lily?' he demanded shrewdly at the gate when I dithered.

'Well,' I said. Lily, she of the laden tea trolley.

'Watch his nibs,' he said, eyes alert under bushy eyebrows. 'Do a recce, shunt in the side door, what? Word of advice. Nick's barmy as the rest of that Battishall crew, what?'

'Right,' I said.

'Decoy, the old feint, frontal attack,' he said in a stentorian voice for secrecy. 'Enfilade, what?'

'Ta, pal.'

'Roberta will be stuffing her fat face – fit as a pole vaulter! Good luck. Shag the girl one for me, what?'

'Er, right, right.'

He marched up the drive whistling 'Lillibullero', swinging his stick and making hell of a din. He stopped at the great sweep of stone steps and shouted, 'All clear!' Daft old sod.

My signal. I walked unhurriedly along the hedgerow, not wanting to be seen lurking. I had my story ready, in case: I came back to see if they'd really meant I was to move in, in two days. Across the lawn, up to the house. Lights were coming on. I could see figures moving, shadows on curtains, an orchestral concert on some radio, the ghost flicker of a TV set. The side entrance was locked, but the back door was ajar. Somebody aged was on the nearby lawn collecting croquet things, probably loading the dice for tomorrow's game. I slipped in.

Blundering about a house gives you the frights. I went up a few blind alleys, answered in a muffled monotone when some lady called, 'Is that you, Winifred?' Up some stairs, down others, hearing loos flush and televisions on the go. Some inane quiz show, audiences roaring on cue and voices quavering answers to some quizmaster know-all.

Then surprisingly I was in the great hall, one central light on in its chandelier. I crossed to the with-drawing room door and knocked gently. No answer. But I could now say I'd knocked. I opened one leaf of the double doors and went in.

A coal fire made me remember home. The room seemed even vaster by subdued light. I shut the door and stood a second. No, nobody lounging on the couch or slumbering in the armchairs. A votive light, blue like for Marian worship, made little leaps of flame from the mantelpiece. The picture was still covered. I crossed to stand before it, listening. No stealthy steps, nothing to indicate I'd been sussed.

Gingerly, I took hold of the little curtain, scared suddenly in case it was the Elephant Man or worse. Moved it and stared, puzzled. Shifted the votive light for safety, and stared some more.

My mind went, Who, *him*?

Prissy, with red lips, blue sash, tartan jacket, neck cravat high, blue bonnet with a grey-white wig, a four-star ribbon of silk shaped like a cross on his bonnet, ornate brown gauntlets. A good fake, really, but wasn't this merely an inclusive copy of the Edinburgh portrait? I peered, disappointed. No wonder it hadn't exuded a single vibe. Modern. I sniffed, but maybe the painter had used one of those fast-drying chemical salts, or oils like hempseed. The Pretender. I'd have to look the picture up. I drew the curtain and replaced the votive light. Some romantic hankering for olden days, perhaps.

Then the light came on.

'Stay where you are, Lovejoy.' My name, meaning they didn't need to gun me down.

Ashley Battishall, no less. My hands raised themselves. 'I wasn't doing anything,' I said in a pathetic whimper.

'I saw him, guv,' Nick's voice said, all self-righteousness.

'You did splendidly, Nick. Wait outside.'

He let me turn, and stood glowering at me while Nick went to apprise the boss lady. I felt a bit peeved that he hadn't even got a shotgun. I mean, I'd done my bit, trembling in my boots, and all for nothing. We stood, each of us out-peeving the other, until Roberta entered, vapid and swooning still, in a different silk house dress and frothy slippers. She was helped to the couch by the lovely Lily, waved her away.

Ashley told her, 'Caught red-handed, stealing the portrait

'Steal?' I almost laughed aloud. '*Steal?* That thing? It's not even a good fake, for Christ's sake! Who on earth'd want to? I could do better with one hand tied behind my back.'

Ashley didn't glance at Roberta. She glanced for us all. We paused a moment, while Lily rolled in a collection of edibles. For somebody in permanent decline, Roberta noshed well.

'I think I could take a little blancmange, Lily,' Roberta whispered feebly. 'And Black Forest gâteau. Yes, a little cream.' Her tone had a rather wailing high cadence before plunging to the punch line. Lily dished up and glided out. Roberta started on the grub, sighing at the effort.

'Listen, love,' I wanted to get this over. I had visions of Nick secretly phoning the Old Bill and me having to explain to the Misses Dewhurst why their little motor was suddenly all over tomorrow's tabloids. 'I'm sorry, but I had to see this. I want to know what the heck we're going to do with *Whistlejack*, for best price.'

'May I tell him, dearest?' Ashley asked humbly.

Roberta sighed a negative sigh. 'No, Ashley. We cannot be sure of his sympathies. He is a beast, an animal.'

'Here, missus,' I said, narked. 'It's you that needs me, remember. You've only to say, I'll be off like a cork from a bottle.'

'We are so *near* success, Lovejoy,' she whispered through a mouthful of cream and cake. 'We simply cannot let you spread malicious lies. Our crusade will save the whole earth.'

'And who are you against that?' Ashley ground out.

'Nobody,' I admitted. 'But you insisted I join in. Is the deal on or off?'

'Yes, Lovejoy.' Ashley hesitated. And Roberta smiled.

Her eyes were somewhat ovoid, I noticed, but electric and malicious. She was thrilled. I was a mouse caught in the cheesebox. No guesses who was the cat.

'You may tell him, Ashley,' she said, radiant.

The spoon rose, pierced her delicious mouth, was closed upon by those lips, withdrawn slowly from that heaven within – the tongue with a parting lick.

'Mr Sheehan has kindly allowed us to overbid you on *Whistlejack*, Lovejoy,' Ashley said. God, he was pompous. He swelled a few times, deflated, rising and falling on his heels, hands behind his back.

'We have the rights on a possible . . .' he baulked on the word robbery '. . . transfer of ownership.'

'Not you, Lovejoy,' gloated Roberta.

The spoon did its fascinating dip, scoop, penetration, tilt, withdrawal. It's staggering what a woman can do even though she's unaware of the effect she has on a man.

'We paid Mr Sheehan a large sum an hour ago.'

'Ashley.' Roberta whispered to him. I couldn't catch it. She was watching me, eyes glittering with eagerness. Maybe she was feeling poorly now the fuss was over.

'Yes, dearest.' He faced me. 'Lovejoy. This is your last warning. Stay in line. You may go. Report here no later than nine o'clock Tuesday evening.'

'Very well.'

He saw me out of the side door. I went without a backward glance, my mistake, because I'd gone a few yards in the gathering darkness when I paused. I listened, but no sound.

Then I was felled by a blow, something hard. Feet scuffed. I tried to run but blundered into somebody, got cuffed down. Fists belted me. Something hard whacked me across the shoulders and back. My leg got bludgeoned. I held my arms over my head, staggering. I couldn't see, but somehow I was on gravel.

'Get the bugger a few more,' somebody grunted. Nick's voice.

I kicked out, but the blows only rained harder and voices cursed me. I eeled away, running, them running beside me clobbering and thumping as I ran. I hit a tree, bush, something anyway. I started shouting, yelling for help.

'Quieten the bastard,' somebody bawled, louder than me.

The battering continued in a way I won't describe, if that's all right. God knows how far I got, tottering about that bloody spread of dark lawns while the blokes – there must have been four – cudgelled me. Then I was on the road, astonishingly solid underfoot, jarring my teeth. A car's headlights showed, and the beating lessened. I ran, still yelling, but the car cruised by and I was running away, the blokes with Nick yelling imprecations and laughing their heads off.

Wheezing and aching, I found a thicket and crawled in for a minute. One of my teeth was loose. My lip was bleeding, and my scalp cut. I thought my ribs were broken. I'd be lucky to last the night. I felt coma supervene.

When I woke it was daylight. I was stiff as hell. A fallow deer was looking at me. A tractor clattered by, its engine roaring, digging tool raised like a praying mantis. If this was having Obverse Zodiac, give me my old birthday every time.

Time to go home. I'd been warned. They were in with Big John Sheehan more than I was. And I was still to do their bidding. Hey-ho. BJS, letting some stranger overbid me, when he'd given his word? It wasn't like Sheehan, but I daren't question it.

Except, I thought, the stakes were suddenly much higher. Assault and battery now, even though it was only me they'd battered. I'd been silly. High time I worked a few things out.

Events proved I was as daft as ever, though, because I killed somebody towards nightfall. And me being me, it had to be a friend.

13

The water was down to a trickle when I made the cottage and tried to have a wash. The Water Board restless at non-payment. The garden barrel was overflowing, so I made do with that and my fabled desert trick – paraffin in a tin can sunk into the grass, a pan of water balanced above. The tea tastes of paraffin, but you can't have everything. I cleaned myself up. No clean shirts, but I found a new singlet somebody'd given me last Christmas, still in its plastic wrapper and 'Love, Always, My Darling!!!' from somebody or other. I wondered who she was, but Christmas was some time back. Soap's a nuisance. It's either worn down to the size of a toffee so you can't raise a lather, or solid and hard so you can't raise a lather. You'd think they'd get organized. I had a wash in a lukewarm splash, bum, balls, armpits, cleaned my face carefully so's not to set my lips off on another bleed, and I was good as new.

Breakfast was difficult. All I found was a piece of cheese going deeper yellow at the edges. The electricity was off, my minuscule fridge trickling water across my flagged floor. Still, tea was something. No eggs, no bacon, no bread, no butter. I gave up searching. Why do I bother being hopeful?

Moving the divan, I lifted the trapdoor and got a candle. Down into my pit of wonders. It's a gungy cellar, no vintage wines or anything, just shelves and boxes of cuttings from newspapers with a file or two. It holds my gleanings: records of antiques auctions, notes I made on the hoof, suppositions when heavy rollers like Big John Sheehan are hard at it. And historical bits, slices of antique lore. I sat and sipped my mug of non-tea tea and perused what little I'd got on Charles Edward Stuart.

'Bonnie Prince Charlie' disappoints. Grandiose romantic ballads and sentiments kindle loyalty to myth. Look underneath for the true story. Sadly, the famed 'Highland Laddie', as the ladies of Edinburgh called him in 1745 when squealing for locks of his hair at his riotous parties at Holyrood, dissolves into something unpleasing. The totally false fable is well known: born a true-blue Scot, this handsome cultured lad struggled for justice against those evil sordid swine the Hanovarian Georges who, by treachery and deceit, duped everybody out of everything. Unfairly defeated, the lad born to be king escaped with the help of various ladies and (cue songs and sobs) went over the sea to Skye and exile. And what caused his lonesome romantic languishment overseas, far from his native soil? Why, what else but the usual treachery, betrayal, perfidy, plus anything else that sounds romantic.

It's codswallop. Sorry.

The truth is a real pig. I honestly find it sad, the ultimate put-down. I've nothing against Charles Edward Louis John Casimir Silvester Severino Maria Stuart – aka Bonnie Prince Charlie – being born an Italian in Rome. Nor against his mum being a Pole. Far from it. But there's something really naff about a bloke who simply got plastered day in day out, lived stuporose, festering his life away. It's as if history tricks us into believing its opposite. Sadly, 'Bonnie Charlie' was really a fat lazy wife-beating drunk, with a '. . . fistula, great sores on his legs, insupportable in stench . . .' He rigged up a complicated series of bells, cords, balanced chairs and alarms surrounding his wife Louise's bed, to sound off should any would-be lover come night-stealing to her. (The paranoia wasn't new; he'd done the same to his mistress, the delectable Clementina Walkinshaw, with whom he lived as Count and Countess Johnson when he converted to Protestantism – though they fought like cat and dog in the cafés of the Bois de Bologne.) Flying into uncontrollable tempers at the least thing, this obese sot used to whale Louise something rotten, screaming drunken abuse about betrayal and being unfaithful, trying to strangle her while she screamed the place down and servants pulled him off. He had sticky fingers, kept the 12,000 livres his sick dad sent him to visit him in Rome; Charlie spent it, and didn't go. Bloated, sores, pimpled, vile in rage, stinking, he was the slob of the century. You've got to feel sorry for him. And his birds.

Actually, he didn't like women much. You get blokes like that. God knows why, when women are pleasant, have a sense of humour, smile more, give you paradise. Of course, they're often a pest, forever telling you off for not tidying up, saying pull yourself together. But that's a small price to pay for ecstasy. Charlie, though, reckoned them 'wicked and impenetrable'. His answer was to clobber them senseless with a stick when he was blotto on hooch, which was usually. But occasionally he did try – like, writing now and then to a former mistress Madame de Talmond in her Paris pad (all 'cats and chamber pots'), but such spells were rare. His brother, Henry the papist Cardinal in Rome despaired of Charlie's use of 'the nasty bottle'. Charlie flitted about the continent incognito as Smith, Douglas, Johnson, the Count of Albany, et cetera, while marriage brokers tried hard to match him up with various unwilling minor princesses. No success – Princess Marie-Louise Ferdinande had hysterics at the idea – until the impetuous, but stony broke, Princess Louise Maximiliana (with 'excellent teeth', vigilant fixers urged) tied the knot in a proxy wedding in Paris. The turquoise wedding ring had Charlie's cameo on it – what wouldn't I give for it. She was pretty, with a good plump figure, and cheery. At first. Except she didn't become pregnant. Charlie, on form, blamed her as month followed month and still she didn't give him an heir. He became morose, got endlessly sloshed in the theatre, and went back to the usual carousel of booze and beatings. It's all chronicled by diplomats, casual observers, and London's unceasing spies. I feel really sorry for Louise. She was an attractive lass, intelligent and bright, interested in art and literature. Naturally, she didn't see why she should play abigail to a snoring soak. She was at least as royal as him. So she acquired admirers. While Charlie blundered about drunk, fixing up his elaborate lover-traps of wobbly chairs and sliding bells, she made bizarre escape dashes in coaches. It became a lunatic comic opera, one particularly rollicking night gallop ending with Charlie kicking at a convent door bawling drunken threats while Louise cowered inside. He even took out a contract on one of Louise's lovers, murder for 1,000 gold sequins. Like all his plans, it didn't work. (Typically, he welshed on the payment.) Henry the Cardinal York yanked Louise to a Rome convent, under papal protection, as London's hawk-eyed agents reported, 'out of reach of any dabbler'. But Louise was equal to this confinement, and enjoyed security from the repellent Charlie while secretly enjoying her lover Alfieri.

It ended in tears. Charlie had a reconciliation with Charlotte, his daughter by Clementina Walkinshaw, before he popped his clogs. She died of cancer soon after her dad. Afterwards, the legend even fails itself. Henry, Cardinal York, the last real Pretender, was dislodged by Napoleon. This once-powerful Vatican Eminence became, at seventy-five, a refugee scuttling frantically ahead of Bonaparte's armies after his cardinal's palace was ransacked. King George III kindly gave him a pension for life.

Whereupon Henry returned to Rome and lived in offensive opulence. He forgot his former holy vows somewhat in personal pleasures, styling himself 'Henry the Ninth' with six-horse coaches and liveried servants, courtesy of handouts drawn on Coutts, the London bankers, paid by Great Britain's kindly King George. Go to Canova's grand marble monument in St Peter's in Rome to see the end of the story. It was compassionately ordered in 1819 by the future George IV. See what I mean, myths being their own opposite?

Oh, I make excuses for Charlie. His dad, James VIII (Scotland) and III (England), lived on handouts from Italian monarchs – not easy. Charlie's mum, the Polish Princess Clementina Sobieska, was demented by James's womanizing. They had terrible rows – James accused her of 'infamous tyranny', called her a hypocrite because she finally hopped it while he was carousing with Lady Inverness *et al*. Poor Little Charlie.

It gets you down. Legends ought to be romantic.

I checked my appearance in the cracked mirror, ignored the symbolism, replaced the trapdoor, and went to the pub, wondering where the heck my planning talents had gone.

Vasco was in the Marquis of Granby, a stroke of luck. He's a discouraging dealer from Aldeburgh and is a mine of forgery fact and fiction. A rough hunched bloke, he always looks just back from bear hunting.

'Wotch, Vasco.' I shook my head with reluctance at Marion. She smiled, drew me an ale, mouthed that I could owe her.

'Wish they'd do that for me, Lovejoy,' Vasco said glumly.

'Jacobites?' I asked, toasting Marion.

'Good or dud?'

'Either, preferably the former.'

'Christ,' he said, turning to look at me. Until then he'd only watched me in the bar mirror. 'Into money?'

'Clients have. Remember those Stuart glasses I engraved?'

'Mmmh. Rose with two buds on one, Amen verse on the other?'

'Remember where they went?' I'd actually sent them to the coast by Tinker to a collector. These two engravings are the commonest on genuine crystal Jacobite glasses. The rose is England, the two buds the Old and Young Pretenders. Verses that end with Amen are the ones to go for. 'I hated doing them. They were genuine old drinking glasses. Made them something they weren't.'

'Don't be daft, Lovejoy. Their value upped six thousand per cent. Dutch bloke bought them outright.'

'What else's sold lately?'

'Jacobite?' He shrugged. 'Sod all. A pendant, lock of Charlie's hair, ha-ha-ha. One of his dud poems about Drinking not Thinking, but the parchment didn't look right. Too yellow, probably Doothie's work. He's gone mad on bloody saffron. Somebody ought to have a word with him. Give us all a bad name.'

'Well, he's getting on.'

'He should age parchment like you do. That dehydration.'

That made me anxious. The trick is to make it feel friable. Any chemistry book tells you how. 'Shush, Vasco. What else?'

He thought. 'The only other Jacobite was a little table, triangular. Opened out on lopers to a six-sider. Had a drawer. Supposedly from Holyrood Castle.'

'That's rare,' I said, awed. 'What wood?'

'Walnut, lovely turned stretchers, three legs. Went for nine thousand quid to some Columbian importer.'

Which made me swallow, because that too was one of mine. Corinth had sold it for me on commission. Montgomery, her sniffer, told me it'd gone for four thousand. I'd got twenty-five per cent. My debtors heard the glad tidings and came a-running. Of all the antique tables – and there's a maddening variety – the triangular-to-hexagon table is without doubt the most useless. It's small, a triangular flat top on three turned walnut legs. The surface unfolds in three flaps to form a hexagon, the flaps supported on lopers (that is, slides). Three rods, stretchers, connect the legs for strength. Lovely, and a devil to make properly, but rare. I'd made a drawer beneath one side – only one, because the table's triangular so you can't have three; there isn't room. Lovely but useless, nothing but trouble. It needs intensive care when you use it. Must have driven maids-of-all out of their minds in case it toppled when they served.

'Corinth's lately interested in Jacobites,' Vasco said.

Come to think of it, she'd commissioned the triangular table from me. I'd been glad. Forgery does wonders when you're starving.

I no longer cared now. 'Who's interested in *Whistlejack*?'

'The big Stubbs painting? Everybody, Lovejoy. But that priory's security's like a bullion bank.'

'Hard, eh?'

'The lads tried last Christmas. Got nowhere. Alarms, radar, heat-seekers. It's a pig.' He sounded grieved, as a baulked antique dealer will when proud possessors guard their antiques from robbers. 'A special gallery to itself.'

'Tough indeed, Vasco.' I had a grim thought. If it was so difficult, why did Ashley and Roberta Battishall want me? Surely not to help them actually nick the damned thing? I went cold. I managed to swallow with the help of my ale. 'Look, Vasco.' I lowered my voice further as a crowd came in on a gust of laughter. Scouse Oliver was among them, a pleasant dealer eager to make a fortune before he was thirty. He'd done it by robbery with violence, and now was trying antiques. He gets off on technicalities.

'Corinth doing anything at Fenstone?'

Vasco snorted. 'Middle Snoring, Lovejoy? I'm sick to death of the bloody place.' He wagged a hand to Marion, who came across to refill. 'I had four offers of antiques, turned up to collect, and they'd already gone.'

My groan was heartfelt, not acted. 'That's terrible.'

He almost wept in self-pity. 'That Dame Millicent should keep her farm going without dabbling in antiques.'

'Aye.' Fervently I blessed my instincts. Jubilation made me add something I immediately wished I hadn't. 'Tryer said the same thing. Must have been the same woman. Big landowner beyond Fenstone proper?'

He eyed me in a way I didn't like. 'Tryer? The Sex Museum nut with that ugly cow whatshername?'

'Chemise, aye.' I felt something was wrong, wanted to get away.

I'd missed some vibe, and I wasn't sure what. 'He was getting ready to leave when I bumped into him.'

'That so.' His eyes in the bar mirror were looking.

Getting out smiling, cheerily waving to Scouse Oliver and his pals, a merry carefree soul, was the hardest thing I've ever done. I'd promised to return the Misses Dewhurst's old Morris Minor, but instead decided to drive to Juliana Witherspoon, hardworking spinster of Fenstone and pillar of the Church. I got a yard. The Americans were crowded on the pavement outside, listening to Gwena, our town guide.

'. . . Queen Boadicea's wild Iceni tribesmen stormed the town,' she was saying. 'And on this very spot crucified the Romans –'

'Lovejoy!' Hilda cried, joyously enveloping me. 'Vernon! Look who's here!' She rounded on Gwena, who was suddenly guilty. 'You said he'd gone abroad, young lady!'

'No, Hilda.' I surfaced for breath and beamed. Gwena hates me because her older sister Tarlene lends me a groat now and again. But what's charity for? It's holy, for Christ's sake. I vaguely recalled, didn't this lot owe me breakfast? 'No, Hilda love. They tried to hire me for, er, the Amsterdam antiques meeting. But I insisted on staying. To see you.'

'Fantastic, Lovejoy!' Hilda cried. They crowded round, talking excitedly. 'We'll be just in time!'

'How long we got?' Vernon checked a fob watch. Lovely, old. That explained the vibes when we'd met.

'One hour, Vernon. Let's go!' cried Hilda.

Beatific, I smiled at Gwena. We left her fuming on the pavement.

14

They had a small coach, fifteen seater for four couples and two extra women. Age range oh, sixtyish down to thirties. Chatty, going for laughs as all Americans do when mobhanded. Hilda asked what I'd done to my mouth. I milked sympathy telling them I'd stumbled in the dark, which got us onto street lighting. They had strong views. As we pulled away from the fuming Gwena we were into suing town councils for street maintenance. God, but Yanks are litigious. They know their rights.

We left town on the eastern trunk road to the estuaries. Then we swung north after a mile or two, coastward but more rural. All in all, a journey shortened by needling, quips, their mood of banter. But I was glad when we made it to the destination.

Except I hated it.

Dragonsdale's no place for me. Rural, bonny river, thatched cottages, fourteenth-century flintstone church, farms, a forest sulking black-green on the horizon, utterly countrified. I groaned miserably as we climbed down.

'Oh, Lovejoy!' Hilda exclaimed, tears starting. 'Isn't this the most pretty, well, England you ever did see?'

'Aye.' Enthusiasm has limits.

'Don't be shy, Lovejoy, boo-oah,' said Vernon. 'That scene is straight out of the most famed landscape Old Masters.'

'It's so . . . *sweet*!' cried Mahleen, a fortyish lady with gold, literally shiny gold, teeth, and gold pendant earrings that touched her shoulders. She wore a gold scarf and had, I assure you, gold-flecked hair on a gold ponytail bee. Her stockings had gold clocks, her heels shone gold. Her astrakhan coat had gold cuffs. She smiled gold lipstick. I thought her gorgeous, though her pals were critical. They made laughing comments. She gave as good as she got.

'Glad you like it.' I wondered why the little lane we'd stopped in was familiar. Two cottages, a distant farmhouse, the church a furlong off. Not deserted by any means, but definitely rural.

Mahleen called her Wilmore, a chubby Friar Tuck, always losing his spectacles so he couldn't see a damned thing. He loved golf, and more golf. That's all that can be said of any golfer, anywhere. He admired the countryside in smiling silence, mentally laying out yet more golflinks.

'Brilliant country, Mahleen,' Wilmore said. 'Two eighteens, before my very eyes.'

Then why not get on with it? I couldn't help thinking. A clubhouse, concrete car parks, lights and civilization out here instead of those silent watching trees, that lurking river, hedgerows shielding vast acres from encroaching mankind. Bring in the neon lights, let roads shove our boundaries out, eliminate Nature's unknown.

'Now, where is it?' Hilda the Organizer demanded of the driver, a taciturn uniformed man hunched from years at his wheel.

'End place, lady.'

'This wayeeee!' cried Hilda, and we were off down the lane.

We walked in the ruts. No vehicles this way evidently, except to make deliveries. Mahleen quizzed me, should she pay Jox to be made a dame or not? I said it was up to her, recalling meeting Hilda and Vern at Jox's daft fraud. I was beginning to work out whether I ought to start it up myself, actually, because Mahleen's friend Wilhelmina – same age, but blues, no gold – from New Jersey said she'd been seriously thinking of forking out for a ladyhood. The price Jox had quoted her set me coughing, especially as I was still owed for dressing up like a pillock.

'Howdy!' Jox thundered, speak of the devil, emerging.

The group enthused greetings. Jox shook hands. I'd never seen so much handshaking. Americans never stop.

'And Lovejoy!' he said, abruptly less hearty.

'Wotcher, Jox.'

'I *love* that wotcher, Lovejoy.' That from Nadette, a slender business lady, always well groomed, from Ark-an-saw, 'not like this bunch.' It always got a laugh. 'We need Lovejoy along because he's a natural. Ain't that so, Jerry?'

'Sure is.' Jerry, her husband, never smiled. He seemed gloomy, except for his plus fours, chequerboard shirt and yellow boater.

'Good!' Jox's enthusiasm fell further. I wondered, natural? 'Mr Hopestone is waiting *where it actually happened*!'

That set them off speculating nineteen to the dozen. I hadn't a notion what we were going to see. Something rustic? As long as it wasn't gruesome, like a two-headed calf. I followed, Mahleen asking about my divvying gift.

'It's nothing,' I said, wary lest I was dragged into something else. I had that silver ditchery to do for Sabrina, some partnership thing to arrange with the Misses Dewhurst, Beth to con out of her antique Bilston enamels, Tinker to find – where the hell was the old soak? – and discover who was going to steal *Whistlejack*. And see Juliana, see if she truly was a forger.

'It sure is!' she insisted. 'You tell me, or I'll – '

'I get a sick feeling from a genuine antique.'

'See?' she breathed, but Wilmore was ogling the landscape with a developer's theodolite eyes. 'Lovejoy's *real*!'

'This land for sale, Lovejoy?' Wilmore asked.

'Hush up!' Mahleen spat in golden fury. 'This isn't speculator land, Wilmore! This is *family* land. History!'

'That's so, Mahleen,' Jox said smoothly, grabbing her and whisking her to the front. 'The ancient lordships hereabouts . . .' His sales pitch. I followed on with Wilmore.

'Our countryside is reverting to the wild,' I joked ruefully. 'Some villages . . . Well, young folk want a town, chance to dance, jobs other than ploughman, milkmaid.'

'Same all over, Lovejoy.' Wilmore still had his speculator's brain in. 'But buy a few farms, set up a Grand Prix course. County championships, a real possibility.'

Something clicked. Hadn't Jox said something about. . . ? 'Somebody set up a wildlife scheme. Ancient deeds scuppered it. But give it a go. I'd rather see anything except a wilderness.'

'We'll talk about it, Lovejoy.'

A bloke was standing by a field gate. Jox introduced him all round. I stood back, eyeing him. Twenty-sevenish, thinning hair, sparse frame, a born smoker doomed to cough his life in bedsits eating baked beans. Jox was making an announcement.

'Ladies and gentlemen.' He spoke in hushed tones. 'This is Mr Hugo Hopestone, countryman born and bred. A churchgoer, he has something of serious consequence to report. First I'll give a little background to Mr Hopestone's story. I think you'll agree it is epoch-shattering.'

Jox avoided my gaze. Hugo was as much a countryman as me, which is nil, nought, big oh. This was another Jox-type plunge to zilch profit, no royalties and no repeat fees.

'Let me first say that our fabled East Anglia of historic renown has a lurid past. Sinister stories abound. Eyewitness accounts, guaranteed reports, made in all good faith, prove these significant events.'

He waxed eloquent, enlarging on local fables. It's sort of true. East Anglia has everything from headless cavaliers to grey nuns spooking the local boozer. I tried not to listen, but Jox's pathetic delivery drew me in. I'm not superstitious, oh no. Not me. I mean, who'd believe junk about ghosts, spirits, poltergeists? It's for kiddies and Hollywood, when real stories have dried up.

'Now Hugo will tell you his tale.' Jox raised a hand, on oath. 'Hugo Hopestone, is your story made up?'

Jox sounded truculent, glaring accusingly at Hopestone there in the gateway of a fallow field.

'Every word is true, sir,' Hugo said. 'Absolutely.'

Our crowd exhaled together, thrilled.

'Go ahead, then.' Jox glared at us – still not me, though – in turn, then with gravity at his stooge.

'I was walking through this field, ladies and gentlemen, in late autumn. I heard a humming noise. A great ball of light passed by. It settled in the field's centre.' He pointed. 'There.'

'There? Right there?' some cried.

'How big was it?' Wilmore demanded.

'I was blinded. It must have been six feet wide.'

They began firing questions: was there wind, was it pitch dark, a moon, was he frightened, drunk?

'I'd been at a friend's house in Dragonsdale. I left at nine thirty. When I woke, it was gone eleven. I was the other side of that wood, in a field.'

'What had happened between those times?' Hilda asked, agog.

'I was abducted by creatures I had never seen before, lady.'

'Abducted!' several shrilled.

Mahleen turned, awed. 'You see, Lovejoy? This is for *real*.'

'Nordic or a Grey?' I spoke up. 'Which were they, Hugo?'

He looked at Jox, who cried, 'Let Hugo speak!'

'The recollections came to me after a day or two.' Hugo gamely stuck to his phoney script. 'They were small, big dark eyes, a slit for a mouth. Pearly skins. So little I'd almost say dwarfs.'

'Little People!' Vernon sighed. 'That phrase is so telling!'

'Greys! They were Greys, then!' Mahleen exclaimed breathless. Wilmore caught my eye. He didn't believe any of this either. He judged the distance along some imagined fairway.

'The question is,' Jox took over smoothly, with one foot on the gate for height, 'what these creatures were. I have the testimony of the local doctor, who examined Hugo the day after the abduction. Hugo had burns along his chest, exactly where the pads of some electrocardiograph would go!'

'They stripped and examined me,' Hugo said. 'They took a sample of blood. Then I just woke.'

'You hear them speak at all?' an intense man asked. He was our one stuffed shirt, forever taking notes and clicking a stop watch. He talked lovingly into a dictaphone.

'Yes. Like a distant twittering. It was non-stop.'

'Hugo,' I said. 'Did you read of the UFO conference at Sheffield? The Nordic extraterrestrials being gentle wizards, and the Greys being evil little trolls.' I tried not to sound cynical. 'Abducting humans for genetic experiments.'

'I haven't heard.'

Jox started up angrily, 'This is a genuine straighforward – '

Then we were interrupted by a portly man in country tweeds. I'd last seen him lighting candles at St Edmund's in Fenstone. He limped forward, one leg trailing.

'This gathering is illegal,' he pronounced in a deep baritone. 'William Geake, parish churchwarden.'

That caused a stir. Americans are all lawyers, being born with law like we get Original Sin.

'Nonsense!' Jox agitatedly tried to hold us.

'Church demesne extends over this land,' the stout boomer said. 'Material use conflicts with religious aims.' But Yanks also know how to complain.

'Outrageous!' Hilda said in a band saw voice. 'We've *paid*!'

'Please, folks,' from Jox, knowing failure.

'That can't be,' I piped up. 'I have a friend in business here. He has a mobile, a Sex Museum, but the principle's the same.'

He fixed me, unyielding. 'There are ancient charters that restrict . . .' et legal cetera.

'Mr Geake. You're in the wrong parish. Dragonsdale.'

He smiled bleakly. 'That gate's the Fenstone-Dragonsdale line.'

Rubbish, of course, but he carried it off, giving his spiel in portentous tones that would have scared a bishop. Another Jox loser. We dispersed, making for the coach. The one-sided argument, Jox versus pomp and circumstance, became heated. I caught up with Wilmore. I needed a sane ally, but a golfer would have to do.

'You using those peripherally weighted golf clubs yet, what, Big Emma? Made a fortune for that Long Island schoolteacher, eh?'

He grinned, pleased. 'Nearly right, Lovejoy. Sure. Great discovery. I never did like graphite heads. Perimeter weighting in metal-wood's all the rage now. Inner septums, o' course.'

'Course,' I said airily, as if I knew what he was on about. I'd heard two golfers talking on the village bus. I've nothing against discoveries, though I'd rather they be rediscoveries, like Hector Berlioz's *Solemn Mass* lately. It gives human life a better sense of fitness. 'Need finance, Wilmore?'

His grin slid into wariness. 'I got most. I just don't know the rules here, Lovejoy.'

Who did? 'Talk again, Wilmore,' I said quietly. 'I know somebody who'll advise you, as a favour to me.'

'What's in it for you?'

I like Yanks. No inhibitions about gelt. If Wilmore'd been local, reaching here would have taken a year.

'A woman friend,' I said, trying to look shamefaced.

'I understand, Lovejoy. Talk again. We're at the George.'

We ended with Jox wringing his hands, desperate not to give refunds. He appealed to me, God, the universe.

'Look,' he said, anguished, 'please explain to Miss Priscilla. It wasn't my fault.'

'Miss Priscilla wno?' from me, suddenly alert.

'Dewhurst. Arranges these astrology tours. They run a – '

The driver ciosed the door on Jox. I ahemed as the disappointed group started chatting and grumbling. Complaints, refunds, rebellion was in the air.

'Look, mate,' I told him quietly, 'you'll have a riot on your hands. How about taking them to, like, Whychwe Priory, down the estuary? I'll do the commentary . . .'

With relief, he set off down the coast road. I made a shy announcement, got a round of applause when I told of the ghost who walks there.

'Can't promise she'll show,' I told everybody blithely. 'But I hear she's gorgeous. Give me first chance, right?'

That set them whooping. We bowled eastwards. Whychwe Priory was where Whistlejack's portrait was. I couldn't help glancing round the merry little group. So these were the Misses Dewhursts', and I the twindles' partner? I learn something new every day, especially about myself. And my mistakes.

As we went, I told a few merry tales of this 'supernatural coast', as some writers call these sealands. There's nothing like East Anglia for phantoms. They do odd things.

On the 'strood', the sea-track to Mersea Island, Roman legionaries stand guard, knee-deep in the North Sea's flowing tides. At Walberswick, the famous Whisperers sigh of an evening on the sea breeze, and the ghosts of the old man and little boy wait for the ferry but never get on, vanishing as the boat approaches the hard. At Cromer, it's the Hell Hound that puts the wind up you. You get enticed into the Wash's murky waters, near Snettisham, by their renowned Sirens, and you may never be seen again, for you'll be shown round their enthralling ocean caves for ever. But you'll never escape the terrible Sea Serpent of Kessingland, near Lowstoft, so don't go strolling their lovely beaches on your own.

To scattered applause, I subsided and sat to watch us approach the low sealands. It's everywhere in East Anglia. The ghost of Cymbeline, Shakespeare's hero, mourns his lost kingdom in my very own village, where his earthwork ramparts loom in the loneliest wood in the world. And the Shining Boy, ten years old, stares ceaselessly of an evening at a house in my lane (not mine thank God; I don't believe in ghosts, and I mean that fervently). And the ghosts of two men fight with scythes, unceasing and murderous, by our old church –

'Aaargh!' I yelped, striking out.

'Lovejoy, honey! Wake up! We're here!'

Hilda, grabbing my arm. I must have nodded off from all the excitement. I blotted my damp forehead and tried a smile.

'Good. I'll take you round.' I came to. 'A lovely Old Master wants to see us . . .' I played it from there, getting them laughing as we alighted and herded through the arch.

But something occurred. If East Anglia was riddled with supernatural phenomena, wasn't it odd that one particular patch was spared anything like that? Very peculiar, to say the least, that the parish of St Edmund's in Fenstone was blessed with yawnsome anonymity. More striking still, no matter whatever *tried* to happen there, nothing – *nothing at all* – ever did.

The suspicion intrigued me, as we went between beautiful lawns where peacocks strolled. Whatever wanted to happen got stymied, stifled, closed down. Even the most innocent occurrence was kiboshed – like Hugo Hopestone's phoney tale of extraterrestrials, for instance, the UFO tales told all over the world, to entertain tourists for a few pence.

Before, I'd only guessed, and not cared much. Now, I began to worry, and I mean really worry. Should I have mentioned the sex display trailer, implicated Tryer and Chemise? There was the celibate priest in St Edmund's, and the pretty Juliana's unshakable convictions –

'Money, please,' the chap in the booth said. 'How many?'

Action time, and not a second to think. 'Listen, mate.' I sprang to the fore. 'Let us all in for half price, and my partners – they're big business ladies locally – promise to bring in ten more coachloads tomorrow. Okay?'

He eyed me with suspicion. 'How can I be sure?'

'Look.' I beamed, exuding honesty. 'Let me explain . . .'

15

We had a whale of a time. I laughed like a drain during that visit. The Americans own the world, but they had me almost falling down at their joshing, leg-pulling, outright onslaughts. It took my breath away when Mahleen, golden she-god of our cavalcade, said with affability when Wilmore made a remark, 'Yeah, well, you can ignore Wilmore, Lovejoy. He's a slave-owning Republican, Sow-therrrrn States, honey chile,' which set everybody arguing heatedly. But it was all over in a trice, and they were back to their exclamations, admiring, pointing out features of Whychwe Priory, trying to get the peacocks to fan tails, doing battle over camera lenses, making us all pose by the roof tower.

We had tea laid on – me the big organizer, the man in the booth my lifelong pal, owing to the backhander I'd promised him tomorrow. Incidentally, I'd agreed on thirty per cent, would you believe, which rankled. I should have beat him down to fifteen. It still narks. Okay, so it was all falsehood, but you have to keep faith, right? I sometimes forget what's made up and what's not.

Maybe this caused me misgiving. But I put the feeling away and went round the priory's great rooms, the chapel (lovely ancient windows, but nicking them honestly never crossed my mind). And we ogled *Whistlejack*. Lovely great oil painting, beautifully lit. Animal paintings are the pits, but this almost made me like horses. It rears, profile view, colours alive and shining. Over the fireplace is a portrait of Stubbs himself, by his pal Ozias Humphrey. The room, sure enough, was lowered to take the massive oil, so two levels, with four gorgeous chairs by 'King' Chippendale. I had to sit down, while my friends worried and sent people for glasses of water and argued –God, Yanks *argue*. In the same few square feet, a Chippendale display cabinet. The William Vile (no kinder man, despite his name) chest of drawers proved enough to bring me round. I was off explaining, loving every minute.

'Course,' I prattled on, 'Tom Chippendale loved these glazing bars. Mahogany'd come in by then. It's tough enough to cut into thin rods, sometimes overhanging the actual glass.' I pointed it out. 'That was an innovation.'

Beckoning them close, I lowered my voice. 'See, Tom loved the ladies. He intended his cabinets for their dressing or with-drawing rooms. He went on a bit about japanned softwoods – it shows the oriental influence better – but the softwood's not lasted like mahogany.'

'It looks frail, Lovejoy,' from Nadette's husband, Jerry.

Thank you, Jerry. 'It'll outlast us all.' Which gave rise to a splurge of gallows humour. I was asked to price everything we saw, from the lovely carpet woven by Lord Rockingham's mum to Joshua Reynolds' portrait of Rockingham – he owned the nag. 'The real find would be . . .' they fell silent '. . . a Chippendale cabinet *not* mounted on a stand. There's only one such of his known.'

'What would that be worth?' Vernon, the golf hawk.

'Don't do it, Vern,' I begged. 'You're thinking: Buy a real Chippendale cabinet on a stand, then cut its legs off and make it priceless.'

Which set them all off, whooping and laughing.

'What's wrong with sharing a fortune?' Mahleen demanded.

'Look, pals.' I had to tell them. 'Some antiques are actually unique. *The Last Supper*, or the Koh-i-Noor in its present 106-carat form. A unique is too well known to fake, unless you've got a buyer. And your price has to be a mint.'

'Seems good to me,' Wilmore said.

Everybody roared, but I was suddenly desperate to convince. I could see their eyes gleaming, avarice in overdrive. They'd be out in the junkshops faking any minute. We're a breed of greed.

'No. Honest. Listen.' I had to talk them back to sanity. 'In antiques, rarity is inversely proportional to fallability. See?' They went agog. 'Once upon a time, there was a great ship. Biggest warship of mediaeval days, Henry V's. Struck by lightning, sank, was lost in the waters. That's an antique worth finding, right?'

'Sell us a treasure map, Lovejoy!' Wilmore, irrepressible.

'No need.' My punch line. 'Everybody's known all along where the *Grâce Dieu* is. Since that terrible day, in AD 1439, she's lain in the

River Hamble. Everybody knows that 3,906 trees were used to build her. Okay,' I said into their quiet, 'tales varied about the enormous ship that occasionally showed at freak low water. Her supposed identity wavered as centuries passed. Locals pillaged, nails, weapons, iron fixtures. Many cottages have her wooden beams in their roofs. But she's there. Carbon dating, historians, records, everything says so.'

'What's your point, Lovejoy?'

'If an antique – *any* antique – is unique, then even if it's lost like the *Grâce Dieu*, the Holy Grail, Michelangelo's *Sleeping Cupid* sculpture – then it become virtually unfakable. See?'

'You mean, forge common antiques, not rare?'

'That's it, Vernon.' I was relieved. Tension lifted.

'Like you do?'

No answer to that except some crack about occasional exceptions, which got us all joking and moving on. I noticed that Vernon was hanging back talking intently to Nadetta's husband Jerry, but put it down to idle chat.

By the time we'd finished our tea-and-wad we were worn out but exhilarated. We stopped at the Gunners Arms in Whychwe Fleet, a low estuary clogged with river craft, exchanging songs and getting sloshed, the driver with us. We had a kitty, Mahleen standing me my sub, and had pastie, beans, chips, followed by spotted dick – the merry jokes on *that* – and custard.

But why was I sick to my soul? What had I done wrong?

It was about tennish by the time we reached the George – yes, breakfast, I'd be along, half-eight precisely, more ribaldry, that sort of good night – and then spoke from the pavement to the driver.

'Where's your garage, mate?'

'Sudbury. You want me to drop you off on the way?'

'Aye, please.' I climbed in.

The town was quiet. The main thoroughfares are High Street and Head Street, always brightly lit. It's not remarkable despite its antiquity. Town Hall, banks, shopping centre hanging fire at night time, a car swishing through as tired as its driver, a lone bobby bored by the traffic lights, a couple coming late from the pictures unlocking their parked car.

'Hang on.'

Something was nagging. For one thing, I wasn't as kaylied as I ought to have been. The driver was merrier than I was, and he'd been pretty abstemious. In fact, I was cold sober. The incident at Jox's UFO scam kept coming to mind. It was exactly what happened to Tryer's enterprise, what was it, some holy well he's dreamt up with his brother from Breakstone. The parish. Tryer had said something . . . I struggled to remember, befuddled.

'Lovejoy,' the driver prompted, 'when you're ready?'

'Half a sec.'

Tryer had said something like, *He didn't exactly say it was blasphemous, but he come near* . . . An outright accusation of blasphemy would have hit the nation's headlines. But an administrative correction wouldn't rate a single breath. I'd mentioned Tryer, when speaking up for Jox and Hugo. And I'd been pretty free talking of Tryer somewhere else – where was it?

'Can you go down the bypass?'

'Aye.' He pulled away, changing gears smoothly. 'But that Leisure place will be closed. Except for the nosh bar, burgers.'

I leant over. 'Get a move on, mate. It's urgent.'

'Traffic lights, Lovejoy,' he said, pointing as we slowed near the war memorial. 'My gaffer'd skin me if I got booked.'

'It's late. Who's to see?' I was agitated, frantic now to see Tryer was all right. 'For Christ's sake, I'd bloody get out and *run*.' One mile, maybe ten furlongs, was all it was.

'You've been tarting about, Lovejoy! It was you stood gaping, not me. We could've been there.'

The lights changed. I stood, swaying, holding the passenger pole, staring out of the sightscreen. When I'm useless, I'm infallibly dud. There's this theory, isn't there, that everything that happens in your life is a fluke, that plans and decisions aren't worth a bent groat? It's all chance. Then there's the opposite theory, that your life is the direct result of your decisions, conscious or subconscious. Both theories can't be right, and they're dead opposites. But at that moment, barrelling down East Hill to the bypass, I know which one I believed. I think I'd been up to no good. Secretly, with sinister intent, I'd chucked straws into the wind to test it. And now I was scared it had become a gale, while I'd dawdled. I just hoped to God it hadn't blown anyone away.

The driver, infected by my anxiety, began hurrying, cutting corners, overtaking on the forbidden inside lane near the river bridge, putting his hazard lights on at the roundabout. He had us swinging left into the Leisure place beyond the fire station faster than I could have run, give him that.

They were at it when we got there.

'Here, here!' I squawked. 'Stop there!' I'd glimpsed, in the swish of headlights, a figure lope across the boating pond's reflected sheen. No illumination, just the skyglow, glaring the wrong way of course. I could see the palish blur of Tryer's trailer.

'What the fuck?' the driver said bemused. He cut his engine. I was out in a rush, shouting him to come and help.

We were a hundreds yards off. I heard somebody bleat. A man's voice, a woman's? Was it a voice at all? There are ducks about, and you never can tell.

'Stop that!' I bawled, out of breath when I'd not done anything except rabbit at the driver. 'Stop! In the name of the law!' I yelled, really pathetic. Running like hell I threw my voice deeper, to sound not scared.

'What's going on there?' somebody shouted, thin and miles away. Always at a distance when you want them.

'Help! Police!' from me, just as useless. 'Stop!'

The shout – voice, unvoice – came from the left, a distance from the trailer. For a mad moment I thought of starting Tryer's engine for its headlights. It was facing that way. But what if it was locked? Precious seconds. I sprinted past the trailer, still bawling my head off, police, help, stop thief, heaven knows what, and heard Chemise calling in fright.

'What is it? Tryer?'

Opened her door, blinding me in the bloody bargain.

'Close that light off, for God's sake!' I hurtled past. She ran out, the door blinding us further.

'Lovejoy? What's the matter? Where's Tryer?'

'Arrest that man!' I howled, outstripping her. By then I was beside the boating pool, reeds whipping my knees. I heard a terrible throaty sound in the gloaming and a faint splash. Something floundered, bleated one last time, and went a terrible *thunk*.

'Bring a light!' I shrieked, bawled, but my throat caught. I stumbled forward in that daft posture we use when groping forward in the dark for something we don't know, crouched, chin projecting, hands swimming the dark before me. 'Help! Over here!'

'What's going on?' That imperious thin voice. Authority, demanding attention but doing sod all.

'Bring the fucking police, you pillock!' I yelled, resumed my ridiculous groping, wading in the reeds.

'Lovejoy? Where's Tryer?' Chemise, behind me. She splashed, took a breath, squelched to the grass. 'He came to meet somebody.'

There was a dreadful pungent stink. It wasn't anything rural, nothing human. It wafted after me, after us. I heard a small disturbance, reached out, grabbed nothing. Now, the children's boating pool is only a foot deep.

'Maybe he fell in, Chem,' I said, trying to stop my voice quavering. 'I'll go and see. Stop here.'

And waded in, to the place I'd guessed that bleat and blow came from. Maybe I was wrong. I used my hands, stepping slowly, trying to look sideways, hoping to catch a glow from somewhere. Then I heard the driver gun the engine, the rotten swine cutting and leaving, the evil pig.

His headlights cut the night. I heard him shout left or right, Lovejoy, the vehicle chugging nearer. What a nice bloke, I thought.

Just as I put my hand on a face and screamed, screeched, howled and flailed like a desperate duck out of the reeds and away from it. And stood sodden like the coward I am.

'Over here!' I shouted, trying to pretend I hadn't been panicked out of my skin. 'This way!'

'Tryer!' Chemise shrieked. 'It's Tryer! Get him, Lovejoy!'

'I am, for Christ's sake!' I waded back in, hesitating, feeling. I couldn't see the pale blob that had been something's face, kept going, feeling, ghost swimming, crouching . . . Bump.

He wasn't floating. His arms must have been touching the bottom, so shallow was it. My foot crunched glass, our yobbos' idea of a joke, to chuck broken bottles in.

'Gotcher, Tryer,' I said, grabbing his collar and pulling, but hopeless, already knowing he was gone. That's me, causing this, then trying to cheer Chemise up by extending her hope that my dramatic non-rescue non-dash, was in time.

115

'Here, Lovejoy.' The driver was with me, us tugging Tryer's body, Gullivers with Lilliput's navy.

We hauled him up the grass, turned him over. Chemise fell on him, stroking and crying. His skull was stove in near the temple. One eye protruded.

'He's going to be all right, Lovejoy, isn't he?' she wailed. 'Tryer? Tryer, darling.'

When the explosion came it almost flattened us all. In slow motion I saw Chemise bend under the blast. I was flung backwards, over and over. The driver's elbow caught me on the face as he was catapulted into the water. I was stunned, came to with the sky lit like on Bonfire Plot, but no fireworks, only a steady roaring whitish fire leaping where Tryer's Sex Museum and his erstwhile fortune had stood. I tried, but couldn't get up. My arm was twisted under me. The driver was near me on the grass, his face black as if scorched in some sooty fire.

Then people, desperate first-aiders, an ambulance, a doctor, a fire engine – how the hell had they taken years to reach us? The fire station was only three hundred yards away, for God's sake. Playing billiards all frigging night instead of getting to the starting line. And finally, at a headlong stroll, the police, who started work by placing me under arrest. Several witnesses had seen me struggling in the boating pool with the deceased. A good witness, especially to constabulary, was the park keeper, who had seen me force Tryer's head under water and kick him to death. Like I say, luck or design, who knows? Actually, I believe those two theories are identical, one and the same. When it's luck, we reckon we've planned it. When it seems like we've worked it all out, it's us conning ourselves. Everything's luck.

Or, I realized, coming to in a police cell, lack of it.

16

They questioned me in their time-honoured way, namely and to wit, telling me what they wanted me to say and to sign their blank sheets. This is so they could all go back to their subsidized boozer in the crypt until their respective tours of duty ended. I said I hadn't a clue, no idea, what on earth were they talking about. I thought of swinging the lead, forgetting my own name and all that. But I'd done it once before. It hadn't worked then either.

They brought me before Maudie Laud, a firecracker who is now the region's boss. She is smart and mistrustful of everybody, mostly me. I'll like her in another reincarnation, because she also distrusts her own Plod.

'Lovejoy,' she began, after telling the tape recorder the date and time, 'you were arrested on reasonable suspicion.'

'Was I?' I brightened immediately, because it sounded like an excuse. I wasn't forgetting I'd gone partly amnesic. Some suspicions *are* reasonable. Over nine hundred years ago, our beautiful Princess Margaret, fleeting to a nunnery for reasons best not gone into, was shipwrecked. Who should help her ashore but King Malcolm of Scotland, who proposed on the soggy spot. (Actually, he already had a Queen, but she soon died suddenly – some pious folk claim her death was St Margaret of Scotland's first miracle.) The convent idea got binned. But King Malcolm was suspicious, for his new Queen Margaret secretly slipped away each day. With drawn sword and seething retinue he followed – to find her praying for *his* soul before a secret altar. History doesn't tell how embarrassed he was: 'Oh, sorry, love. Er, just out strolling with a column of armed knights in this, er, barren cave, er . . .' Sort of scrape I get into, but not out of. Where was I? Being reasonably guilty.

'Indeed,' Maudie said crisply. 'Several corroborating witnesses. However it seems you appeared on the scene after the event, and in company with a charabanc driver in whose company you had been all day.'

'Had I?' Her lips thinned in anger. She controlled it, game lass.

'Yes. With Americans presently residing at the George Hotel. You took them to Whychwe Priory on an outing.'

'Did I?' Frail and sagging.

'Therefore,' she said, with a visible effort not to have me shot for bad acting, 'I am dropping charges for the time being. You can leave.' She told the tape recorder the time and date, and explained to it, seeing it really cared, that the interview was over. *For the time being* is their threat to us law-abiders.

'Thank you,' I said, rising with a distinct totter.

There were three others in the room, two uniformed Plod of serfdom rank, plus some stout silent bloke with malevolent eyes. I hated him and his fancy waistcoat back.

'Lovejoy,' Maudie said. 'One word. If you don't mind.'

If I didn't *mind*? Had the planet spun off course? I waited as they left. The stout plainclothesman hung back.

'Thank you, Wilberforce,' Maudie said. The door closing on his hot steady eyes.

'New chaplain?' I said. Mistake. Jokes always are, I find. Jimmy James, funniest ever comedian, never told a single joke.

She was still seated and looked up with a calculating expression. She lit a cigarette, which surprised me. I wanted to remind her, no smoking in the nick, but wisely didn't.

'Ideas, Lovejoy.'

Not a question. Tell who killed Tryer, Lovejoy, or else. They'd not said if the driver was recovering, or moribund in hospital. Nor Chemise.

'Dunno, love.' I returned her stare. 'Honest to God, I'd tell you if I'd even an inkling.'

'You see my problem?' Mild of manner, a genuine question this time. She inhaled, took a shred of tobacco off the tip of her tongue, every gesture deliberate. I'd hate to make love with Maudie Laud; you'd never know what bits were acting. Mind you, I never do anyway, because I'm too busy entering paradise. 'I believe you could guess, but will not say.'

'You're wrong. I've just said.'

'You will seek out and do to death the perpetrator?'

'Me? I've never done anything like that.'

'Which is the most evil way a police investigation can end, Lovejoy.' She went on as if I hadn't spoken. 'Loose ends make untidy stitching. They fray in my mind, fraying away.'

'Yes.'

'My suggestion is this: go about your lawful business. But before you do anything, ask even the most innocent question, call, personally, at my home if need be, pass word by your smelly reprobate Dill. Understand?'

'Yes.' Christ, they talk like the League of Nations. It comes with an inflation-proof pension. 'Can I ask?'

She didn't move. 'I'll listen.'

Aha. She really did know zilch. 'I decided to call on Tryer, ask about his eviction notice, the council's watch committee, con another meal out of Chemise. Did Chemise see anybody?'

'No perpetrator. Nor the driver.' She added with unconcealed bitterness, 'The fire services did their usual job of obliterating every footprint on the greensward.'

'Good that they came fast, though,' I said without thinking.

Her expression changed. 'So you remember we were last on the scene?'

'Aren't they always?' I said, blithe. She wasn't fooled.

That was that. I had no injuries to speak of, a few scratches I could live with. I said good morning and left. I reached the car park before my way was impeded.

'Yes, Mr Wilberforce?'

He stood, metabolic rate burning fat, sweating hate.

'I've heard about you, Lovejoy.' He smelled of garlic. His moustache was brownish at each end. His waistcoat glittered. 'Your record stinks. I know you, Lovejoy. You ponce, filch, thieve, cadge, nick, beg off everybody. You're disgusting. You know it. I know it. So I'm going to get you, hook or crook.'

There's no point in replying to policy statements. They've all got them, from social workers to the Fraud Squad. All they translate into is: we're in authority, and do what we frigging well like. Which is why the UN is utterly useless, the Olympics corrupt, the EU bureaucrats rich beyond the greediest imagination. I read somewhere that declarations of war simply weren't, and that most wars just start without any gentlemanly preliminaries like polite exchanges of notes. Wilberforce was just another psycho in office.

'No answer, Lovejoy?' Flecks of spittle spattered the air. I wondered if he had a wife somewhere, children.

'What was the question?'

'Willy,' somebody called just as he drew back to take a swing. He didn't relax, but didn't clout me. A uniformed Plod was standing on the steps looking down. 'You're wanted.'

We all looked up. Maudie Laud was at a window. Quite a tableau. I gave her a nod and departed that place. All nicks have steps. Noticed that? Sometimes, I speculate on the reasons. Nothing architectural, I'll bet.

There's a book called *Spotlight*. It pictures all actors, gives names, sometimes a little statement of their perfections. It took me forty long minutes flicking through before I came across Hugo Hopestone. He looked better than in real life, with more hair, good teeth. Sneakily I wondered if photographers touch the prints up. I phoned his agent, a woman sounding a toxic chainsmoker, and lied I had another job for Hugo. He was miraculously available to meet.

With relief, I went for breakfast with my tourists, but they'd gone to some cosmic seance with a lady called Beatrice I once made smiles with down the estuary. Her mate is Barnacle Bill, a nautical salt of enormous stature and paranoid suspicion. I was really narked, because I'd only had one measly plate of bacon, egg, fried tomatoes and beans in the nick. I hadn't complained when they'd short-changed me on the toast because I'd expected a proper breakfast with Hilda, Mahleen and Nadette while the others provided a merry backdrop. Bitterly, I got the old Morris and drove out to Fenstone to see Juliana Witherspoon. It's coming to something when you have to visit a churchwarden instead of having a breakfast you've been promised twice. It's not fair.

Looked at in the cold light of drizzle, Fenstone appeared stuporous. Maybe it once bustled in the Middle Ages, been a thriving centre of mediaeval commerce. Now it seemed on its last legs. Usually, an East Anglian village has farm carts, impatient motors, prams, old folk working out how long before the children must be met, a shop with football notices, cricket matches, the whole humdrum swirl.

This was like the bomb had dropped. Some farm tractor had gone through, deposited a stetch of clay on the road. It had remained undisturbed. The one old lady walking a dog actually turned to look as I drove in, giving me a quizzical What, a motor car? sort of gander. It had not burgeoned during my enforced absence. The FOR SALE signs still bristled, posters still bleached, weather-torn. I managed to find a parking space (joke) in the main street. There was one other motor, its front tyre flat. A notice stuck on its windscreen announced POLICE AWARE. It's how the Plod take dynamic action on abandoned cars The Bull pub was having another lie-in. The church looked as lively as its churchyard. It was all happening in Fenstone. I had Miss Witherspoon's address – not that it would have caused me any difficulty if I hadn't.

Juliana's cottage was set back at right angles from the main road near the tavern, with a once-paved space showing where farm carts had pulled in before the adjacent barn. A light was on. Some vandal had imposed fanlights in the lovely old treble tiling. I almost shivered, something I don't often do because I'm a warm mortal, but the mist was already clinging. Any self-respecting East Anglian mist should have cleared off by now.

'Wotcher, Juliana. Did it get nicked, then?'

'No.' She didn't even bother to look round.

'Why not? Seemed a pretty good painting.'

She was seated before an easel, working hard on the fine detail of a small painting. I went in, stood looking. Normally I'd have dithered at the door and asked. But she'd established different rules for us. I couldn't help staring at her nape. There's hardly anything more interesting than a woman's nape, with its wisps of hair trying to get loose, looser. The place was larger than she needed. Partly completed canvases stood against the walls. Wattle and daub, I noticed, with ancient beams above, maybe fifteenth century.

'August Macke, love? That original in Berlin, eh?'

'Juliana Witherspoon,' she said with cold ferocity.

Artists feel like this, even excellent forgers. Most, including Packo Orange, who would die if they thought for one minute that their forged paintings would for ever be thought legitimate. They need

121

fame, like all artists, and hope that one day they'll be unmasked and admired. But the art establishment sees them as fraudsters, and wants them dead – the only state that guarantees nil productivity plus profit.

August Macke was a German Expressionist. Brave lad, he volunteered for the Great War, and lasted only a few weeks. His paintings are small, evocative of that lost era of long frocks and hat boxes. I think them beautiful. Juliana was doing his tiny oil, *The Woman in the Green Jacket*. (Tip: Fake Expressionist paintings, currently almost unknown, will become epidemic in three years' time, so buy soon.)

'You're terrific, love.'

'Thank you, Lovejoy.' Cold. Her hand did not waver as she put her small sable to the foreground. 'Praise indeed, coming straight from a police cell.'

Rumour still got through to Fenstone then. But I was narked. 'I was cleared. Which means,' I added, 'that I'm declared innocent, unlike you.'

She dropped her brush, retrieved it. 'What do you mean?' She reached for the turpentine. I wish I could afford sable brushes. They cost the earth. She had a dozen, tips under inverted plastic freezer bags. Same trick I use.

'Meaning you can't criticize Miss Witherspoon.'

'Lovejoy,' she said wearily. 'Why are you here?'

'To ask what other paintings you've done, love.'

'Why should I tell you?' I cleaned her sable, gave it back for her to thin the point.

'Don't you clean with petrol? I do, unless it's a forgery. Then I use turpentine or white spirit. Are you okay, love?'

She was suddenly droopy, as if it was as all too much. 'You can look.'

I wandered about the improvised studio. She sat on her stool staring at her unfinished Macke. I searched among the ones leaning against the wall. The light wasn't good. Most artists in East Anglia swear by a 'good northern light', which is why they knock holes in lovely old buildings. The two fanlights were the best Juliana could afford. God knows what she'd have done to this lovely old barn if she'd been rich. Maybe not forged at all?

No doubt about it, Juliana Witherspoon was of exceptionally high standard. In fact, the one she was doing now I'd have paid for, knowing it a forgery, at a sale.

'Where did you train?'

'Italy, mostly. I wouldn't have minded Russia.'

'You use good canvases?' I saw she didn't understand the trade lingo. 'I mean genuinely old canvases.' I'd seen at least one that still gave vibes, but it had been drastically cleaned of its original antique painting.

'Some.' That listlessness again. I tried to cheer her up.

'Look, love. This isn't signed yet. It's straight Eliose Harriet Stannard. Date it 1864, sign it with her name. You're allowed, by law, as long as you don't sell it as a genuine Stannard. Wasn't she Alfred Stannard's daughter, Norwich School? Know what I'd do? I'd pencil in – use Borrowdale graphite, though – Alfred's name, and some sentiment like, 'Excellent, my dear!' That'll remind buyers she attended her dad's art classes. It'll go like a bomb.' She looked at me. I faltered. They were not happy eyes. 'That is, if I *was* a forger and wanted money. Put a saver on it, your name in flake white under a coat of emulsion on the reverse. Forgers escape prison that way.' Me too, I thought, but did not say.

'I can't make you out, Lovejoy.'

Hard to smile under the circumstances. 'I'm transparent, love.'

'Now you've seen my art, what will you do?'

'Keep a weather eye on auctions, love.' I crossed to look at the Macke – well, the Witherspoon. 'Not going to give me a list of your forgeries?'

'I've only done these, Lovejoy. And the one – '

'In the vestry?' I nodded. Motive, never much use, was clear here. She wanted to help her priest. I could understand that; she was head over heels. Means? Well, she was a talented artist. 'You wanted me to say it was a genuine, then you'd have nicked it; claimed on the insurance?'

Her shoulders drooped further. 'It seemed so sensible. He's paid out a fortune to insurers, Lovejoy. Surely he is entitled to some return?'

She didn't mean the Deity. I felt sympathy.

'You've not done another lately, for somebody local?'

'*Here*, Lovejoy?' She gave a laugh worse than any groan. 'If you know a customer, let me know. You're the first caller I've had in a fortnight.'

'Isn't there some farm lady interested in antiques?' It was a shot at hazard. 'A farm labourer told me she raised wool, some new animals . . .'

'Dame Millicent. Quite barmy, all weird speculations.'

Brightening, I knew I'd done right to come. Time to visit Cockcroft Manor, chat up the loony old crone. I thanked Juliana, said if there was ever anything I could ever do . . . Then I remembered I was nutritionally compromised, and hesitated.

'Juliana. Have you anything to eat? I was up early in the nick.'

An hour later I made Cockcroft Manor, but not until I'd had a worrying chat with Hugo.

17

'I felt a right prat,' Hugo said.

He didn't look very well, or even very bright. Shabby, resigned, like he mustn't be late for some impending defeat. We'd met in China Miles's yard near the Welcome Sailor. It's a new nosh bar, founded on everybody else's credit. I was running up a slate there because I'd once done China a favour by spotting that he'd bought a twiffler – a flatware piece, basically a pudding plate. (They were handmade before the 1870s, when machinery took over and killed passion. Because people don't look properly, they're missed times out of number. I've seen four this year in car boot sales, going for a warble.)

'You did well, Hugo.'

'Pretending I'd been groped by some UFO alien?'

Well, I thought, dedicated actor and all that.

He waxed. 'See, Lovejoy, the stage is famine or feast.' He stooped to his plate and scooped the pie and mash I'd bought him. I watched with fascination, knowing I'd try it at home. He put his mouth on the plate's rim and shovelled the grub horizontally into his open gob. Horrible, but you have to admire dexterity.

He spoke with a full mouth, much more horriblerer still. Queasy, I resolved not to try it after all.

'Jox told me to flannel the tourists. Lent me a book on UFOs.'

'If I had a job, Hugo,' I spoke with care, not wanting to prevent public demand dragging him off to Stratford, 'private, country house stuff, family situation, nothing illegal. . . ?'

His eager grin was one of baked beans, sausage, dangles of bacon. Jesus, but we're an ugly species.

'Like, Agatha Christie? That murder-in-a-vicarage game? I'd do it like a shot!' He babbled on, me dodging the shards as he spoke. 'My friend did one! Earned plenty!'

'Yes, but with special rules.' I hadn't anything planned, but wasn't going to ditch a possible ally. 'China?'

China emerged. His caff's literally a converted scrap-metal dealer's yard. China isn't Chinese or anything, just runs a credit scam with his wife's cousin, who is and lives in the Far East sitting by her facsimile machine. The scam's easy, a product of the Age of Communication, and is the very best argument against owning a credit card on earth.

'How're you going to pay, Lovejoy? Credit card?'

Which gave me a laugh. China earned the yard and kitchen from credit-card frauds. He was a waiter in an Aldgate restaurant. When diners paid by plastic, he would photocopy the credit card, facsimile it to the Hong Kong cousin, who would instantly 'swipe'—the term—the details onto a blank. China would return the card to the customer in seconds, with a grovelling coat-at-the-door farewell. Before the diners had reached home, their replicated credit card would have been used to buy jewellery, gold, withdraw money. Nobody is any the wiser – until the monthly statement comes through. But by then China was in the clear. A humble waiter, busy restaurant, what was a dispute between some bank and some diner to him? It works well. The 'plazzie', as it's known, has become a contender, from pennies to quarter of a billion in three years. I'm glad I'm not credit-worthy.

'Lady asked, Lovejoy. Said don't forget the biggin.' China made prominences of his cupped hands. 'Lovely eyes on her.'

Sabrina wanting action for her auction scam. 'Ta, China.' We parted amicably. Outside, I asked Hugo, 'One thing. That stout bloke, whatsisname. Put the spoke in.'

Hugo looked edgy. 'Don't ask me, Lovejoy.' He looked definitely deal's off. 'I want no stick trade, nothing heavy.'

Heavy? I looked blankly at him. What the hell was he on about? 'I was only wondering if he was some neighbour of Jox's.'

His brow cleared. 'Thank Christ, Lovejoy. Didn't think you were GBH. William Geake. He was round earlier when Jox was rehearsing us, browbeating. He's got it in for Jox. Big peeler. Retired. Jox told me he'd top the bastard if he could.'

With Jox's record, he'd be daft trying. Thoughtfully I watched Hugo plod off. Was Jox capable of doing somebody like Tryer in, though? Forget why, just think possibilities. And anybody can do anything. For a second I dithered whether to call in on the Misses

Dewhurst and demand explanations, but finally decided to drive out to Dame Millicent, that crone of increasing significance.

Tryer came to mind. I'd tried not to think, wonder how Chemise was doing. That's not because I'm a hard-hearted swine. It was because, once you start dwelling on some terrible event, you give in, go to pieces. During the hours that had passed since I'd splashed into the boating pool, I'd concentrated on being angry at the police. I'd composed bitter letters to my Member of Parliament about unlaw, made imaginary speeches on telly crime programmes and roused the nation to indignation. Childhood gunge, but it stops you breaking down. With luck, I could keep myself from ever remembering. I was busy, and memory's a luxury anyway.

Cockcroft Manor Farm was a tenth the grandeur of its name. You'd take it for an ordinary farmhouse, as you whizzed by on the A45. It seemed uncertain what to be in the modern world. Probably was a useful farm in its heyday, churning out produce, keeping folk in employ, a rural epicentre. Now it seemed prepared to sell its soul. A trestle table stood at the gate with boxes of apples, cabbages, potatoes, tomatoes, and a notice: 'Please serve yourself!!! Money in the tin!!! Thank you!!!' Commerce had arrived at Cockcroft.

Except the three beehives on the uncut grass were empty. The pastures held a couple of tired horses. The stables looked nigh derelict, door reaching slantwise for the ground. A tractor rusted patiently. Some other implement petrified awry, corroding on the skyline. The manor house itself could have done with paint, some tiles, yards of cladding, panes of glass, a skilled chimney straightener, and a pargeter to restore the lovely old pargeting flaking in chunks off the gable ends. The farm covered forty acres, give or take, which isn't much. Forest extended across the rising distance. A river worked abstractedly to form an oxbow lake; a millennium should see it through. As I stood daring the drive, a red-coated horseman emerged from the woods with a scatter of hounds like wafted oats in front. He stared, rode across my field of view and vanished into the stand of young deciduous trees. Neither of us waved. Geake again.

'You there!' an imperious lady shouted from the farmhouse. I cupped a hand. 'Put – money – in – tin!'

'No,' I bawled.

'Bounder!' she called.

'Snotface!' I bawled.

She froze, then laughed, wagged her stick, rocked her way inside. I drove in, parked.

'Dame Millicent Hallsworthy,' I said into the gloom.

'In here, you vulgar brute.'

Advancing gingerly, I bumped against something huge. It growled and moved aside, came padding along. I swallowed and wondered if I should be here. Trying to be pleasant to a dog the size of a lioness is impossible. I had a bird who was addicted to dogs. She had three pinschers I hated. I lasted one day. Feeding time was carnage incarnate, so to speak. This hound was a mournful thing with trailing ears. A door was open.

'Lovejoy.' The words just reached into the room. I followed.

Long, practically bare, a log fire keeping the stone-flagged flooring free of ice. I'm not often cold, and when I am it's mainly emotional, but this place was ridiculous. Damp walls, fungus the size of tumorose saucers on the pelmets, cardboard and plywood plugging several windows. One sprung sofa. The dog had followed, growing larger meanwhile, staring in sorrow.

'You're the antiques man with the gift,' she said. 'Late!'

Her face was lined, not pale, her smile full of blackened teeth. She wore a beret. A moth-eaten (literally) fox fur dangled round her neck, glassy of eye, limbs pendulating. It looked warm, but chilled me further. Nowhere to sit except on the metal springs leaping in still life from her sofa, so I stood with the dog, at least as dejected.

Gift? It was her dog, so I agreed. 'Yes, Dame Millicent.'

She eyed me perkily. 'You're wondering why a titled lady lives in squalor, Lovejoy.'

'No.' The dog sighed in threat. 'Yes,' I amended.

'Don't be afraid of Malapert. He's harmless. Come closer. Let me look at you.' I stepped cautiously. Malapert came, too. The word means saucy, blunt of manner. She eyed me. 'I'd have eaten you, Lovejoy, a few years ago. Now . . .' She shrugged, winced. She was bent with arthritis. Her hands were gnarled, looked crushed from some accident, except the accident was only accumulated life. She clutched a metal ball. Her knees were bulbs, calves mere spindles down to deformed ankles. 'I can't get up in the morning without

128

my electric blanket.' She sighed. Malapert sighed. So I sighed. Crawler.

'Anything I can do for you, Dame Millicent?'

She smiled. It was beautiful, the gaunt room instantly warmer. 'I do so love you people,' she said. 'You will have noticed my accent? Balkan, of course. I shall leave you guessing. Foreigners call me Dame Hallsworthy. They called Sir Ralph – wrongly – Sir Keeler, Mister Sir, any combination! This island never falters, though!'

Politely I laughed, remembering the scandal. It had wobbled a government donkey's years before. Somebody's suicide and a cluster of resignations had faded. It was resurrected by desperate newspapers every few years. Sir Ralph was an august MP of peculiar bent.

'You like my antique pome?' she asked slyly. The metal ball. Hollow, plugged with a shapely stopper. The dog glanced at me.

'Great,' I lied heartily. 'Er, a beautiful pome!'

She grimaced. 'Well, it *might* deceive somebody, Lovejoy. I've been trying new polish, coats it silver.'

'Aye. Sorry.' I honestly felt it for the old fraud.

A pome is a metal ball, usually silver. You fill it with hot water in some vestry, and the priest carries it through his stone-cold church service. It's simply a handwarmer. So there are no embarrassing gasps as his frozen fingers drop the chalice. Exquisite ones were made by brilliant London silversmiths. Some are nothing more than silver cases holding a glass bottle. Few dealers recognize them, thinking them portable travelling flasks.

'The blacksmith makes me things. This, those pilliwinks.'

'Finger crushers?' It's a mediaeval instrument of torture for cramping digits, lever action. Very collectable. You can torture one finger at a time or several together, depending on your need for truth, as it were. I would have had a closer look but for the hound. 'He seems to've been pretty deft.' Maybe I should sell for her. Ironwork's easy to pass as genuine.

'Yes. I was sad to lose him. He wanted to stay.'

'But he was made to leave?' I asked, innocent.

'His lady spurned him, Lovejoy. She loves . . . another.'

Aha! Juliana Witherspoon, hopelessly smitten by the priest, ignores Jolly Joe the Blacksmith, who departs forlorn?

'So Fenstone shrank further still, eh?'

Her deflected fingers reminded me of old gardening implements. She gestured with them.

'I've tried everything, Lovejoy, from farming imported exotic animals to tourism. I've even tried pretending there's ancient treasures in my fields.'

'No!' I gasped. She got the joke and laughed herself into arthritic agony.

'You bastard,' she wheezed, subsiding. 'Knew you'd be a crook, soon as you shouted that insult.'

'Who puts the fruit and veg out?'

'Me and Malapert.' She explained. 'I have a Dutch dogcart. He hauls it beautifully. I gather produce piecemeal.'

She indicated the fire. I went and chucked another log on it. It spat at me, spent charcoal all over the hearth.

'Willow wood never burns well,' she said. 'But it's the only material I can get. The orchards failed. Blight.'

'Don't you spray?' Believe it or not, they use five different sprays in orchards.

'I thought last autumn would save me. Took a loan to buy chemicals, hired machines. Vandals holed the drums, poisoned the vegetable garden.'

Surprise surprise. 'Who's your neighbour? Huntsman.'

'That's Geake, churchwarden. A would-be gentleman.' She stopped herself chuckling by holding her ribs.

'Look, Dame Millicent. Your dying village has five activists.' I counted. 'You, Father Jay, Juliana, Jox, Geake.'

'That's about it, Lovejoy. Jox is useless. Can you believe his grandfather was a Royal Navy captain, a hero?' She went nostalgic. 'Times change. When Sir Ralph was alive, he kept trouble at bay.' She smiled, wistful. 'He had a klendusic quality. You know those plants that, whatever the onslaught, have already prepared some protective mechanism? Dear man. Friends in high places!' She smiled at me with pride. 'My lover, of course. The parties we had, Lovejoy! Now, nobody comes near. I've not had a letter for over a year.'

'Sorry, love.' This kind of thing makes me uncomfortable.

'It is for me to apologize.' Dignity regained control.

'We should all meet,' I told her. 'Throw a party, just the six of us. Hatch a Save Fenstone plan, eh?'

'Would you come, Lovejoy?'

'As long as Juliana did.'

She smiled. 'So you've met Juliana. And liked her?' Her bright eyes fixed me. 'I suggested you to her, Lovejoy.' And explained before I could ask, 'I knew of you from Priscilla.'

Of course. I was lost. The Dewhurst biddies were everywhere before me, with the American tourists, Jox's scam, this old lady. I limped gamely after. 'You know the Dewhursts?'

'Doesn't everyone? They've made a superb discovery. It's the Obverse Zodiac. Works every time! Priscilla should cast your natal chart, Lovejoy. Perhaps you and Juliana are ideally suited! You are just the man to wean her from that turbulent priest.' She became suddenly testy. 'What good is a woman who isn't *used*, Lovejoy? I *hate* silliness. Life's simple if people would only open their stupid eyes! A man must be loved. A woman must be used. I get *mad*. I'd make it a law.' Anger wore her out. She leant on a cushion, spent. Then resumed, conversational, 'Priscilla is the more prescient of the twins, don't you think, astrologically?'

Which led to more pointless prattle of astral planes and things planetary. Which led to me sloping off as soon as I could. I found some change in the glove compartment, and bought two pounds of apples (money in the tin) for the Misses Dewhurst. The trouble was, I was now broke which meant defrauding somebody of an antique for money.

See how I'm forced into crime? And people still go about saying things are my fault. I should talk to Chemise, if I could find her. Wondering who did for Tryer, I realized I had the very best evidence, in the form of bruises. Nick and his henchmen, courtesy of Roberta and Ashley Battishall! Motive? I didn't know. I didn't care. They would pay. Time was crowding me. I drove onto the A45, and got a ticket for speeding.

18

In the woods near where I live stands a small dwelling. It's part of a theme park now – lakes, meadows, forests, miles of yawnsville where folk feel Close To Nature. I'm not one for this, but I'd heard they were about to date it, so went to see.

Half a dozen idlers were standing about outside. I'd had to park our car a furlong off. A bedraggled scientist was explaining. Like all scientists, he looked John the Baptist in trainer shoes.

'This country has a great resource,' he was saying earnestly. 'The Nottingham Tree Ring Dating Laboratory. Our master sequence is around 1100 to about 1750 . . .'

Around? *About*? A king of scientific precision. I wanted him to do the frigging thing, drill a core from the beams, then we could all go home.

'We take cores,' this wretch intoned, 'pencil-thin, exterior to centre. We measure two hundred rings, compare their widths from trees felled on known dates.'

'How accurate are you?' I asked. Spectators shuffled in embarrassment, such insolence to this fount of knowledge.

'Within a year,' he said, smug. 'The oldest mediaeval peasant's cottage so far tested is AD 1335, Malpledurham in Oxfordshire, fifteen years before the Black Death pandemic.'

Somebody whispered, 'Don't rub him up the wrong way.'

'Wotcher, Wilmore.' I was surprised. He was wearing a dark golfing mac. I whispered back, 'Shouldn't you be with Gwena the Guide?'

'Astrology session.' He grinned the enthusiastic grin of an escaping American. I couldn't help liking him. 'Recovered, hearing of this development potential.'

'. . . was never intended as a manor house,' the cachectic saint of science was intoning. 'Its roof's two timbers are in a curved, upturned

V configuration. Manor houses had those two main timbers held by a cross beam, a letter A . . .'

'Will it be preserved?' I asked this scarecrow.

He said, just as stern, 'We already have a preservation order. Our conservationist group has a plant watch.'

He started to show his implements, a drill, tubes to hold the cores. Me and Wilmore drifted away. I'd seen it.

'Ring dating's not bad,' I groused to Wilmore. 'Radioactive carbon dating isn't so good.' I was sad that Mahleen the Golden wasn't waiting by the motors.

'I was hoping they might release this area, Lovejoy,' Wilmore shrugged. 'Maybe the cottage won't be old after all. You can't blame me. One in five of Britain's stately homes has been sold since the 1970s, right?' His face showed a developer's rapture. 'The British Isles has one million registered golfers, Lovejoy, 52.76 per cent of Europe's registered 1.9 million! England, Scotland, Wales, total 32,286 golf holes, on 1,974 greens! Anti-golf maniacs say we're world wreckers, creating sterile environments. But golf is the greatest ever sport . . .'

'Good heavens,' I murmured politely, switching off.

Such numbers! Everybody uses statistics to bend arguments. It's all fraudulent. Stockbrokers spend billions – and a six-year old chimpanzee beat Sweden's top stockbrokers *by chucking darts at the companies list pinned to a board.* Okay, I know that figures frighten. I mean, the USA's eastern seaboard holds the record for lightning, when the great blizzard a few years ago produced 59,000 cloud-to-ground flashes, peaking at 5,100 flashes an hour overall. Strikes numbered 0.16 per square kilometre near Tampa, Florida. It doesn't reassure me that East Anglia's lightning isn't a contender. I distrust forests, because rogue elephants kill two Indians every three days – in India, of course, but so? It doesn't mean I'm less scared in East Anglia. When one single crazed beast kills forty-four poor villagers, charging trumpeting from the countryside –

'Eh?' He'd said something important.

'. . . the Battishalls' place. Excuse me?'

'Dragonsdale? Your group is at Dragonsdale?' I wanted at least one strand tied up, at any price. So far only the slow obliteration of Fenstone linked with Tryer's death.

'Sure is. I've asked Mahleen to examine its potential after that zodiac session. What's the matter, Lovejoy?'

'Nothing,' I said heartily. 'The Battishalls are, er, friends of mine.' I swallowed the lie, but I'm courageous at heart. 'Jaunting out there, Wilmore?'

'Now why don't we do that, Lovejoy?'

At last. Two birds with but a single stone. High time.

As I drove the valley on the old B road, I reflected on how we discover, uncover, reveal. There isn't a tabloid in the land that isn't packed with 'personality girls' exposing How He Performs In Bed, all that. And every morning brings news of the latest: 'Another *Tyrannosaurus rex* Found!!!' Except impressions mislead. So far they've only found fourteen *T. rex* skeletons in the entire world, South Dakota their planetary mecca. We mesmerize ourselves into whatever's fashion. And the latest is discovery at all costs.

Discoveries are always seen as exciting things. I sympathized with Dame Millicent, whose instincts were sound: pretend that some ancient gold/tomb/battlefield/whatever lay on her derelict property, and cash in as the world beat a path to her door. Okay, so she was baulked, just like Jox. Just as Juliana and Father Jay in that echoing church.

Yet Dame Millicent was right. It *could* be done. As I drove and Wilmore chuntered on about Japanese green fees, a gillion ideas for her crummy farm occurred. You didn't have to find a *Grâce Dieu* or a German submarine – like the U-534 that sailed from Kiel in May 1945, to its watery end in the Kattegat, to resurface half a century later when Dutch salvagers hauled it from the ocean. Or, the Sutton Hoo Viking ship that yielded priceless treasure. Flukes – you know *those* – do happen. Like to those Jesuits of Dublin's Leeson Street, who hadn't thought much of their painting, *The Taking Of Christ*, that hung lopsided in their refectory. By some minor Flemish artist, worth only a few quid, right? Well, no. Works of Michelangelo Merisi da Caravaggio, the painter of this (fanfare, please) 'discovery' go at seventy million slotniks. The kindly priests gave it to a gallery. Is there a God?

Tryer said he'd tried with a holy wishing well. Jox's latest go was Hugo the Thespian's UFO performance. I'm not knocking these notions, for all placed growth comes from fib or fame. The ultimate examples are Glastonbury, Tintagel, where folk market the mighty Arthur; Lourdes, Assisi, battlefields like Waterloo and Gettysburg. And the inn, in France's Auvers-sur-Oise.

Which is where a thirty-seven-year old painter arrived from a year in a Provence lunatic asylum, for a short while before he shot himself. Everybody knows how Camille Pissarro suggested Auvers (peace, beauty, that precious northern light), how Vincent turned out seventy paintings in seventy days. And how Van Gogh borrowed his wine-merchant-cum-innkeeper landlord Arthur Ravoux's pistol to scare away crows, then shot himself. And returned at dusk, answered, 'Oh, nothing. I've hurt myself,' and ascended the two flights to his bedroom. And how Vincent calmly smoked his pipe when two rude gendarmes came in, superbly answering their bullying abuse, 'I am free to do what I want with my body.' And how he died thirty hours later in his loyal brother Théo's arms, while Vincent's friend Dr Paul Gachet mourned impotently. The Auberge Ravoux has a restaurant now, a bookshop, Vincent's sparse room as it was, and the attention of the world.

Now, we can't have those treasures already discovered. So sinful humanity finds treasures where there are no treasures at all. I support Tryer's scams, stick up for Jox's daft exploits. But everybody does it, makes money from people's dreams. The Church's income's been boosted by prostitutes' rents for centuries. The United Nations – no mean exploiter of myth – bureaucrat who ran a call-girl scam at the High Commissioner for Refugees Geneva HQ is one example. UN vehicles 'donated' to pals, food aid in Uganda sold on the black market, UN stores whittled away to pals . . . It's routine. Against that lot, I'm a saint.

And some priceless objects discovered years ago get rediscovered, to the joy of a select few. Like the Trojan Treasure excavated in Turkey by the scandalous Heinrich Schliemann in 1873. (Scandalous because fraudulent – his American citizenship was got by fraud; he ditched his Russian wife for a Greek lass he got by mail order. An accomplished smuggler, and a chiseller in more ways than one.) Its nine thousand gold artefacts were disputed in Turkey's courts – Schliemann got fined the odd groat; Berlin's museums paid a whack. He then gave the Troy treasure to Germany. The Soviets captured it in 1945 from its secret hidey-hole under a railway station beneath Berlin Zoo, and off it went to Moscow. Result of the new modern co-operation? Acrimony, shrieking headlines, wholesale hatred. And why? Because we're gold struck. Historically famous gold creates wails of avarice.

We parked in the hotel drive and Nick was immediately there, watched us approach.

'Wait, Lovejoy.' Nick glanced at Wilmore. 'I'll ask the mistress if you're allowed.'

'Hadn't you heard, Nick? I'm a resident.'

We made it past Nick without assault. He looked for my suitcases, but I pulled out my pockets to show impoverishment. Neither of us smiled. I thought, you wait, Nick, just wait. There'll be smiles a-plenty.

19

Not long since, I knew this woman. She had a shop near Bury St Edmunds, sold toys. Only secondhand, hardly mendable. She was nice, nothing between us, but sometimes I'd stop, pass the tea hour, admire her gunge. Occasionally she'd pick up some teddy bear, usually a fake Steiff – the most sought-after are German from 1903 on – with wrong stitching and a phoney stud. I'd explain to Mary that even if the Steiff stud was correctly clipped to the bear's left ear it still might be a fake. (Remember that Theodore Roosevelt refused to shoot a tethered bear cub in 1902, which started the teddy bear epidemic, so teddies dated 1889 must be fake. If you find a genuine one used at Roosevelt's daughter Alice's wedding as table ornaments, you've arrived.)

Well, me and Mary went on for aeons, she finding toys, and me miserably telling her no, it's a repro Lancaster bomber toy; they are advertized in mail order. We'd have a laugh, and off I'd go, belly a-slosh with tea. Until the day she was diagnosed as dying.

She'd felt off colour, and was told the very, very worst. She was in a state when I called. I stayed a couple of nights, ran her shop while she told her family. Tears all round, until double happiness! Because, that third afternoon, I was handed a genuine Ernst Plank toy locomotive engine, boxed, trademarked, 3-inch gauge, beautiful tinplate, tender and carriage complete. In a joke, I offered the bloke a quid. He took it, leaving me gaping. Mary's brother rang just then. Mary was staying over a few days, so I left the train set with a prominent note full of excited congrats about finally making the find of the century, pointing out the functional spirit-heated boiler, pistons and all.

Then, tragedy. Because Mary came home, still stunned from her calamitous news – and *without reading my letter* absently sold the train set to a collector for five quid. Which is like giving away a

Richard Wilson oil colour for a loaf. The following day her doctor, puzzled, had the sense to check on the hospital laboratory's findings. And Mary was fit as a flea, didn't have the dreaded death sentence after all !!*!$!! Whereupon, Mary danced home, and delightedly welcomed me the following week with the good news. Life! Rejoicing!

Eventually I asked about the Ernst Plank train set. Genuine Nuremberg, maybe as early as 1884, eh? Fortune! Whereupon the following:–

Mary: What train set?

Me: (smile fading) The one I left you on your counter.

Mary. (aghast) Lovejoy. *What train set*?

Me: (shrill, with panic) The frigging genuine Plank boxed set I frigging left with that letter, you stupid old bat.

Mary: (screaming) *What letter*?

You know what? Nobody's ever seen Mary smile since. She's the most bitter, morose bird you'd meet in a twelvemonth. I avoid her now. Her reprieve from death is forgotten. The agony of being, for a trice, at death's dark door has been eclipsed by her terrible grievance, as if she'd been cheated. See what happens in antiques? Each dealer knows his own personal El Dorado. Even being saved from death can't equal it.

Mary's now a wino bagging round the sailing club dustbins down the estuaries. The threat of death couldn't ruin her. But losing out in the antiques trade finished her.

If I had the sense I was born with, I would have remembered Mary's tale with its hint of death, and been a lot safer. But I haven't so I didn't and I wasn't.

'Lovelock!'

'Lovejoy. How do, Jim.'

'He was in my regiment,' old Jim Andrews said chattily to Wilmore. He looked about three hundred years old, and stank of rum. His eyes darted furtively under his fungating brows. 'Subaltern, tanks, western campaign.'

'Er, no. Wrong generation.' I caught the old soak, who tottered. 'Look, how about you have a lie down?'

'Nurse banned me in the bar, Lovelock. Two's my ration.'

'Right, Jim. Give me some help, Wilmore.'

'Sure.' We helped the reeling Mr Andrews to an armchair.

'In the drawing room,' the old man quavered unexpectedly. 'Talking about their Restoration society. Can you credit it? Off their silly bloody noddles. Mark my words.'

'Er, right. See you, Jim.'

We knocked gently on the double doors, Nick hating me but smiling benignly whenever Wilmore caught his eye.

Ashley was pontificating. '. . . a brilliant politico-religious movement. It mirrors the needs of the times. Think! If only those wondrous days would come again!' His eyes shone with strange fervour. 'Everything for Europe, and the world!'

The tourist group applauded, exclaiming approval. Some waved welcome at me and Wilmore. They'd noshed a light supper and been slugging back the wine. Roberta sat in her semi-reclining Manet posture but without a nubian slave. She looked beautiful. The portrait of Bonnie Prince Charlie, looking even tawdrier, was unveiled. Something had leant against its surface and dimpled the canvas. Why didn't they straighten it out, for God's sake? Takes a minute. Sloppiness with even fake antiques galls me.

'My wife Roberta will speak on Romance and the Prince!'

'Thank you, Ashley.' Roberta sipped wine for strength. The full glass sank to a mere drop. Some sip.

'We founded Carolean Restoration Now, CAREN, because we feel so passionately about the story's romance,' Roberta said wistfully. 'Sweet Flora Macdonald, the prince's love all his life . . .'

As she spoke this pack of falsehood, I took out my grubby handkerchief and dipped it into a glass of water and crossed to the portrait. Gingerly I lifted it down and propped it against Mahleen's knee. If you lean canvases together the corner of one can indent the canvas of the other. It causes an ugly dimple that stays, distorts the picture's surface. I touched the dimple with the wetted handkerchief, and pressed it round in concentric circles, wetting the canvas.

'. . . So month after month, Prince Charlie was led to safety by the loyal Flora. Imagine the scores of times when, sleeping in the cold mountainous highlands, the faithful Flora, roused the Pretender, and led him . . . over the sea to Skye.'

'How lovely!' Hilda said, tears filling her eyes.

'So wonderfully *real*!' said Nadette.

'In later years,' Roberta said, wistful to the rowlocks, 'after starvation, the faithful Flora sailed overseas to mend her broken heart. After enjoying the splendid democracy of the USA, poor darling, she returned to spend her last years sighing alone for her lost love, handsome Bonnie Prince Charlie!'

Applause. More wine, to celebrate this rubbish, and the visitors started praising Roberta for the wonderful work she was doing, keeping alive the most wonderful love story. I didn't clap, because a con trick always earns my respect. And Roberta, shrinking violet that she was, carried it off. My friends were captivated. Vernon, Jerry, Wilmore even.

They talked of the lovely Flora Macdonald, wondering if she'd been near their home towns or not. I said nothing. I hung the painting. Then I saw what had been making me feel off colour. The former veil curtaining had been replaced by a piece of silk, fawn in colour, floral patterned – purplish lilac, white pink-spotted lilies, carnations, a creamy chrysanthemum.

'Lovejoy is critical,' Roberta said, watching. 'I shall replace that old faded silk with new brocade!'

'Shut your frigging mouth, silly cow.'

We all looked about. I too looked in astonishment, wondering who'd been so rude. Then I realized. Me.

'Oh,' I said in lame apology, but I'd meant every word.

Roberta cried, 'Ashley! Lovejoy is abusive again!'

He advanced, but I was past caring. I stood glowering. She had the grace to cringe, Pearl White before the bully.

'Listen, you simpering bag of spanners,' I said. My throat felt cold, my cheeks tingling. 'That piece of silk – see it? You probably got it from your attic, found under the floorboards as insulation. But it's worth a hundred times you, and your precious toadying Ashley.'

'Lovejoy!' Hilda exclaimed. The others were deploring my conduct or standing appalled as I ranted. Except I was speaking almost in a whisper.

'That piece of silk was woven in Spitalfields in 1744. Know how, Roberta? No, you don't. Let me enlighten you, you idle overfed cow.' In fury I dragged her across to stand before the painting. I pulled the silk close.

'The people were Huguenots. They'd come to escape massacre after the revocation of the Edict of Nantes. They lived in Spitalfields, London. Starving, struggling to survive. This silk was wound onto quills by malnourished three-year-old children. Whole families living and working in one room. The looms never stopped, hand-thrown silk growing an inch an hour. Poverty that overstuffed gannets never knew.'

I glared at Roberta. She was weeping. It was the end of the world, somebody not worshipping the ground she simpered on. I glared at the rest. They were staring, silent now.

'The women and children were winders and throwsters. If their looms were slashed by bastards who ran a protection racket then the women went to stand in Spitalfields Market, to work for strangers at three shillings a week, not enough to keep alive.

'Inform on the loom-breakers and there was retribution. Oh aye, the slashers got hanged all right, like those outside the Salmon and Ball pub in Bethnal Green. But those who asked the law for help got stoned, like poor Daniel Clarke in 1771. The mob chased him down the alleyways – and stoned him to death, for weaving silk.'

'In England?' somebody said, I think Hilda. 'London?'

There's no telling some people. 'Slump hit, caused wholesale deaths, starvation. Spitalfields – a stone's throw from the Bank of England – was a nightmare of gunshots, riots, tumult, murders, barricades in every street, explosions. Into that horror there came from a quiet Lincolnshire parsonage a lass called Anna Maria Garthwaite. Alone, she travelled into this pandemonium, lodged in Spitalfields.'

Silence. Even Roberta listened, no limelight for a change.

'What happened to her?' Mahleen asked.

'She wove this.' I let Roberta go, suddenly I was sick to death of the woman. I didn't want to be here. I wanted my cottage, to stay there with the curtains drawn, have a bath and feel clean. Somebody had finished Tryer, and it hadn't been his fault. I wasn't sure that it wasn't mine, but I was too tired.

'This? She made this silk?'

'Went freelance. For a pittance. For you, Roberta. To veil that poxy phoney portrait of a drunken bum that you romance about. But don't knock it, or Anna Maria Garthwaite. She's worth a dozen of you, love.'

'Lovejoy.' Jerry, Nadette's husband, decided to speak up for chivalry. 'We came to this gracious lady's home, as your friend, to hear her wonderful tale of the marvellous links between our two great countries – '

'Jerry. Don't say it.' I was worn out.

'I have to, Lovejoy.' He was adamant. 'Our country plucked that poor heroine Flora from the perfidy of – '

'It's a con, Jerry.' In for a penny. 'Can't you see?' I stood ready in case they called Nick's men in to cudgel me to oblivion.

'Con?' Mahleen and Wilmore said together. They knew con.

'Flora Macdonald was only with Charlie eleven days. When he'd gone, to drink himself stupid the rest of his life, she was fêted in Edinburgh and London. King George himself extolled her. She returned home laden with gifts, married a Macdonald, settled down in fair prosperity. She went with her family to the New World – and fought *against* your new republic.'

'Against?' somebody croaked.

'Her spelling was atrocious, even in North Carolina. But everybody liked her. Seven children, they did well for themselves. Until the War of Independence. Her husband's Royal Highland Emigrants fought disastrously at Moore's Creek Bridge. For two years, Flora was separated. She had a grim time under the American Patriots. No fêtes or presents this time. Possessions gone, family scattered or imprisoned. Your Americans' Loyalist committee abused her shamefully. It was *then* that Flora was brave. She escaped to Nova Scotia, and came home, reunited with her husband on the Isle of Skye.'

More silence. Vernon and Wilmore exchanged glances. I offered lamely, 'Richard Wilson painted her portrait . . .'

Ashley was apoplectic, Roberta was near to a swoon. I stood embarrassed, as the party broke up. I went with them to the door. Gwena was driving the charabanc this time. I avoided her.

'No, no,' I said smiling a bit shamefacedly to everyone who asked if I was coming with them to the George for a nightcap. 'No, thanks. Actually, I'm staying a few days.'

'Thanks.' Wilmore shook my hand. 'See you, Lovejoy.'

'Maybe I'll call round tomorrow,' I said, not meaning it.

Then a strange thing happened. Mahleen stepped close, gave me a buss. As she did so – we were on the steps, Ashley being gravely formal to the ladies – she whispered, 'See me triple urgent, Lovejoy. Antiques! Money!'

And was gone. I thought I'd imagined it. I waved them off to spin their departure out. Nothing for it. I went inside, and took my medicine. It was different from what I expected.

Ashley was with Roberta. She was being supported by her angry husband. If looks could kill.

'. . . suppose I shall have to, Ashley.'

'Must you, dearest? It always leaves you exhausted.'

'I know, dear.' She was in tears of self-pity. 'But the Cause. I have the most awful premonitions.' She broke down.

Ashley told me to ring for a maid. I didn't know how. He lowered Roberta into a chair and rushed to pull a naff quid-a-yard braided cord beside the naff modern repro hall mirror. A maid appeared, pushing her hair into her maid's lace cap. She'd thought she was off duty.

'Lily, help the mistress to her bedroom suite, would you?'

'Yes, sir.'

'And, Lily,' Roberta murmured feebly. 'I think I could manage some gâteau, a little of that trifle, with cream, some marzipan torte – you know the one – and a dish of fruit salad.'

'Yes, ma'am.'

'With some peeled grapes, not those thin dark ones; the fat white Italian. And a selection of tartlets. Have you any from Gunton's? They agree with me best.'

'Yes, ma'am.' Lily darted me a sideways glance as Roberta was assisted to the lift. I know that all glances are supposed to be oblique by definition, but there was something congratulatory about Lily's sideways look that should have enlightened. But I'm thick at the best of times. At the worst, I'm pathetic. The lift doors crashed, making Roberta whimper. It whirred away, leaving Ashley.

'What you said, Lovejoy, was reprehensible!'

'I've seen too many scams, Ashley. If you wanted me out, you shouldn't have dragged me in. But you set your hoodlums on me, force me in. So take me, warts and all. I've kept up my side. Tell me what the scam is, who we're conning out of what, and I'll do what I'm made to. Then I can get the hell away from you and your winceyette woman. Where's my room?'

His cheeks glowed red, generating a scarlet fluorescence that could have lit our village. For a fleeting instant I saw a silhouette against the sheen of the children's boating pool, and knew it wasn't him that had beaten Tryer to death in the park. His orders, though?

'Third floor, Lovejoy. Knock at the blue suite before entering.' He said it like a penance. Jesus, I thought, what's in there? A hit team, torturers?

'Look, Ashley,' I said showing the chicken in me. 'I meant no harm. These causes, like your Bonnie Prince Charlie crap – er, project. I see ten a week. They never, never *ever*, turn out the way you think they will. They can't.' I heard the lift returning, to carry me to another battering.

'You do not know. Our Cause is the hope of mankind.'

'They always are, Ashley,' I said sadly. 'But mankind is hopeless. He wants sin.'

God, he was stubborn. And nobody's more stubborn than when bent on fraud. 'Truth got left at the starting line aeons ago. It's a folk memory, like boggarts and fairies.'

'Cynicism is evil, Lovejoy. You will be punished for it.'

So it was to be a belting. I sighed. Escape was out of the question. I tried to wheedle. 'It isn't cynicism, Ashley. It's experience. Of antiques, of people who want a fortune for a clothes peg, of dreamers – that's all of us – who claim that their bit of broken glass is the Hope Diamond.'

'You will do as you are told.'

'Right.' I eyed him, curious now. There was something I'd missed here. 'But if you're running an antiques scam, Ashley, you're going about it all wrong. If it's simply money you want, you'll fail.'

'You will stay here three days, Lovejoy,' he said, tight-lipped. I swear he hadn't listened to one blinking word. 'Understood?'

'Aye.' The lift crashed gently. I went towards it.

Ashley barred my way, in a new fury. 'Only the mistress uses the lift. *Stairs*.'

He stayed in the grand hall. As if I'd taken away his toffee-apple. I wondered if all murderers were childish, or if it was an act. No answer on the first flight of stairs, none on the second. There was one on the third, of a sort.

20

The landing was almost threadbare. Blue suite, indeed. As I stood at the door, scared to death it would be Big John Sheehan inside ready to chuck me out of the window – his favourite ploy – Lily emerged wheeling a trolley. I cleared my throat a couple of times. She looked delectable, bending forward, curves moving.

'Er, all right in there?' I asked. My voice squeaked.

'You'll find out soon enough, Lovejoy.' Sideways, that glance again. 'I hope you survive.'

Dear God. 'Look, Lily. Pass on a message for me. To Tinker Dill. Tell him –'

'Do your own dirty work, Lovejoy.' Hate, so soon?

'Er, ta.' I was desperate to leave some rock carving so future astronauts would know I'd been this way. 'Give my regards to . . .' To the world, anybody. 'Mr Andrews,' I ended feebly.

'You know old Jim?' Direct look this time, no obliquity.

'Old pal,' I said, grasping at straws. 'From way back.' It sounded Lone Ranger. I amended eagerly, 'My dad's war pal.'

'I'll tell him.' She paused. 'Be yourself in there, Lovejoy.' And went. There was a service lift on the landing.

Be myself? I prayed to be somebody else for a millisec, thought, oh get on with it, and went in.

A sitting room, furnished in warehouse gunge. And blue! A television muttered, somebody groaning? Music of the egg-and-beans-for-table-three sort droned.

'Hello?' I called. 'I'm here.'

Nothing. At the far end a door stood ajar, the pale TV screenlight reflected through. A window, curtained, gave me an instant's mad hope but I knew from experience that goons would be prowling outside. Dejectedly I edged forwards. Bedroom? Chamber of horrors? Both?

'Hello?' I said, louder.

The door gave onto a bedroom, eggshell blue. Roberta was in a round, white, frothy bed, eating from a tray. It was modern pressed plastic painted to resemble silver. Honest to God, a mansion this size, servants, and she dines off a chunk of stamped compound. I swallowed, realized I was hungry.

The television showed some woman, groaning in the throes. A corn porn video, eight ninety-nine from Hamblesons in Wyre Street. This was the only torture.

'Er, am I right, missus?' I didn't want Ashley to come charging out of the wardrobe with his psychotic mob.

'Shhhh.' She shushed me. The mound of grub was enormous. Lily's knowing glance came back to me. Roberta's eyes didn't leave the screen.

What to do? I stood like a spare tool. The lady selected some little sweet things, that they give out at posh parties. I watched her. Delicately her mouth opened, the morsel went in with no unnecessary expenditure of energy, then that lovely smooth hand returned to waver, decide, dip, select out one more tasty titbit for that luscious paradisical mouth. And one more time.

The cake was a huge gâteau. My mouth watered. I tried to smile at her, but it felt cardboard instead of silent endearment. She tilted her head slightly. I edged aside, partly in the way, and the groans from the television came faster. I tore my gaze from the grub to look. The woman, rolling her eyes. Close-up of the bloke on her starting to thresh. Pan to their conjoined bodies, limbs writhing. The woman shoving her breasts at him, rolling over on a sandy seashore, to straddle him. Him crying out as he curved his body up to thrust into her, she laughing, head back, riding him like a bucking beast . . .

God, but the grub was tantalizing. I couldn't keep my eyes off it. Roberta cut herself a slice of some chocolate-covered thing. How didn't she turn into a giant squab? I heard myself moan with lust. Roberta, I noticed, as she started on the new slice, was slowly shedding her nightdress, one of those white satin garments with foamy collarettes.

Her breast appeared. She ate on, baring her shoulders. The nightdress's skirt was out over the satiny quilt. Her eyes closed, ecstatic at the taste. Her tongue flicked her lips.

The groans had become yelps out there as the waves beat on the seashore. Close-ups of hands, buttocks, limbs going.

'Can I pass anything, missus?' I was desperate to get nearer the grub.

'Shhhh.'

How she said it with her mouth filled I don't know. I watched her press a chocolate marzipan in. It was marvellous to watch her eat, except the word eat sounds too indelicate for the way which the morsels were chosen, inspected, and elegantly assimilated into that beautiful mouth. To think it actually became part of her, a total act of union. Like watching osmosis to music.

The grunts became yelps, screams. The screen's flicker was swifter, electrons straining to keep up. Roberta beckoned. I advanced hopefully. Food? Moi? My belly rumbled. I tightened it to shut it up, passing the message that I was doing my best, before this selfish bitch swallowed the universe. There was flan left, a dozen of those little cakes, some buttered scones, a quarter of that chocolate sponge, a gâteau, and a swirly thing in a tall glass. Three plates stood empty, with two glasses showing they'd had their swirl tastefully excised. I was astonished at the pace.

Then she reached out, fumbled to find my belt one-handed. Her eyes were still on the screen. She tutted once, some finer point of technique I suppose. I started to undo the belt myself. She resumed her nosh. Her alacrity was mind-bending. Not even in Woody's or China's had I seen food disappear this fast. Yet she ingested – and even that's not elegant enough – gently, seemingly hardly bothering to eat at all. It was dining with balletic grace, the consumption Olympics. The nosh drew me, then her mouth, then she was pulling it and tutting at my shirt.

The screen showed several couples were watching from rocks. Excited by the coupling, they all started to make love. I groaned, because the gâteau went the way of all flesh with a movement that can only be called a caress. It was beautiful to watch the selfish bitch eat while I starved to frigging death. Then the covers parted slowly to admit me.

There wasn't a single crumb in the bed! Unbelievable. I've only to have a slice of stale bread and my cottage is a mass of crumbs. I keep finding them days later. Roberta had cleared the best part of a vicarage nosh and her fingers, the sheets, pillows were untainted. She reached over me, which accidentally brought us closer, as the television started up multiple passionate cries.

Roberta finally slowed her repast, turning her attention to me with, at first, casual acceptance rather than interest. Then she waved, and the TV went silent. Another stretch, and the lights dimmed, images of fountains and flowers appearing on the ceiling. No music.

By then I was in no fit state to notice anything environmental, and found myself a new Roberta, one who exclaimed and exhorted. It was not elegant. She became savage, demanding savagery back. It was wonderful, even though I still didn't know quite what was going on. It was ecstasy, because it always is. I abandoned all other appetites in appeasement of the greatest human hunger. She was superb, everything a goddess could be. Craving, worse almost than me, working with passionate abandon. I knew I would love her for ever and ever, do anything she wanted. I was hers, no two ways.

Eventually we slept. Dunno why, but women are always cold, going to bed. Even in summer with a head start, they're perishing. They amaze me. How can you make your feet so freezing? Even their bottoms are frigid, and a bottom's at the very centre of things, so to speak. Icy knees too, and I've never met a hot breast yet. In the morning, they're warm.

And they snore, in two episodes. One's half an hour after they drop off, lasts forty minutes. The other's at four-thirty, and is a long chuntering hour. Dunno why that, either. I woke in darkness. The magic romantic pictures on the ceiling had faded. I reached, found a plate of something, scoffed the lot. I found another – small sweet things – and engulfed those, put the plate carefully under the bed. Got a third and gnawed through a thick marzipan cake. Then a flan. Crumbs, I thought. These sheets would need washing, because I'm hopeless. Chocolate spreads so.

About then, she gave a stretchy kind of groan, and her hand called me to attention, as it were.

She was twenty times better than any of the television. Within seconds I was babbling undying devotion, and I meant every endearment most sincerely. Lily's remarks came to me between passions, though, and that odd complicity of Ashley. I was now on their strength, a devoted member.

Came dawn, I found the side table cleared of grub and the gorgeous Mrs Battishall gone. It was shoving back the curtains to see the countryside staring in – I quickly drew them again – that I realized that, if Ashley had ordered Tryer dead, then Roberta must have agreed. Or worse, for she was boss.

Bath, shave, dress, then tell Ashley how antiques could raise money the right – i.e. wrong – way. Outside, I heard activity on the gravel. I peered out. To see Stubbs's brilliant portrait of Whistlejack being carried in. Real? I couldn't feel the vibes at this distance.

Things were too fast. I had to see what Mahleen's whispered promise ('Antiques! Money!') meant, see what Ashley was playing at, find Chemise. And gather the five Fenstone survivors at Dame Millicent's. And see Big John Sheehan, ask could the rules be moulded. Then to Farouk, maybe, ask him if he needed help to burgle Dame Millicent's. Then Corinth, maybe, if I could reach her. Sabrina would have to wait. And so would my own non-existent antiques dealing.

For once I felt an ache. Roberta was marvellous. I wondered if that was all, a see-what-I-can-give carrot ahead of the donkey (me). I scented food, hurried into the day.

21

Swanning downstairs, I felt as if I could run over houses. Lovejoy of the three-league boots. Ashley, shaking with rage (did the blighter ever do anything else? He was getting tiresome), was glaring in the hall. But he was the one who'd sent me up to, er, rest in his wife's bedroom. I could smell breakfast.

'In,' he ordered me.

The drawing room was aired, light, clean. Roberta was leaning against a flower stand. She looked radiant in a camelia house dress, fortuitously in a shaft of early morning sun. I advanced smiling, but halted stricken when she raised her eyes. Hate? So soon again again?

'Lovejoy,' she said, voice shaking. 'How *dare* you!'

Eh? *She'd* raped *me*, for God's sake. I'd had no chance of escape. 'Eh?' I was confused. 'Ashley sent me to, er, you. And you encouraged . . .' But you mustn't tell how sex is, or women get mad. Euphemism rules. 'Didn't you, er . . . ?' Beg me to beat you, use crude foul language? 'Invite me?' I ended lamely.

'That is not in question, Lovejoy! What is, is that you are a thief!' She was shaking like an aspen leaf, though I wouldn't know an aspen from a daffodil. Some poem I'd learnt as a little lad, willows whiten, aspens quiver, little breezes. Quite good, for a poem. Whoever wrote it should stick at it, maybe make a living.

'Eh? I've nicked nothing, missus.' What was worrying me was that I'd seen the great equestrian painting carried in, yet so far I'd felt not a single chime. Forgery, rearing its head in Dragonsdale? I brightened a bit. All was not lost.

'Ashley? Summon Lily.'

We waited. Lily entered, stood mute with clasped hands. They could search me until the cows came home. I had the perfect witness in Roberta herself, right? She'd all but reamed me. I'd been naked, in no position to hide anything stolen or otherwise.

'Lily,' Ashley demanded. 'Did you remove the food from the blue suite bedside table?'

'No, Mr Battishall. The plates were empty when I cleared away, sir.'

'Thank you, Lily. You may go.'

Food? *Food?* I listened. They *were* off their frigging heads.

Click, the door went. Silence. Roberta's furious stare was now triumphant. I felt lasered. She was livid because I'd eaten the remnants of her gargantuan midnight nosh in this madhouse?

'There, Lovejoy! How dare you *steal my sustenance!*'

Ashley wore a smug gotcha smile. The sanest person in this bedlam was drunken old Jim Andrews, and he was completely off his trolley.

'I'm sorry, Mr Battishall.' When in doubt, grovel. When in serious trouble in a loony bin, grovel more. 'I hadn't eaten all day. I was afraid it would go bad . . .' Et lying cetera. Christ, Roberta had scoffed enough to fuel a regiment. Why couldn't I have a mouthful while she slept? Yet I'd been shagging Ashley's wife. He'd planned it all, condoned everything. I wanted to go back to my cold empty cottage.

'Lovejoy, you will be severely punished for your treachery.'

Roberta swayed. Ashley leapt forward with a cry of alarm, helped her to the couch. She reclined. He dashed for cushions.

'I will see to him, dearest.' Ashley rounded on me, flushed with all this excitement. 'Lovejoy. You will begin work immediately *without breakfast*. Inspect the Stubbs painting, estimate its value. Advise on its sale – *now*.'

'Why?'

Roberta wailed faintly. Ashley looked fit to marmalize me, but I stood my ground. The aroma of breakfast out there was driving me insane. I was starving. I honestly felt I'd earned a crust, a cup of tea. Time I escaped from this frigging zoo, get to the Misses Dewhurst Lorelei nosh house . . .

Ashley controlled himself with visible effort. 'The Cause,' he said, reverence in his voice. He almost knelt.

'Money,' I said. 'Is that what you mean?'

'But the Cause must be financed –'

'You're going about it wrong, Ashley.' I walked to the portrait of Charlie, moved the burning votive light further from the precious

Garthwaite silk. 'You'll get nabbed. So will Roberta and all your daft supporters. Serve you right, too. I hate a poor-quality fraud.'

Mrs Battishall's shriek was so loud it fetched Lily. She retreated under my bent eye.

'Ashley, dear,' whimpered Roberta, 'shall I be arrested?'

'Within seconds, love,' I answered for him. 'This place will be sold to pay lawyers,' I added. 'I'm only being kind.'

'Don't trick us, Lovejoy.' Ashley still wanted an execution.

'No, Ashley,' I said, sorrow coming over me. 'That Stubbs painting is a fake. If it was genuine, a mighty antique that size, I'd be staggering, being sick on your sham Isfahan carpets. As it is, I could eat a horse.' Mental apology to Whistlejack.

'Don't be stupid, Lovejoy. You are simply trying to deceive us.' He was calm in ignorance. I was frantic with fear in my cold certainty. 'We paid highly to Mr Sheehan for the privilege of having our own true retainers take the Stubbs. It can't have gone wrong.'

'Don't say I didn't warn you, Ashley.'

Ashley was so sure, every second of his life just so. Must be an unnerving feeling. 'You've already decided on some betrayal scheme. Try it, and you will have to take the consequences.'

'No betrayal intended,' I lied, with a sad countenance. 'But I'm a peaceful bloke. All I want is my usual life. It may not seem much, but I live down among the bread men. It's what I'm for. Okay, I'll raise money for your daft cause. You have the whip hand. I give you my word. Honest.' That took some saying. I was quite sincere, as far as I could tell.

'In return?'

'You just leave me alone afterwards.'

'But?' he said, warily.

The best rule when lying, I find, is to make a condition. I pursed my lips, eyed Roberta's languid form.

'Two conditions,' I said, chancing my arm. 'You let me arrange your scam, the money-raiser. I alone do it. It will bring in a huge sum. I keep penny in the pound. I promise you'll control every groat, start to finish.'

'Very well. You will market our Stubbs?' *Their*? See what I mean? Possession is fluid stuff, ownership a myth.

'Promise. Hand on my heart.' He ahemed. He knew what was coming.

'You mentioned two conditions, Lovejoy.' Frosty.

'Yes.' I looked at Roberta, went a bit red, not acting. Did I say euphemism rules? I stammer when embarrassed. 'The main condition.' I gave a rueful grimace by way of apology. 'I want to . . . visit Mrs Battishall. Er, spend the night in conversation with the lady, just once more.' 'Conversation' meant physical intimate contact. Translate the word in old novels by sexual intercourse, heavy petting at least, and you're there.

'Dearest?' Unbelievably, Ashley passed the query on.

She sighed. I noticed she had a mark on her neck, and looked away in guilt. Somebody had been gnawing Mrs Battishall in orgiastic detumescence. And her milk-white cheek was also darkened by a faint bruise, skilfully cosmeticked not to show. I had some too. Only she knew where.

'Very well, dear.'

For the Cause, I thought, but did not say. She'd been more explicit than any soft-porn video.

'We agree, Lovejoy,' Ashley explained, as if they'd been talking in some secret lingo. Maybe they were. Chinese women in the olden days developed a special language, for writing to one another so nobody outside their circles could follow. I wonder how often the code was cracked. Linear B had been, and Samuel Pepys's mirror diaries. Maybe Ashley's docile agreement and the plump luscious lady's compliance meant what had happened to Tryer?

Breakfast now? But they were looking at me in expectation. Up to me. I needed a scam that gave me freedom.

'Here's what we do. We arrange an exhibition of frauds, forgeries, fakes, Sexton Blakes, shams, lookalikes, duds. Scores, hundreds, maybe.' They were quite blank. I paced a bit, energy starting to flow. 'We claim nothing, just tell the whole wide world that we've got a variety of forgeries. It's quite legal. The British Museum's done it, earned itself a fortune. Every antique . . .' I panned with outspread palms, being a huge advertising sign '. . . is a genuine forgery! At knock-down prices! Get your Monet, your Rembrandt, here! For peanuts!'

Still silent.

'Don't you see?' I cried, marching to and fro in enthusiasm. 'We'll pull the selling ploy when we open!'

'The selling ploy?'

'Yes!' I beamed, laughing with excitement now I was motoring. 'We announce that somebody has actually found a genuine X, Y, or Z in the sale, bought a *real* Rembrandt, Tompion clock, Turner, whatever, for a song! Don't you see? They'll come in droves! We'll seed the exhibition with a dead obvious *genuine* antique, ask a colossal admission fee!'

'Where do we get a genuine antique, Lovejoy? We only have the Stubbs painting, and daren't advertise *that*.'

'You two aren't in the real world. We sell *any* antique to some delighted customer for a bob, aye. And tell the world, do a broadcast on the evening news. But it doesn't mean we *have* one, see?'

'No,' Roberta said. She looked good enough to eat.

My patience gave. 'See it as we go. Leave it to me.'

'But we'll get very little from selling mere forgeries, Lovejoy,' she said doubtfully. 'They are surely cheap?' She was recovering before my very eyes, her vapid ailment vanishing under the glow of imagined money.

I sighed. 'Just trust me. Fraud's as routine as drawing breath.'

'But fraud is so rare, Lovejoy.'

Well, I had to laugh. 'Look, love.' I cast about for an example. 'Ashley here uses a mobile phone, right? Well, that instrument is the fastest-growing source of fraud in the universe. Let's say you're travelling abroad, Bangkok, Malaysia, London, wherever. You want to phone home. But it will cost the earth, right? So you simply go downtown to the public phone banks *anywhere on earth* and stand there, looking willing. Within five minutes, honest to God, somebody'll whisper, Want to phone home, cheap? They charge one US dollar per illegal minute. They're called phreakers.' I spelled it for them. 'You can even *buy* a number for three hundred US dollars.'

'Buy a number?' Ashley scoffed, but he was worried.

'Then you simply dial, on any phone. The phone company bills the registered owner of the mobile's number. You merrily phone Alaska, Australia, Jamaica. Talk all you want. Why not? Somebody else gets the bill.'

'Lovejoy,' Roberta said in a small voice. 'You are a crook.'

'I didn't nick the Stubb painting, love,' I shot back.

'Ashley . . .' Her lip trembled. She began to wilt.

'Sorry, love. It just came out.' I made to advance, possibly to offer consolation.

'Two problems, Lovejoy.' Ashley interposed himself. 'This show of forgeries. Will it be open to the public? We don't know how to organize such an exhibition, or make money from it.'

'It's all the antiques trade does, most of the time.'

He blinked, but his wife took it in her totter.

'I take it these fakes would have to be excellent quality,' she said. 'Where will we get them?'

'Love,' I said, with more sincerity than I'd felt for days, 'the world'll provide any number, any time.'

'Honestly?' Her eyes went round.

'Well, no,' I admitted. 'Not honestly. But,' I added with fervour, 'genuine forgeries by the train load. Deal?'

'Deal,' she said, modestly lowering her eyes.

She didn't need to refer to Ashley. I was pleased. As long as she stayed boss, I stood a chance of getting out of this unscathed, not least by Big John Sheehan, Ashley's minions, and Maudie Laud and her constables.

'Done, then.' We smiled at each other. Ashley didn't smile at all. I decided to push my luck. 'Is it breakfast?'

A reasonable nosh in the communal dining room, with Jim Andrews asking me what my platoon thought of the new batch of Lee-Enfields, and a gaggle of elderly twitchers itching to trudge the fields looking for birds. And Lily, sardonic with her non-smile when I wanted more toast. Then to the cellars, to see the great Stubbs painting.

Nick and goons rigged lights up to show it off.

Well, it was bonny, right enough. The huge horse, colours just right, rearing on that genuinely ancient canvas. And the frame had the right marks. I looked, sniffed, felt. All in all, a really good forgery. Well done, Juliana, I thought. Gold star for effort. But fake. Not a chime of the genuine about it. She'd probably used the phenol-formaldehyde trick – this chemical ages an oil painting in a fortnight. Everybody does it. The oil plus pigment swiftly hurries to the necessary hardness. I was disappointed, though. She'd used French *vernis craqueleur*, varnish that imparts a realistic fine surface cracking. Only takes thirty minutes, and a new oil painting looks 150 years old, but it's still the mark of an amateur forger. Very sad she'd used Lefranc's ageing varnish. If she'd used frame gilder's *assiette à dorer*, extra-fine grade, she wouldn't have needed to. It's upsetting to come across a good job spoilt. Ha' p'orth of tar, and all that.

'Thanks, Nick,' I said heartily to the swine. 'You pulled in a winner there, Ashley. I'm sorry I doubted it. You nicked it without a mark. Brilliant!'

And left them. One day, I thought, one day. I got permission to leave for an hour, to go to the library.

22

The racecourse at Tey sounds better than it is, a few fields, fluttering flags, white railings, and those box things nags start from. Big John was pacing the ground and taking camera photographs. That is to say, he was sipping whisky from a lead crystal tumbler while villeins of various intellectual calibres did the work. He was on a chair beside his Rolls.

'Morning, Lovejoy,' he said. 'Interested in racing?'

Any Big John question is fraught. I dithered. 'Well, I can see the attraction, John.' I'd rather watch fog.

'Fascinating sport,' he said. 'See that young stallion?'

'Eh? Oh, aye.' It looked clumsy, born stupid, chewing grass. Three blokes and a bird attended it. Post-operative humans in major surgery don't get that degree of care.

'Forelegs straight and close together, sign of a born stayer. Ever seen anything so beautiful, Lovejoy?'

'I was just thinking that, John. Lovely.'

'Do you know,' he said, swivelling to look up, 'the eejit owner wouldn't sell? Not even for a fair price?'

Nearby goons growled. I growled along, chameleon colouring.

'But he did eventually?' I surmised, shrewd.

'He did that, Lovejoy.' His hoods relaxed with satisfaction. 'Why is everybody too thick to see the obvious? Every single time there's trouble I've to send my lads to sort it. Not good enough, Lovejoy.'

'It certainly isn't, John,' I said fervently.

'It's a decline in moral standards, Lovejoy.' He heaved a sigh. 'There's a stallion right now at stud. Cost chickenfeed, £5,000. But its progeny are raking it in. So where's the money?' He eyed me, delight in his eyes. 'In the stud fees, that's where! Hundred grand a stand. Take your mare along, get her serviced by the stallion. Shags ten mares a week when he's on the go. Can you imagine?'

I could, and moaned softly to prove it. 'Will this one?'

'Earn that? When he's won his races, Lovejoy. I'm arranging the details now. I don't care about the odds.' A magnanimous forgiving tone.

That was good of him. Time to strike. 'Oh, John. Glad I bumped into you.' Like, I normally go strolling across the barren wastes to admire dank foliage every day. 'Er, you remember my wanting a hold on the Whistlejack snitch?'

'I do, Lovejoy.' He shouted to one of the photographers, 'Further over!' He tutted, sipped. 'I don't want the competition put off their stride until three furlongs out. Not sensible.'

'No, I can see that.' I let him settle. 'Well, Mr Battishall in Dragonsdale said you let him have a go.'

'Mmmmh? Mmmmh. He paid up, Lovejoy. You didn't.'

I drew breath. The stallion was walking about, the serfs holding its string. I drew breath: *But you promised me, John.*

'That's right, John,' I said. 'Sorry.'

'Not at all, Lovejoy. Anything I can do?' I'd helped him once over his two sons. His tone was condign, really friendly. I was glad things were working out for him.

'No, ta, John. Good luck with the horse.'

'Luck's no good. Lovejoy,' he said. 'Odds too long.'

'How true, John.' Well, I'd tried. I said so long to his nerks and walked to the Morris. Ask a silly question.

Passing the railway station, I bought a newspaper. It announced that, during the night, a famous painting had been filched from an old priory down the coast. Believed to be a Stubbs horse portrait once exhibited in the Tate Gallery. A spokesman announced . . .

Which would have worried me, except with Big John around I suspected that I would be a superfluous worrier. He'd given the Battishalls permission. Their look out from now on, right?

The priest was strolling his churchyard among the graves, reading his breviary. He wore a biretta, a black cassock, almost other-worldly. The wind had risen, whipped the weeds and trees about. An elderly lady rose from tending a grave, slowly rocked her way through the lych gate.

He moved with even paces, pausing, turned, walked back. The

church door was ajar. More confident than other churches these days, or fewer treasures? I sat on a tombstone, legs dangling. Nature reigned in Fenstone churchyard. A squirrel raced, froze, raced. Birds knocked about. You could see several cottages. The chimney of one smoked, and it was a cold fresh-wind day. Whoever wrote *The Deserted Village* must have been local.

'Morning, Reverend.'

'Lovejoy. Time for a cup of tea?'

Coffee time, but I was gasping. 'Ta. Not interrupting?'

'Of course not. My Latin's appalling. Comparatives I found simplicity itself. The conditionals are a dreadful risk.'

'I often think that.'

'*Oratio obliqua* caused me nightmares.' He chuckled softly as we fell in step. 'Prohibitions expressed by the subjunctive! Subjunctive tenses following the rules for sequence! Ugh!'

'One long hassle,' I agreed. You have to sympathize. Yet who would care a jot, if he forgot his Latin, chucked his breviary and gambled his church on Big John's nag? The Almighty, maybe? Fair enough. But Juliana would gallop off rejoicing into the sunset with him.

We went into the vestry and he brewed up. He saw me look about for heat. 'Sorry, Lovejoy. We can't afford warmth. Miss Juliana is marvellous, and Mr Geake finds funds from somewhere for Sundays so the heaters can go on for mass. That's it, I'm afraid.'

I smiled to show I was basking in his church's tropical clime. 'I came to ask your help, Reverend.'

'Anything I can do, Lovejoy?'

Big John had asked that. I didn't want Sheehan to know I associated with papists. 'Fenstone has a problem.'

'Problem?' He carried the tea over. I perched on the modern – hence sham – vestry chest. 'Miss Juliana said you can solve any problem there is.'

We chuckled. I subsided first. He was as wary as I was. Maybe priests have to be like that? My village has had a succession of guitar-playing roisterers in sandals and ponchos. Maybe God makes episcopalians folksy, harmonicas part of the gear.

'Dame Millicent, Jox, Juliana, you and Geake. The famous five, Reverend. The remaining villagers are batting out time or leaving. Isn't that Fenstone?'

'Probably, Lovejoy.' He came and sat on the other end of the chest. 'We have hardly been blessed with good fortune. I suppose Dame Millicent told you about her guanacos? Then Jox's schemes. They all failed. He had a wonderful little restaurant near the tavern.'

'I've never seen the pub open.'

'Didn't you hear? The licence has been withdrawn.'

Pubs are licensed to sell alcohol, by magistrates. Anybody can speak out, for or against.

'Tough luck.'

'They're an old couple, the Creeds. They'll go to their daughter's at Walton-on-the-Naze, a small hotel there.'

One more? 'It's odd that everything in Fenstone seems to atrophy, necrose, implode.'

His expression was one of absolute rue. 'Isn't it the way of life nowadays, Lovejoy? The old order changeth, giving place to new. Young folks want cities, towns, action.' I'd said all that. He snarled the word, in humour. I laughed politely, wondering what had suddenly gone wrong since I'd sat down with the hot mug. Something had. 'We've lost our post office – uneconomical. Once a village's population fritters, it reaches stalling speed.'

'The same in the old Wild West, I suppose.'

'And Australia's gold mining towns when the gold ran out.'

Except I couldn't see there'd been much gold, or any local equivalent, in Fenstone. 'I proposed a meeting to Dame Millicent, Reverend.'

'Of who?'

'Those struggling to resuscitate Fenstone.' I explained. 'Look, Reverend. Once a place dwindles to sod all – sorry, to nil – then the county council withdraws all services, road maintenance, buses. You're down to one detour bus twice a week. Then it'll be water supplies, the mobile library. Soon, it'll be gas, electricity . . .'

'If you insist, Lovejoy. But I really do think it hopeless. We need young vigorous families, get the school back, interests, a growing community. Meetings? We've had them all.'

His tea was horrible. 'How did you come, Reverend?'

'What?' He was startled.

Wasn't it mere chitchat? 'Where from, what parish?'

'Oh. The Midlands.' He smiled. 'Busy, every problem you wished for. Or not!'

That made me chuckle. Oh, such a chuckle. 'How long were you there?' I helped his silence. 'Do they move you around, parish to parish? I mean, from the Black Country's thousands to a fading handful.'

'The bishop sends you an "obedience". Sort of posting order. You may have a discussion, to give you an opportunity to refuse if you don't want to come.'

I smiled. 'Fenstone might have got some irrascible old coot!'

He too smiled. 'Maybe they have – in disguise!'

'Ta for tea.' I got up. 'What happened to the painting?' It had gone from the vestry wall. 'It was quite good.'

He wasn't interested. 'Miss Juliana is trying to sell it.'

'Send it across. I might be able to get a bit on it.'

'Thank you. I appreciate your interest, Lovejoy.'

He saw me out, closed the church door. I drove to see Priscilla Dewhurst and her twindle, start the forgery scam.

Antiques at last – well, fakes. Time I returned to decency.

'Listen, Maurice.' Maurice was in the Arcade looking after Tramway's stall. The Arcade is merely a narrow covered way between two walls that look off a bomb site. Dingy alcoves are equipped as 'shops' – a plank, stool, maybe a lamp. Each dealer rents a space, hoping to con some tourists out of honest coin for sundry grot. Our antiques trade.

'What?' He takes orders for non-existent animals that, sadly, always die on mysterious voyages. They are dumped overboard, 'to escape Customs and Excise', he tells the animal collectors who, of course, lose their deposits. These non-animal animals are rare species of parrots, tortoises, things like marmosets. His real love, though, is antiques.

'Money, Maurice, money.'

Antique dealers dropped from the rafters at the word.

'Whose, Lovejoy?' He's been bald ever since his wife flitted with an Aldgate silver merchant, leaving Maurice three children. I babysat for them until his sister joined forces. 'Commission?'

'Aye, oh Hairless Shrewd One. Except you pay me the commission, see? Unless your antiques are cheap. Then I'll buy.'

'An exhibition, Lovejoy?' He started to smile.

'Free to all comers. Pass the word, eh?'

'But who'll select?' He plucked my sleeve. 'You?'

'That's it. How're the kiddies?'

'Fine, ta. What's to stop us shelling in forgeries?'

'Nothing.' With my best smile. 'It's called *Forgery and Fame*.'

'What's it mean?' he called. Other dealers started asking, scribbling notes, the Stock Exchange on Friday. 'And when?'

'God knows,' I called back. 'And any day now.'

'Put me down for six, Lovejoy.' Big Frank from Suffolk loomed up, dusking the daylight.

'Nothing illegal Frank, eh?' I've been his best man at some of his bigamous weddings. He's our silver dealer, knows nothing else, and precious little about that.

He fell about laughing, almost shredding two alcoves.

'Can I do your advertising, Lovejoy?' from Cyril. Keyveen glowered in the background. Maybe it was a new sulk.

'Advertising?' I wished I had my sunglasses. He glittered in a gold lamé sheath frock coat adorned with winking Christmas tree lights. Mahleen would be dead jealous. 'How will you advertise?'

'Oh, simply *stand* there, darling.' He admired his purple fingernails while everybody laughed. 'Who'd need more?'

'Don't be stup . . .' I coughed as Keyveen stepped menacingly close. 'Of course, Cyril!' I said quickly. 'Who else would I ask? That's why I came. Tonietta said you were this way.'

Actually, I would need adverts. I couldn't just rely on word of mouth, saying that a forgeries exhibition was at a hotel belonging to our town's chief magistrate, a loon.

'Me, too.' Addie Allardyce slipped me a note. 'You *promised*, Lovejoy.' Said with meaning. I pondered, remembered nothing.

'Addie. Tell Tonietta she's got three slots, okay?'

'Me six, Lovejoy.' Harry Bateman from his ailing shop in Bury St Edmunds, trying to keep up with his errant wife. Antiques plays havoc with marriage. I've heard.

'Right. Send Tinker a note.' I've a soft spot for Harry.

'Forgeries okay, Lovejoy?' Inge boomed, popping lightbulbs.

I winced. Subtlety isn't Inge's strong point, though she'd say it was, and I would instantly agree.

'You got any? I warn you. I need hundreds, love.'

'Eight or nine, Lovejoy. Furniture mostly, some jewellery.'

'Okay. I'll be auditioning.' Groans all round at that.

'Coins and medals, Lovejoy?' Igglesworth, a devout train spotter who prayed, actually hands and knees, for engines with meaningful numbers to hurtle through our station.

'One slot, Iggie.'

They started coming thick and fast then as word spread. Edwardian bureaux, precious stones with dubious settings, some Tom Keating Old Masters done a few years since, Victorian furniture, household ware, treen, armour, weapons (weapon collectors are among the most knowledgeable maniacs in captivity), costume (biggest crowd-puller, but the least gelt after books), toys, stamps (never to be touched at any price), hats, locks and clocks, farm implements, tools, rare pens, Victorian kitchen utensils . . .

'Tinker!' I cried at last, as the stinking old devil shuffled up in his shabby old greatcoat. 'Where the hell've you been? Been trying to find you.' Not true, but what can you say to a friend you'd forgotten?

'In nick,' he gravelled out. The crowd edged back, giving his stink room. 'They did me for that flute you sold some Tewkesbury bird.'

'Eh? Oh. Tough, Tinker. How'd you get out?'

'No fingerprints, were there? Silly cow'd cleaned it.'

We'd passed off a silver-plated flute, modern Japanese steel, as genuine silver. Somebody – no name, no pack drill, as they say – had imposed a silversmith's mark, illegally. I breathed relief, but Tinker never bears grudges.

'Tinker. Take deposits, slots in an exhibition. I'm calling an audition for forgeries, fakes, naffs. Anywhere, soon.'

'How much a slot, Lovejoy? And where do I see you?'

'Misses Dewhurst's Lorelei Tearooms.' I whispered, 'Charge plenty. Sting everybody. Hold IOUs one day only.'

'Right, Lovejoy. Here. She wants to see you.'

'Who?' Even Beth's Bilstons were in a queue.

'Chemise.'

A sudden silence. People shuffled uncomfortably, nudging each other, remembering Tryer in the Castle Meadow.

'At your cottage. I said she could go in, Lovejoy.'

'Oh, great,' I said heartily. 'Good. I'll, er, call in.' I took him aside for a chat, learned quickly about Farouk.

As I eeled out a girl tagged me, saying nothing. Puzzled, I went a hundred yards among the shoppers, then stopped. I couldn't for the life of me remember ever having seen her before. Blonde, not more than sixteen.

'Miss. Why are you walking with me?'

'I've come to help your antiques, Lovejoy,' she explained as I stood there like a lemon.

'Who are you?'

'I'm Holly. Can I move in?'

That stopped even me. I thought I'd heard everything. 'You'll have me shot. No. Anyway, I've got an apprentice.'

'She's away,' Holly said. 'I'm younger and prettier.'

'Well, I'm staying somewhere else,' I said weakly.

'You'll hate it, Lovejoy. That hotel's a cesspit.'

Muttering, I hurried on. Coming to something when you're ravished in the High Street by tiddlers. I made the Lorelei Tearooms at rush hour. There were five people in, my tourist friends. All I could think was, what do I tell Chemise?

23

The Lorelei Sweetmeat Delicatessen and Tearooms offered varied welcomes.

'Lovejoy! Honnnnnee!' from golden dazzler Mahleen.

'Good morning, Lovejoy, dear.' Philadora and Priscilla.

'Hey, ma man,' from Jerry. 'Thet husband find you?'

Amid jocularity, Miss Priscilla tutted at Jerry's words.

'Take no notice, Lovejoy. It was only some tiresome auctioneer gentleman. Mr Mulrose, he said. Some message about a salver.' Everything ornamental, old, and/or silver is a salver to the Dewhurst sisters. Gulp, though, because Mulrose is the surname of Sabrina, she of the rapacious Sundays.

'She attractive as Roberta, Lovejoy?' needled Hilda.

That's the trouble with reputations. They never fade. Like the 4th Earl of Sandwich, inventor of the sandwich. He invariably gets the world's worst press except for Judas, just as unfairly. Reference books tell of Sandwich's useless Admiralty career, his repulsive neanderthal appearance, his occult sex orgies, depravity, gambling, disloyalty. Every schoolkid knows these. But Sandwich's 'casual mistress', Martha, shot dead by a killer's flintlock outside Covent Garden, was Sandwich's true love for over sixteen dedicated years. He was parsimonious because he started off – and finished up – poor, after a lifetime's dedicated patriotic work. True, he was ugly, but so am I. And he did join in the sex orgies at Medmenham – wouldn't we, if we could have?

Against the tide of supposition there's always a neglected truth. Like, the endless recycling of General Gordon's Mysterious Death at Khartoum. Wasn't it truthfully depicted in Charlton Heston's film . . . ? Well, no. Mursal Hamuda, one of the 'Mad' Mahdi's black riflemen, did it quite unintentionally in the turmoil. But the image of G.W. Joy's painting of the brave soldier facing the delirious enemy is so admirable it's what we want to believe. Like a woman's reputation (pick any). Once people slag her off, she's marked for life.

'Mrs Battishall?' These Yanks were red hot at gossip.

'We saw the glint in her eye, Lovejoy!' Nadette said.

'Want to see an exhibition of antique forgeries?' I asked, eyeing the Misses Dewhurst hurrying food.

'Sure do! Where? When?'

'Chance of finding any genuine antiques there, Lovejoy?'

'Sure is.' I caught myself. Americanisms infect. 'Possibly.'

'Will you divvy for us, Lovejoy?' from Wilmore. I'd begun to like Wilmore. Now I wasn't quite so sure.

'Certainly. And I promise to give you first offer.' I smiled, an honest smile being the essential accomplishment for falsehood. These were my friends. 'It's at Dragonsdale, the Battishalls' hotel.'

'Will we be here?' They started discussing dates, could Gwena alter a visit here, a trip there.

Priscilla brought over some toast, eleventh hour.

'Here you are, Lovejoy, to start you off. Lovejoy,' she announced proudly, 'is our partner. Libra, with a tilt –'

'Please, love,' I begged through a mouthful. 'Not that zodiac thing. I can't stand –'

'Oh, don't, Lovejoy!' from a soulful Mahleen. 'We had a fascinating session with Roberta. No amount of criticism can alter the Obverse Zodiac . . .'

Switching off, I heard their non-reason reasons for believing dross. They seemed really into the Barmy Battishalls' society. Hereabouts, we have the Richard the Third Society, which argues that Dick was innocent, never murdered the Princes in the Tower. I let them get on with their stories. (Mahleen: 'I *saw instantly* the bitch was a Scorpio, and you know *them*, right?') My mind drifted. I would have to make sure that Corinth and Montgomery Mainwaring, Litterbin, Bog Frew the thespian, all knew about the exhibition. And Farouk. One thing nagged: if Dame Millicent was so poor, why didn't she simply sell the one genuine antique Farouk wanted, that valuable piece of Danish furniture?

'Your friend, Lovejoy?' Vernon indicated a girl pressing her face at the window.

'Oh, that's Holly,' I said airily. 'Runs errands for me.'

Miss Philadora rushed to shoo Holly away.

'Natal chart readings prove Roberta right,' they were saying when I came to, Nadette leading. 'Until the Misses Dewhurst discovered the O.Z. there was no explaining deviances.'

The twins demurred with simpering modesty. 'Yes,' Priscilla said. 'That's why Mrs Roberta must —'

'Miss Priscilla!' three of them interrupted together. 'How about more coffee here?'

'Must what?' I asked.

'Nothing.' Vernon did the denial, laughing. 'Hey, Wilmore. That new golf course by that river . . .'

We joked into a sideslip then, so Vernon's deflection had worked. I wondered exactly what we were raising money for. The Old Pretender Society, or something else? I noshed at increasing speed, Mahleen admiring my talent. I was suddenly in a hurry. Things were linking. Ashley did Tryer, sure. But who *were* these tourists? Nice people all, but too many coincidences carouselling round them.

'Look,' I said, managing to lever my foot from under some lady's sole beneath the table. 'Sorry, but I've to leave. Don't leave town until you've seen the exhibition, okay? You might find a bargain!'

Ha-ha cheeriness to that. They promised to catch me up.

'You never breakfast, Lovejoy!' Hilda complained. 'Supper tonight?'

'A deal. I'll be at my cottage. Give me a ring if you're at a loose end.' The phone was cut off months back. I didn't tell them I was going to see the bishop. 'Philadora, can I use the back door?'

Holly might be lurking.

Usually I'm relaxed when I've to see one dealer, forger, collector. It's because I like them. Look at Noah, an old furniture faker of renown. He is the most patient bloke on earth. Looks a gorilla, soul of an angel. Never cheats anybody, just turns out three pieces of furniture a year. Sixty-five if he's a day, selects the right wood, glues, makes his own hand-filed screws. He's the only bloke in East Anglia who can make a genuine forgery of a tripod tea table, except me.

His workshop is a thing of beauty, set behind a flower garden on the bypass. It's so small you have to open the door and stand outside talking in. He's called Noah because he makes little wooden animals for a children's hospital.

'Wotch, Noah. Going okay?'

'Nearly done, Lovejoy.' He looks like Pinocchio's dad, bushy eyebrows, specs, leather apron. I wonder sometimes if he's caricaturing himself as somebody else. Like, say, Juliana's Reverend Father Jay?

'Lovely, Noah! You've dished the top!'

He smiled shyly. The mahogany tripod table was beautiful. 'I hate forgers who dish on a lathe, Lovejoy.' He sighed. 'No patience these days, fakers. God knows how they'd manage without an electric drill!'

We tut-tutted along. I looked at his table. 'Sell anywhere, this, Noah.' He was still caressing the surface eccentrically so it wouldn't show the dishing absolutely central, only lopsided. 'Can I measure?' Nearly three-quarters of an inch difference. 'Lovely, Noah.'

'It's only common sense, Lovejoy. Wood shrinks over two centuries. It does it across its graining. You'd think they'd learn.'

'Isn't that a bit much? Nearer a half-inch, eh?'

We discussed degrees of shrinkage. I'd have made it a smaller difference, something less obvious, but Noah is a craftsman so I gave in. All his wood was evenly darkened – old wood has shadows in exposed areas – except for the bit where the table top exactly covered the underneath block. The four little supporting columns, forming the 'birdcage' on which the table turned, stuck out proud from the upper block. Really authentic, for wood shrinks in its diameter, not its height. There were small bruises matching these protrusions underneath.

'Want it sold, in an exhibition of forgeries?'

He pursed his lips. No forger likes to be called a forger in public, only on the quiet. 'From me, Lovejoy?'

The old man's pride. 'Invent a name. Anybody worth a light will know it's your work.' Class tells.

We agreed, Tinker to collect. I was lucky. His piece would lend the exhibition style. I didn't want my fakes to be polythene and acrylic garbage, home-cast resins from kits. There are tons on every street barrow. I wanted style.

In an hour I'd seen Spoons, he of the silver forgeries. I'd discovered him via his fake silver spoons, hallmarked 1630-ish, but with the bowls too wide, too regular at the margin, and the finial's saint always too ornate. He works in a garage mending motors, all axles and revving engines. He has a little furnace at the rear, to work silver in his break. He offered two fine silver candlesticks, but was narked when I rejected his Spanish mariner's silver astrolabe. He was astonished that navigational instruments had to be robust, and silver isn't.

'But I've wasted months on the frigging thing, Lovejoy!'

'Melt it down, Spoons.' They go on making the same mistake. Like Noah says, no patience. 'And no more mug-to-tankard switches, Spoons,' I added, heartless. 'The country's awash with the damned things.' I left the garage to Spoons's cries and his workmates jeers.

Why silver forgers can't leave good antiques alone is beyond me. Every bloke with a gas burner thinks it clever to buy a genuine antique silver mug and convert ('switch up', in the trade) it into a jug, imposing fake hallmarks. Can't understand them.

From there I 'teamed in', as dealers call assembling a mob for an up-coming scam, a good mob of forgers. For quickness, I restricted the journey to a seven-mile radius. But even so I got Speckie to promise me three long caser ('grandfather') clocks. He still had girlfriend problems, but I trust his work because he's red hot, making the seat boards as authentic as possible. The seat board's often the giveaway in long case clocks, because it's inside the clock anyway, and who bothers to remove the hood and examine where the clock movement sits? Speckie always uses age-compatible wood, and he's never yet turned out a clock with a seat board having *two* sets of aligning holes instead of one, the correct number. You can't trust forgers these days. It's come to something when you have to confess that.

Linnetta teamed in. I like her even if we've never yet made smiles because she never shouts at me. She specializes in porcelain, does lovely marks that she practices weeks on end before ever firing a piece. She reads a lot. She's the only ceramics forger we've got careful enough to exclude chrome when faking tin-glaze wares of the eighteenth century – chromes tint the ceramics a faint pink, and chrome wasn't around until the nineteenth century.

Jewellery is always a riot. Amberoid pressed from spare bits to copy genuine whole-piece amber is easy, but has interfaces that you can see miles away. (Tip: just shine a reflected light through). Phoney diamonds are commonest – though with conductivity meters it costs only fifty pence to test one diamond, however big. Pearls are good, but their availability nowadays is such that you might as well not fake them with fishscales at all, just buy the real thing if you can. (But don't, please, dip the silken thread into nail varnish to make them easier to string; solvents dissolve them.) Brown diamonds are in vogue, so I wanted to keep off them. Solid carbon dioxide turns diamonds brown, having got trapped in the crystal in the earth's mantle some 245 miles deep down.

To be careful, I teamed in four jewel forgers, plus Phoebe the Slave (her choice of nickname, not mine). She works in the Arcade, midweek. Her husband's a politician in London and she wants to experience lowlifes. I approve. What she gets up to behind the tarpaulin at the far end near Woody's caff with Mincer – beer bellied, tattoos enough to print him as a comic – is her own business.

Paintings were more difficult. I'd need Juliana (Miss) and maybe find time to look out some more of those I'd got in my workshop. For watercolours I got Doothie, making him promise to buy the right paper off Cloana in Aldeburgh. She makes the stuff, deckles it in her little cottage, any age of watermarks you want. The trouble is, she has a waiting list as long as your arm for her authentic replica genuine fake papers. I was in too much of a hurry to argue, simply told Doothie (he's in his eighties, but the patience bit, remember?) to make sure he included a couple of Buckingham Palace watercolours, with Marble Arch in the entrance to its forecourt like it used to be. 'Copy the view from the park, Doothie,' I said, 'like Joseph Nash's paintings of 1846 that the Queen has, okay? Sell like hot cakes.'

'Anything else, Lovejoy?' he asked, all eager.

'Far East scenics, early Indian Empire. Days of the Raj stuff. But none of Chinnery's Hong Kong or Chinese drawings from Sotheby's bloody catalogue. Everybody's doing them. I'll take two dozen watercolours. You can buy in, but subbing's your own deal.'

I like the old geezer.

'Can I take orders if they sell, Lovejoy?' he asked.

Honest to God. Do you believe some people? He gets on my wick.

He honestly said that, like he was making Bakewell puddings at a
fête. I didn't answer, just left, shaking my head. Eighty-four, still daft
as a brush. In that happy state of endogenous depression, I drove
home. Help everybody, what do you get?

24

The cottage looked different. I realized I'd not been home for donkey's years. I stood at the gate – there's no gate; it rotted. The gravel drive was free of weeds. The grass had been cut, a swathe beside the path for neatness. Smoke ascended. And, miraculously, washing on a washing line. I didn't know I had one. A white thing blocked the window. I pondered for a while, then my megabrain went *curtain*! Hesitant, I made the porch.

'Hello?' I thought, this has to be a bird. Tinker only clears me out of booze, leaves a sour smell.

'Hello?' A bird, from indoors. 'Is that you, Lovejoy?'

'It had better be.' I wondered if it was safe.

She came to check. 'Wipe your feet.'

'Sorry.' I wiped, entered, stood like a lemon. She was in my kitchen alcove. 'What's that funny smell?'

'Bread.' She was up to her elbows in dough. Very satisfying, to watch a bird who knows what she's about, kneading dough. When you think of the technology in bread, you realize the bedrock of expertise that domesticity rests on. All woman-made, lovely to see, and Chemise so natural. How did they know? Are they secretly shown how by each other? The cottage hadn't ponged new bread for many a moon. I don't bake much.

'Nice, love.'

'Perhaps, when I find a single utensil, Lovejoy.'

That earned a sigh. No sooner in the door than they start ballocking me. Utensils? Our grandmas slogged with hardly a thing, did wonders. I remembered about Tryer.

'Mind your manners, or I'll evict you. The rent's dear.'

'Where have you been, Lovejoy? I've been waiting weeks.'

'You can't have,' I pointed out. 'Because . . .' Because Tryer was only recently murdered? 'I called, not long back.' Lame, lame.

'Your shirt's aired, Lovejoy. Clean trousers, jacket. Secondhand, the charity shop, but . . .' She shrugged, didn't look. She meant my attire was shambolic.

'Right.' I went brisk, this was all routine. 'Tea on?'

'Will be soon. Get yourself washed and changed.'

See what I mean? Even mild agreement is a declaration of war. But I forgave her. She was only keeping going. I went magnanimous, Big John Sheehan with cowardice.

'Hot water, is there?' I asked to keep her on her toes.

She swivelled. '*Lovejoy!*' exasperated.

'And the bath?' I'd been using it for washing some old parchment, giving it a really good soak before illuminating a fourteenth-century devotional Book of Hours. A 'carpet' page, just like the gorgeous Lindisfarne Gospels, makes a fortune.

'Cleaned, ready.' She added, needling, 'Soap waiting.'

Stung, I went to the bathroom, giving her my silent reproach, and undressed. Then a cold draught struck.

'Hey!' I said, grabbing a towel. 'Keep out, you cow!'

'Found anything I haven't seen, Lovejoy?' She grabbed my discarded clothes, slammed the door to. 'If you have,' she called, irate, 'I'll call Doc Lancaster. He'll be fascinated.'

'Ha – de – ha – ha.' The water was really hot. I like it tepid, so cooled it and climbed in.

She came again, washing my back, shoving me to reach my nape.

'Hope you've washed that frigging dough off your elbows?'

'Keep still,' she said. 'Worse than a child. You stink like a chemist's. You been with some tart?'

Roberta was no tart. I told Chemise to mind her own business. She lathered me like I was a Crufts dog, rinsed me until I gleamed. Then she hauled me out, dried me though I tried to grab the towel, her saying all the while not to be silly and stand still. Then I heard her laying the table by slamming plates down. I was out of breath. Being helped takes a compelling degree of fitness.

She was at the table when I emerged. She wore a pinafore (where from?), chin on her interlaced fingers. Bread, marmalade, jam, tea, scones, clotted cream, a cake, fruit salad and runny cream. Roberta would love it. She had the stool, left me the chair. Well, my house, right? She poured, cut bread, sat watching. I'm used to this, because

173

women don't eat much, would rather watch you nosh for some reason. You'd think they'd get narked, seeing their grub engulfed in a trice, but no. Like I've always said, women are hooked on appetites. God knows what they get out of it. Roberta Battishall was a mutant.

'Strawberry.' Chemise pointed. Strawberry jam. Yesterday's date. She was telling me it was newly made.

'Mmmh.'

'Cherry.' In silence. Another index digit, read that label.

'Mmmh.' Meaning I'd get round to it in a sec.

But here's a strange thing, I thought as I noshed. Look at Roberta and Chemise. I know it's wrong to make comparisons, because no two women are alike. But there was lovely Roberta, throttling anorexia by gulping calories by the truckload while making out she was your shy retiring wallflower, going beserk with rage when I nicked a crumb. And here was Chemise, plain as that, yet somehow relishing watching somebody clear her table.

Not only that, Roberta was rich. Chemise was poor, had nothing, not even her crummy Sex Museum, and her bloke, Tryer . . . well, wasn't.

Chemise waited until I slowed. She stoked the table, more provender. I resumed, slowed, eventually chugged to a stop. She'd given me the unchipped mug. Roberta would have had me hanged for selfishness.

We sat. A dunnock entered, for crumbs. Another came.

'The place will be heaving with them,' I wanted to say, but couldn't, so just sat there until the birds were gone.

A squirrel flirted with the door, skipped off. My hedgehog came, trundled slowly round, then left. It was all happening. We were an hour before somebody spoke.

'Lovejoy,' she said, 'what are we going to do?'

Ten minutes more for me to answer, and then it wasn't much of one. 'We rest for a while, love.' Be decisive – postpone. 'Move. I'll do the divan.'

It unfolds. Usually it's left out for ease, because you've only to get it out again if you've been so careless as to fold it away. I was surprised how nice it looked, sheets all clean, pillowcases white. I drew her to it, pushed her on, and flopped down beside her just as we were. She fell asleep immediately. I'd known she would. I bet she hadn't slept for days, not since Tryer . . . well, whatever.

Oddly, I too slept. She shoved into me so we lay like two commas. And that, said Alice, was that.

'Christ, you're a randy bugger,' said a girl's voice. 'Why shag an ugly cow like her, Lovejoy?'

A blurred Holly stood nearby, looking down at Chemise. I'd thought I was dreaming, but wasn't. Chemise was sitting up, staring.

'I'm Holly, Lovejoy's new assistant. I'm in, you're out.'

'No, love. You're not, you're not, and she's not. Hop it.'

'Who's the cow?' said this educational product.

'She *is* my helper, love. I can't manage two.'

Holly tittered. 'My dad says you manage several.'

Who? 'Who?' I said aloud, shrugged to show Chemise I disclaimed Holly, dad and all. 'Sod off.'

'You need me, Lovejoy. I know the chief magistrate.'

'I'm legal clean, love. Close the door as you leave.'

She left, but I had the notion she'd not go far. Chemise was looking after her, craning, the divan tilting.

'Lovejoy. What are we going to do?'

That's women. *They've* a problem, it's what are *we* going to do. It means you've to solve it while they criticize and tell you, down among the muck and bullets, where you're going wrong. But you have a problem, then it's tough luck.

'We?' Time to marry some ends, make many problems become fewer. 'We, love, are going to the bishop.'

'Bishop? As in church?'

'No. As in cathedral.'

The phone rang. I stared, amazed. It hadn't done that for yonks. I picked it up gingerly. 'Oh. Hello, Sabrina.'

'Have you somebody else there?' she rasped out.

'No, no. Just the, er, post girl delivering a parcel.'

'Leslie suspects, darling. Forget this Sunday.'

'Right.' I pulled a face at Chemise, apologies.

'I'll come early tomorrow, bring the biggin.' Hell. I'd forgotten her manky auction. 'Maybe we'll have a little playtime before I have to run, mmmh?'

'Mmmh,' I said, trying to be casual for Chemise's sake and rapacious for Sabrina's.

'Eight o'clock, brute lover?'

'Right. Eight.' I returned to Chemise. 'Look, love. How about you stay here, while we're rigging this exhibition?' I added sternly, 'I start early, okay?'

'Very well, Lovejoy. Will the bishop solve anything?'

'Who knows until we ask?' I hauled her up. 'Have you any dosh?'

'A little, Lovejoy.'

'Hang on.' I rang, got Doothie. He was narked, having his nap. 'Get faking, not kipping, you geriatric. What if you popped off? Where would that leave me? Is Juggernaut out?'

'Yes. Left prison last week. But going straight, Lovejoy.'

Juggernaut's Doothie's money-hugging engraver. 'I need a forged Bank of England One Pound banknote. Number Two was sold in Spinks of London, price of a freehold house. Description in their catalogue.'

'Number . . . Two.' The old idiot was taking it down.

I ask you. 'No, Doothie,' I said, broken. 'Tell Juggernaut to make me Number One, see? Number Two is famous.'

'Very well, Lovejoy.'

The receiver down, I told Chemise that we'd let somebody make a fantastic find at the exhibition. We'd advertise it as a forgery.

'Somebody can buy it for a song, and we'll say it's genuine!'

'Why, Lovejoy?'

'Stop asking daft questions. Find the bishop's address, love.'

Honestly, people rile me. They have all sorts of brilliant skills, but can't be bothered to see the obvious.

The bishop offered us tea, despaired when we refused.

'What newspaper are you?' he asked, a benevolent, twinkling old gent. He really did wear gaiters. I was thrilled, for Trollope's sake more than mine, standards hanging on.

'We're from the north, m'lord.' I was proud of my clean shirt. '*Bolton Journal Express . . .*'

'Ah, yes. The vicar in a dying village?'

'Yes, m'lord. We always run a weekly article on underpopulated areas. I gather there are several villages face extinction?'

'Indeed.' He heaved a mighty sigh. 'We have several. Quite the most affected is Fenstone. The few loyal people there have tried everything to rejuvenate the community, all to fail.'

'How do you choose a priest for a village like that, m'lord? Do you have a cadre of specially trained priests?'

'Heavens no!' he said. 'I wish we had. Incidentally, not all clergy wish to be called vicar, parson, rector even. The present Fenstone incumbent is known as Father. Leanings towards the papacy, perhaps? Ecumenical times, though, what?'

'Oh aye, m'lord. Isn't that reverend, er, Anglo-Catholic . . . ?'

'Hardly. Very sparse in this area. No, Jay Smith only arrived three years ago. Midlands seminary, religious teacher in a school, returned to parish work.'

'Which seminary?'

'Oh, closed.' The bishop winced. 'Sign of the times.'

'So sad.' I brightened. 'How d'you dispose of all your antique seminary furniture?'

Pain struck my leg. Chemise, the cow, had kicked me.

'I'm sure you do your very best,' she said sweetly.

'Thank you, my dear. Do write a few lines about our seminaries. So little financial support these days . . .'

That was it. Chemise and me had a principal ally in Father Jay who seemed at least as much a fraud as I was.

We drove to Dragonsdale. I got a private audience, and told Roberta and Ashley – in mid-tea, still not losing weight – that I'd have to stay at my cottage for a couple of nights, because at vast expense I was arranging their exhibition.

She looked miffed at my having to stay away, probably narked she'd have only Ashley to criticize. I went all meaningful, hinted that I already missed being away from her, even though I'd been chastised for natural hunger. I got in six good *double entendres*. She managed to look sad for a millisec, between tartlets. I'd left Chemise at the crossroads. I wasn't having Nick adding two and two.

'Can I have a private word, Roberta?' I asked, businesslike.

'Very well. Ashley, stay within earshot.'

Ashley went. I looked down at Roberta. The pace of her noshing slowly lessened. She sipped a dainty cup, replaced it in its saucer.

I yanked her to her feet hard. I sucked her mouth until she went limp for air hunger, let her go.

She dragged air in, reeled back onto the couch in a faint. First time it had ever been legitimate, I'll bet.

'Now, love.' I was cool. 'Remember that I want you more than Ashley ever will. If anybody is to help your Cause, it's me and only me.'

'Lovejoy,' she gasped faintly, 'you're jealous!'

'Don't, darling. I'll be back. I'm in the phone book.'

And swept out. All lies, of course. I wasn't in the book any more, been cut off too often. But if she and Ashley had done Tryer, then eventually she'd be out of it. I'd see to that. (No, I really mean that the police would see to that, not me.)

Chemise was waiting. Father Jay wasn't celibate for religion. He could wed Juliana any time. Theology for once was no obstacle, an all-time first for that shifty science. I told her what I'd said to Roberta. Now, Chemise knew as much as I did.

'What now, Lovejoy? The exhibition?'

'Ah, no, love. Tonight we burgle a friend.'

'You burgle a friend's house?' (Note that singular, *me*? It's their minds.)

'No, love.' I was patient. '*We*. You plus me. And I meant *for* a friend. Farouk, I think's his name.'

'Lovejoy,' she said after a bit. 'I'm scared.'

'First-night nerves, love. Once you've done your first robbery, you'll be cool as ice.'

'On my own?' she said, near panic.

See? Give them a job, they go to pieces. 'No,' I lied. 'With me beside you. One thing: can you lift a table on your own?'

25

There's a funny thing about countryside: word spreads like a moorland fire. Barkers, those hard drinkers who ferret out antiques, are the real gossip experts. They can leach news and clues from a passing breeze. Once, I was given a lift home from a village cricket match, twenty miles off. An old bloke at his cottage door, top of my lane, saw us pass and raised his thumb. I asked the bird to stop, walked back. 'How did you know we'd won, Bert?' I asked, curious. He'd no phone. I was the first back. 'Weather, son,' he said. See? Pigeon post, maybe, osmosis. Who knows?

We went in to prepare for the robbery. There on my mat were three scribbled notes from dealers, plus another two carefully pinned inside the door. Chemise was angry, thought it terrible, said we ought to fit a lock. (We, note.)

I told her, 'Dealers steal other dealers' notes, so their own antiques'll get chosen, see? It's life.'

She still bridled. The phone rang. Its machine had clocked six messages. God, I'd started something. It was Margaret Dainty, lame, vaguely married, attractive middle age, deplorably honest, wanting in.

'George Chinnery, Lovejoy, for some exhibition? Decent forgeries?'

'Well, ye-e-e-es, love.' I owe Margaret. She's been a haven for me after many a stormy voyage, but I really *hate* owing friends who expect me to keep my promises. It's unfair to tax friendship, the rotten swine.

'I'm so sorry, Lovejoy. But I do need help.' She's the only real aristocrat we have. I listened in anguish, wanting to say no. 'What we've been to each other shouldn't come into it. But my brother's boy, Jaddo, *is* talented. He does Chinnery like a dream. Please, Lovejoy?'

'How many?' I'd already warned Doothie there was a surfeit.

'Several, Lovejoy.' Hope lit her voice.

George Chinnery was a scoundrel, son of an amateur painter in these parts. Young George was a pal of the immortal Turner at the Royal Academy. He spent half a century swanning around the brand new colony of Hong Kong, Portugese Macao, Canton in China's Kwantung. Opium figured large in his life. He was always being chased by loyal women, including his missus. He actually *complained*, can you believe, when his wife loyally followed him up the Pearl River. He said how good it was that China stopped wives 'from coming and bothering' him there. The poor lass, forbidden to land on sacred Chinese soil and join the jocular swine, died of smallpox. Quel boor, right? But he painted, drew, sketched like a dream. Scenes now revered as the truest depictions of the culture clash, ours and Chinese, in Hong Kong, Macao, Kwantung. Even economists scramble for Chinnery's work these days.

'Okay, send Jaddo's stuff, but listen.' I cut through her thanks. 'Tell him pencil, ink, and pen, okay? And scenes of junks, river scenes, Flower Boats – Canton prostitute vessels – signed Lam Qua, Yin Qua, Fal Qua. If he can't hack the signatures, tell him I'll do mangled ones. Don't let him frig about ruining good forgeries.'

'Thank you, darling. I'll never forget this.'

'Tell your nephew that Chinnery mixed his own colours, and loved thin – meaning *thin* – canvas. Ellery in Lowestoft weaves it for Geckle in Limehouse. Tell Jaddo Chinnery was crazy for vermilion. Make sure he puts Chinese white flecks in.'

Chemise read the notes. 'They're all offering forgeries, Lovejoy. French furniture, porcelain, pewter, silver, jewellery, English Regency. Motor cars, even.'

'So?' I was impatient, nervous. She had to go a-burgling.

'Is there so much fake antiquery about?'

'It's everywhere, love. And it's beautiful, done right.'

She stared, uncomprehending. 'How can it be, if it's dud?'

'Because a forgery can be a sacrament.' I sat beside her. 'It's holy from the work within. Just as a woman becomes beautiful.'

Bitterness crept in as she repeated the words, 'Look at me, Lovejoy. Am I beautiful?' Her smile was tearful. 'Nobody else thinks so. Except Tryer. I know he was a poor specimen. But he liked me,

Lovejoy. And he took me in, an act of forgiveness. And you know *what* he forgave?' She sniffed, tears dripping. I felt horrible, not knowing what to do.

'Don't, love,' I said, uncomfortable.

'Tryer forgave me my ugliness, Lovejoy.'

'Shut up, you silly cow.' It was out before I could think. 'You're stupid. Every woman has her own beauty. It's those bloody magazines. Beanpole girls with coat hanger shoulders and no breasts. Fashion is a con, love. You can't have fashions in women. Women are what we must have. Her beauty is that she understands it's how things are.'

'Oh, Lovejoy.' She wept on. 'He wasn't fit, Tryer. Drank too much, never exercised. You knew him. He wasn't as tall as . . . who hit him. I saw him go down, glow reflected from the water.'

She cried it out, except that's only what people say. You can't cry grief out. It bides its time, comes stealing back.

'Who was it, love?'

'I don't know, Lovejoy. I glimpsed him against the water.'

We stayed like that a bit. I got her moving by saying the burglary she was going to do would help to pin the swine. I didn't know if it would, of course, but a grieving woman has to be fetched back into life.

We drove to Farouk.

'It's like this, Farouk,' I explained. He owned a restaurant. I wouldn't go into the kitchen, that place of raw carnage, so we sat where people came to order takeaways. 'Mr Sheehan allows three weeks. Your time's running out.'

'There is time yet, Lovejoy.'

He scribbled an order while I paused. A couple wanted a load of grub that made my mouth water. They waited watching TV, some quiz show with inanities.

'I can do it tonight for virtually nothing.'

'Why would you go to such trouble? We are not friends.'

'Because I am organising –'

'Your exhibition?' He smiled. 'I see! You want my Danish piece out of the way beforehand?'

'Correct! Don't want it turning up among my exhibits.' People often give you the reasons they want to hear.

'A sound argument.' He paused. 'Are you expensive?'

'Not very. Pay me on commission,' I said, munificent. 'Three per cent, to get the trade.'

We laughed at that, the second oldest commercial falsehood. I rejoined Chemise.

'It's on, love,' I said. 'You know what to do?'

'No, Lovejoy. I'm worried sick.'

'Honest to God!' I exploded, starting the motor and pulling away from Farouk's nosh house. 'I'm not asking you to do much. Get it into your stupid noddle, you daft bat! I chat the old dear up. You creep upstairs and steal the furniture. Christ Almighty, it's simple!' She said nothing. I yelled at her for always interrupting. 'Your trouble is I've been too good to you, you whinging moron. I do *all* the donkey work . . .'

It wasn't much as supportive psychotherapy goes, but being worried sick was my job, not hers. She'd got the easy bit. Do it properly like I'd told her and I'd be in the clear. The risk to her was minimal. I seethed in anger. Women complain when they've nothing to complain about.

There was a faint light in the house when I drove up and parked, banging the driver's door, swaggering like auditioning for *The Student Prince*. Dame Millicent came to answer, pleasure lighting her features. I felt a cad, nearly.

'Lovejoy! You want more farm produce?'

'Ha-ha. No, I came about the meeting.' I shoved the mat with my foot so the door couldn't close.

She plodded in, sat with a groan. Her dog was asleep, thank God. I carefully closed the room door. The logs had run out, the fire dying. She had three candles about the room.

'They gutter, Lovejoy, most irritating.'

'I use candles too, sometimes. You make them?'

'Mr Geake. He renders the fat down. It's country free.'

'Good old countryside.' She was sipping whisky. I shook my head. 'Dame Millicent. What are the chances of buying Juliana's forgeries?'

'Juliana is in the unfortunate state of love,' she said, acerbic. 'I'm never sure these days about that condition. Is there now such a thing?'

'I'm lodging a bird who was loved,' I said. 'I think.'

'You see, Lovejoy? We do not know. Possessiveness comes into love. Quite terrifying, how far one will go to keep the loved one.'

'If I wheedle her into thinking it's for her priest?' I put my feet on the dog. It snored, contented.

'Like a shot. But she's a bright lady. She must be convinced. Which raises questions, Lovejoy.'

'Does it?' Her old eyes glinted in the candlelight.

'Indeed. Like why are you really here. Why, when you are the only divvy, the best forger, do you need Juliana Witherspoon? You haven't fallen for the girl yourself?'

'No,' I lied. This lie's easy, because I fall for them all. 'I'm forced to help the Battishalls. They're pals with a Mr Sheehan.' Best I could do on the spur of the moment. She nodded. 'I'm scared of Sheehan.'

'This exhibition. I heard,' she said to my face, 'from Mr Geake. He stopped by an hour ago.'

And well off the premises by now, I prayed. 'It's an exhibition of fakes, forgeries. Replicas, even copies. Have you got anything I could put in?' Clever Lovejoy.

'In this place? I sold everything long ago, Lovejoy.'

'Well, if your country set pals want rid of silver, anything antique, let me know.'

'I promise, Lovejoy.'

The conversation went from there to reminiscences about her old affairs, splendid parties, her old lover who'd been admired throughout the land . . . Only one candle was burning by the time I rose to say my good nights. I'd given Chemise enough time to steal the roof, let alone a dressing table.

She was waiting where I'd told her, a furlong down the road. We couldn't get the dressing table in the car, so I had to tie the damned thing on the roof with rope.

'Lovejoy!' She was elated, but disliking what she felt. 'I'm a *burglar*!'

'Hmmm?' I was disturbed, because she'd nicked a fake. It didn't feel like any antique I'd ever sussed. 'Well done, lass.'

'You don't understand, Lovejoy.' She turned to me, solemn. 'I mean I am a *burglar*. I actually robbed a lady's *house*.'

'You've done what everybody else on earth's done, does, is doing. Now for Christ's sake stop boasting.'

'I'm not boasting, Lovejoy. I never knew I *could*.'

This always brings out the sighs in me. 'Everybody does it, love. You're just a late starter. It's like love – me and Dame Millicent were talking about it. When you make love, you actually *make* the stuff. Including nuns and priests. Celibate, perhaps, but read some saints. Nicking things is the rule, not the exception. Forgery's the mortar, antiques the bricks. Together, they are the building, love.'

'Why are you not excited? I thought you'd be ecstatic!'

'It's a forgery, love. Was it the only piece there?'

'Exactly as you described, Lovejoy.' She started to cry, sniffing again. I'd suffered this evening. 'There was no other furniture, just a bed and a wardrobe.'

'You did well, love,' I said. 'I'm proud of you.'

'It's strange, Lovejoy. You know what is most disturbing?'

Well, I did, but you have to say you don't. 'No?' I said in a puzzled kind of fashion.

'It's that I'm thrilled. It was exhilarating. And worse.' She looked defiant. 'I'm delighted you're pleased.'

'It's how it always is, at first, Chemise,' I said. She took my hand, laid it on her knee, and me driving between hedgerows struggling to see the way.

'Look, love,' I said, nervous. 'About you staying. Sooner or later I'll have to go back to the Battishalls'.'

She took some time replying, then said, 'It's all right now, Lovejoy. If it's all right with you?'

Well, I thought piously, I deserved recompense for the fake Danish piece. I'd done her a favour by letting her take the risk instead of me. And taught her a new trade. Fair's fair.

Except breathing heavily and all but ravishing her there and then in the motor as I turned in to my garden, I couldn't. The way was blocked by a large limousine. The lights were on in my cottage, and music split the night. Laughter, corks popped, glasses tinkled. And there was a delicious aroma. The Americans had come, bearing gifts. Party time at Lovejoy Antiques, Inc.

'Who *are* they, Lovejoy?' Chemise was outraged, almost as if she'd actually wanted to –

'American friends.' I recognized faces moving past the window. 'Love. Suss out Father Jay, okay?'

We advanced, musing. Once, chance; twice, coincidence. But a third time it's a Genseric the Most Terrible.

26

'Hey, Lovejoy!'

The whoops began before we were in the door. Mahleen was first, followed by a shoal. Gwena, slightly less frolicsome, was pouring the vino and dishing cakes. I brightened, joined in.

'What's the occasion?' I asked. 'Is anybody welcome?'

Hoots of laughter, during which people eyed Chemise. The women marked her down and wrote her off. They can handle ugliness in others, quite like it in fact. Beauty means she's a bitch, in the old comedienne's music-hall joke. Chemise was no threat.

'So you're our ally, Lovejoy!' cried Hilda, though she was immediately silenced by a few, 'Hey, gal!' cries. 'Sorr-ee!' she screamed, unrepentant. It was only supermarket sixpence-off wine, but who knows the difference? Like most things in life, labels rule. I wish I'd remembered that.

Mahleen came to chat. Chemise seemed to be enjoying herself.

'We're proud of you, Lovejoy. You've jumped the gun!'

'I have?' I was pleased, done something right.

'But I want a quiet meeting, like I said.'

'Oh. Sorry, love. I got tied up.'

'We'll be unstoppable,' she whispered. A compact player was belting out decibels, the cottage reeling. People jigged.

'We will?'

'Money, glorious *money*, Lovejoy!' She waved to Wilmore, who clasped his hands, boxer style. He seemed high and on the kilter. Vernon sang 'Over the sea to Skye,' pretending to row in a choppy sea. Never such merriment at Lovejoy Antiques, Inc. So why'd I gone cold?

'Listen up, everybody!' Vernon shouted, pinging his glass. Glass? I had no glasses. I often wished I had.

'A toast!' They began shrieking for silence.

'We have here tonight,' Vernon boomed, wobbling on the divan, 'the most superb divvy! Who has – ' he held out his hands to suppress applause ' – who has joined our Group!'

Roars, joy unbounded. Mahleen sank me in her golden cleavage. I'd never seen so much cosmetics unbottled. She was beautiful. I'd not eaten for a decade. I was squiffy on wine.

'This, friends,' Vernon went on in the sudden hush, 'betokens certain success! And Lovejoy, sensing our Cause's inherent truth, has already started the assault!'

I had? I was grinning like an ape. Gwena looked ratty, as ever since she realized I was seeing her sister. Says my intentions are dishonourable, mistrustful cow. Me, dishonourable? It's prejudice.

'And so we've decided to stay, friends, and help! We,' he shouted, trying to keep upright, 'are his troops! Lovejoy our general!'

'Shhh!' Mahleen was signalling to Wilmore, shut Vernon up.

Vernon toasted in tears, 'The King over the water!'

He waved his glass, the ladies shrieking at being drenched in white wine. I groaned, less jovial. This lot were part of Roberta's daft mob. And converts, the very worst sort of believers, poisonously fervid. Jacobites used to make this toast, passing their wine glass over the fingerbowl in allusion to the absent Bonnie Prince Charlie. Hopelessly romantic, fable founded on fraud founded on fable. Most political rebellions flourish, strange to relate, by their opponents' help. The Yanks mostly financed Russia's revolutionaries. And Charlemagne's spiritual affection for Aix-la-Chapelle, that drew him to live there, wasn't anything of the sort; he simply liked the hot springs, swam there in the afternoon.

'We're *what*?' I asked, Vernon blowing an imaginary trumpet.

'Going out on campaign, General! The action starts here!'

By then we were all three sheets to the wind. I'd never been so drunk that fast. We piled out and into the big limo. Chemise caught me, stuffed yet more messages in my pocket and stood looking after me. I tried shouting I'd be back, have the kettle on, but we were off, piled in a heap like an undergraduate rag day stunt. I was under Mahleen, or possibly on, I don't know. During the journey she found my ear, whispered to meet in room one six. I fell about laughing.

The George lounge was quiet, only the vestibule bar still honky-tonking away. A few couples were having one last drink before making smiles. Maudie Laud was there. She just smiled, waved me over.

'Wotcher, Maud, sorry but I'm with friends.'

'Not be long, ladies,' she told them politely. 'I'll let you have him after a chat.'

Warily I sat opposite. The lounge always has a log fire. It's comfortable, a sense of timelessness.

'They really are tourists, Maud.' I didn't want her leaping to conclusions about innocents, including me.

She watched them go. 'Which, Lovejoy?' she asked.

That narked me. 'Get your questions over with. Or shall I answer straight off, save time?' She nodded, smiling. I would have liked her in another incarnation. In this she was putrid. 'Yes, I'm organizing an exhibition of forgeries, fakes, duds, shams. Yes, all will be clearly labelled as such. Yes, wholly legal. Yes, the funds will be declared for income tax purposes. Yes, it will be a charitable fund-raising. Yes, it will be open to all, including your Plod. No date yet, but soon.'

'Thank you, Lovejoy.' She made to rise, paused, her smile hard. 'Why are you doing it?'

'An obligation to a lady. No money, just obligation.'

'The ailing Roberta?'

She knew a hell of a lot of intimacies. 'I never betray a lady's confidence.'

'I'll accept that for now. She rose and stretched, knowing the effect on me. 'Let me guess, Lovejoy.' She thought, finger under her chin. 'That gold lady, room sixteen?' And when I said nothing, 'You will tell me if anything. . . ?'

'Police helmets, truncheons, insignia from the peelers? I'd pay a good price, love, for police museum items.'

'You would?' She looked dangerous, but I was past caring, wine being what it is.

'You know the curator, young Freeth.' I can give as good as I get. 'Nice wife. Kids in school now, eh?'

'What're you saying, Lovejoy?'

'I said I pay a good price, Maud. Just remember.'

She stared for what seemed a week, but it can't have been more than half that. She was mad I knew about her and Freeth.

'I see. You know who did Tryer,' she said softly, her brow clearing. 'You wouldn't be so determined otherwise.'

Am I that transparent? I hated the bitch. 'Haven't a clue, Maud. I'll buy old police dictating machines, prison plans, percussion weapons, anything like that. Oh, ta for keeping Tinker in your nick just when I needed him.'

'Rol Freeth and I are simply colleagues, Lovejoy.' She would have killed me, but for witnesses. 'If you –'

My sigh almost blew the rafters down. 'Look, Maud. I can't stand here gossiping about you having a bit on the side.' I paused, one up for once. 'What room number was it?'

Having this last word felt like a mouth full of sawdust. I watched her go. The rest of the lounge was taking no notice, talking softly, passion impending. It made me disconsolate. I could be with Chemise. Or, with Roberta, for my payment in kind. I trudged up the stairs, looking for room one six. I couldn't endure more jollity, probably getting even more sloshed now, on the hard stuff.

'Wotcher.' I knocked and entered, stood surprised. Nobody, semi-darkness. I couldn't see a damned thing. 'Sorry, er . . .'

'Lovejoy! I thought you'd never come.'

'Mahleen?' And alone? I fumbled for the light.

'No lights. Follow my heat, hon.'

So I did. I felt a brief sorrow for Chemise, alone in my cottage, but a woman makes you forget everything, including others.

If love's been made right, something comes over a man. It might seem like sleep to passing observers. Younger women assume you've just nodded off in dismissive indolence. Older women, though, know better. They realize the man has briefly left terra firma, for some astral plane where others cannot follow. From the inside, it feels terrible, a kind of premonition of death, and can't be mucked about with. The wrongest thing a woman can do, biggest mistake, is light a fag, say, 'Hey, *let's talk*!' This ghastly fudge remark is not only the commonest flaw in TV scripts, but the most ruinous utterance in human love. Any woman whose blokes keep walking out on her should learn this: after making love, a few moments of quiet will weld him to you for ever and ever, because he'll love you for nowt thereafter. You might be the most useless woman in the history of beds, but *he won't know this* if you treat him to that slight mercy.

God knows why birds can't see this, but only one woman in a hundred cottons on. And she's *always* an older woman. Hence, they're best, for ever. That's all I know about relationships, but it's worth any number of agony aunts and marriage guidance agencies. When I hear women exclaiming about some plain woman, nothing going for her, who seems miraculously able to keep a handsome devil against all odds, I smile and think: aha, a wise lass.

Now, Mahleen lay still, awake, quiet. I was in the pit of despond, expecting to be dragged back to the world by a jokey outburst of calamitous babble. Then I came to minutes later to find her watching me along the pillow. She brushed my hair with her hand, said nothing.

'Thanks, love,' I said, my voice thick.

'Thank you.' She mouthed it.

We lay in silence. She put her hand on me, closed her smiling eyes, and we dozed. For once blissfully detached from worry, in this merciful woman's arms I floated free and dreamt.

Sometimes, the opposite of what is right, is right, if you follow. Guess what's the eeriest, most scary noise in the whole wide world. It's not an approaching warplane, the flap of Dracula's wings. Nor a gun's safety being snicked to fire. None of the above.

It's the sound of a bamboo, growing.

Just saying that seems daft, like the old Buddist problem of what's the sound of one hand clapping. Unless you too have slept near it. It's not like a tree, say, that simply shushes in the breeze. It's weird. You're settling down to kip – perimeter lads vigilant, say, scanners for once not on the blink, quiet night, right? Not where there's bamboo.

Because the bloody stuff whimpers, shrieks, squeaks, groans. It's a herd being strangled, torture chambers magicked from Torquemada's Dominicans. Bamboo even on a good night sounds like a horde weeping, howling. Worse, it's not continuous. Between the chunks of noise come serious blocks of quiet that have you gripping your rifle with clammy hands, preparing for the worst . . .

What I said was wrong. It isn't the sound of bamboo growing. It's the terrible silences in between.

We woke together. She was holding me, saying, 'Shhhh, it's all right, honey,' like I was some scared kid, the silly cow. I shoved her away, sat shivering on the edge, feet dangling.

'Sorry,' I said brightly. 'Thought I heard somebody.'

'It's two thirty, Lovejoy. Leave it for morning.'

'You're right, Beth.' I slid back under the bedclothes.

'Nearly,' she said without rancour. 'Mahleen.'

See? A little kindness goes a long way with a man, but a little mercy goes all the way. We made such gentle love, unbelievable. Came dawn, I asked her what she wanted me for. Being a pushover comes with being male.

'Support us, Lovejoy. That's what I want.'

'Okay,' I said. I didn't even ask who's us, doing what. Like she'd said pass the marmalade.

'It's my country's one hope,' she said, tears coming. 'It's legal, necessary, and morally right.'

'What is? Nobody has that much money, to –'

'To put America right? No.' Her voice was soft now, her eyes shining with love. 'But what if the Pretender's descendant was found! We *know* that Bonnie Prince Charlie was offered the constitutional monarchy of the US of A!' She placed a silencing finger on my mouth. 'Think, Lovejoy!'

'You actually want to –?'

'No, honey. We aren't that dumb.' She was sad about being so wise. 'But, think. Such a focus would be a unifying burst of patriotism! It wouldn't even matter who, would it?'

I was itching to know who. 'You've found him, her? The Pretender, to the American throne?'

'Yes. We know.' She was in raptures. 'We only need enough to set up a court in exile – anywhere. Sure, our president, the government, will pooh-pooh it, ignore the idea. But people won't be *able* to! We need something to weld us into one nation again – even our half-million illegals pouring in annually. It'd be the magic of kingship! The one, true, annealing power!'

Well, I could see the problem. But kings are not always glorious. Splendid Louis XIV, 'Louis Le Grand', bankrupted France. There are plenty of examples. Even monarchs bucking for sainthood, like Isabella of Castile, were repressive sadistic oppressors, whatever the files being prepared for her beatification claim. And what *is* kingship? A young Pole in 1755 nipped niftily up the servants' stairs in St Petersburg's Winter Palace, and became King of Poland by being good in bed; the future Empress Catherine knew how good. And our own cricketing hero C. B. Fry was offered the throne of Albania nigh a century ago – he wisely declined; it was snapped up by King Zog.

Mind you, mere politicians haven't the same appeal. Disraeli fathered illegitimates – a daughter Kate on a French bird, a son Ralph by the flashy cigar-puffing Lady 'Dolly' Walpole Neville. Hearing this, you go, like who cares? But a descendant of King This or Tsar That's a different kettle of fish.

'It's Roberta, isn't it?' I said, feeling the way. 'Or Ashley?'

'I promised not to say, Lovejoy. We're sworn.'

She'd said it was legal, necessary, and morally right. I don't know anything that's all three. I got as far as, 'Where do antiques fit in – ?' before she reminded me that we only had an hour before breakfast, so it was soaring wings and swelling strings and brain on hold as she straddled me. Lovely, yes, but in the bamboo dream I'd seen mirages, even visions.

The only bloke whose shape fitted the glimpse I'd had, on Tryer's final night, was Juliana's Father Jay. No motive, but what has motive to do with murder? Motive is always irrelevant, just as alibis have nothing to do with innocence. Motive and alibi are the falsehoods of murder.

'Can I have breakfast, love?' I asked when we were dressed.

'I love a greedy man, Lovejoy.'

That narked me. 'Wanting breakfast's not greedy.'

She advanced on me smiling. 'I mean pulling me into the bath.'

'Saves water.'

She fluffed her nape hair like they do. 'You shall have a dozen breakfasts, honey. Give me ten minutes. Come in from the car park. Tell Wilmore you got a lift into town.'

'Leave the excuses to me. Women can't do them. One thing. Can I borrow a few quid? I'm broke.'

That set her laughing. 'Don't be long, Lovejoy.' She made a mock-tartish exit. I hoped her nocturnal activities weren't too revealing. You can't tell if a bloke's had a night of sexual carousing, but it's impossible for a woman to hide that look.

192

Somebody knocked. 'Lovejoy?'

Thank God it was only Tinker. He entered belching.

'Morning, Lovejoy. Got a note? I'm broke.'

'Morning, Tinker.' I passed him half of Mahleen's largesse. 'How've you got on organizing my durbar? Anything forged, faked, duff, haul it in. I'll audition soon.

'You already told me, Lovejoy. I done it. It's now.' He sprawled on the bed, filthy and stinking. The maids'd wonder what Mahleen'd been up to.

'Eh? But I've not had my breakfast.'

'The Welcome Sailor, five minutes, Lovejoy.' He offered me a bottle. I declined, to his relief. He swigged. I leant away from his niff. 'You're allus mob-handed. Yanks here. Them Fenstone nutters. Now everybody in frigging antiques. Nobody left except the Serge.'

'Police aren't invited.' I'm used to Tinker knowing my movements without being told.

'Any specials, Lovejoy? I still got a few minutes.'

'Aye. Juliana Witherspoon. And bring that printer, the one with the daft dog that climbs trees.'

'Ked? He's shacked up now, a lass who makes bronzes.'

'Bring her. Doesn't matter if she's useless. And Fatsine.' She's a disappointed linguist, hampered by a lack of grammar. Compensates by making antique Chelsea pottery. 'She can show Wedgwood as well.' Her Wedgwood's pathetic, but the others aren't bad.

'What about the duds? There's already plenty in the queue.'

'Tell them yes, but promise nowt.'

'How many items we after, Lovejoy?'

The heart of the matter, for everything hinged on this. 'Trust you to depress me.' The old soak was grinning, his prune features showing merriment. I started laughing.

'Fill the ground floor of . . .' I searched for some large place. He'd never been to the Battishalls'. '. . . of the Magistracy.'

'Right, Lovejoy.' I pulled him up. He coughed, deafening the birdsong for miles around. I go deaf for an instant. He quivered, wheezed back to his normal colour. 'Here, Lovejoy. What we want with that Holly?'

'Nothing.' I was puzzled. Why mention her all of a sudden? 'She's hanging about. I sent her packing.' Then I remembered she'd said something about the senior magistrate . . . Tinker had just mentioned her in the same breath as the Magistracy.

He saw my bafflement. 'Holly drives Heanley to distraction.'

My mind went, hang on a sec. Heanley, the law court custodian, had a wayward daughter. 'Den Heanley? Holly?'

'That's her. Trouble.'

My belly gnawed my middle. Was I never going to get a free nosh from the Yanks? 'Look, Tinker. I'll just have a quick breakfast. The Yanks –'

'Leave off, Lovejoy. They don't fry in the right grease, not like Woody's.' He opened the door. 'There'll be riots if you're late.' As we went downstairs, he asked, 'That oldie goldie a good shag, is she, Lovejoy? She has some fair-sized Bristols on her. But then you always did like tits . . .'

So, with this Beau Brummel of the modern age, I went hungrily towards my antiques audition. The one good thing was, I now knew it was Juliana's beloved Father Jay who'd done for Tryer, not Nick or the Battishalls. I felt a glow of relish. Wreak vengeance on clergy, you can't go far wrong.

The Welcome Sailor was heaving, harassed police controlling the forgers and antique dealers that were queueing all the way to the car park.

27

'This your doing, Lovejoy?' old George asked-said in the Plod's God-on-the-Mountain voice, accusation with enquiry, that puts all innocents in the wrong.

'What's up, George?' Stout, ageing, a typical peeler.

'It's my coffee time, Lovejoy.' He's a gloomy old sod.

There were thirty or so dealers, barkers, whifflers, shuffers, forgers, surging about the Welcome Sailor, and more arriving. Inside looked like a bookie's on Derby Day, people shoving and calling out. I was instantly surrounded, dealers battling to come closer, wanting my approval for their assorted crud. News spread that I'd arrived, and more joined the mob engulfing me.

'Christ, George!' I gasped, buffeted. 'Get me inside.'

Two more Plod battled through, somehow thrust me in, following, calling angrily. It took half an hour because people kept coming in through the side door, windows even. Things quietened after two squad cars arrived. Nervously I peered out. An orderly queue formed, police wearily trying to keep the pavement clear.

'Eighty quid, Lovejoy.' Harlequin came at me.

'Eh?' Harlequin's the publican's nickname. We don't use nicknames more than one syllable, much, but Harlequin insists. He dresses himself and his missus up as Harlequin and Columbine at Michaelmas, a lost bet of years gone by. I used to know Columbine, to make smiles. She tells me he's not crazy. 'I'm broke, Harlequin. Got any grub?' I added for George's sake, 'got done out of breakfast.'

'You've cost me eighty quid opening at this hour, Lovejoy. Pay up, or it's the pavement with this caper.'

'Gimme a receipt.' I counted out the residue of what Mahleen had paid – I mean lent – me. 'Fifteen, sixteen. That's it. Any chance of you doing the costume bit, Harlequin? That's why I told Tinker here instead of the Lamb and Flag.'

'Me? Now?'

'Course.' I went all soulful. 'I really didn't want this charity to get off to a bad start. I'm really sorry.'

'Charity?' Columbine – she's plain old Andromeda Haythornthwaite really – emerged in her sexy dressing gown, really unfair. She changes her hair colour every week. Today, blonde with a jet streak.

'It's okay, love,' I said, broken but noble. 'I understand. Your lie-in today, an hour's peace. I've been up all night, slogging for this New Baby Unit.' I turned my pockets out, stony broke. 'Harlequin's taken my very last copper.' I showed a glimpse of hope, dare I believe in people, will Tinkerbell live? 'Can I owe Harlequin the rest of the eighty quid, Columbine? The little babies I'm slaving for would be grateful.'

My eyes brimmed with real tears, I was so moved. Well, to labour, endlessly unfed and penniless, for cots filled with neglected infants, was true charity. Nobody could deny that. George spoilt it by blowing his nose in a handkerchief the size of a parachute.

'I've not had coffee yet,' he reminded the world.

'You just keep quiet, George!' Columbine reprimanded.

Outside the mob were hammering on doors, tapping windows. Voices were raised. This, note, to bring forgeries for sale, which says something about the antiques markets. Can't think what. 'You demanded *money*, for a *baby* charity?' Her voice has a commendable vibrato when she's being mad or sexy. Her husband shook.

'I'll try to pay the rest, Columbine,' I said, St Alban in chains.

'It's only right!' Harlequin said defensively, but I'd won. 'Lovejoy's dealers – look at them! They're animals!'

'*Give it back!*' Quaver, vibrato, tremble, fury, were all in there. I wish I could do it. I tried, when we made smiles once in the pub yard but I can't do it. Infants can. You'd get away with murder with a voice like that.

Harlequin repaid me. I handed a note to Columbine. 'Love. Could I have a glass of water? I haven't had a thing since yesterday. I don't want to keel over during my charity.'

She blazed, 'I'll make you a decent breakfast!'

She drove Harlequin out. He beamed hate, but what had I done except given him the chance of doing a little good in the world? I honestly can't understand some people.

'Which New Baby Unit, Lovejoy?' George asked. 'My daughter's due in seven weeks.'

Some people really do irritate. 'The one in, er, Moon Morrow, George,' I invented, narked at the silly old goon. 'It needs cots and, er, spoons. Let them in.'

He shuffled towards the door. I'm thankful I don't have his bad feet. 'We'll have a whip round at the station, Lovejoy. The lads raised a fortune for the surgery unit.'

'Ta, George.' Already I was worn out and I'd not even started. Kindness is tiring. All administrations are set up to exploit, by the pretence of giving service. Harlequin ushered in Juliana Wither-spoon, her face white.

'Lovejoy!' she said. 'Where is he?'

'He?' I asked, blank.

'My brother. Doctor Dill said he's here, needs me urgently.'

'Oh. It was a mistake.' Tinker's surname is Dill. 'Got a note-book?'

'Notebook?' She looked like she had a terrible headache.

'Aye. We're listing people to, er help Father Jay. George, let them in. Single file.'

George opened the door, was trampled by the inrush of antique dealers with forgeries to sell. Hear them talk, you'd think they'd never seen a fake in their entire lives. Put out the whisper that you'll buy any dud from their stock, and you get flattened by the stampede.

The Plod poured in with the yelling crowd, struggling. They managed to resuscitate a huffed George, and the auditions were on.

'Gold ecus, Lovejoy.' Tapper's named for his skill in forging tap-and-die strikers for making medals, coins. Actually a presentable young banker, but I don't ask.

'Gold content, Tapper?'

'Nought point one above genuine.' He spoke with justifiable pride. Italians set this precedent, forging King George V gold sovereigns with fractionally higher gold content than the real thing. Very hard to prosecute people who manufacture fakes worth more than your original.

'You're in, Tapper. Your own security display case, proper labelling. Take his name, Juliana, put ECU.'

'What?' she asked, bewildered. I sighed. This was going to be one of those days.

'For God's sake, Jul, set up a frigging desk. You're mucking about doing sweet Fanny Adams.'

'I have no notebook, Lovejoy,' Juliana wailed, distracted.

'Next, George.' I ignored her. Women haven't got enough to do. Ask them to do a hand's turn, they crack.

'Morning. I'm Jackery.' Stout, balding, tired shoes, daubed corduroys. 'I've one forgery, Lovejoy, but they're lovely.'

Jackery. Closing my mind to Juliana's whingeing I rummaged in my ragbag memory. Lavenham, three years ago. An obsessed lunatic, one painting that he does over and over.

'Seurat's nudes?' The plural for singular gave him away.

'It's not fair, Lovejoy.' He spoke earnestly. 'They always call them names, They're beautiful.'

'Isn't it in the Barnes Collection in Philadelphia?' Barnes was an eccentric American doctor who amassed an art collection, 1900s. Major stuff, over 2,000 works. In 1915 he wrote his notorious book, *How to Judge a Painting*. Critics howled with laughter. He got his revenge, though, by guarding his possessions with paranoia. 'How did you see it? Dr Barnes's will stated his collections should never be reproduced, lent, even colour photographed.' Jackery's famous for this, his one forgery. The original, Seurat's three nudes, *Les Poseuses*, is nearly as famous (joke).

'They came to Paris.' His eyes went dreamy. 'I went. Lost my job over it.' He spoke without rancour. 'And my wife. She didn't understand.'

'Thank you, Jackery,' I said. We shook hands. 'You've done a great thing for mankind. I'm honoured to have your forgery in the exhibition. Your label must say it's for sale.' He started to protest. I waved him away. 'You don't have to *sell*. Name an impossible price, see?'

His lip trembled. 'What if somebody agrees to pay it, though?'

'No, Jackery. A stated price is legally only "an invitation to treat". Say you've changed your mind. Give your name.' I indicated Juliana, who was finally getting round to scribbling, distraught. 'Tell her to get a move on. Next.'

We got going, faster after Columbine brought a fry-up in for me. I had to send her back for more, but eating was a refreshing novelty. I took some really risky decisions as the offers came in.

A trio from Cambridge said they'd faked some silverware and two gold emblems from King Croesus's famed Lydian Hoard. Turkey recently sued for the original treasure, got it back from the USA. Quite right too, I say, because somebody stole it back in the 1960s, and smuggled it to unscrupulous buyers via international fences. I'm not making allegations here, because New York City's Metropolitan Museum of Art will want to remain anonymous and I respect their privacy most sincerely. I believed this trio of walking derelictions, because one had a goldsmith's segs – small hard nodes of skin on his right index finger.

Sadly, I rejected some copperplate letters 'by Sir Walter Scott', done by an old lady. Scott wrote *Guy Mannering* in under six weeks, had a voluminous output, especially after Byron grabbed the poetry market from him. Forged letters from writers are useless, unless you've some originals to compare. She tried showing me parchment fragments of *Cardenio*, Shakespeare's lost play, but everybody has cupboards full ever since that American chap found it – he says – in the British Museum Library. I felt sorry for her, but what can I do?

'That was despicable, Lovejoy!' Juliana stood over me.

'I'm trying to help you snaffle your bloke. This isn't a charity. This is fakery!'

'What was that, Lovejoy?' from Columbine inside the kitchen. 'I mean I want donations, Biney,' I amended quickly. 'Everything must make a profit. Those barns need blankets and bottles.'

Juliana lowered her voice. 'Lovejoy. I mistrust this whole enterprise. I shall watch you every inch.'

'One thing,' I said, just as softly. 'How would your Whistlejack forgery do if I subject it to electrochemical abrasive stripping voltammetry?'

'My what?' She recoiled. I only know the words, not how to do it.

'It uses graphite electrodes, Jul. Measures pigments almost without failure.' I smiled. The dealers outside were yelling, George in distress. 'Don't blame me, and I won't blame you. Deal?'

'You declared it genuine, Lovejoy! Ashley told me so.'

'I lied.'

She was pale. 'What else have you lied about?'

'Next, George.' Practically everything, except antiques.

They really started then. I clocked them about sixty an hour, one after the other. I became dizzy. There were the usual things – furniture promised by the truckload, paintings galore, enough silverware to plate East Anglia, fake bicycles – more of these than you'd think; they bring high gelt these days. Where there's wheels, dealers say these days, you get nutters. In that first hour I had a lad who'd faked Daimler's prototype 1885 motorbike, Otto four-stroke engine and all. I asked him if he'd a pal who could forge S. H. Cooper's original steam-driven bicycle, pre-1870, but he hadn't. I accepted the lazy devil. I'm not really into engines.

Some were fascinating. A school teacher from Northampton produced photographs of a cupboard house.

'This is a Dutch fake, or ours?'

He went shy with pride. 'Mine, Lovejoy. I made every item. It's in a genuine old cupboard, too.'

It stopped my breath. An Ince corner cupboard, lovely, untouched.

'You didn't damage it?' I asked.

'In my family generations, Lovejoy. Pristine. I lined it with clean cardboard, then made the doll's house Regency furniture. My wife makes tapestries and candles.' He pointed, pleased.

In Holland, these 'baby houses' were fashionable a couple of centuries ago. Brides got married about fourteen or fifteen years of age. They liked these things. Many were made by skilled craftsmen, some for advertising purposes, others for selling to newly wedded girls. See an original, it blows your mind. They are made in exquisite detail.

'. . . six hundred items, Lovejoy. Regency chandeliers . . .'

'Accepted,' I said, wondering how I could get his Ince cupboard from him without disturbing the doll's house furniture.

Some things just had to be rejected, even though a commensurate amount of effort had been expended on them. I refused a Stortford bloke who'd faked a fragment of the 7000 BC linen found lately in Asia Minor. He left in tears.

'That was wretched!' Juliana, storming the Bastille again.

'Hold it, George.' Wearily, I drew her behind the counter and shoved my fist in her face. 'Listen to me, you stuck up bitch. I know what I'm doing. You don't. Understand?'

'You are a disgusting, retarded beast, Lovejoy. I've heard about your scrounging off women, your cheating –'

'That does it. George? Evict this bird. She's useless.'

But she stayed, only so she could sulk. We resumed, Juliana sitting in mute reproach while I worked. I was furious, because everything on earth is possibly fake, isn't it? I remember hereabouts a nerk called Coacher selling plants by post, until he was arrested by Maud for mail-order fraud. He advertised the Military Orchid, thought to be extinct until some Sherlock found one in 1947. Notoriously fickle, there are now two hundred plants growing in secret, watched by vigilantes. See? Everything's fake until proved otherwise. And people are desperate to join in a fake. Somebody calculated that if you send a pyramid letter to five other people, in four months everybody in the world would have received 13 million letters. Mind you, statistics aren't. I mean, the average peal of twelve church bells, ringing one peal every few seconds, would take 38 years of ding-donging to complete all possible changes. So?

But some things are less fake than fake. In 1863, the famous antiques expert William Chaffers decided that Chinese porcelain was actually all made here, in Lowestoft to be precise. In tribute, I accepted the works of a potter from Harwich. He'd forged Chinese porcelains, complete with bizarre inscriptions.

'See the inscriptions?' he enthused over his photos.

When Western traders placed orders for special pieces, Chinese potters made blunders, not knowing our language. Families wanting particular decorations simply wrote out inscriptions on paper, which were then taken to Canton for the designs to be copied on the porcelain dinner services. One Swedish chap drew his design he wanted on a page from his son's exercise book, on which his little lad had scrawled, 'Mother is today in an even worse temper.' The Chinese service was brilliantly manufactured with his son's acid comment in the design.

'Are they this good?'

'Honest,' he said. I'd seen some of this bloke's early Nantgarw ware, good in spite of the duff glazing.

'Accept. Ten pieces, separate labels. Name to the lady.'

Accepting forgeries can go in bursts. In one heady spell I nodded a score of clever items, all manufactured by enthusiastic amateurs. I took a forgery of Michelangelo's sketch *The Holy Family with the Infant John the Baptist* – it was sold for millions not long since at Christie's. Nobody even knows where it was discovered, because Major Robb of Great Tew, Oxfordshire, isn't telling. I grinned at Juliana, who looked away, though I could tell she was dying to see the drawings the girl showed me. I accepted a bloke's copies – poor things, really – of Picasso paintings, for notoriety value, because he was well faked during his lifetime. And Salvador Dali, who was forged seemingly with his own connivance.

I turned down an electronic mugger, who looked decidedly shifty. This modern crime's very simple. You set up a machine outside a bank at weekend when it's closed. Your printed notice announces that this machine is a new ATM, automated teller machine. When people insert their cards, it flashes a signal saying sorry, folks, but it isn't properly installed yet. The ATM spits out your card, and you go on your way grumbling. But it has secretly copied your plastic, which the electronic mugger simply uses for his own high-spending purposes.

But I jumped at the chance of a dozen forgeries of St John Lateran's famed possessions. The Mafia, or somebody neff, bombed this 'Mother of Churches' in Rome, ruining precious frescoes and God knows what. Hearing this, a scammer called Doper Tone had gone, passed himself off as a visiting curator from Bermondsey, getting details of which antiques had gone the way of all flesh. He then came home and worked solidly for a year to replicate them. I shook his hand, delighted at such loving care. He'd even got a photo of himself near the pope, looking aghast at the explosion site. I really admire dedication.

We had a break. I went to visit Columbine in her kitchen. Juliana would have come too, but I stopped her.

'Get those lists into columns, Jul,' I advised. 'You spend too much time grumbling.'

'*Lovejoy*,' she ground out, white again but this time with fury. 'Tell me one thing men can do better than women.' Tension was tearing her apart. Why? 'Well? Thinking up an idiot answer?'

'No. Still thinking about the question.'

Honestly, you can't help some people. I was pleased with Columbine, though. Harlequin was in the yard barreling up from the brewer's dray, so I was some time resuming. And you know what? Juliana still wasn't straight. I honestly don't know. Women lack organization.

By mid-morning I was flying, the queue dwindling. The police were at ease. New forgers trickled up asking was this where Lovejoy's auditions were.

There's only four sorts of antique dealers: tiddlers, fiddlers, diddlers, and middlers.

Ignore tiddlers – they see the Mona Lisa as a couple of pints or a new handbag, forever think small. Ignore fiddlers – they'd improve that enigmatic smile by a wash of acrylic emulsion from the hardware shop, forever wanting DIY action. Ignore diddlers – they try to sell La Giaconda to nine different buyers at once, always tricking themselves into trouble and out of a fortune. But those middlers, as I call straight batters, are rare and, dare I say, honest, giving you the right change, willing to take back something if it's proved rubbish. Such a gent was Brig. He brought photos of his collection of First-Day Commemorative mugs, from when Buckingham Palace was opened to the public. I looked. Not antiques, but well done.

'Sorry, Lovejoy,' he said, ashamed. 'I know. There *were* no First-Day special mugs, and they're not antiques anyway, seeing the Palace was only opened in 1993, but they'll go like trifle. And I can bring some antique forgeries along.'

'Sure, Brig.' Normally I'd have rejected them, but his wife has some disease that stops her walking. 'And?'

'I've been asked to kiln some . . . sorry, Lovejoy, droppings.'

'Eh? As in . . .?'

'Fake dinosaur droppings. There's a market now.'

Food for thought. I've heard of every scam on earth. There's a bloke in Sweden sells earrings made, I assure you, of varnished moose poop scooped from the wilds. The other side of the coin, as it were, is the London auction sale of 'dinobilia' when Bonhams culled a fortune for ten sauropod eggs from China said to be seventy million years old. Dinosaur droppings from Utah yielded less than a tenth of that sum. This proves two things. Collectors never change – if they want it, they'll sell their grannie's teeth for it. And second, everybody, but everybody, has an opinion. Like those Australian kiddies who found a monster egg, two thousand years old, of the extinct Madagascan Elephant Bird. (That's the scientists' description. Can we trust them?) When a minister declared it government property, the kiddies reburied it in secret – and the whole nation took sides. See? Everybody has hard line opinions, for or against. I love it, a sign of life.

'Brig, tell the lady to list them in a foyer display, Cabinet of the Weird and Wonderful.'

It got stranger still, as the auditions went on. I know a bloke who swears he's never seen a true Byzantine fresco, in a lifetime's work on Byzantine wall paintings. He says they began them on fresh plaster, building up layers of thick opaque paint in glues or lime over the fresco ground colours. I had a nasty argument over this. Tesco brought in drawings of some Cypriot church wall paintings he'd forged. The originals are in Houston, Texas – after being excitingly smuggled out of Turkish-occupied Cyprus to Munich, thence to London. It was Juliana who interrupted our chat, saying we'd wasted ten whole minutes.

'Sorry, Tesco,' I apologized. 'She's new. I have to nurse her along.'

'It's okay, Lovejoy.' He's a craftsman. 'I've nine free-standing panels, the history of the Mediterranean region.'

'No. You get two framed cards, eighteen inches by twenty-four . . .' Nuclear war ensued, and I had to get George to drag him out, yelling abuse, oppression, et jingoistic cetera. I warned Juliana's thin lips, 'Not a word, Jul.' She kept silent, maybe learning.

Some indefatigable old dear had painstakingly reproduced the diaries of Tom Lewin in his own handwriting. Even I'd heard of the fabled 'Thangliena', who ruled India's North-East Frontier in the Raj. Fluent linguist, brave to the point of madness, this humble ensign fought through Bengal until he became King of the Lushai Hill Tribes. He assimilated languages somehow by breathing the local air.

'You a relative?' I asked her.

'Bless you, no. But we mustn't forget our brave Victorian lads. Mr Lewin became a friend of Meredith and Burne-Jones, don't y'know. An artist and musician, too.' She spoke with personal pride.

'Was he crazy?' I asked, curious for her opinion.

'Certainly not!' She bridled. 'He *was* eccentric. What if he did ship oysters from Fortnum's in Piccadilly? He was entitled! Ruskin admired him!'

'How long did this take you, Mrs Boyson?'

'Only five years. I invented letters from him to his beloved Lushai concubine Dari, during his retirement in England.' She coloured. I looked at the manuscript. It was several hundred pages. 'Thangliena was, how can one say, a man of certain strong *desires*. Understandable, a gentleman far from home.'

'Thank you, love. Accepted.' She looked shabby. 'Name to the lady, please. Tell her to get Tinker to arrange a display case, copperplate label.'

'Oh,' she exclaimed, flustered, 'I can't do copperplate, Lovejoy! Though I received a Sunday School prize when I was eight for spelling –'

'Get on with it, for Christ's sake!' I yelled, practically hurling her across the tap room. 'George! Next!'

On and on. My pal Chess the printer from Tooting Bec arrived, with examples of Hoyle's works on games, including his rare London first edition of 1751 about the game of brag. An ancient British gold torc – simple, but resplendent – of the kind dug up hereabouts, very easy to fake but from genuine solid gold with the right trace elements. I took it sight unseen because, although I didn't know the girl who brought the photograph, a child of six can fake one in an afternoon, given the right tools and the gold. She also showed me a photo of a Moche warrior-priest. I inspected it, puzzled.

'You do this, too?' It looked like gold. The pre-Inca Moche civilization's not much understood, but what we do know is dazzling. Just right for forgery to blossom. Date, about 1700 years ago. The antiques world is clamouring for Moche gold and silver ornaments from these Peruvian burials, first to eighth centuries. Forgery follows newly discovered antiques like seagulls follow the plough.

'No. Daddy. He's redundant. He started this hobby a fortnight since.'

She was no more than thirteen, specky, braces on her teeth. I questioned her a bit. No, her dad, a lowly clerk, had never done this before.

'What metal, chuckie?' I asked. Thirteen, you don't know whether to offer them a lollipop or a fag these days. She wondered should she take umbrage, opted for peace.

'Daddy melted down a garden pot to make them. Mum got mad.'

'Did he indeed.' Daddy had class. 'He make his own moulds?' He was highly talented. The international black market in Moche antiques only began about 1987, though long ago Mrs Hearst – fawning mamma of little Randolph – paid for excavations in Peru's coastal regions in the 1890s. The sale of forged die-casts had not yet reached East Anglia. Until now. Handled right, this neophyte forger might be the find of the year. I watched her for evasion, but the child came straight out.

'He used up all our Ted's plasticines. Ted got mad.'

So Daddy had improvised, against family opposition, and come up with a convincing pair of fakes that, given the right gold alloys, guaranteed a new career in forgery. Daddy had potential. I glanced at Juliana, cleared my throat. 'Tell your clever Daddy that Lovejoy says to see Tinker immediately. His, er, models are accepted. I've got a new job for Daddy.'

The morning surged on. Faked ivory was much in evidence, though the real thing's still not hard to come by in spite of pious droning by sundry governments. Fake bronzes are always about, the staple fare of fakedom, and paintings, paintings galore.

Some forgeries were so excellent they hardly qualified as fakes at all. One bloke I'd never met called Oomoo showed me pictures of a svelte lady in a royal blue sheath dress, a similar emerald dress, a tight calf-length scarlet dress with dated mandarin sleeves. I looked up at his worried face, baffled. 'What's the catch, Oom?'

'They're glass, Lovejoy. The dresses. Big in 1911, 1912. Spun whipped glass. My woman does the embroidery. She says *point lancé's* the only stitch that works.'

I'd heard of these, seen a lovely chequered spun-glass headband once, for all the world like silk. 'Accepted. How many can you bring?' See? Hardly fake at all.

Then there was the opportunist faker, Washer. He came with five Pablo Picassos and two Georges Braques. The *La Femme aux Yeux Noir* Picasso wasn't too bad, but the rest were awful.

'You didn't finish the Picasso sculpture, then?'

He grinned sheepishly. 'No, Lovejoy. The newspapers only showed pictures of the paintings after the robbery.' Washer meant the Murph-the-Surf-style break-in at Stockholm's Museum of Modern Art. Once a painting's reported stolen, it's the signal for forgers to get to work – for who knows whether the 'right' one's eventually recovered or not? We call it the Mona Lisa effect. I gave Washer the nod.

Inevitably, when the last had gone, she started up.

'This is *wrong*, Lovejoy! I suppose you know that?'

I was drained. 'Robin Hood is famous for pulling this caper.'

'It's dishonest! You are encouraging forgeries. All those people.' She was almost in tears. 'The whole world seems to want to take advantage of poor honest buyers.'

'Poor honest buyers?' I felt my temper give. 'Do you know anybody who'd walk past a priceless antique Gainsborough on offer for a quid? Would you, love?' I could have clocked her one.

'What's going on there?' called Columbine, but pleased I was ballocking off some other female.

'That's always you, Lovejoy.' Juliana came close to a sneer. 'Criticizing a person's plight, never your own greed!'

'My own greed?' I'm honestly baffled. 'Who's greedy? Who do you think paid for the restoration of Leonardo da Vinci's *Last Supper*? An industrial combine called Olivetti, that's who. And that shy retiring USA firm Coca-Cola forked out for restoration work at Russia's Hermitage. And who funded the cleaning of the Sistine Chapel's ceiling but Japanese TV moguls? And don't tell me that restoration is right and proper. It's mostly ruination. Once restorers started using synthetic materials to restore old masterpieces, they were simply awarding themselves jobs for life. Don't get on to me.'

'This whole enterprise is a sin, Lovejoy!' Red dots of fury appeared on her cheeks. 'I'm aware of your philandering with the landlord's wife this morning. I heard you tell Constable George to keep a look out in case! Your conduct is disgusting! I want nothing more to do with you!'

Too narked to continue, I shouted thanks to Columbine and Harlequin, gabbed Juliana's lists, and stalked out. A few latecomers scurried after me along the pavement, offering me pictures, scraps of paper and exotic descriptions.

Things irritate you when you want to calm down. Where the hell was Tinker? And Chemise, now I needed her? Idling about doing sweet sod all, that's what. I saw her waving from across the road from the George.

'Where have you been?' I demanded in a yell, my half-dozen followers clubbing up against me like dominoes.

'I found it, Lovejoy,' Chemise called, embarrassed. Everybody in the High Street was looking.

She made it safely through the traffic while I audited the remaining fakers. The engravings of the National Gallery – the grand building that replaced the squalor and filth of the St Martin-in-the-Fields Workhouse – seemed okay, I told Jemima's cousin Gabbie, new and not much idea. 'But why not add the washhouse chimneys that stood there? Engravers missed those out to make it look grand, but sociologists and other dumbos'll buy them. They love slums.'

'My auntie's a social worker, Lovejoy.' She too was angry.

'Er, dumbo's a term of endearment, love,' I invented. 'Means, er, all-hearing, big ears, see?'

She left, mollified, while I accepted some Regency silverware, a set of fake homemade keys made in a foundry down Canvey Island, ten Wedgwood tiles 'by Nunn', a great name, a mass of powder flasks for flintlock weapons – the easiest things to fake. Finally, best wine to the last, a trio of fake Regency 'pier glasses', mirrors in giltwood, leaf moulded frames, by a quiet drunkard called Haymake. I was pleased to see him alive, and gave him licence to bring along some Art-Deco figures he was making, lovely women in innocent erotic postures. The ones to look out for are fakes by the enigmatic Viennese craftsman F. Preiss in bronze and ivory, cast-and-carved, as dealers say. If Haymake claimed his were 'nice' I felt convinced they'd be superb. I accepted a cluster of Napoleonic memorabilia, all forgeries, because it included an ivory rotunda framing a statuette of Bonaparte. It was offered by a walrus-shaped bloke who startled me by also wanting to bring some Chippendale-style cherrywood candle stands that his long-dead uncle used to turn out for a hobby.

Job done. And here came Chemise, women noticing her surpassing plainness with sly sideways looks.

'About bloody time,' I groused. 'Found what?'

'Reverend Father Jay, Lovejoy,' she said. 'He's not.'

And the sun rose.

28

'Look,' I said to Valetta, who runs the George's booking desk. 'My American friends invited us for lunch, but we were feeding the old folks so I couldn't get here.' I smiled, martyred. 'Okay to go through?'

'No, Lovejoy.' She was reading a paper, uncaring bitch. 'They're on a trip with Gwena.'

'But we're starving. Look.' I leant forward. 'I'm doing a deal. That Wilmore, y'know, developer. He's buying the Red Lion.' It's the George's big rival. She turned a page. 'I could get you details, if . . .' Chemise was embarrassed, but I stared her down.

'Really? I've not heard about that.'

'It's got to be kept quiet. Property deals, all that.'

She relented, wrote out a chit for me to give to Aldo, when a familiar voice harrumphed. Misery enveloped the world.

'Lovejoy! It's time to arrange the sale.'

'Sale?' I groaned audibly, my hand outstretched for the chit. 'Can't it wait, Ashley?'

'No. And,' he added, nasty, 'you haven't time for lunch.'

The aroma of food wafted from the carvery. They'd all be on their starters, a thick creamy soup, or maybe those mushrooms fried in batter. I almost folded, belly cramp.

'Can't it wait while I get some sandwiches?'

'Probably a lie, Lovejoy,' the unfeeling swine said. 'Roberta insists you settle everything today. Seeing,' he added, 'you have filled my hotel with workmen under the control of a filthy tramp.'

Tinker, getting on with it. Chemise spoke up.

'Mr Battishall? I have the information you're referring to. Lovejoy delegated responsibility to me. He decided that the only way was to organize the auction at your hotel during the exhibition. It will require a separate space, of course.'

'Well, ye-e-e-es,' he said.

'Accordingly, I have contacted sixty major buyers. One may assume with some confidence that potential bidders will be among those who attend the exhibition?'

Gaping, I looked anew at Chemise. Still with those teeth, that hair, those spindly legs. But she smiled with a veteran scamster's certainty.

'Be that as it may,' Ashley began. Well, he was used to the rapacious Roberta, so it was no contest.

'Excuse me, sir.' She had a really lovely smile. 'If you could allow Lovejoy a few minutes in the restaurant to set the seal of approval . . .'

Pedantry for pedantry. The seal of approval, for God's sake.

'Very well. Ten minutes only, Lovejoy.'

'Yes, Ashley.' I snatched the chit from Valetta and streaked into the carvery, seizing a plate and queue-hopping to where the chefs served the grub, apologizing as I went. 'Sorry, lady, but my auntie's ill and I'm due at the hospital . . .'

Chemise collared a table. I fell on the grub as she went for a salad. Anything to get out before Ashley trapped me.

'Maybe,' I spluttered eagerly, hacking and noshing, 'you could distract Ashley while I eel out through the kitchens. He'll go mental when he realizes you were lying about having it all organized.'

'I wasn't, Lovejoy.' She waved a notebook. 'I have the lists. Have your dinner.'

Women are truly beautiful. 'Where'd you get the names?' I flicked through her – no, *my* notebook. It had been in my hidden cellar.

'I was tidying in your cellar.'

Aldo came across. 'Who's paying, Lovejoy?' I gave him Valetta's chit. 'It's for one.'

'Hellfire, Aldo!' I exploded, while he tried to quieten me. The diners were looking. 'Is it my fault that your staff can't write numbers down clearly? God Almighty . . .' He retreated, hands raised, such a quaint laugh. I continued conversationally, 'Good girl. What about Juliana's holy roller?'

'That's just it, Lovejoy. He's no such thing. Last night I went to Birmingham.' She moved her salad about her plate. 'You didn't come home. That golden lady, I presume.'

'No,' I said, innocent. 'I stayed with friends. Too late, no buses after ten.'

She pretended to believe. 'I found the old bursar of Father Jay's seminary. It's closed now. He accepted Jay's education certificates. A seminary in South Carolina, USA.'

'So?' I helped her to finish her salad. Waste is sin, my old Gran used to teach. 'Doesn't matter where, does it?'

Ashley was back, peering, timing us by his quartz digital, his gnawing ulcer close to popping.

'Yes it does, Lovejoy.' She was even calm contradicting me. 'If it's a diploma shop. Degrees by post.'

That stopped me. 'He isn't even a padre?'

'He did it in two months.' She was justifiably proud, pink with pleasure at the effect she was creating. 'Sent forms, paid the fee, got the diplomas. The lady on the phone told me that I could have three theology qualifications, and be ordained minister by the first of next month.' She smiled, radiant. 'They're equal opportunity, Lovejoy. Even you could become holy.'

'With testimonials from churches where he'd served?'

'Yes. They do an after-sales service, certificates from alleged churches. Though,' she added, going serious, 'we shouldn't condemn, Lovejoy. These institutions might do some good, seeing the moral gap undoubtedly existing –'

Oh aye, my mind went. I said, to shut her up, 'I often think that, love. But you've missed one name out.'

'Who, Lovejoy?' She riffled through the notebook anxiously.

'He's not in there. But send him an invitation anyway.'

Ashley came marching down the carvery. I rose to greet him as Chemise asked me to spell his name, pencil poised.

'Sheehan, J.,' I said quietly, then loudly, 'Wotcher, Ashley. Time for a pudding?'

This next bit's about money, so I'd miss it out if you can't take it.

Quite a long time ago, some university don at the Brunel tried to work money out. Who hasn't? He depended on formulas connecting us with different ancestors across Time. It told you the value of a house, pig, day's wages, in modern dosh. He'd reckon the cost of a loaf on, say, 10 August 1989, apply algebraic mumbo-jumbo and hey presto! There it was! The price of your loaf in Year of Grace 1167, whenever, was X in modern money! Tables and charts followed.

Even I scribed him a missive, Dear Sir, Please explain how . . .
Reason? I wanted to use his system for pricing antiques *today*. And
you know what?

It didn't work.

It didn't work for centuries. It didn't work across a few months,
years. I tried every period I could find records for. No avail.

For some twenty years, Sotheby's coined an Art Index to show the
changing values of master paintings. Investors clung to it like sailors
reaching a life raft – but the violent swings of the 1990s sank every
known formula. Newspapers denounced the Art Index as balder-
dash, claiming that even Sotheby's own experts shrugged it off, that a
'basket' of fewer than forty paintings, many of which were never even
auctioned during any one calendar year, was unreliable. Prediction
accuracy about auction prices scored little more than thirty per cent.
(And anybody can score fifty per cent just by spinning a coin, heads or
tails.)

Supposition ruled, guesswork was king. And who did the guessing?
Answer: auction houses who got the biggest cut when they sold Old
Masters, that's who.

So currently only two systems work: the 'DT Art 100', that prices
the auction sales around 250 auction rooms, internationally, of 100
American/European artists' works, and records an Index in Nominal
Prices – 1975 prices are the base level – of 1,000, in US dollars.
Though I hate to boost a newspaper's sales, it's the best yet, if only for
artists' products, and not for all antiques. Second system is my own:
to measure time. Get this year's annual average wage, and represent
what you can get for *any* antique as a fraction of that, in wages. If that
wage is, say, 10,000 (pounds, dollars, slotniks), and the best offer you
can get for your antique is exactly that, then it's earned you a year. If
it will yield only 5,000 then it's worth six months, and so on. This way,
you've a reliable comparison.

I tried telling this to Ashley Battishall, no use. When we arrived,
his place was in uproar. A few elderly residents were enjoying the
hullabaloo, getting in everybody's way. Tinker was already three
sheets, reeling and giving orders. He'd hired a team of vannies and
auction whifflers to build display stands. He'd paid them all in my
IOUs, the goon. I'd told him not to. Actually, I didn't mind, because
my blokes outnumbered Nick's. Battishall finally went and bought

the DT Art 100 booklet, and I let him play about with that. Secretly, we fixed on a reserve price for the Stubbs painting.

It would be auctioned during the exhibition. Tinker and Chemise, off their own bat, had fixed it for two days' time. I warned them not to get uppity, but I was at a loose end, now that I knew that Reverend Jay Smith, beloved of Juliana, had done for Tryer.

Time for the Fenstone meeting? I felt like looking into his killer's eyes – while well protected, of course, by Dame Millicent, Mr Geake, Juliana. I'd take Chemise.

As I went to shout my usual 'Where've I left that motor?' to Chemise, who had forgotten to remind me, I saw a nervous bloke by the hotel steps. He'd been listening to old Jim Andrews. He followed me, a thin, edgy individual. A poor clerk who'd pressed every worn thread to go posh for an interview.

'Lovejoy?' he stuttered. I was pleased, because I do too.

A pause, then I tumbled. 'Daddy? Gold modeller?'

His brow cleared. 'Fred A'Court. I hope my Lana wasn't impertinent. It's been hard for her. I got your message.'

'You've brought another forgery?'

Shy, he held out a folded tissue. I unwrapped it. A filigree brooch, nearly the right weight. 'Lead?' Its interlaced golden strands were pitted, as if for small gemstones.

'My own alloy. The relative density – '

'Oh aye.' I cut him short. Techniques are only as good as the finished fake. 'Looks good.'

'It's a fake golden butterfly, Spanish treasure fleet off Florida, 1715.' He went red. 'I use magazine pictures.'

'Look, Fred.' I gave it back. 'It's high time somebody did a flock. You're good enough.' You have to encourage talent. 'A flock is a gradual release of antiques, fakes, whatever, supposedly from a single source. Like, the *Santa Cruz* treasure ship. She sank off Pembrokeshire in 1679 with two hundred chests of gold. Mark your butterfly, Cast From Original Found In Ocean. It'll get everybody thinking, *What* original? They'll think, *Some sod's found another Spanish galleon*! Can you do more? When we get a few tickles – enquiries from dealers – we can sell scores of gold forgeries.'

He was looking anxious. 'A black market, Lovejoy?'

'Governments create black markets, Fred. Not us.'

'Okay, then, Lovejoy,' he said, doubtful.
'Help me to load this dressing table, will you?'
And exit smiling.

29

'Wotcher, F'rouk. Lend me somebody to unload?'

Behind his nosh bar was a narrow alley, the sort you always get behind every eating place. I often wonder why. Do they choose the place, or does the place choose them?

He stirred two idlers to action. They were disgruntled at having to leave contemplation of the racing results, but did the job. They wanted to simply drop the dressing table with a crash. I stopped them. Farouk smiled apology.

'Relatives,' he sighed. 'Why are obligations one-way?'

He sounded like me. I was starting to like Farouk. 'Mmmh. Not a scratch, note.' I got ready for the difficult bit. 'Er, mind me asking, mate, but why didn't you do the job yourself? You knew its case.' A case is the layout of a place, alarms, patrols, of a theft.

He didn't smile. 'I knew the man who'd delivered the piece, three years ago when money was freer. I drove the van for him. But I wouldn't go there now.'

'So?'

'I had trouble. A policeman Lovejoy.' He waved at a diner. 'I planned a caff in Fenstone. He did everything but torch the place to prevent me.'

And I knew. That limp, the familiar face that wasn't. I'd known all along. 'Geake, William Geake?'

'Yes. He's retired, an invalid. Some accident.'

'Poor chap.' I paused. 'Heard of my exhibition?'

'Forgeries? I'll be there, Lovejoy.' His smile faded. The dresser was standing forlorn. 'You don't mean this is fake?'

'Good one, F'rouk, but duff. Send it in the exhibition if you like. See Tinker.' I got in and fired the engine. 'Same fee, though.'

He shouted persuasions, how could I demand antiques prices when I'd nicked a fake? I didn't stay. A deal is a deal.

William Geake had been a peeler, then. Now reminded, I could place him. Not uniformed branch. Accident, invalided out of the Force, retired to a village, involved in church activities. Lucky for Farouk, unlucky for Fenstone.

They kept me waiting an hour. She came with that dismissive assertiveness they're trained to use when the public interrupts tea. Her file slammed impatiently on the desk.

'What now, Lovejoy?'

'My exhibition, at the Dragonsdale Hotel?'

'Yes.' Her wintry smile invited applause, as if she'd sherlocked it out of tight-lipped townsfolk.

'It's in premises owned by the town's senior magistrate, don't forget. Law and order rule!'

'Presented as a public-spirited exhibition that warns buyers against today's forgers, Lovejoy? We know that angle.'

There were wall photos, former plod. 'Geake here, Maud?'

A millisec's delay. 'Why do you ask?' Like drawing blood.

'Mmmh?' I was casual. 'Wasn't there some accident?'

'Car crash, line of duty.' She decided to go casual too. 'I wasn't here then. A good serving officer.'

'Oh.' I snapped my fingers. 'Clean forgot. Anything I should watch out for? Stolen silver, shipments?'

'I'll deliver a list within the hour. Incidentally, Holly Heanley's in council care.'

'Don't tell me. Tell her dad. And keep her out of my hair.'

'She's waiting in *your* car, Lovejoy. Giving my police yard a bad name.' She smiled a sleet-filled smile.

Holly was in my passenger seat. 'Where's the frigging radio in this crap heap, Lovejoy?'

'Waiting to be invented, love.'

Narked, I drove to the law courts, found Den and introduced Holly to him like I was Beau Nash.

'Den, she's a pest. Can't you chain her up?'

He'd brewed up in his alcove, shared his tea like a gent. 'How do some parents manage to get their daughters settled, behave?' He looked tired.

'Den. William Geake. Remember him?'

He was surprised. 'Geake?' Peeler hurt in a motor wrap.

Why didn't I remember this? A wrap is a smash-up where the car is totalled. 'Mmmh. What the hell do I do with Holly? She's a nuisance.'

'If you ever find out let me know. I just thank God she's stopped hanging about the Magistracy. I'd rather her be with you. You're barmy, but not sick.'

'Cheers, Den. Your tea's rotten.'

In the motor, Holly was still sulking, but eyeing up youthful miscreants parading in and out of the courts.

'Battishall, Holly?' I hadn't asked about her cryptic remark.

Teenage smugness is annoying. I knew how Den felt, wanting to give her a clout knowing it would be wrong.

'He paid me, Lovejoy. Always after me, couldn't get enough.' Triumph, I saw, is what she was feeling. 'He used to blub like a kid. I made him beg.' She laughed, harsh, a nutmeg grater. Scorn, pride, disgust all came into it. 'Great magistrate, Lovejoy. You know what he does?' She looked with wonderment. 'He sends people to gaol! He kneels and cries afterwards, says he's sorry.'

Jesus. 'You still see him?'

'Nar, Lovejoy. He's disgusting. Still tries it. I make him pay, then nothing.' She did her laugh, the thrill of money for inflicting punishment. What happened to childhood?

'Why did you stop?'

'*He* made me.' She sounded bitter. 'Caught me shagging His Honour in a lane.' She glared, eyes hot.

'He interrupted you?' I felt ill. Past misdemeanors crowded in, the knock on the windscreen, footsteps, police sirens while the lads fought in the lay-by over a vanload. Christ.

'No. Too sly. He told me off later. Said he'd have me put away.' She filled with contempt. 'Didn't say a word to His Honour, oh no.'

Streetwalker crudities poured out of her. This was no baffled child. Holly's language was milder than Tonietta's, but curiously more offensive. Who'd caught them?

'Did he say why he was there?' And explained when she frowned, 'I presume you were in Battishall's motor, lantern hours? Only nightwalkers – poachers, twitchers – prowl after dusk.'

'Must have stood watching in the dark. Ugh!' She shivered. 'Give me the fucking creeps, them do.'

Like a fool I misunderstood, hadn't the nerve to ask her outright who it was. And her dad Den worked at the law courts, after all.

'Where did you meet Mr Battishall, Holly?'

That laugh, screech of an outraged barn owl. 'You're thick, Lovejoy, you know that? Dad had me put in care for staying out all hours. The Magistracy's where I met Ashley. He kept me for a serious talk.' She minced the word, mouth a prow.

I sighed. 'Where else?' But something had to be done with the lass, for God's sake. You can't just write people off. 'Listen, Holly. I'm in trouble. Serious.'

'With the law, Lovejoy?' she breathed. 'Same as me?'

'Aye.' I invented, 'Er, they'll put me in soon, Maudie said. So I'm going to do a scam. Will you help?'

'I knew it, Lovejoy! You're always doing things, you.' She'd come alive, almost squirming. 'Will it be dangerous?'

'Very.' With luck I'd think of something. If not, I'd warn Den. 'There's a risk, love. One thing, though. Leave off blackmailing Battishall until it's over with, okay?'

'Right, Lovejoy.' She laid a hand on my leg. I shifted it quickly. I was in enough trouble. 'You can get me at home.'

'Eh? Oh, right. I'll be in touch.'

She alighted, peered in at the window. 'How soon, Lovejoy?'

'Forty-eight hours, Holly. Be ready.' I drove off, resigned. God knows what I'd do for the child-as-was. I don't have prescriptions for the world. I only live here, as crooks say.

They told me at the Arcade that Carmen was in the Fleece. I caught him almost before he was sloshed.

'Carmen!' I greeted. 'Missed you at the audition.'

'Out driving.' Carmen's our local celebrity. He never looks at you. He claims to have invented carjacking. This game's prevalent, but as little as two years ago it was rare. You collide with another vehicle, day or night doesn't matter. You then rush up to the victim car, create a hullaballoo by smashing windows, yelling, whatever, while robbing the motorist of his valuables. Yobbos carjack for wages, antiques, boxes of jewellery. Carjackers are called hit-and-hoppits. That's it.

'Just thought I'd ask, Carmen.' (Car . . . men, get it? He has this team of drivers and hoods.) I like him because he doesn't hurt folk.

He'll even call off a jacking if he sees kiddies in the mark's motor. Even on hot days, Carmen wears a thick sheepskin, leather outside. I hate to think what weapons he's hiding.

'Lovejoy, a moment. If you will permit me, Carmen?'

'Hello, Montgomery.' Even to myself I sounded wary. Corinth had entered, eyebrows questioning. The lads all switched to maximum lust. She was made way for at the bar stools, the quicker to get her legs on display.

'I have a replica of a motor.' Mainwaring, ever the gent, smiled for approval. 'An electric Oldsmobile. They were around a lot, once.' He harrumphed, amused. 'Before we opted for pollution!'

'Who made it?' An electric motor car won the USA's first recorded motor race a century ago, beating the petrol-drivens.

'Bought in.' Montgomery smirked, knowing but not telling. 'Corinth wants it *in* the exhibition, not outside with the dross.'

'Got any more? Anything similar?'

'Maybe.' He did that double brush of his moustache. 'Litterbin's fetching Corinth's Angkor Wat loot over – nudge, nudge, Lovejoy, what? We shall chop it. Made by Miss Corinth's own factory. Original umber.'

Cambodia's a lesson in what not to buy, if you want to stay legal. Lately realizing that it had some of the world's great antique treasures, Cambodia issued another appeal for people to stop looting. This plea is always a signal for international dealers to start a looting frenzy. Cambodia's new Constitution even states stern penalties for treasure traffickers. It's no good. Every dealer in Europe knows how to reach traffickers – two phone calls, and you're through to the Munich dealers who'll promise, and bring you, a seven-hundred-year-old temple carving, a Buddha's head, a whole temple in container loads (via Thailand, Indonesia then Holland). Cambodia's fighting a losing battle. Angkor Wat's very size, 100 square kilometres, limits security. There are scores of other sites. Western dealers have been in raptures about the sacred royal Khmer Empire's sites ever since the Tokyo conference pledged money, aid, protection. It's a laugh, though a tragic one. Such pious gatherings only serve to publicize the treasures' availability. My prediction: Angkor Wat will whittle down to zilch, like Rome, Venice, Yucatán, in two decades. Fini.

'Original burnt umber? You sure, Montgomery?'

There's been a terrible row between the French and India about Camobodian antiques. Indian restorers 'restored' some of Angkor Wat's temples by cleaning the stonework, changing the colour from a lovely umber to bright sandy hues. The French went berserk, accusing India's restorers of ruination. India said sandy was the original colour. See? International co-operation is a contradiction in terms. But Montgomery's news was good. One phone call to London, the East Coast Express would be heaving with cheque-book dealers by morning. The railways ought to send me a turkey every Christmas.

'Include them, and you can bring your motor inside.' This was news to me. Corinth never had, hasn't, will never have, a factory of fakers. Mainwaring and Corinth must be diddling Litterbin out of much. I wouldn't mind getting cheated by Corinth, as long as it was in my line of duty.

'A wise move, Lovejoy!' He drifted. Me and Carmen watched.

'What goes on there, Lovejoy? Him and Corinth.'

'He loves her. She exploits him. Tit for tat, Carmen?'

'Right. I've got a load of antique toys, mechanicals, car mascots, little pot houses. Not much to look at, but I want rid. From a good genuine antique business.' He sounded aggrieved.

'Carjacked *and* genuine?' Stolen stuff would have my exhibition impounded in a flash by Maudie Laud. 'Can't do it. Maud's Plod in every bush.'

'How'll I shift it?' he demanded, as if I was to blame.

'Take it to the M18 service station, Saturday night, nine o'clock.' I gave him the name of an Ulster lass, Nuala, who comes across with her dad. It's a secret non-secret non-market, if you follow. You can actually place an order for a yet-to-be stolen antique, then simply turn up, pay up, and drive off with it all on the same day. (For legal reasons I can't name it, but it isn't a million miles from Hawksmoor.) 'Say I sent you.'

He bought drinks, but one pint makes me waterlogged. 'Okay, Lovejoy. Tit for tat. Your Geake's a wobbler. My lads hated the bastard. He chased a carjacker, doing a ton. Topped some poor bleeder, a wrapper.'

Which being translated meant William Geake was a weirdo.

Chasing a carjacker one night, he crashed at 100 m.p.h, killed some innocent, car a write-off.

'But these things happen, Carmen.'

He looked straight at me, an all-time first. 'Lovejoy. *There was no carjacker.*' He allowed a second for it to sink in. 'He told the Plod a tale. I'm sorry he recovered. He should have died, not the padre.'

'What padre?' I was lost. Geake pursued a non-existent carjacking priest?

'Some old git, God rest him.' Carmen was losing interest.

'Amen,' I said. 'Cheers, Carmen.'

Geake. Ex-policeman of this parish. Chased a mirage, and killed somebody in the process?

30

The hotel was in uproar. I was worried about the cost of so many blokes. I didn't dare ask about Tinker's IOUs. They were all busy unloading, shouting, carrying furniture, paintings, pots. Illicit labourers, unrecorded by the Inland Revenue, are freely (not free-ly) available in East Anglia. In Lincolnshire alone there's 20,000 known gangmasters. One call brings an army, ready to slog for pay on the hoof.

In a second I was surrounded by dealers and vannies, all holding out chits, chops, papers. I signed every one unread, to buy breath. Tinker was a hundred yards off, waving they were all okay. In three seconds I paid out more bribes than India's Redline bus contractors of New Delhi, and they hold the galaxy record.

'This is exciting, Lovejoy!' Miss Priscilla and Miss Philadora were thrilled, actually applauding when they stepped out of the motor. 'And such a worthy cause!'

The Americans were having tea on the lawn with Roberta and Ashley. A lovely picture. Old Jim Andrews was watching. I hung back. The Dewhursts fluttered ahead.

'You're Lovejoy. Anzacs, gunner, Western Desert, right?'

'No, Jim. Lovejoy, antique dealer.'

Today he looked old. I smelled whisky. 'Could have sworn,' he muttered, then focused. 'See that end van? Not been unloaded properly. Wouldn't last a day under fire. Rabble!'

Four pantechnicons stood nearby. One had its tail locked and chained, ready to go. The others stood tail down, furniture, paintings, clocks, packing cases, being unloaded.

'It has, Jim,' I explained. 'The driver's locked it.'

'Ignoramus.' He shook with vehemence. 'Should be put on a charge! That's what's wrong with this country! Backsliders!'

We were far enough away for his senile quaver to be lost in

the open air. He pointed with his stick. I had to prop the daft old coot up.

'Measure a vehicle's capacity! There was one foot width times height times length missing from its contents.'

'They took out *less* than its volume?' I was doubtful. If he really was barmy it meant nothing. If correct, though, it asked what was huge in surface area, but thin. A big oil painting?

'Its interior is lopsided!' He pointed triumphantly. 'One wall's a foot thicker!' He became sly. 'We'll create a diversion, set something on fire, maybe the truck itself, during which – '

'Er, good idea, Jim.' I'd seen too many burning vehicles lately. 'Tell you what. I'll suss things out. You keep watch.'

He winked. 'Good, son. Recce before guns.'

God, I thought, agreeing to his lunacy and going to join the rest. I'll soon be as daft as him. I was frantic about William Geake. Juliana was on the steps, scurrying with her list. Chemise saw me, waved with a smile. Tinker grinned from the verandah with a jug and glass, in clover, calling instructions. Sundry aged folk wandered.

'All happening, Lovejoy!' Mahleen called loudly. Roberta winced, raised a hand to her temple, reclining on her chaise. Ashley leapt with a shawl. Teacups tinkled. Idyllic.

'What's the agenda?' I asked.

'Money,' Wilmore said, all happy. 'My home ground!'

Whoops, laughter. I found an iron garden chair, joined the circle. Nadette darted a sharp smile from me to Mahleen, more gold than ever. Vernon and Jerry tapped calculators.

'Anything you fancy, Lovejoy?' Nadette cooed sweetly. 'You've not sampled *all* the antiques, have you, dear?'

'Whose money?' I'm always worried by women's wars. Women's logic is for losing track of.

'The Cause's, Lovejoy.' Vernon the Sincere. 'How much d'you reckon the exhibition will make?'

Hildra cried, 'Thousands! Look at all those *fakes*.'

'It's too much,' Roberta said faintly. 'That Miss Witherspoon must go instantly.'

'I'll do it, my dear.' Ashley rose to hurtle off.

'No. Roberta. I need Juliana.' I wasn't having it.

'Ashley!' Roberta whimpered.

'Roberta knows nothing, Ashley.' I didn't let him stare me down, not with what I now knew. 'Your place, your exhibition. But if I leave, your enterprise vanishes. I set it up. Juliana stays. No argument.'

The Yanks went quiet. The Dewhursts coloured. Miss Priscilla, peacemaker, put in gently, 'Lovejoy *does* know forgeries, Roberta. And his obverse – '

'That's right, Priscilla. I'm the obverse, okay? My guess is, it'll all go. Fakes,' I added drily, 'often go faster than genuine antiques. Honest folk know why.'

'But the expense, Lovejoy?' from good old Wilmore.

'Antique dealers operate on thirties. Thirty per cent's the least possible profit. One third's the most they'll pay. Three times the buying price is what they ask.'

'But that's terrible!' If Priscilla had been wearing her apron she'd have thrown it over her head in horror. She does it at calamity.

'Sounds right.' Vernon and Jerry were nodding.

'How much, then, Lovejoy?' Wilmore asked.

'I'll estimate the total once the exhibition's set up. We'll take sixes – that's two-thirds. The rest goes to the owners.'

'My hotel's expenses!' Ashley threatened, but he didn't worry me now. All I saw was him blubbering beside his car begging young Holly for a shag, offering fistfuls of notes.

'Any more questions?' I looked round.

'That *ugly* girl ruins the ambience,' Roberta said.

'More than ambience'll be ruined.' I'd had enough malingering. 'Chemise is worth any ten. She stays.'

Wilmore spoke up. 'Lovejoy. I want to ask you a serious personal question.' For a second my heart stopped, thinking of his golden missus. 'Can we make this exhibition an elastic commodity? Keep the income flowing after?'

'Yes.' I cleared my throat. 'I've to find a safe centre to operate from. I've found one.'

'How do we finance it?' Vernon, from the heart. 'Loans?'

'No banks, for Christ's sake.' The Misses Dewhurst cried out at my language. I said sorry, forgot myself. 'We make the dealers raise the bread. We provide the market.'

They were doubtful. '*What* safe centre? Will it cost?'

'Not much more than your holiday, Jerry.'

They spoke a little while I collared some cakes, minuscule one-calorie toothfillers. Wilmore was elected spokesman.

'Can't be done, Lovejoy, on no overheads.'

'Really?' I rose, scooping the last plateful into my pocket for the journey. 'Wilmore, don't ever go into antiques. Borrow your motor, Priscilla? I'll be ten minutes.'

Chemise followed my beckoning. 'Know what?' she said. 'Juliana's resigned. Couldn't face it.'

Couldn't face seeing her painting forgery auctioned off as the real thing, more like. We got in the motor. Chemise asked to go back for her coat, the weather was turning chilly.

'What made her chuck it?' I asked. 'She was okay when I arrived.'

'That old man with the walking stick interrupted her. She burst into tears and left.' She shivered. 'I'm freezing.'

Women always are. Never known one with warm feet, and I've searched, I've searched.

'We're going the wrong way, Lovejoy,' she said after a bit. 'This is to Fenstone.' She was looking at me in a way she never had. 'Left, Lovejoy.'

I yelled, 'Don't you ever frigging well shut *up*?'

'I'm sorry, darling.'

You can't tell them. They never listen. *Darling?*

During the journey, I reflected on how things had turned out. Maybe some dealer did for Tryer? Antiques is a game of snakes and ladders, millions of snakes and hardly any ladders. But something I'd said lately kept coming to mind: money's the only thing without value. Psychotics, politicians, and accountants don't know this. Somehow I'd entered a world where all money schemes were undermined, ruined. Jox, Tryer, Dame Millicent, the lot. Therefore the weirdo was as sane as you. So I'd to look among the normals for the nutter. Except, why did I?

Chemise was watching me. I thought she'd been asleep. 'You don't have to, Lovejoy.'

'Sorry. I talked my thoughts?'

'Some.' She stared out. It was coming on to rain. 'I miss Tryer, Lovejoy. He didn't take me seriously, not like you. But he treated me grand.' She smiled the woman's non-smile. 'Me so ugly!' I had more sense than try to talk her out of her self-prejudice. 'He already had a wife.'

That I knew. 'What do you think of this lot, love?'

'The Americans?'

'And the Battishalls, the Cause.' I was surprised about the Dewhursts, but astrology makes people do daft things. I said as much.

'It's not so crazy, Lovejoy. A cause can turn massacres to musicals, Vietnam for *The White Horse Inn*.'

'If you say so,' but I was uncomfortable. We passed Fletchinghurst, where Easter festivals hark back to sacrificial days, even children's skipping rhymes sounding sinister. It got me thinking.

There was a report once, dated 23 February 1809. Manuscript only. You still find copies in bookshops: Napoleon in America. It stated that one French frigate with 150 men could 'capture Pensacola' from the mouth of the Mississippi, having taken Spanish Florida and Louisiana. I'd had to look up Pensalcola. Once head of the USA, Bonaparte would be 'possessed' – the manuscripts always spell that wrong – of Canada, Mexico, all North America.

Royalty's funny stuff. You don't need voting in, for a start. And, if you're voted out or executed, you're the dragon's teeth – somebody else takes your place. Execute Charles I, there's always a Charles II *et seq*. For the Cause, the eighty-ninth cousin umpteen times removed will do. And you don't need a multi-megabuck Human Genome Diversity Project to prove it, like the Italians have in Turin to prove that the pre-Roman Etruscans are still around. You can mislay the heir to a throne, but you can't eradicate royalty.

As I write, the King of All the Gypsies is being crowned. Okay, it's Romania, there's a rival somewhere, but so? Par for royalty's course. A crown of jewels and over three dozen gold coins, bestowed outside – *sic* – the Orthodox cathedral in Sibiu is a powerful symbol, even if the King's a coppersmith. The point is it's *now*, not in the Dark Ages. It's the same in Buganda, which crowns its thirty-sixth King. Gremlins, however, might decide that by the time anybody reads this . . . Naturally, constitutions change. No country stays the same. Hence Australia, Fiji, Papua New Guinea change the face on their postage stamps. Fine by me. It's what countries do. Politics is

226

mutation by decree. So kings may come and queens may go, but royalty lives, even if its earthly representatives don't linger.

Like take Russia's 'Nicholas the Simple', as acid-tongued writers call Nicholas II. Now, I simply don't know whether the last Czar of All the Russias was right to assume personal command of his entire army in 1915. Or why he believed his friendship with Rasputin, that Siberian holy nutter, would bring the House of Romanov closer to the Czar's beloved narod, his people. But read the Czar's love letters to his Czarina Alexandra – they wrote daily – your heart almost breaks. And she was only 12 when they fell in love, at her sister's wedding. Take away the conventional silliness of lovers ('My darling, Sunny . . .') and you well up. Leave aside Anastasia – was she, wasn't she – and you still question who the Pretender Czar actually is/was. Conventional history, that old fibber, depicts Czar Nicholas standing with his baby son Alexei in his arms to face the execution squad. Terrible, sure, and there are witnesses. But who exactly *was* that quiet laboratory technician who passed away only last year in St Petersburg, whose colleagues *knew* was little Alexei himself, the last Romanov Czar of All the Russians, whose tiny bones were never found in the excavations of the disused mineshaft at Ekaterinburg . . . ?

'I'll drive, Lovejoy.' Chemise switched off the ignition.

Struggling with the wheel, I exploded. 'You silly cow! You'll have us in the bloody hedge!'

She was maddeningly calm. 'You're muttering and demented. Get from behind that wheel, for Christ's sake. Twice you've nearly collided.'

My hands were damp and shaking, sweat running down my armpits. What on earth had I been thinking about? Worse, the arrogant bitch turned out to be a superb driver, double declutching and all.

We arrived at Juliana's studio in Fenstone as dusk fell. No sign of life. I told Chemise to keep the engine running, and walked about a bit to recover. The wattle-and-daub wall would have been simple to cut through, but I picked the lock because I'm a conservationist at heart. Inside, just her plain studio, neat, clean, things put away. When I'm painting, tidiness goes. I found the painting she'd shown me that Sunday morning. It still felt unconvincing. Yet I felt queer.

At first I put it down to getting myself all unglued while driving Priscilla's old Morris banger, but kept finding myself walking along one wall. It was plenty tall enough. And there were marks on the floor. Not exactly grooves, but shiny scored marks – smooth wheels running in an arc?

The wall held a stack of shelves. I took down a dusty book on painting, Mayer on artist materials. Old edition, long superseded. I looked at a pot. The solvent had evaporated, leaving a crust. Dust, dust. In a studio so excrutiatingly tidy?

'In other words,' I said aloud, 'you are Juliana's place. The wall is someone else's.'

'Whose?' a voice said.

'Not yours, Reverend.' I was cool, safe. Chemise was out there still. He was tall, lean, looked fast on his pins. And hungrier than usual. Except I didn't know his usual.

He moved quietly in, closing the door. It didn't swing open. I must have picked it well, no damage.

'Then whose?' He shrugged, helpless, but I'm too canny to be taken in by tricks, and moved away. Casual, but casting about for a heavy object. 'You see, Lovejoy, I badly need to know precisely what you know.'

'Where is Juliana?' I asked, throat drying fast. He was athletic, strong. Every damned thing I'm not.

'She had a journey.' He seemed surprised I'd asked.

'I came to see when you'd meet with Mr Geake, Juliana, Dame Millicent, get the village going again. I've a couple of new schemes.'

His was the sorrow of a grimly penitential monk. Except he didn't seem monkish, not celibate. I felt he was nearly as interested in women as me. I wondered if he knew about the painting Juliana had hidden behind the wall. Maybe he'd helped her set the hiding place up. But I'd better not ask outright, I warned myself, but with horror heard myself say, 'Did *you* make Juliana do the fake?'

He imitated even more surprise. 'Fake? You mean the little painting Miss Witherspoon discovered in church? No.' He smiled, and for a second I thought things were going to be all right, that my thumping chest was wasting its time. 'I heard about your coming forgeries exhibition, Lovejoy. And the wealth it will bring the great Cause.'

'The Cause?' I grinned, a skull peeling layers. 'Barmy sods, begging pardon.'

He held an axe. *He carried an axe.* You don't get priests with axes. Him standing there, under the one electric globe, in this remote dying village in the marshes, that low mist stealing up. Dusk had turned solid, no street lights. I realized I couldn't hear Chemise's motor. He hefted the axe like he wanted to show it off.

'Chemise!' I croaked. No answer. 'Chemise!'

She didn't come.

'The question is, Lovejoy, if you know, please tell me. I,' he said with his confessor's grin, 'shall judge if you speak truly. I have experience in these matters.'

He stepped closer. I grabbed a paintbrush, frantically wondering if I could chuck a bottle of turpentine in his face, make a dash to where Chemise had obviously nodded off, the disloyal mare.

Backing, I fell over an easel, scrambled upright, scared now. He stopped, judging me with dispassion. I knew how the victims of the Inquisition must have felt.

'Why are the Americans here, Lovejoy? What *is* their Cause? Truthfully, now. I know falsehood.'

I ahemed gravel from my throat, found I'd backed away against the wall. No door or windows, only two canvases, no guns, weapons of any description.

'They've joined the Battishalls, I think,' I cried in panic, not wanting to be misunderstood, to reveal all.

He stepped closer. If I moved a pace forward, he'd be within a swing of an axe. His axe, my head. He must have been a boxer at his non-existent seminary.

'The bishop said you'd made enquires, Lovejoy. As had your lady friend.' His grin faded away, his axe lifting an inch. I'd no chance to move. 'I learned by telephone.'

'Look, Reverend,' I shrilled, sweat stinging my eyes. 'So what, you didn't take holy orders? Neither did I!' I laughed, a squeak. 'Plenty of people pretend . . .'

His eyes bored, murderous. 'Pretend what they're not?'

I drew ten lungfuls in one go, bawled, 'Chemise, love!'

Laconic now. It would take one smash. 'I'm afraid I had to ask her to leave urgently.'

Chemise, my lifeline. Gone? The faithless bitch. I'd kill the stupid mare, leaving me alone with a maniac who'd topped Tryer and was now going to top me.

'Gone?' I tried to say. My lips felt blue.

'To Dame Millicent's. Not far, just far enough.'

'For what? I've told you everything. They're into genealogy, lunatic stuff about the zodiac.' A true friend of the Misses Dewhurst, I had to keep them out of it for their own safety. Except they'd *want* to be sacrificed, surely, to save me? 'The Dewhurst sisters put everybody up to it. Nothing to do with me.'

He turned, the prelude to assault with weapon. I'd seen the stance in pub fights. I drew breath to plead, beg, whine, but stayed transfixed, rabbit and stoat.

'The law . . .' I got out.

'Law is a joke, the lawcourt its clown.'

'Please. I'll not tell you killed anyone, honest.'

To this day I don't know if I got the words out or if I only thought them. He seemed to make a judgement, and lifted his hand.

And then something beautiful happened. Geake, ex-policeman, churchwarden, stepped through the door, foot slurring, and said evenly, 'Father Jay? An intruder, I think?'

'Yes!' I yelped, leapt forward, wrists out for mancles. 'I surrender!' I babbled this until William Geake, rescuer, told me in resurrected Plod tones to shut up.

'Done any damage, has he?' Geake said, looking.

'Nothing. I think, Mr Geake. I heard noises. Lovejoy had this axe. I relieved him of it. I was about to call you.'

This wasn't true. I gaped. He'd brought the bloody axe.

'Very well, Father Jay. I'll see to him.' Geake tilted his head. I moved thankfully out of the door. No car, no Chemise. Geake followed, gestured to a motor across the road. 'Miss Witherspoon's, Lovejoy. She'll be along any second, give you a lift, unless you want to wait for that ugly lass.'

'No, ta, sir.' I fawned, grovelled, grinned, wrung his hand. 'Thank you, sir. Any time I can do anything, sir, Lovejoy's the name, antiques the game. Any auction, I'm your man. Okay?'

'Lovejoy,' he said wearily, 'you wear me out, y'hear? Now sod off out of Fenstone, and never ever return.'

'Sure, sure! Willco, Inspector!'

Sweating now with sheer relief, I went and sat in the motor. I was shaking at the escape, my bloody teeth actually chattering. Lovejoy the Cool, trembling. The keys were in the ignition, but the thought honestly never crossed my mind. The mist had closed in, darkness impenetrable.

Across the road, I could barely see the studio glim, making true opaque fog. No wonder the young folk had decided to leg it out, civilization here we come, leave Fenstone to its sombre mists and loony priest. I thought, uneasy for reasons I couldn't fathom, what if there's a frigging bomb in this motor? Planted by Juliana, off her rocker from love of this priest . . .

A dark figure loomed. I screamed, scrabbled for the door, fell from the car, scraping my elbows – to be raised by this female, her high heels scraping.

'Lovejoy? Are you all right?'

Second time in an hour I'd been rescued, by somebody I'd suspected. I almost wept from relief. 'Oh, there you are, Jul!' I said gruffly. 'Mr Geake said you'd give me a lift.'

'It's dreadfully inconvenient. I've things to do.'

'That fake, eh?' I sat while my heart slowed.

'Fake?' She didn't switch on.

'That thing you found in church, remember?' I wagged a finger as if I'd meant that one all the time. 'We've been using French *vernis à vieiller*, haven't we? And with the Daler Bristlewhite 8 round brush. Tut tut. Just because that stuff ages patina within twelve hours doesn't mean it's right, love. Impasto takes on an umber hue that's a dead giveaway, like a tart's face whose mascara's run – '

'Lovejoy.' She alighted angrily, taking her keys. '*Walk!*'

'No, love. I've sussed the bloke you're crazy about.'

So we drove off. Ten minutes later, we encountered Chemise in the lanes, driving Dame Millicent. Even Juliana couldn't mistake an old Morris in the mists. I told her to beam them down, and explained to Chemise that there'd been a mistake. I left Juliana, having done all the asking I wanted to do. We took the old dame home. She gave us some of her home-brewed pear wine, and a merry evening was had by all.

On the way home I was too weary to upbraid Chemise as she

deserved. I just told her how I'd nearly met my doom by the mad axeman of Fenstone, been saved by Geake, my hero. She said nothing.

Worried, about midnight I phoned Maudie Laud. She treated me like dirt when I told her Father Jay killed Tryer, that he'd almost done for me too.

'As soon as you arrest him I'll make a statement – '

'Lovejoy. Mr Geake just came to make a statement.'

'And you've let that lunatic go free?'

'Lovejoy, Father Jay's also here. I'm perfectly satisfied there was no wrong-doing, except for your illicit trespass . . .'

That night Chemise and I made smiles, to her utter astonishment and my paradisical bliss. I felt calmer and more relieved than I had for weeks. It was now all straightforward.

Day dawned on my riotous exhibition, about which I was glad. It also dawned on Ashley's illicit auction, which was really bad news.

31

We lay there in my divan bed. Chemise was astounded I still smarted at Maudie Laud's dismissal of my story.

'See?' I complained bitterly. 'Who do they believe when the chips are down? An axe maniac, or a decent law-abider?'

'Maybe she's got a plan, Lovejoy.'

Boiled eggs chopped up in a teacup with pepper's the only way to eat eggs, except for fried both sides, eight slices of bread and butter, with hot tea. She'd done well, but I was still narked.

'Plan? They were in her office, laughing. What the hell's Geake playing at?'

'His friend.' Chemise shrugged. She didn't eat much, dry toast like they all do. 'Maybe Geake can keep him under control.'

'Like he did befo . . .' I ahemed, pretended some egg had gone down the wrong way.

'Something's wrong, Lovejoy.' She was still. She had no night-dress, wore my tatty dressing gown. I was naked. It's no good dressing up to go to bed, I always think; you only have to take it off. 'If Father Jay was really going to . . . you know, then why didn't he eliminate me too?'

'Eh?' I paused in mid nosh. I hate logical women.

'He would have had to, wouldn't he? Otherwise, what could he say when I got back? Instead, he sent me to bring another witness, Dame Millicent. He'd have had to murder three instead of just you. See?'

'Oh, that's frigging charming, that is!' I yelled. I almost chucked my breakfast at her in rage, but they don't come my way often enough to waste. 'Look, you daft sod. It was *me* in there with that axe killer.' I almost fainted, remembering.

'That's the point, Lovejoy,' said this soul of reason. 'He was simply trying to frighten you.'

'A loon with a hatchet succeeds.' I resumed eating, then stopped. 'Why?'

'He kept asking what the Americans wanted. You told him?'

'Aye. Wouldn't you have?'

She made me recount the conversation in excrutiating detail, word for word while she fried more bread. She refused my tea sugar this time. I'm surrounded by psychotics.

'Then you didn't,' she concluded, coming close. I budged over to keep her place's warmth. 'You didn't tell him they want to establish a Pretender to the USA.'

We contested like children, I did, you didn't, I did, until I had to concede, because I hadn't.

'But that means I'm wrong about Father Jay doing . . .'

'And you can't be wrong, Lovejoy. Is that it?'

'He's innocent because he's a holy priest, right?'

'Nothing at all to do with it, Lovejoy.'

And she meant it. Each of us has different ideas. But I remembered my law: everybody's salvation meets at gold.

She sat in silence while I finished my grub, and slid down beneath the duvet.

'Admit it, Lovejoy.' She smiled, her features radiant. 'You're wrong about Father Jay. I'm wrong sometimes. Like thinking you'd not look at me twice, me being ugly.'

'That's because you're thick,' I explained reasonably. 'Women have smaller brains. Women and men are . . .'

But she was working me by then, growing in confidence. I decided to postpone my explanation, having forgotten it.

Time for loose ends. I remembered a bloke called Fish from Halstead who forges copper tokens – halfpennies, farthings, even silver ones. I got him on the phone, third try, told him to mount a display.

'I've only ninety, maybe a hundred, Lovejoy,' he said.

'Everything you've got, Fish, okay? Bring your bleeper along.' We call him Fish because he uses a Fisher metal detector, trespassing away merrily through the candle hours. He supplements his field finds by forging Georgian trade tokens in his brother's workshop. The populace was short of change three hundred years ago, so shops struck token coins to help trade along. 'Tinker'll set you up in a cabinet. No need to give proper identifications. Let them be mystery finds, see?'

'But forging, Lovejoy . . .' He's always nervous, from run-ins with gamekeepers.

'They're tokens, not coin of the realm, Fish. And who's to know? You only *found* them, see?'

'That's right, Lovejoy!' He brightened, said he'd be along.

Three more calls brought a promise of an old ship's figurehead, 1795, that I'd last seen Peter Duck finishing in Lowestoft. I wasn't too lucky with some Edwardian jewellery – Pinner Joe'd just sold a load of his forgeries to some German antiques collector, but he said he'd bring what he had left. I managed to threaten, bribe, inveigle Hulldown from Wolverhampton to bring his forged insurance firemarks; he's the best faker of these copper/lead plaques for showing Georgian London that your business was insured and by what company; the 1800s began the real heyday, and Hulldown was the best in the business. The loon didn't really want to come, Wolverhampton Wanderers playing at home. I lied that Big John Sheehan wanted his support personally. After that I didn't need rhetoric.

'Chemise,' I said awkwardly as we got ready, 'thanks, love.' She said nothing. We hit the road to the exhibition – where as it happens the first person we clapped eyes on was Tinker, paralytic but focused, sitting under an old mulberry in a ring of tins and bottles, some still awaiting their turn.

'Lovejoy,' he said, slurring. 'See them cars?'

There must have been four hundred, all over the grass and two adjacent fields. We'd been stopped by a bobby, made to park three furlongs away. Chemise was furious, like women are, wanted to argue. I'd walked on alone.

'Aye?' No people, he meant.

'Know where the folk are, Lovejoy? In a frigging queue waiting for tickets, that's where.' He cackled, started coughing, spewing phlegm onto the grass and tumbling over. I propped him up, shaking sense into the old sod.

'Tickets?' I asked. 'God above, what tickets?'

'The big auction, Lovejoy. I've announced you're going to auction the whole exhibition off in private this evening, see? First three hundred get tickets, the rest get told to piss orff!' He did another roll in the aisles. I dragged him vertical to explain, but Chemise came storming to his rescue, What-are-you-doing-hurting-that-poor-old-etc, etc.

'He's cruel, missus,' Tinker croaked. 'Me an old soldier, all the work I've done while he's been shaggi – '

'Here.' I gave him two notes and the bent eye. 'What auction, Tinker?' I smiled innocently at Chemise, confiding, 'He needs his chest thumping when he coughs.'

Tinker wheezed, 'You didn't show up much while me and this lass were arranging things. I reckoned you'd be shagging that gold-coloured Yank bird, so – '

'His mind wanders,' I told Chemise weakly.

'I told the dealers you was auctioning everything, no chop no chip, no paddles.'

'Paper?' I wondered should I slay him now or later.

'Paper, Lovejoy. Then it'll all be done today, see?' His rheumy old eyes were weighing me up, which way would I go.

Paddles is the growing Continental habit of issuing little wooden bats with numbers stuck on. Each bidder has a distinct number. No cheating, therefore. The absence of paddles is a plus to the trade. So Tinker'd earned one point for survival.

To chop is to share in the deal when buying an antique. A fraudulent auctioneer might well ask for a 'chop' – a fraction of the price paid – to be slipped illicitly to himself. This is strictly forbidden and illegal, but, like rain, is perennial in East Anglia. Tinker's 'no chop' promise to the dealers who'd already arrived meant each dealer would keep all resale profit. Two-nil for Tinker.

'Chip' is the auctioneer's slang for Value Added Tax, currently at 17.5 per cent. Tinker's promise that there'd be 'no chip' meant that fraction would go into the dealers' already overstuffed wallets. Three thumbs-up to nil for Tinker. And 'paper' meant IOUs would be welcomed. This is always a problem, because somebody would have to seek out those antique dealers still owing after thirty days – the limit of patience, after which the ground war begins, with blood-soaked motors being found abandoned on the M25 road.

No wonder the dealers were queuing. Well, I'd wanted them to see my exhibition. But I also wanted them buying, in huge numbers. I

236

realized Tinker had now won four-nil, the cunning old soak. Every single visitor would be a dealer, since Tinker's lads would now exclude the public. And they'd all keep silent about the looming auction. The important thing was to keep the news of the auction from the exhibitors. I was being rushed into risk when I wanted time. I hoped the Dewhurst sisters were in arranging flowers or something.

'Thanks, Tinker,' I said. 'You did really well.'

'Anything for you, Lovejoy,' he said. 'Are we for it?'

For a second I stood looking down at him, sitting there on the damp grass. Filthy, decrepit, still with his old army medals, greasy, drunk, stubble obscuring his stained face. But friends don't come better. He could have legged it, could be tottering along the bypass thumbing a lift to safety, but he'd stayed in spite of my rotten temper, and knowing that the worst was yet to come. I gave him the rest of my gelt.

'Chemise? Give him your money.'

She opened her bag. 'Yes, darling. How much?'

Tinker brightened at the option of a more slotniks. 'I need a drink about now, missus,' he said, choking with one careful eye on her handbag. 'Clears me windpipe, see.'

'Cheers, Tinker. See you at the auction, eh?'

'Right, Lovejoy.'

Inside it was bedlam, but gradually nearing order. The Dewhursts were there, fussing. Old Jim Andrews was in the foyer, wearing his campaign medals, barking instructions, only falling silent when Ashley happened by. People were arranging display cases, anxiously saying hello when catching sight of me. Notices were being arranged on easels. Some of the forgers were already standing by their products, worry mounting at the thought of close scrutiny from possible buyers. From upstairs came the sound of hammering. Some exhibitors waved, beckoning, wanting me to tell them they'd done right.

'Lovejoy!' Priscilla said, all floral and lace. 'Isn't this *exciting*? The whiffling gentlemen are *so nice*!'

Philadora blushed becomingly. 'One *whistled* at us, Lovejoy! What on earth would Mother have said?'

They tittered. I watched them. Tinker had promised the dealers that the entire exhibition would be auctioned off later. I'd have to plan.

'A cross lady rang up, Lovejoy.' Their humour faded. 'She had some silver for you at her home. Mend its shoulder, I think she said, or else!'

Sabrina, wanting her genuine silver made into a let's-pretend fake. Which made me think of auctions, and those terrible words, genuine and fake, so ve-e-e-ry similar, don't you find? Tonietta's lovely antique tortoise-shell fan would go brilliantly. I'd make sure of that. Must remember to tell Tinker to go to Tonietta's stall for it.

'Lovejoy!' Ashley stormed up, brimming with fury. 'Where have you been? I have sixty-seven instances of damage to my hotel! Your hoodlums have knocked a wall down in the terrace room! Furthermore, hundreds of indigents are queuing the length of the conservatory – '

'Knocked a wall down?' I yelped in anger. 'I'll put that right, sir! I'll follow you there in a trice! I must just give an instruction to my ladies.'

'Just make sure you do, Lovejoy!'

'Oh, Ashley. Remember that colander? Would you please lend it to that fifth pottery display, evidence of a *real* antique? Tinker will see you get a certified receipt.'

He nodded, strode off for it.

'Ladies,' I said quietly, watching him march away, 'you and I have a truly horrid task before us.'

'We . . . *we* have, Lovejoy?'

'Get your coats. Meet me by the servants' entrance. If anybody asks, say your cat's ill.'

They looked doubtful. Priscilla said, 'We have no cat.'

'No, Priscilla,' I said wearily. 'Just pretend.'

'A deception, Prissy!' Philadora breathed. 'Like when we did Father's waistcoat buttons the wrong way on Grotto Day!'

My patience had finally cracked. I slid off, shouting to the exhibitors standing by that I'd be back in a sec, just going to the loo.

We drove into town at speed, meaning we notched up double figures near Thunderford where the A12 trunk road finally shows willing and becomes a sensible dual carriageway. I was all but screaming with impatience when we reached Roman Road. I parked outside Sabrina's house. Let the chintz curtains twitch, see if I cared.

'Now, ladies.' They were all serious. 'Be *seen*.'

'Seen?' they asked together, apprehensive.

'I want to create an impression of reliability, honesty, truth, patience, decent family values.'

'How very pleasant, Lovejoy!' said Priscilla.

'With you here, I'm in my sinless phase, okay?'

Alone, I went to knock on Sabrina's door. She herself opened it, alarmed. I stood to one side, and she looked past me.

Her husband was on the stairs. 'Who is it?'

'Lovejoy Antiques, Inc.,' I said. 'Me and my partners are to collect a silver – '

'Shhh, Lovejoy!' he said. 'She's got it here. No delays for Christ's sake.' Sabrina winked openly at him, and he retreated upstairs.

'Come in for a second, Lovejoy. I'll see it's wrapped.'

She closed the door, wrapping herself hungrily round me so I could hardly breathe. We grappled, Sabrina groaning with lust and setting me off doing the same but scared to death in case hubby came a-prowling. I was saved when the door behind me opened. We sprang apart, gasping, me trying to straighten my garb, to see the Misses Dewhurst there, so sweet.

'We wondered if you needed assistance with the silverware, Lovejoy,' Philadora said gently.

'No,' I managed to get out, mopping my brow. Sabrina, instantly pleasant smiles and not a hair out of place, was cool as a cucumber, but then women have this knack of covering up, literally and metaphorically, in a millisec. She brought the biggin, already packed.

'Thank you, Lovejoy, in anticipation,' she said with meaning. 'Payment is the usual rate. Agreed?'

'Er, yes. Ta.'

We left, me driving. At the traffic lights Philadora said, 'Lovejoy? Was that lady inviting *undue attentions*?'

'Sabrina?' I looked at them both in the rearview mirror. 'Certainly not! She's a married woman!'

'Our apologies, Lovejoy.' They sounded unsure.

At Beth's house I made sure the Dewhurst ladies were first up the garden path. I let them do the knocking and introducing, safe because I'd phoned ahead. Beth invited us in. I graciously allowed

239

the Misses Dewhurst to pack the Bilstons. They approved because the packing cloths had been boiled clean.

'Thank you for letting your Bilstons be used as display items,' I told her formally. No sign of her husband.

'Not at all, Lovejoy,' she replied with equal formality. 'It's a pleasure to meet someone whose interests have passion.'

'You are so very kind,' I said, regressing to a St James's level of foppery. 'I am indebted to your good self for your inestimable generosity. Please believe me, madam, we shall have your antiques back with you before ten o'clock tonight.'

'I have every trust . . .'

Sickening, but we kept it up, flowery assurances tripping lightly off the tongue until I almost puked. The Misses Dewhursts loved it. I let them carry the enamels to the car, hung back for a swift grope, Beth greedier even, clawing at me behind the door until I heard somebody give a light cough. I stepped out, getting enough breath to say decent thank yous.

And, on the return journey to Dragonsdale, the Dewhursts didn't speak. By the time I'd collected up seven more antiques, all on the understanding that they would be returned by the evening, they'd begun to freeze, hands primly folded in accusation.

In fact, their disapproval got me seriously narked. I pulled in a mile short of the hotel. By now, cars were streaming along in the same direction, but I ignored the honking and shouts of abuse and gave the two ladies a mouthful.

'Listen, the pair of you.' I did my grimmest bent eye. 'I want no criticism, not a word. You hear?'

'Lovejoy.' Priscilla grasped the nettle. 'We observed an *implicit liaison* between you and at least three of the ladies visited. We heard you promise to return these antiques, knowing it is impossible to do so in time!'

'I know.' I hesitated, decided in for a penny, in for a pound. 'I need your help. In a fraud.'

Philadora was wide-eyed. 'Prissy! Did Lovejoy say *fraud*?'

'I did.' Looking into those eyes was like staring at four brilliant blue saucers. 'Know what a roup is?'

'No,' they said faintly.

'A roup's an old Scotch country auction. Items were numbered in a roup-call, meaning a list published before the auction day. Then you sell all, higher bidder wins.'

'But we haven't a list, Lovejoy – '

'Shut up, for Christ's sake!' I shouted, deafening myself in the confines of the small motor. 'Just listen!' I forced a smile and waved as two honking saloons cruised by, their drivers recognizing me at the last second. Then I rounded on the two ladies. 'A roup nowadays has a special meaning, different from the Scotch original. It's now a *fraudulent* auction. I publish the list after – *after* – the auction, to pretend things were all right at the time, see?'

'But the dealers will complain that they never saw the list until it was too late, Lovejoy.'

I could have banged their stupid heads together. 'That's where you come in. You will stand at the exhibition entrance giving out a pamphlet, forgery in general, *caveat emptor* and all that.'

'No list?' Priscilla asked, guessing the answer.

'No list,' I agreed. 'When the auction's over you will deliberately litter the car parks and fields with discarded lists.'

'We've had no time to prepare a list, Lovejoy!' They were aghast.

'No.' Why can't people see the obvious? It wears me out. 'The items won't *be* listed, just loosely grouped.'

'But what about the exhibitors, Lovejoy?'

'You,' I said firmly, 'will arrange a large supper party for them all. At the Welcome Sailor. I, er, like the landlady. Take them there in charabancs at Mr Battishall's expense. A celebration.'

'We will?' said Priscilla.

'Yes.' I started the engine. Mustn't be late for my own fraudulent roup. 'During which,' I added, keeping the ball bouncing, 'you will abscond, and return to help me.'

'To help you what?'

I leant back against the headrest. God, I had a headache to split the Pennines. 'Sell the whole exhibition, love.'

'Have you got permission from all the fakers and forgers who actually *own* the exhibits, Lovejoy?'

'No.'

'Then how on earth can you possibly – ?'

'Not me, you stupid old faggots!' I yelled, apoplectic. 'You *and* me.

We will do it! There's no way to stop it now. *We've* obtained a load of antiques by criminal deception. There's no going back.'

Furious, I drove into the column of vehicles, ignored the signals of old George at the crossroads.

'Lovejoy,' Miss Priscilla said timidly as we arrived.

'What now?'

'Does this mean we're whifflers?'

That almost calmed me enough to smile. God give me strength. 'Yes. Until the auction. Then you become ponders, people who pretend to make bids randomly. But,' I added hastily in case, 'don't do it in earnest, okay? Or we'll lose every penny.'

Philadora started up. 'Lovejoy, are we *criminals*?'

'Aye,' I said, harsh. I didn't like that, because I'm no criminal, never have been.

'Oooh!' they moaned in horror.

Priscilla was made of sterner stuff, patted her sister's hand. 'Courage, Philadora,' she said quietly. 'Lovejoy doesn't want weak-willed vicarage ladies. He needs partners of mettle. Remember his obverse and our own zodiac meet at resolution!'

'Yes, Prissy,' Philadora whispered.

We alighted like troupers, marched in like that bit from 'Gunga Din'.

32

They gave me a load of ribaldry, whistles, jeers. I made for the steps, flourishing a hand in airy rejoinder.

The queue of dealers was no longer the orderly line Tinker had described. It was a seething mob, some 250 strong.

'Where the hell, Lovejoy?' from Litterbin, smoking a cigar as long as his arm. 'We've been waiting frigging days.'

'Ten minutes to go, Binny.' I consulted an imaginary watch, checking the crowd. They were all here, Farouk and his nephews, Montgomery and Corinth, Addie Allardyce and her jealous husband, Chemise taking notes on her clipboard, Bog Frew from the Old Vic in cape and ermine hat, ominously Big John Sheehan's Cavern and Tomtom looking in from some neanderthal landscape, Vasco, Big Frank from Suffolk, Harry Bateman and his Jenny, who loves effeminate Klayson – don't ask me how – and scores of other faces familiar, half-forgotten and unknown. The Brighton circus was in, the Liverpool lads – BJS's connection there – some Glasgow blokes. I felt really quite proud, the lot all haring in on my say-so. Even Jox, ready to notch another failure.

Oh, and Holly Heanley, eyeing me steadily. Now, I didn't want her here, lest I be accused of assisting the hotel owner's Lolita obsession.

'Ladies and gentlefolk,' I began into a chorus of derision, 'today sees the biggest exhibition of forgeries ever shown. I promise you: it utterly eclipses the British Museum's Fakery exhibition. At great cost, it shows that you can't trust appearances when buying antiques.'

'What else is new, Lovejoy?' some wag yelled.

'What else is *old*?' somebody gruff capped, causing roars of laughter so I couldn't hear myself.

'Any police here?' I called. It shut them up, heads shaking all round. 'This is the order of play, then. You enjoy the items, place orders if you wish. But Customs and Excise people will be in as ordinary women, okay?'

'Women' means innocent members of the public, if there is such a thing. Dunno how the term came about, but it's everywhere.

'So no mention of any auction, or you'll all get dunned for Value Added Tax. So, silence until the exhibitors leave, okay?'

The crowd growled anger. I understood the resentment. Robber barons still prowl our fair kingdom despite Magna Carta. They are called civil servants, and their creed of brutish rapacity government.

'What about this auction, Lovejoy?' Litterbin called. The throng silenced. Blokes like Litterbin tend to be Monday experts – dealers who only know when it's all over, the hindsight-blindsight brigade. They remain know-alls all their lives.

'It starts at six precisely. One mention of it to any exhibitor means it'll be cancelled. And I'll spread the word tell who was the blabbermouth. Understand? I'll be auctioneer, to ensure fair play . . .' A roar of jeers and laughter. I wafted them down, smiling but worried in case some of them didn't go along with the notion. It had to succeed, or I'd be done for. 'In the hotel dining room. Tinker's whifflers on the doors, nobody in after the first hammer, okay?'

'The women and filers, Lovejoy. What about them?'

'Any public will be shunted at the five o'clock close. The exhibitors will be bussed away at five-thirty by my helpers. None will remain. That'll leave you miserable lot and me to the auction. Teas and snacks in the entrance hall. Questions?'

'Why're we limited in numbers, Lovejoy?' a Liverpudlian voice spoke up. 'We've mates due in an hour.'

'They can see the exhibition, but only you lot get auction tickets. I want eyes.'

'Faces' are hoodlums; 'eyes' are recognizable friends. I was pleased with the response, everybody nodding yes, that's okay, sensible.

My cue to bang on the door. Tinker opened it, decidedly the worse for wear. He had three whifflers, all blokes I knew, and the Misses Dewhurst. They had books of tickets at a desk, were busily initialling them.

'Charge high,' I whispered to Priscilla, and sailed by.

The stampede began, up the steps, into the corridor. I strolled in, looking for something to eat. Maybe that pleasant serving maid Whatsername would prove kindly to a hungry benefactor like me. I do nothing but help people, get little enough appreciation.

The exhibition would have graced London's best showrooms in its complexity. I made a quick tour of the whole place, partly from bravado, but also to boost morale.

The exhibitors were all in place, many of the blokes wearing their best and standing by their stands. They were all checking their watches, nervously asking each other the time – all exhibitors at any trade show do this. Visit one, see if I'm right. I drifted through like a dignitary, my usual down-at-heel self.

Noah was there, I was pleased to see, more like Pinocchio's dad than ever, twinkly of eye, leather of apron. He had two glorious forgeries, including the mahogany tripod table.

'Good of you to come yourself, Noah.'

'Nice to get out, Lovejoy.' He smiled from underneath his bushy eyebrows. 'Can't help wondering what the catch is.'

'Suspicious old get,' I said. 'Seen a maid called Lily?'

Spoons was on the second landing. He'd brought his daft old – i.e. new – Spanish mariner's astrolabe in sterling silver, but his candle-sticks were lovely against a cloth of royal blue velveteen. I told him off for not doing as I'd said.

'Leave off, Lovejoy,' he grumbled. 'I brought my special, so don't give me earache.'

It was lovely, Rare, these Dutch baby-in-the-cellar cups. Silver, made from Elizabethan times up to the nineteenth century. The Hollanders call it *Hansje in den kelder*, 'Little Hans in the cellar', which is odd until you realize what it's for. Fill the bowl with wine, a little silver babe rises up underneath a silver dome – whereupon everybody present gets sloshed, because it's the traditional toasting vessel when a baby's imminent. Like most antiques, its name's wrong – the 'cellar' isn't, and why Hans anyway? Dunno. But Spoons had done a lovely job.

Speckie was there, tidy for once, with a *new* new pretty girlfriend to polish his longcase clocks. I told him to stop her or she'd put everybody off. A woman's work is never done, but a forger's work has to be finished well before the first customer happens by.

Linetta, one of my favourites, was quietly there, smiling beside her precision porcelains. For a while I thought of asking her if she was married/engaged/available, but got distracted by a glimpse of Juliana. I was almost sure it was her familiar figure that flitted across the landing as I inspected old Doothie's watercolours. He'd done sixteen, the paper bonny old stuff, with another thirteen views, suspiciously Turner. He had his bottle specs on to show he was ailing fast and therefore vulnerable to buyers' greed.

A nervous youth, stranger, was standing by a series of paintings near the dayroom, his stand on a wall table's grey-beige cloth. It looked really naff. I was about to explode, when I remembered who this might be. The paintings were Far East, simple fakes done beautifully. They looked real, without that giveaway stencilled appearance. From a distance they were Chinnery.

'Lovejoy?' he asked apprehensively. He was clean, presentable, looked sixteen and frightened. 'Auntie Margaret sends her . . .' he blushed, inspected his feet, 'regards,' he ended, embarrassed at his aunt, actually over thirty, feeling love.

'You Jaddo?'

'Jaddo Dainty.' He spoke defiantly. 'I done these pictures.'

'You're as good as your auntie said. Look, Jaddo.' I lowered my voice because other exhibitors were drifting across to see. 'Stay with the main mob of exhibitors, right? You'll go to the Welcome Sailor for a meal. But see me, Monday. Your auntie'll find me. You've a career ahead.'

'Will they sell?' he asked, desperate. 'Only, my dad's in trouble and –'

'Fear not, Jaddo,' I told him. 'Give your auntie my love, okay?' He reddened, mortified. I drifted on.

Even if I say so myself, it was extra special. Tapper had his coin collector's cabinet, hallmark of the medallist. He wore a three-piece suit, every inch the banker in pursuit of sidelong gain. Jackery had made the trip from Lavenham. His forgery of Seurat's nudes was beautiful. God knows what would happen when he returned from the Welcome Sailor and found it sold. But you can't make an omelette without breaking Jackerys. Is that true or not?

The trio of gold fakers from Cambridge had come with a remarkable amount of Croesus's Lydian Hoard treasure – fake you understand – and had rigged up odd display strobes I'd never seen before. Talent abounded. They'd got ancient-style music fibrillating the curtains, but I wasn't having that and said to shut it up. I wanted discretion, muted voices, murmurs of appreciation.

Daimler's 1885 motorbike was there, with an exploded diagram of the Otto four-stroke engine artistically done, going round on a circular dais, just like in the Motor Show. Really elegant. The lad had two mates along, with remakes of old model steam engines, two working. They'd been set up outside the conservatory, looked really good against all that greenery and glass.

The schoolteacher's cupboard house was brilliant, in a genuine Ince cupboard just as I'd hoped. I'd have to tell the Dewhurts to watch the price on that one.

Doper Tone, the non-curator not from Bermondsey, his photo with the pope highlighted, had brought his stuff not from St John Lateran. All brewing well.

Oddly, the real attraction was Brig. His mugs-and-droppings stall was crowded out as soon as people started coming through. I was ahead, but by the time I reached his display – by the steps leading down into the conservatory's tasteful jungle of plants and white ironwork – a press of spectators was already at his commemorative mugs, plates, plaques. I forced through. He was harassed but pleased. Several people were questioning him about the prehistoric artefacts – read dung – on his other stall on the verandah, the Weird and Wonderful section. He was issuing cards, saying price, telling the tale. I left smiling, shaking my head ruefully. Why *do* people *buy* some things?

Tesco had fought hard for space for his Mediterranean history show. I suspected the swine of having hidden the massive free-stander legend panels somewhere until I'd gone by, but hadn't time to fight. It looked all right. Mrs Boyson, with a new hairdo, was showing her clever forgery of the Thangliena diaries in Tinker's display case. I gave her a buss. Terrible to think her whole life's work would be in the hands of some undeserving buyer very soon.

My headache came on then because Ashley stormed up. We sidled into an alcove where he went ape.

'Lovejoy! I demand an explanation . . .' et Ashley cetera. He'd heard from the Misses Dewhurst about the auction.

247

'Ashley,' I said, 'don't you want the money?'

'Shhhh! Of course! But the residents dine at six!'

'Then they'll have to wait. Tell you what,' I placated him. 'Tell the Misses Dewhurst to give them supper with the exhibitors! And staff! My expense.' I smiled with the lie, being kind.

He hesitated. 'Treat?'

'Yes. Miss Priscilla's arranging it now. Be an outing for the old dears.'

That cooled, I said hello to Chess, my old printing pal from Tooting Bec. Jemima's cousin Gabbie had done mmmh, well, *nearly* a good job on the London watercolours, meaning pretty neffie really but then Jemima's been a close friend once or twice and emotion argues when common sense has no voice.

One other stand that pleased me was Fred A'Court's, neophyte gold modeller. His daughter Lana was with him. They looked nervy, polished as if going to a function. I talked as long as I could, with max psychotherapy. He'd managed to scrape together seven items for his launch into the flocking trade. I winked, said today was the first day of the rest of his life, call at my cottage Monday to decide his career plan.

But time was pressing, because the Ashleys of this world are never pacified long. I found Roberta. She was reclining, feebly managing to scoff a trolley load of cakes, biscuits, tarts, trifles, savouries, to restore her from all the work she hadn't to do. Life is one long slog.

The votive light was burning, the curtains drawn before the duff painting. I approached her chaise longue on tiptoe.

'Roberta?' I sank to my knees, offered her the soft centres. She selected three, blind. Her eyes fluttered open.

'Lovejoy?' she managed to whisper.

'Yes. Look, er, darling.' I had only a couple of minutes pre-Ashley. 'I'm committed to your cause. I've fallen for you, Roberta. That night was the most wondrous. I can't live without you. Get rid of Ashley . . .' I did about four minutes of pure soul, really naff. I tried edging a cake near where I could nick it but she was too slick and ate it with a weak sigh just as I thought I was close to a calorie. 'Darling. I want to pay *you* the money tonight, not Ashley. Your name, your bank account, darling, you alone.' Saccharine to the gills. I reached for her. If I couldn't grab grub, I'd grab solace.

248

'I knew it, Lovejoy.' Smug with self-satisfaction, having conquered all. 'I, too, was *slightly* carried away. You do have a certain passion. We need that . . .'

Her cool breast was just about to leap free when Priscilla entered with Ashley, carrying a pile of photocopy sheets. Presumably the roup-call lists for scattering.

'I apologize, Roberta,' Priscilla said, firmly not noticing my swift spring away. 'But we have a problem.'

'Ah, the payment for the Welcome Sailor?' I gave them a sincere beam. 'Chemise has already seen to it.'

Ashley glared from me to Roberta. 'Is this true, Lovejoy? Nothing you've said so far has been!'

See? No trust these days, reliability a dirty word.

'Roberta.' When in doubt appeal to authority. 'Nothing can stop us now, except doubt –' I glared at Ashley '– among loyal friends!'

'Ashley,' Roberta whispered faintly. 'Do as Lovejoy says. For me . . .' He voice trailed off. She reached for a trifle, whimpered when she couldn't find a spoon. I passed one. I hate to see hunger suffer.

'Thank you, Roberta.' Ignoring Miss Priscilla's gaze, I went quietly out, lost myself in the thickening crowds.

33

Chemise was worried, but worries come too late to be any use. So I put my brave face on, with the Misses Dewhurst on the steps, ready to wave everybody off.

'Is this all right, Lovejoy?' Chemise asked. The Americans got aboard, Mahleen squeezing my arm with a 24-carat clang of undisguised lust, making me go red.

'See you later, honey!' she breathed. 'I've got what you want.'

'I've got you a ladyship title, Mahleen. The call just came through. It'll cost about eighteen thousand quid. But genuine. In East Anglia. The titles mean little nowadays, but they're legally transferable.'

'You've . . .' She stared. 'Like Jox's titles?'

'No, love. Honest and true. You've been good to me.'

'Lovejoy –' She was swept away by a late rush.

Exhibitors shook my hand. They'd had good orders.

'Our American visitors will share the celebrations!' I said, grinning. 'See they get a good nosh, eh? Look after Mr and Mrs Battishall.' I walked to the charabancs. Grinning's hard. If I'd been a candidate I'd have got elected there and then. 'They will follow in the limo, all right?' Roberta was glorious in amber chiffon with white silk mandarin sleeves. I could have eaten her, would with average luck.

She smiled back, shivering, delicate as a flower. I bussed her as the first chara revved up and moved off, the exhibitors all waving, chatting of the successful day.

'See you, doowerlink,' I told her. I patted Ashley on the back, wishing I'd palmed a knife. 'The Welcome Sailor'll do you proud.'

'I shall try to eat,' Roberta promised bravely. All little girl, she stood on tiptoe and kissed me. She drew away, looking at me properly. It was not altogether pleasant, that eagle-eyed search. 'Lovejoy?' she asked.

'By nine you'll be home. Everything'll be sorted, love.'

'Ashley,' she said, 'I'm cold. My shawl . . .' He belted away. 'Nothing's wrong, Lovejoy, is it?'

The other charabancs revved, pulled out, everybody waving. I looked to see Lily, my favourite, smiling down. No sign of old Jim the irascible. He was probably ballocking the driver for fuel impurities or something barmy. The old guests pulled out immediately after, black smoke fuming the countryside.

'Wrong? What could be wrong, love? The Cause's made a fortune on commission?'

She looked at the dealers' waiting cars. 'They will go soon?'

'Aye.' I did my best sigh at the unrelenting dedication of all those antiques dealers. 'All except the chosen few.' I winked. 'They all want to be the last to leave, in case some rival dealer offers a discount. I'll take a few last orders. Don't worry.'

She placed a hand on my chest. The limo driver, a pimply St Osyth bloke, tried not to notice this. We stepped away.

'And the Stubbs will be sold?'

'Auctioned for a fortune. Payable to you only, dwoorlink. There'll be a dozen bidders only.'

'You'll stay, Lovejoy?' Her tongue touched her lips. 'It's been a revelation, you here. We share the same obverse, you and I.'

'So you're a Gemini with a . . . ?' A touch of what, Aquarius? I'd forgotten. Astrology's a woman's toy, not for blokes.

'Libra,' she corrected. 'I should have listened to Priscilla years ago, at school.'

'Eh?' Ashley came into view, three shawls. 'School?'

'We were all at school together, Prissy, Philly, and I.' She watched Ashley hurtle towards us. 'It doesn't entitle them to any licence, Lovejoy. You understand?'

'They're just helpers, love.'

'Be sure that's all, Lovejoy. By tonight, I shall have funds enough to declare myself. I need a dedicated advisor. I do not mean Ashley. You understand, darling?'

'E₁, no?' Declare what?

'Declare my position as the Pretender to the USA.'

My mind reached for a splitting headache, gave up. Where's a headache when you need one? 'You?' I gaped.

'Of course. I've been the subject of news items in the past, all unbearably flippant. From now, I shall be serious.'

She ignored Ashley, stepped into the motor. Ashley climbed in babbling how he'd hurried, so sorry to delay, the whole grovelling mess. I ascended the steps, after gaping at the skies for a while.

'School pals, eh, Priscilla?' I said accusingly. Her sister flushed. 'There was me thinking we'd all just met.'

'Oh, Lovejoy, that was *years* ago!'

'Who else?'

'Heavens!' Priscilla laughed, colour in her cheeks. 'Hilda *was* at the same school for a little while – her father was something in their Embassy! Goodness, we were practically strangers!'

'Oh, aye,' I said drily. But strangers who'd kept contact, visited, shared the same loony Cause, were willing to expend time, money, effort on its furtherance. Still, no threat. There's a society somewhere for everything, from Save Our Toadstools to Down With Richard III. And there's a society of collectors of anything and everything. And everybody's got to go to school somewhere, right? No need to change any plan, right?

'Listen, ladies. The auction's fixed, Chemise?'

'Yes, Lovejoy. Gavel, desk, notepads, ballpoints, two dummy handsets like you said. One mobile phone.'

'Mobile's you, Chemise. Miss Prissy, you take one wall phone, Miss Philly the other, okay? When I cross my feet – *don't look*, corner of your eye, okay? – you'll raise your hand as if listening to a phone-in bidder, then nod. Once. Got it?'

'Why, Lovejoy?'

'It's the old pretence again, Priscilla.'

She turned to her sister. 'We dissemble, Philadora. There won't actually *be* anybody telephoning.' Philadora registered this world-shatterer. 'Correct, Lovejoy?'

'Yes,' I said, near to collapse. 'Chemise. Got the stickies?'

'Yes, Lovejoy.' From a holdall she brought out a roll of white adhesive paper discs. 'Numbered to 831.'

'God Almighty. That many?' I drew breath to ask if she'd checked, but saw her steely glint and desisted. This was the lass who'd operated Tryer's mobile Sex Museum through countrywide opposition. She handed me a tabulated list. Valuable lass, Chemise.

'Ascending order, the way I went round the exhibits when it was opened, okay?' I didn't want to auction the wrong items. I'd seen that happen more than once.

'I *know*, Lovejoy.'

'The sanads?' The Dewhursts drew breath together, but I got in first. 'They are chits, papers giving authority that bidders sign. Remember what I said about deposits, money or written cheque with each? Tinker's whifflers'll know, and bring each to you, Chemise, okay?'

'Do they get a copy of the auction list, Lovejoy?'

'Once the doors are closed, aye. Not until.' I looked at my three helpers thinking, God. Not much of an army.

The great pantechnicons stood silent on the forecourt, now eight of them. The end one didn't look at all different, but had a thicker wall, according to old Jim Andrews, that possible Alzheimer. The huge van had a solid-looking wall, sure, but didn't they all? Well, no.

For a second it made me shiver, because there wasn't a single chime from the pantechnicon. I felt cold, looked to see where the chill was coming from, but not a leaf stirred.

'Chemise. Did Tomtom and his mate Cav give you a message?'

'Yes, Lovejoy. They're waiting for you, said to tell them when you want to move something in.'

So the great Stubbs was still inside this van?

'Where's Tinker?' When weapons come out, find your mates.

'He's with them. He's drunk, Lovejoy.'

We went in, Chemise silent, the biddies chattering excitedly. Tinker was telling Tomtom some tale, cackling.

'And Lovejoy says he owns the frigging firm —'

'Sorry, Tinker.' I winked at Tomtom to show him I was only pretending, innocent ears abounding. 'Come with me. Tomtom, er, that large extra object you wish auctioned. Could you bring it in on my nod, please? You can stay out here if you like, have a drink.'

'No, Lovejoy.' Tomtom spoke his monotone straight at me. 'We'll be with you every second.'

'Oh.' Sweat ran down my arms. 'Glad of that, Tomtom.' I couldn't lose for winning today. On a roll. Grinning scared, I told Chemise and the Dewhurst ladies to go ahead into the dining room where it would be held. I could hear the hum of voices even from the hallway, gusts of laughter. 'Just nip to the loo.'

My hands were almost a giveaway, shaking. Tomtom remained by the end of the corridor. His mate Cav went on by, to stand blocking the light from the fire escape. God, they were hulks.

'Tinker. Listen. Can you drive a pantechnicon?' I had to mop my face with the towel, splashed a bit on my brow.

'Drive anyfink, Lovejoy.' He frowned. 'Why? Which?'

'Soon as I start the auction, Tinker, that end van. Drive it away. I've no keys or anything.' My frigging teeth chattered.

'Right.' He thought a bit. The mirror looked back at me with that sneer mirrors get when you're ridiculous. 'Where to?'

'Have I to think of everything, for Christ's sake?' I almost raised my hand to clout the drunken old soak, my anger shuddering to a halt just in time. 'Anywhere,' I said, tired out. 'Vanish the damned thing.'

'We in trouble, Lovejoy?' he gravelled out, watching me.

I looked into my horrible eyes. 'Not you, Tinker. Me.'

'Not on your own, son,' he said with a cackle. He made a fist. 'I'll marmalize the lot.'

'Ta, Tinker. Look after yourself.' I left, putting on fake jubilation. I didn't want compassion getting in my way at this stage.

The dining room was thronged. I should have been pleased, but wasn't. I waved cheerily, all those familiar faces. Many dealers were from outside East Anglia.

A sadness was on me, as I stepped to the dais. All these people. Maybe it was the occasion. The building was packed with phoney fame, re-created in forgeries by human skill. And I'd done it. Not by my own hands, but I couldn't escape blame. If it hadn't been for me there would be no auction, no forgeries. And every single item in the whole place would appear within days on the antiques stalls as 'genuine, original'. Don't misunderstand. I've done my share, God knows, hundreds. I stood there, gavel in my hand, wondering for a sour second what fakes do for an ancient genuis's reputation.

The trouble is that fame isn't. In the Middle Ages, the teeming mediaeval centres of learning were thronged with the savants – Rome, Bologna, Liége, Paris, Oxford. Even among these glitterati, one bloke's name was on everybody's lips, the toast of mediaeval

Paris. His learning, brilliance, his carousing worse than any Macheath, this riotous English scholiast from humble Wilton was admired, copied, praised and envied from the Danube to the Atlantic. The world worshipped. And (fanfare) here comes his name: Serlon. Your mind goes, *Who?* Fame, like I say, isn't. Looking around at the sea of expectant avarice, I wondered sadly if we deliberately exterminate the reputations of the great. Is it that's what greed does to anyone honourable?

'Lovejoy!' somebody said. 'Don't stand there like a prat.'

'Sorry. Just checking.'

Holly was at the corridor door, arguing with a whiffler. She was one problem I could do without. I passed my index finger along my chin, the sign of rejection. Whifflers bundled her out. Not a head turned. I saw the whifflers stand sentry by the closed doors, registered the Dewhurst sisters at the wall phones, gavelled once.

'Lads and lasses. Please be aware that the management cannot claim that *all* these items are authentic antiques. Okay?' There was laughter, cynicism rampant.

'We've got to be out of here in lightning time. Let's go. Item one.'

Tinker was by the door that led into the kitchens, waiting on my signal. The hatchways were bolted.

'Tinker, check those corridor doors, okay?' And coursed on as he tottered out to comply. 'Item one: a mosaic said to be Roman, Balkerne Hill site, two yards square. Quick . . . ?'

The mosaic I recognized, one of three exhibits fetched by Sampan, a grave robber from Harwich. It was genuine, unlike his other two. He does them well. And it had begun.

Before I knew it I was into the low twenties, thirties, then the sixties, really motoring.

'Item seventy-two,' I was rattling on, when I saw somebody slip in at the back, smiling apologetically. Now, you don't slip into a roup auction. But Mr Geake was sure of himself. I saw Zem, one of the whifflers on loan from Podge Tater's place in Kings Lynn, look doubtfully at his mate but let him through. Well, so? He'd saved my life. 'This painting, manner of Seurat I'd say, start me off, a thousand . . . ?'

And crossed my feet. Instantly, not even a decent pause, Priscilla's hand shot up. She spoke into the phone.

The painting got knocked down to her for a fortune. She was pale but game, rising to join the queue at Chemise's table where the successful bidders were signing chits, flashing wads, arguing the toss but getting on with it, the old cinema writer's joke engraved on their minds: it's not the price, it's the money.

Lot 100 came and went, then 150. At 190 I knocked old Mrs Boyson's writings of Thangliena down to a phoney bidder called Squire Malpassant, carefully avoiding the use of double-barrelled names that posh London houses go for when fraudulently knocking lots down to phoney bidders 'off the wall'.

Tinker was gone. I surged on, selling everything in the exhibition. Some things astonish you. I've seen seventy-year-old antique dealers rendered speechless by coming across some trick that they've never seen. You never stop learning. I mean, who'd have thought that a handful of poor quality sketches of old boxers, badly aged by simple dilute tea – a child's trick – would go for the price of a new semi-detached house? I'd thought twice before admitting them. I myself had scrawled their illegible dates in pencil, in the interests of authenticity, because Manda, though beautiful, hasn't the brains of a rocking horse.

We were into Lot 434 before I noticed the room go quiet. I realized that Mr Geake was bidding. Then I saw. Every time a slumped figure in the ninth row started to bid, Mr Geake bid instead, cutting him out.

The slumped figure was Father Jay.

Now, there's nothing sets antennae quivering at an auction like rivalry. And this appeared a definite 'frog', as dealers say. Mr Geake was definitely 'pulling a frog', and Father Jay, wearing a dowdy tweed trilby, was missing out. I don't know what made me do it, but I thought swiftly, decided to up the lot by taking imaginary bids off the chandelier, as the saying goes.

And the bids raised, raised, lifted off, soared.

I checked to see what the hell 434 was. A few so-say diaries, fake birth certificates, old photos. I'd only agreed to let this particular lot in because it showed how badly forgers can fake. Every auction had these family reminiscences. This was a real hotchpotch. Fakers usually form up job lots, and slip in a taster, a near-authentic bit of scribble, letter or some certificate, that might hoodwink the unwary. The taster is usually a faked up Christmas card from a queen, a printed card supposedly to some lady from King Edward VII, or a note 'evidently or said to be from the hand of' some princess having it away with a bodyguard. The Kennedys are another favourite, especially in fake job lots of USA origin. I couldn't for the life of me remember what was in the damned box. Woodwork had knocked the lot together – not too crude a description. I'd find him after and see.

Everybody knew it was dross. I get fed up. To save Mr Geake a fortune, I knocked Lot 434 to Father Jay, called out, 'Sold to that gent in the hat,' and cruised on.

The auction was going a bomb. I forgot the stupid 434, and gavelled, joked with ribaldry, rushed on, yelling, pretending anger, getting them all laughing.

The room thinned after the first hour. Cars began starting up outside as one by one the dealers left, having stumped up on the sanads and collected their items. The whole building was shaking as the whifflers helped the dealers load. The stairs thumped. People swore outside. Humpers cursed the loads aboard, rushed back for the next. Sanads were even bought and sold before the items were out of the door. It's usual.

The doors were ajar now, as the dealers left. The trouble is, the ones who've finished always think everything's over and leave bragging loudly. I had to keep calling for quiet.

One piece was a laugh. Old Doothie makes me chuckle sometimes. He'd faked a series of Intelligence Quotient studies from that old codger – Dr Cyril Burt, was it? – who faked the racial purity studies on IQ. Doothie'd forged this so-say research from University College, signed by the defunct doctor, on improvements in IQ caused by people listening to Mozart's sonatas. This 'sonata effect' was only proved in the autumn of 1993, and at a blow negated all the IQ studies done everywhere before that date. Doothie's a sly old devil. I got a decent price for it, not a giggle among the dealers even when I pointed the joke out.

The hard core was still there, though, waiting for the one true antique, the nicked Stubbs. As I hurtled on through the 500s and 600s, and reached the 760s, I found my eyes drawn to them. They weren't sitting as one group, like I wanted. I could see French Saunders from Hartlepool, looking a neat youth, but actually a killer aged forty plus. Barnet, not from Barnet but because he has a wig

(Barnet Fair, hair), was reading: he reads until he decides to bid, then he ahems, looks up, nods, and it's back to poetics. He's got two art galleries in Ponder End. And, bad news, Ammster from Amsterdam, Indonesian knifer with, they say, poison-tipped blowpipe arrows secreted about his person for swift use and swifter escape.

And Corinth and Montgomery Mainwaring. Bidders for a sum with noughts all round the pelmets? Looking confident, Corinth causing all the males to breathe harder. Costigan from Spain's Costa del Crime, bank robber and, now, TV magnate on the proceeds. With his lass, Ack Emma, supposed to carry a gun in foreign parts, so to speak, willing to do Costigan's bidding (sorry) any time. And Patch Halliwell, he of the corporate spying triumphs in Russia. Survival seemed a problem.

The Misses Dewhurst caught my eye. I saw Miss Priscilla's benign gaze on me before she glanced away. I raced through a series of new bids. I'd told Chemise to leave the rubbish to the last, was pleased the dealers drifted quicker. Penultimate was a set of dornick vestments, superbly done by two strange embroideresses in Galashiels, worth a mint. I got very little for them, considering the work involved.

The last item was a set of old golf clubs, feather balls included. Everybody's faking them nowadays. You can hardly give them away. I sold them to Harry Bateman, who gave a yelp of glee and paid Chemise after getting her to stamp his sanad.

Until only the main group, the money core, was left. Tired, I signalled to the two remaining whifflers to close the doors and push off. I gave Tomtom and his oppo the nod.

'Now, ladies and gentlemen,' I announced, voice shaky, 'you all know why we're here. We expect a large sum. There is a high reserve price. This work of art is world famous. Bring it in, Tomtom. Back the pantechnicon up to the side door. See the corridor's closed off, eh?'

They went. Chemise and the Misses Dewhurst were totting up, comparing notes, who'd bought what. My heart was where it had been for hours, in my mouth. There was the sound of feet pounding up to the door. Cav burst in, aghast.

'It's gone, Lovejoy!'

'Eh?' I rose, at least as aghast as Cav. Tinker, thank God, had nicked the pantechnicon. 'It can't have!' I yelled.

'The fucking pantechnicon's *gone*, Lovejoy! It's been halfed!'
Half-inched, pinched in Cockney slang.

'With all these people around?' I thundered, well, bleated.

Tomtom appeared, talking with quiet malevolence into a mobile phone. My knees actually quivered. He was on to Big John Sheehan. The world was for it, especially the bit with me in it.

At times like these I have to consider my future. A friend would defend his mate, deny all knowledge of the theft, postulate thieving strangers. But I knew I'd be for it, because I always am. But I had to stand by Tinker, even if it meant sacrificing myself. I gagged. Sacrifice *me*? Had I gone mad? My voice opted for survival.

'It can only have been Tinker,' I bawled in rage. 'The bastard. He said he'd check the van . . .'

The room emptied of Tomtom and Cav, following by the money bloc. Mayhem they knew well, but when it was about to be sprayed around by BJS, who dealt out punishment in a wanton manner irrespective of blame, they didn't want to know. Corinth gave me a backward look, speculative and suspicious.

They melted, leaving me with Chemise and the Dewhursts.

'Pals,' I said, voice shaking. 'Time you got going. Take the money, the chits, lists, the lot. I'll see you . . .' I passed a hand in front of my eyes '. . . at the Welcome Sailor.'

'Lovejoy?' Chemise said doubtfully.

'Lovejoy?' echoed Priscilla. Philadora just looked.

I smiled. 'Two hours, okay? Just hop it.'

They went, and now I was on my own. A few cars revved, doors slamming, then nothing. Somebody shouted, probably Tomtom. They would scour the world for Tinker, maybe even do him in. A door slammed in the building. The place was empty.

Silence. That is to say, nobody.

No body.

Meaning me.

34

Curious how empty a place can feel. I wished I'd told the Dewhurst sisters to stay, kept Chemise for company. Except there was no way round it. Now to get Big John Sheehan on the blower, tell him the truth. I couldn't have announced the Stubbs was a dud, not to the bidders. They'd have lynched me, disbelieving swine. I'd *had* to blame Tinker, set the goons after him, to keep me alive. Anybody could see that. I listened. Outside, blokes were shouting, calling go left, try those trees, bring more torches. A hunt's a terrible thing. I swallowed, made the hall.

Phone, one public phone in the main hall. I peered round the corner. Nobody. Darted to it, the cartoon mouse, utterly exposed. I wanted the mob to scatter after Tinker, not stay poking the bushes in the hotel grounds. God knows where Tinker had driven the pantechnicon. I fumbled for a coin. Get Big John on the blower, tell him the tale.

And no change. I almost collapsed with fright. Those thoughtless bitches, leaving me without even a coin to phone my way out of trouble. Thoughtless. Just when you think women have finally got their act together they let you down. They should have stayed to protect me.

Ashley's office? I brightened. On the ground floor near the steps that led down to the indoor jungle of the conservatory's split-level terrarium. I'd been in once to complain. I dived along the corridor, made Ashley's posh door, slid inside.

'Ask Lovejoy,' somebody howled outside, close. Was a window open somewhere? 'Where the fuck's Lovejoy?'

'He come out with you, Sonk? Fucking well look, prat.'

A clumping somewhere inside – *inside*, floor shaking.

Dark, with torchlights – how'd Tomtom got so many so fast? – flashing among trees, once a glare touching my face making me duck and almost brain myself on Ashley's desk.

Phone. I grabbed the thing, knelt, cunningly didn't switch any light on, and waited for the burr of the dialling tone.

No burr.

'Hello? I said quietly, louder. 'Hello?'

Silence. I pressed buttons, hope fading. Nothing.

Maybe it needed you to pull some aerial out by the little red diode thing?

No aerial, no light. I ducked lower. Somebody was coming along the terrace, shining his torch in, yelling to Tomtom. Sonk's treble bass. I shrank to midget size. Sonk had done the Brussels truck job, 'straightening' as we (I mean they, psychopaths who kill for a living) say, two Dutch vannies who'd hijacked a container load belonging to BJS.

The torchlight flashed over the room making bizarre shadows. A basket on the floor went through a million contortions. Sonk boomed, 'The motors, Dave,' and crashed through a flowerbed.

Gone? I eeled along the carpet, opened the door, darted out into the light. I lay on the corridor floor gasping like a landed trout. They'd find me, in the building. If I switched off lights it'd be a giveaway, and in they'd storm after me. Why me? Because Sheehan would tell them to, that's why. Thank God they hadn't got bloodhounds.

Opposite was the glass wall of the conservatory. I stared at it, face on the corridor carpet. A wall of thickened glass. I'd been in to see some ugly growing fronds, old Jim Andrews telling me the Burmese jungle was the place, eat two leaves you don't get gut-rot up country. Sanctuary? Big as half a football field, filled with monstrous plants, no lights, enclosed in glass but practically impenetrable. Just the place to hide until everybody pushed off, then nip out and . . . and what? Hitchhike to my cousin Glen in Lancashire, just passing through.

Just my luck for the door to be locked, but it wasn't. I crawled through, closed it. I was frightened by a sudden whirring, terrified lest automatic lights illuminated me, tomato in a greenhouse. Only some auto sprinkler system spraying the confined forest, activated by cooler air as I'd entered.

Doors slammed. Running feet pounding, a curse, regular thudding of a heavy bloke upstairs.

It was a wet little universe in there. The steps black iron, slippery with permanent drizzle making your face and hands clammy. It felt horrible. When I'd been in before it had been daylight. I hadn't taken much notice, just bored stiff. Now I wished I'd paid attention to doors, exits, tools, weapons.

Struggling with my feeble memory, I recalled the layout. Outside, an expanse of lawn, a distant lake, gravel paths, bushes, a summer-house. Somebody's flashlight swept over the grass. I heard shouts, stayed on the steps hanging head down. Movement gives your position away, not stillness. Freeze, you're a shadow. Move, you're enemy.

The torches receded. I swarmed down. The steps were spiral, wetter nearer the bottom. I should have counted. Anyway I was scared, wanting to get away from that door up there. It's where they'd come through after me. When the exhibitors and staff returned, I'd blithely invent some crazy tale – dozed off, cracked my head on the slippery steps, anything. Or maybe I'd hear them return, nip out and nick some clothes . . .

Except . . . Jesus, I sighed, weary, there seemed a hell of a lot of excepts in my plan. First thing, the exhibitors would want their exhibits. And I'd sold those. The second thing they'd want would be me. They'd simply join the hunters.

Go into the thickest jungle, that was military training, wasn't it? Was it? My old grandad used to say, stay away from thickets, just keep low. But that was the Great War. Or was it when you had a horse? I was suddenly conscious of the conservatory's terrific heat. Tropical, the air thick as slush. Already I was running with sweat, my clothes sogging from that water mist. Whoever'd built this place had been barmy.

Down I eeled to the runny floor. Tiled paving, Ashley boringly explained that they were non-slip so elderly residents would stay firm of foot. I felt my way.

Many plants were on trestles, banks of them along the glass walls. The air was filled with giant tendrils, fronds, trailing vinery, hanging pods, succulent fleshy branches with spatulate leaves. But I wanted the floor crowded too. One aisle between the trestle tables had duckboards. Plant pots stood on these with stacks of trays and sacks of gunge. I crouched to search for a nook where I could lodge maybe until daylight.

Light came through the glass walls up above, washing the dark of the conservatory. It wasn't convincing, that gloaming, because mercifully tinted glass cut it down. Thank heavens. If it had been clear glass, this place would have been quite easy to suss for miscreants. As it was, the darkened glass neutralized the corridor's light. It was the best place. Surely I'd be safe? The hoods couldn't fire the plants to smoke me out. Like all goons, they were addicted to flash gear, style shoes, custom suits. I've seen bruisers looking like bulbous pears argue for hours about fashion collars. They wouldn't have the heart to search in here. Would they? Spoil their tennis and strides.

Feet shook the corridor. Somebody calling, 'Not here, Tomt,' and Tomtom shouting check that nosh place, did Lovejoy come on wheels . . . Getting scared, his boss, Sheehan, on the way and like to turn his cold Ulster blues on whoever made the worst report.

Nobody came. Doors opening, slamming. Because the conservatory was all glass, were they assuming it was the last place on earth anybody would lurk? Torches shone, but I was down among the pots. Moisture and humus set me gagging but not enough to make me stroll out for a breath of fresh air, that was for sure.

Urgent talk, 'Do it again,' in angry yells, Sonk shouted about a cellar, another yelling, 'That bird, frigging hell,' Sonk booming to check who she was . . .

Bird? Juliana? Or Chemise? I almost stood up in relief. If Chemise was here too, there was a witness.

'Bar that end door, Sonk,' a goon shouted, too close. A lumbering shade passed along the glass wall. A safety door clanked, some metal bar sliding into place, then feet pounding past. Quiet.

Alone. I sat on the wet paving. A count of a slow hundred, then the corridor lights went out. No sound, just a gush of dark blacking out the moderate gloom. Still a faint wash of grey from the sky, and a trace, if you imagined hard, of reflected light, then that too drained away.

Shouts in the building still, but lessening as the search beat further afield. Once there was a faint ruckus, quickly stifled as the mistake was discovered. Somebody ran past. A car engine started up, tyres spitting gravel as the car tore away. Tomtom grasping at straws?

Drenched with the air spray, I sat back in relief among the

sculptured plants with their dripping leaves and thick muggy un-breathable air. I was safe. Any minute now they'd hoof out to scour the countryside. Then Big John Sheehan would arrive, before or after the exhibitors returned filled with jollity, with the hotel staff, residents, the barmy Battishalls and I'd be able to escape . . .

A hand grabbed my wrist and he said quietly, 'Lovejoy?'

For a second I didn't think, almost said hello, wet in here isn't it. Then I squawked and struggled but I was held by that firm grasp and fell onto my shoulder, scraping my face, peering, trying to see. I knew who it was.

'Mr Geake?' Relief dampened me further. 'Shhhh!' I said like a fool. 'They might have left somebody in the hall!'

'They're away.' He must have been in here all the time. 'Thirteen, I counted. Not enough to search a building this size.'

Reassurance overwhelmed me. A mere instant ago I'd been scared witless. Now I was in the hands of this ex-policeman. Who'd saved me once before, a real pal. I could have wept.

'Thank God. You're sure?'

'Positive. Listen.'

We listened, me straining, imagining I could hear somebody creeping . . . But he was a trained man, alert, clever. What rank had he been, inspector? A match for those goons any day of the week. I smiled. If he said it was safe, it was safe.

'You're right. They've gone. Can we go, then?'

'Ah, no, Lovejoy. Not now.'

He was right. 'Better safe than sorry, eh?' I chuckled.

'That's right.' After a beat he asked, 'Why did you knock that job lot down to Father Jay, Lovejoy?'

'Eh?' Surely he wasn't narked at that? 'Saving you money, Mr Genke. It was dross. You can pick up better job lots any day of the week. Get you some, if you like.'

'No, Lovejoy. I do not like.'

'Don't get narked, Mr Geake.' Had to be pleasant to him, he'd come to save me, right? But who was the antiques man here, him or me? 'There couldn't have been anything in it.'

'There was, sadly.' He really did sound sad.

'What?' I wanted to get out of here now. Like a drowned rat, worn out from being scared, I wanted some air far away from this quiet intent bloke's hangups. I was still grateful, mind, just warier.

'Letters.'

'Oh, sure, but poor quality fakes.' I chuckled, except my chuckle wasn't working quite as well as usual. 'I've even forgotten who sent them in. Look, why don't I do a few for you? I know blokes who'll do anything from the Declaration of Independence to the Old Testament.'

'No, Lovejoy. Those.' He sighed. 'They said the wrong thing, you see. Purported to be about an illegitimate child born hereabouts during the war.'

'Eh?' I felt cold, in this enervating torrid zone. 'Don't worry, Mr Geake. Letter forgers spray suggestion like that around all the time. Like, titled Victorian ladies having affairs, social scandals, politicians becoming homosexual, spies, film stars . . .' I tried to sound happy when I wasn't. 'It's a standard ploy, see? God, half the published letters about the royal family are duff, neffie, anything to make, fake, a sale! It's what people want to believe. Ask any London tabloid how many they've had *this week*, supposed letters about presidents, kings, tsars. It's practically the national pastime!'

Why was my voice shrill, when I was trying to whisper?

'Was it those letters from . . . that Camelot bloke, became President of the USA? I remember now. Cityman talked me into it, his faked letters.' I chuckled. 'I think he's Tinker's pal.' Had there been some supposed letters from randy old King Teddy too? 'Look, Mr Geake, if you wanted to sell them to the Americans at the George, I'll get you something really worthwhile in that line, okay? Who're you interested in? Can't just be that randy Yank politician, can it?' I tried to stand, but he kept his grip on my wrist.

'No, Lovejoy. Your interest in the American visitors is too close for your own good.'

'You mean Mahleen?' I'd done as I was told by everybody on earth.

'The fake letters. I wanted them destroyed, Lovejoy. It's a service I have done these many years.'

'Buying fake letters from antique shops just to *burn*?'

'I think you know, Lovejoy.' He was whispering in a monotone. 'The magic man himself was briefly stationed in East Anglia during the war. Torpedo craft. It was inevitable, to father a child on some barmaid. Happened a million times, troops everywhere. But past sins are disasters – for some. And opportunities for others.'

Sins? Opportunities? 'I don't know what you're on about.'

'Oh, but you do, Lovejoy.' He paused. I could tell that he was listening. He relaxed, continued. 'Or why would you knock the lot down to Father Jay?' He did his weary sigh. 'Poor man. I have felt pity for him all these years. I learnt of his origin – cousins, you know, he and I. His mother was the illegitimate wartime child. She unwisely left a diary about it after the Dallas tragedy. She was frightened, the political dynasty proving so lethal. Jay was her only offspring. She died in a road accident.'

'Father Jay?' I couldn't think. 'But his name's Smith.'

'He made sure of that. Built up a convincing past. Entered the one remaining occupation where celibacy would protect him.' He sounded so whispering reasonable. 'Stay a priest and, however exotic his diploma-mill holy orders, he'd never have to reveal his origin.' I knew he'd turned his head. I couldn't see a damned thing. 'Marriage is the canker, Lovejoy. It exposes a man to every possible interrogation. Hourly, for life. I had to assume the responsibility. See the village's demise was accelerated – schemes failing, restaurants contaminated, Dame Millicent's herd infected, ancient land rights blocking developments.'

'Listen, Mr Geake.' Suddenly I wanted Big John's goons to haul in. 'The Americans are here to help Mrs Battishall. She's quite scatty, says she's descended from Bonnie Prince Charlie. Claptrap. But she'll make a killing – er, fortune – claiming the American throne. Barmy, off her nut. There isn't one!' I laughed. He made no noise. No wonder Father Jay had looked thunderstruck when I mentioned having to meet my American tourists. I rushed on with my promises. 'I won't say anything about Father Jay topping Tryer. Honest. Soon as I'm out of here I'll –'

'No, Lovejoy. No "out of here" for you.'

'Not . . . ?' I echoed, daft. I couldn't see what he meant.

'I did Tryer, poor chap. Ignorant, stupid. Utterly useless. God knows, I'd had enough run-ins with his like when I was in the force. Tryer's death kept the village out of the limelight. I couldn't possibly have silly letters claiming that America's golden politico had left a by-blow here on our fair shores, could I?'

'But it's made up!' I yelled. 'The whole fucking exhibition was forgery! It was even advertised as fake, start to finish!' I shed tears. Threatened by honesty. Usually the opposite does me down.

'You know how fakes get represented in the tabloid press, Lovejoy. They are the true fakers, are they not?'

'Sir. Look, please.' I wished he could see I was really fawning, grovelling to agree with anything. 'Father Jay – whatever he's really called – he was bidding too! I knocked 434 down to him! He's safe!' I injected a cheery laugh.

'Did you really not know, Lovejoy?' he asked mildly.

'Course I didn't!' *Geake was lame!* I'd seen that dragging foot. I could run, get away. I shifted my weight experimentally. His grip tightened, iron. Was he armed, a gun? Even bobbies aren't allowed them.

'So much untruth, Lovejoy. Where is the real thing? Like my injury. I had to run down the old clergyman. Maudie said that you'd been asking.'

'You deliberately . . . ?' I couldn't get it out.

'Wrapped the old man's motor? Of course. Thus providing Father Jay with a remote country incumbency where he could live in anonimity. He only had to apply. What other priest would want a dying village?'

True. Vicars go crazy for an active parish.

'I had a hard time proving disability. The medical profession can be most obliging, when threatened.'

Bloody hell. He was fit, didn't need to limp at all. And a huntsman. I'd seen him riding at Dame Millicent's. 'Look, Mr Geake. I'll –' Promises, coherent and otherwise, babbled out of me.

'Get up, Lovejoy.'

I rose, blubbering and clutching at him. I felt my fingers touch cold metal. Christ, a gun? I heard myself groan in fear.

'Up you go. Head for the stairs.'

The pig had hold of my wrist. I got up and shuffled. I tried a despairing lunge to one side, blundering into a huge plant. He laughed a low laugh at my antics, put the barrel against my cheek.

'Be good.' Like giving me a parking ticket.

'I don't know which way,' I stuttered, trying.

He propelled me along. He'd do me in here, or maybe up in the corridor, be in the clear. With angry hoods scouring East Anglia for me, who'd suspect a retired peeler?

'They'll hear, Geake!' I fell over my feet.

His grip held. 'No they won't, Lovejoy.'

Won't. So he didn't intend to shoot me. Of couse, for weapons are traceable. Unless I made a run for it he'd not fire. I blundered into the bottom of the spiral staircase, felt for the railing.

'Slowly, Lovejoy. Step at a time.'

One. Two. A third. I was whining in a continuous shrill supplication. Five, six, a slow seven. I'm pathetic, always terrified, always losing, hopeless.

What would he do, club me senseless at the top and send me hurtling down? No, for I might fall safely, except it was a hell of a way down, for here came steps eleven, twelve, thirteen. But near the staircase there was only that flat non-slip paving. I'd be sure to slam myself vertically down onto that, dashing my brains out . . . Sixteen, seventeen. God Almighty, who builds a conservatory with that height to the entrance? Some lunatic architect trying for effect, that's who, never mind the safety of people like me . . .

'Please, Mr Geake,' I tried one last time, 'I'll help you –'

He sounded so reassuring, 'I'll make it quick, Lovejoy. I've never been vindictive.'

Then close to my face a voice screamed, 'Mind, Lovejoy!' I ducked, terrified, flailing to one side and almost tumbling over the frigging railing as something swiped past my face, tendrils whipping by my forehead and almost taking my eyes. There was a horrible bump behind me. The grip went from my wrist. I scrabbled for hold as I felt myself fall sideways, caught hold and clung for dear life, while that screaming went on and on and I thought, run for it you stupid little cow instead of standing there on top of the spiral iron staircase screaming your silly little head off . . . It was me screaming.

And then tried finding a foothold because I was dangling, managed to get my right leg hooked round the railing, clawed myself back to the top step. I made a dive for where I guessed the door might be, knocked myself practically cold on some iron, fell groping, groaning, found my hand taken in hers. Cold corridor air wafted over us both and we were running demented along the corridor towards the light at the end.

'Shut up, Lovejoy!' she said. 'They'll hear us!'

I didn't care. I wanted everybody in the world to hear me, alive, say I was under arrest, anything away from that madman. But she seemed to have guessed right, and had got me free, so I stopped yelling blue murder and ran obediently in silence by Holly's side, through the blinding light of the hall, out through the open door and into the night.

35

The night, cars swathing the trees, a rising wind, distant shouts, the hotel behind us glowing like a Christmas tree. And me and Holly. I had to halt, winded, after a million-league dash, beyond the lawn pond. What was that about hiding in a thicket? I was done for, gasping in a hollow, a terrible stitch in my side. No moon, of course, lazy swine too idle to come and help. We could just about see the pallor of each other's face. My stitch cramped me. The shouts began.

'This is exciting, Lovejoy!' she said.

'Shhh, you silly, er, child.' I hadn't to forget she was only sixteen. 'They'll hear!'

We'd been lucky. They'd already searched this field, moved on.

She sounded thrilled at all this excitement. 'They're looking for you! Will they kill me as well?'

I grabbed her throat. 'I'm going to get clear.'

'Fucking marvellous, Lovejoy.' She went dreamy. 'It feels –'

'You're off your head, silly mare.'

'All that attention!' She sounded envious. Water was seeping into my shoes. 'Is it for killing Chemise's meat?'

Hateful hearing a lass, practically an infant, talking crude slang. 'I didn't. Geake did.'

'Serves the bastard right,' she said piously. 'Why didn't you go back down and shoot him with his gun? I'd have done it. You bottled out.' A child telling me I did wrong not to murder? It must be TV.

A motor started up, lumbered round the fields, quartering the area where the cars had been standing. I raised my head from the grass, saw another motor start, beam headlights moving. Somebody climbed into a third. Two came from the lane leading to the Battishalls' drive. The sods were hunting in. Several blokes started to trot from the hotel. Every light in the place was on. Were they in league with Geake? Had he told them to go out and get me?

Some night creature rustled past, unconcerned.

'Look, Holly.' I licked my lips. I could escape without her.

'Yes, Lovejoy?'

'Help me, love. They'll find me if I stay here. My only hope is to nick a motor.' Two more cars arrived, presumably Big John's entourage joining the fun.

She giggled. 'Did you see Mr Geake tumble? I hit him with a pot I could hardly lift! I had to guess where his head was. It must've been lovely to see him go.' She made a whining sound, falling, went, 'Thump! I wished I'd a camera. It was Mr Geake caught old Ashley with me. The laugh's on him now.'

'Aye, hilarious.' Piety and murder are pals.

They would give chase if they saw somebody running through this country gloom. But she might get shot or something, if they were as serious as I thought. But only a swine would think of sacrificing this life-saving bird to save his own cowardly skin.

'What do you want me to do, darling?'

'Decoy.' Darling? Too many darlings spoil the broth.

'How?'

'Like this,' I said. 'When I say, run hard to our left. They'll follow you. Hide, duck and dive as long as you can. Meanwhile, I'll escape, see? I'll get to, er, Norwich.'

'Where will we meet up, sweetheart?'

Bad news this. 'Er, Havelock's Auctioneers, Norwich.'

'I own you now, Lovejoy. Save a life, own the life.'

Who'd said that? 'Yes.' I chuckled, unconvincing.

'I insist on a trial cohabitation, Lovejoy.'

'Eh? Oh, aye, sure.' I swallowed. What do they teach them at school these days? To my surprise she pressed her mouth on mine. I pulled away, pushed her off. 'Get going. Good luck.'

She'd need it. There'd be a good two dozen hoods after her. I saw her wriggle along the hollow until it gave out and then she ran fast. I waited until the shouts rose, then eeled through the darkness in the opposite direction. I'd thoughtfully shoved her towards tangled thickets, leaving me the open lane. Maybe, deep down, I was anxious for her to escape, at least give them a run for their money. Or maybe I meant me, more like.

Five minutes, I made the hedgerows beside the winding lane

leading back to the hotel. The lights behind me were a godsent beacon. I plodded skittering along the undergrowth towards the trunk road's orange skyglow. I was shaking and damp. I heard the cries begin behind me, tried to run but only fell over more roots so slowed to a cautious trudge. No good breaking a limb. I'd never get away if I did that.

Then I heard her screams and thought, poor Holly. In fact I almost halted, maybe to turn back and try to help her. But what good would that do? Reason came to my aid in the nick of time. Holly'd saved me, true? And willingly gone haring off to decoy them away so I could make it to safety. What would be the point of throwing away Holly's sacrifice? She wanted – *wanted* – me to escape, game girl. It was her plan, for heaven's sake. Relieved my guilt was conquered, I moved on, edging round the thicker obstacles, silently holding the boles of smaller trees to avoid splashing in puddles. It was that caution that saved me from walking into Sheehan's roadblock.

Not long after I hit the lane, I saw a small motor, very like the Dewhursts' Morris, trundle past towards the hotel. I'd dived for cover, mistrusting any vehicle on this lonely lane. I'd gone maybe a couple of miles further when I heard the same decrepit engine coughing slowly up behind me. I ducked aside, just as I smelt cigarette smoke. Two faint red glows showed ahead, very close. I stilled.

The motor halted with a squeal of worn brakes. It was the Dewhurst sisters. I could see their outline in the dashboard sheen. Their headlights illuminated two of Sheehan's hoods standing smoking beside their huge hunched saloon.

'Did you go to the hotel?' they called.

'Yes.' Priscilla's voice. 'There's such trouble! They were calling for everybody. They've seen somebody running across the fields. I do think the farmers will be cross, if their crops are damaged.'

The hoods talked together. One got into the saloon.

'If you join the hunt.' Priscilla said, 'would you please leave Mrs Roberta a message? The Misses Dewhurst are rather tired and shall ring her in the morning. Would you do that, please?'

'Right, love,' in a voice that said some hopes.

They gunned the motor, screeched in a tight one-eighty. I watched their lights recede. The Morris chugged into the layby. Its engine cut.

I waited, thinking, a trap? But their headlights stayed on. Why? Then suddenly the interior light came on. They spoke quietly to each other, then Philadora stepped out, climbed into the back seat. They sat. I watched from the hedgerow.

Then Priscilla wound her window down, and called softly into the night, 'It's safe, Lovejoy.'

The interior light went off. The headlights dowsed.

Frightened, I slipped close, got in, sinking to the floor in a ball. She clicked her headlights on, and drove off without a word.

36

The alleyway behind the Lorelei shop was the place for illicit snoggers after dark. I told Priscilla to drive down it, headlights searching out rutting witnesses. Then return, alight, open the back door of the Lorelei Delicatessen, and enter leaving the door open for me to nip from the motor and slip inside.

Once in, to my astonishment they were jubilant, squealing with laughter as though they'd won some unimaginable prize.

'Shush, for God's sake!' Maudie Laud's peelers might come hang-gliding by any second. I didn't want them finding us celebrating, having maimed Geake and pulled off a robbery.

'But you're safe, Lovejoy!' they said, eyes wide.

They saw my gloom. 'Find me a hiding place, love.' I addressed Priscilla, the leader. 'They'll come with a search warrant.'

'Heavens!' Priscilla was delighted, breathing wonderment. 'This, Philadora, is *real life*!'

'Oh, Priscilla! Our opportunity, at last!'

They applauded. I felt out of it, another wrong guess.

'Lovejoy. Tonight you shall rest, while we construct a priest hole! Like the Roundheads and Cavaliers!'

'Then tomorrow, Lovejoy,' Philadora said with a gentle blush, askance, '*our plan*.'

'The future imperative!' from Priscilla.

Eh? 'Right, loves. And ta for the rescue.'

'*Rescue!*' they shrieked. I had to shush the silly pair.

With the doors locked, they rushed about, showing me their flat above the tea shop, the side room where I would sleep. It was self-contained, a loo, basin, bed that let down. They provided a nightshirt, colouring as they offered it. I vaguely wondered if they had many gentleman visitors, but dutifully had a bath, noshed their hot grub, drank their tea, and was asleep in seconds. They were real planners, that was for sure.

And I dreamt a dream like Genseric the Most Terrible's, all seeming benign – at first. I dreamt I heard Priscilla saying, 'We did right, Philadora.'

And Philadora the Most Timid saying, 'Really, Prissy?'

'He has come to us as we predicted all these years.'

'Oh, yes! And we must be resolute!'

They advanced on me, slowly looming larger . . . and I woke with a scream in my throat.

Empty. The room was empty. I drank some water, mopped sweat from my body, and slept the sleep of the just.

Next day, they knocked and entered, solemn. I sat, had the breakfast they'd brought, asked for more – they had it all ready in some contrivance. They perched far as possible from me, for a while shyly averting their eyes from my naked torso. In ancient days, kings allowed their subjects to file past and watch them nosh. I felt a bit self-conscious.

'Thank you, partners,' I said simply. 'Say when I've to go.'

'Mr Geake is dead,' Priscilla said. 'Heaven rest him.'

So Holly had guessed with unerring precision.

'Fell down the conservatory staircase,' from Philly.

'The police are interviewing the antiques dealers.'

'The . . . whifflers,' Philadora brought the word out proudly, 'caught a girl called Holly. A vagrant, Lovejoy.'

I listened, watching their faces, to and fro like Wimbledon.

'She aimed to *doss down* in the hotel but saw nothing.'

Good old Holly. My exhalation might have been a giveaway to anyone else. But what did these know except their zodiac?

'We perpetrated a deception, Lovejoy,' Priscilla composed herself, 'by telephoning the police at regular intervals during the night, asking for your whereabouts.'

'Partners, after all!' squeaked Philadora. 'They knew nothing.'

'I'd better be going, then.'

They shook their heads. 'The police are seeking Mr Dill.'

'The Americans have decided to stay in East Anglia, Lovejoy. And become antique dealers.'

Rivals, or yet more partners? I wondered.

'With a golf club, in Fenstone.' Priscilla said cheerfully, 'Dame Millicent's land.'

'No obstacles, like Mr Geake, RIP?'

'Father Jay has vanished, they think abroad. With Juliana.'

A reformed character, then. Brand plucked from the burning. Better marry than burn, some holy fraud said. Good old Juliana.

'So I'm in the clear?' I cried, ecstatic. They smiled sadly.

'No. Everybody's after you, Lovejoy.'

'But,' Philadora said patiently, 'we have the Seurat painting, the Thangliena diaries, and sundrys. The ones you made us bid for. In store.'

'Brilliant!' I cried. These were partners worth having.

'For a consideration, we will unite forces, Lovejoy.'

'Really?' *They* trying to do a deal with *me*?

'There's a meeting here in a few minutes, Lovejoy.' Miss Priscilla coloured a little. They rose. 'We suggest you bath and dress. Your linen's washed. You might care to listen. You will not be seen.'

Ten minutes, I was clean, sitting on the stairs like Christopher Robin. The tearoom door kept pinging as visitors arrived. Miss Philly served tea, coffee. Conversation was only about the auction.

'All the money will be in by weekend,' Chemise said eventually, down to hard facts.

'Can it be cleared without Lovejoy?' Mahleen homed in.

'It sure can!' from Wilmore. Hilda and Nadette agreed.

'I saved Lovejoy's life,' said Holly. 'He owes me.' She should have been in Norwich. See how unreliable birds are?

'He is our partner,' from Priscilla. 'He owes *us* more than anyone.' Which was a bit much, seeing I'd been born in the right hour, proving their stupid Obverse Zodiac. 'My sister and I have promised a substantial reward to the newspapers. That is why we asked Miss Laud to attend.'

'Which is?' said Maudie Laud. I almost yelped. This was getting hairy, the chief peeler downstairs.

'Ten thousand pounds, for information leading to the safe return of Lovejoy to his cottage.'

There were murmurs of appreciation. 'We have advised the media, television,' said Philadora proudly. 'We are solely interested in rescuing the poor lamb from his loneliness. He might be on a ferry to the Hook of Holland, anywhere!'

'Maud,' said Mahleen earnestly, 'no charges will be brought against Lovejoy or those who contributed to the auction?'

'No.' Maudie spoke with reluctance. 'I've seen the printed list. All items were listed as forgeries, fakes. Perfectly legal. We would like to have Lovejoy's statement as soon as possible, though. There's an antique stolen from Dame Millicent. He might also clarify events leading to Mr Geake's accident. And explain some details of Father Jay and Miss Witherspoon.'

There was talk about what might have happened, how the Sheehan hoods were all making statements down at the police nick. I smiled wrily. Those summaries would be useless. Good old Dame Millicent, though, bilking the insurance companies by pretending her fake Danish mock-up was antique. I couldn't wait for them to leave, and almost shouted with joy when the door pinged shut behind the last of them. I was upstairs getting my coat on when the Dewhurst sisters followed me.

'Lovejoy.' They stood like a deputation, hands folded uncertainly. Except they weren't all that uncertain.

'Ladies,' I said fervently. 'Ta. I'll be off –'

'No.' Priscilla was between me and the door. 'You stay here. With us. In a state of . . .' It was her timid sister who astonishingly brought the word out.

'Cohabitation, Lovejoy.'

They were both red as fire, meeting my gape with difficulty.

'Eh?' I kept my smile on, puzzled. 'Stay here?'

'It is impossible for you to leave, Lovejoy.' Priscilla pointed to the window. 'Miss Laud has a constant police watch on our tea shop. Since you are already inside, you will be safe until you try to leave.'

'And Chemise is residing at your cottage.'

'And Mahleen has filed for divorce, to marry you.'

'And Roberta, forward hussy, has similar designs.'

'And Sabrina has taken out a summons against you for robbery. Silverware.'

'And Beth has done the same. Bilston enamels.'

'And Holly, who is impudently young –'

'And –'

'Listen.' I finally made it. 'This cohabitation thing. It's impossible. For a start –'

The teashop door went ping. I felt myself pale.

'A moment, Lovejoy.' As I frantically tried to stop her, Priscilla went to the top of the stairs and called, 'Would you care to come up, please?'

A heavy tread sounded. The ultimate deterent, Big John Sheehan, stood there. He looked pleased to see me.

'Look, John,' I said. My knees gave. I sat on the bed. 'I made Tinker nick the pantechnicon, sure. Because –'

'Because the Stubbs inside was a copy? I know, Lovejoy.'

'You knew?' I got narked at that, otherwise I wouldn't have come straight out with it. 'John. You're no divvy. Only the one who –'

'Ladies.' They scuttled downstairs. 'I couldn't let somebody steal it. Not after I'd put a preserver on it.'

'You swapped it for a dud, which Nick, er, nicked for Ashley?' Big John's honour was intact among us thieves. 'But that's . . .' Unfair, treachery, repulsively devious. He was waiting. 'Great, John,' I finished.

'Can't have our honour betrayed, Lovejoy,' he said, dead serious. 'You stay here a fortnight, Lovejoy. I've fixed it with the ladies. Give me time to clear things up.'

'Two weeks?' I bleated in protest. His head tilted. 'Er, fine. Ta, John.'

'Tinker had the sense to take the van to my place in Aldeburgh.' He tapped my chest. 'Any time you want rid of Tinker, tell me, Lovejoy. Good old soldier, Tinker.'

'Right,' I called feebly after him, 'Ta again, John. Good luck with that horse!'

And sank, trembling. I heard the downstairs door ping. The two sisters came slowly upstairs.

'So you see, Lovejoy,' Priscilla said.

'Look, Miss Priscilla –'

'No, Lovejoy. Priscilla, please.' They exchanged glances.

A *fortnight*. I looked at them. Cohabitation?

Priscilla spoke firmly. 'We are not exactly experienced, Lovejoy. But since meeting you, we realize the time has come.'

'Has it?'

'For us, Lovejoy. And you. We have no . . . sexual understanding.' She coloured, pressed on. '*You* are our chance.'

'I am?' I'd edged back, behind the bed. 'Of what?'

'Of realization, Lovejoy. All our lives have been chaste. We see that you and sin are *far more thrilling*.'

Philadora put in, 'You *are* ours, Lovejoy. The Obverse.'

Their frigging zodiac. I was sick of the damned thing. 'Look,' I said, desperate. 'I made a mistake. My birthday's June –'

Priscilla took out a birth certificate. 'No, Lovejoy. We got it from London.'

'The question is, which of us will sleep with you first.' Priscilla faced me. 'I am the elder, it is my duty.'

'No, Prissy,' said Philadora. 'I must sacrifice –'

'Philadora, I've *decided*. Lovejoy, please bear in mind our relative ignorance. Inform us of your expections. Will you require the two of us in succession, or night and night about?'

A headache came on.

Casually, I drifted to the window, surreptitiously looked out. Sure enough, there was a police motor across the street. I ducked back. Wilberforce the Hateful, fingers drumming on the wheel. And another motor with Tomtom and Sonk reading newspapers. Holly and Chemise were having an argument on the pavement with Beth and Sabrina.

'We will fall in with your wishes, Lovejoy,' Philadora said gravely. 'And give you every . . .'

'Satisfaction,' Priscilla said. 'No shirking, Philadora!'

Well, Roberta was their contemporary, and I'd been delighted. So they dressed vintage, but so? It might be the fashion or something. I surrendered, ever the pushover.

'Very well,' I said. 'We'll start this afternoon. Look, any chance of another breakfast?'

Better go for nourishment, or I might not make it through the week.

279

FOR THE BEST IN PAPERBACKS, LOOK FOR THE

In every corner of the world, on every subject under the sun, Penguin represents quality and variety—the very best in publishing today.

For complete information about books available from Penguin—including Puffins, Penguin Classics, and Arkana—and how to order them, write to us at the appropriate address below. Please note that for copyright reasons the selection of books varies from country to country.

In the United Kingdom: Please write to *Dept. JC, Penguin Books Ltd, FREEPOST, West Drayton, Middlesex UB7 0BR*.

If you have any difficulty in obtaining a title, please send your order with the correct money, plus ten percent for postage and packaging, to *P.O. Box No. 11, West Drayton, Middlesex UB7 0BR*

In the United States: Please write to *Consumer Sales, Penguin USA, P.O. Box 999, Dept. 17109, Bergenfield, New Jersey 07621-0120.* VISA and MasterCard holders call 1-800-253-6476 to order all Penguin titles

In Canada: Please write to *Penguin Books Canada Ltd, 10 Alcorn Avenue, Suite 300, Toronto, Ontario M4V 3B2*

In Australia: Please write to *Penguin Books Australia Ltd, P.O. Box 257, Ringwood, Victoria 3134*

In New Zealand: Please write to *Penguin Books (NZ) Ltd, Private Bag 102902, North Shore Mail Centre, Auckland 10*

In India: Please write to *Penguin Books India Pvt Ltd, 706 Eros Apartments, 56 Nehru Place, New Delhi 110 019*

In the Netherlands: Please write to *Penguin Books Netherlands bv, Postbus 3507, NL-1001 AH Amsterdam*

In Germany: Please write to *Penguin Books Deutschland GmbH, Metzlerstrasse 26, 60594 Frankfurt am Main*

In Spain: Please write to *Penguin Books S.A., Bravo Murillo 19, 1° B, 28015 Madrid*

In Italy: Please write to *Penguin Italia s.r.l., Via Felice Casati 20, I-20124 Milano*

In France: Please write to *Penguin France S.A., 17 rue Lejeune, F-31000 Toulouse*

In Japan: Please write to *Penguin Books Japan, Ishikiribashi Building, 2-5-4, Suido, Bunkyo-ku, Tokyo 112*

In Greece: Please write to *Penguin Hellas Ltd, Dimocritou 3, GR-106 71 Athens*

In South Africa: Please write to *Longman Penguin Southern Africa (Pty) Ltd, Private Bag X08, Bertsham 2013*